THE WAR
BETWEEN
THE HEARTS

Nann Dunne

Praise for Nann Dunne and
The War Between The Hearts

The countless women who passed as men to serve their nations in times of war have barely been accorded a footnote in history. But Nann Dunne honors them in bringing us a truly memorable heroine, Sarah Coulter. Sarah's journey as a Union spy, and a woman finding her true self and her true love, makes for page-turning reading.
  —Jennifer Fulton, author of the Moon Island Series

With strong characters, romantic tension, and an engrossing plot, The War Between The Hearts is a book you won't be able to put down until you finish the last page. Highly recommended.
  — Lori L. Lake, author of the Gun Series and other books

Courageous, headstrong Sarah Coulter rides off to war and gallops straight into danger, disaster and heartbreak. This historical romance is both entertaining and surprisingly believable. A good story, well told.
  — Jean Stewart, author of the Isis Series

THE WAR BETWEEN THE HEARTS

ISBN 1-933113-27-8

THIS TRADE PAPERBACK ORIGINAL IS PUBLISHED BY *INTAGLIO PUBLICATIONS*, GAINESVILLE, FL USA

CREDITS

EDITOR: *STACIA SEAMAN*

COVER DESIGN BY *SHERI (GRAPHICARTIST2020@HOTMAIL.COM)*

Acknowledgments

If one author, miles away, can be said to hold another author's hand in constant encouragement, that description fits my longtime friend, Lori L. Lake. With each book, a writer undertakes a new journey, and Lori took the time from her extremely busy schedule to help smooth my path. She supported my first steps, picked me up when I faltered, and bolstered my confidence all along the way. Her unselfish generosity is endless, and so is my gratitude.

Other friends who contributed their generous assistance include Laney Roberts, editor, who went above and beyond the call of duty to keep everything consistent and make sure the loose ends got tied together; Day Peterson, editor, who recommended words and phrases that so perfectly fit the period I wondered whether she lived there in another life; Patty Schramm, first reader and Civil War buff, who gave the story her hearty endorsement; and authors Jennifer Fulton (The Moon Island Series) and Jean Stewart (The Isis Series), who offered their interest and encouragement.

Thank you to Kathy Smith, Stacia Seaman, and the Intaglio staff for their ongoing consideration and attention to publishing my story, and to Sheri for the gorgeous cover she created.

My constant and eternal gratitude goes to another miles-distant and cherished friend, Karen Surtees, whose persistence in demanding more stories from me (including two books we coauthored) instilled my passion for writing.

And finally, thank you to the women who served on both sides of the Civil War. Approximately 700 are known, but the total number is assumed to be in the thousands. Firsthand accounts of their military service are unanimous in praising their patriotism and attention to duty.

With few exceptions, the towns and battles in this story, while as authentic to the era as I could make them, are fictional, as are the characters.

Dedication

To my family and friends who have always been supportive, and especially to my father and stepmother whose sincere interest in my writing is a never-ending source of delight and motivation.

A special dedication to my brother, Mike, who left us this past year, but whose golden spirit remains with us always. You are missed.

PROLOGUE

1862—WESTERN VIRGINIA

W ait until you see me wearing a beard and mustache."
Sarah-Bren Coulter strode swiftly along the sidewalk,
bent on finding the costume shop. Her shorter companion's bonneted
head turned toward her.

"You'll make a handsome man," Lindsay Coulter declared. As
she hurried to match Sarah's pace, she stumbled on a loose stone and
pitched forward, about to sprawl into the path of a horse-drawn
wagon full of lumber.

"Careful!" Sarah-Bren grabbed her sister-in-law's arm and
pulled her back to the sidewalk. The driver, apparently oblivious to
the near accident, guided the horse on down the brick-paved street,
while creaking wheels swirled eddies of dust in the wagon's wake.

"Thank you." Lindsay's blue eyes were wide. "I didn't expect
shopping to be so dangerous." With one gloved hand, she tucked a
loosened strand of black hair beneath the edge of her bonnet. Her
other hand brushed at her long, brown skirt, scattering a puff of dirt
motes into the sunshine.

Sarah's lips curved in a wicked grin. "Shopping with me is
always dangerous." But her voice shook a little at the thought that
Lindsay had come close to being seriously injured, perhaps even
killed.

Sarah continued to be surprised at her love for the small woman.
Disdainful of most of the girls she had grown up with—their life
goals centered on catching a suitable husband—she had expected
merely to tolerate anyone who married her twin brother, Scott. But
Lindsay walked right into her heart and became her sister and
confidante.

11

Tightening her grip on Lindsay's arm, Sarah steered her to the opposite curb. Once safely out of the street, she released her hold and fished a piece of paper from the pocket of her dark green dress. Two staring men tipped their hats as they walked by. Lindsay's polite nod barely acknowledged them, while Sarah ignored them altogether. Her unusual height often captured attention, while her dark brown hair, cream-colored complexion, and unusual amber eyes turned the attention into admiration. Her bearing, however, drew the most notice. She glowed with confidence like a beacon in the night. She believed she could do anything she set her mind to and, so far in life, had done just that.

She unfolded the paper, checked the shop's address, and looked farther down the street. The Coulter women were on a mission. Or rather, Sarah was. She had invited her co-conspirator to accompany her on a supposedly innocent shopping trip, and when Scott offered to mind the baby so his wife could go, Lindsay jumped at the chance.

Sarah tucked the paper back into her pocket and sketched a wave toward the buildings. "We're on the right street. The costume shop should be somewhere along here." They gazed around the area and scrutinized all the likely signs.

Downtown Wheeling covered a flat finger of land squeezed between the Ohio River and a few steep hills. The town had spread along the river and partway up the hills, and because of its location along the busy Ohio, it had grown into a center of activity. Besides a young steel industry and various retail and commercial establishments, the town boasted theatrical stage shows that provided entertainment for the whole region. The theater, in turn, spawned shops catering to the professional needs of actors and actresses, and this was what had brought Sarah and Lindsay from Fairmont, two hours' train ride to the south.

"Let's try down this way," Sarah suggested and started walking in that direction. As they passed a number of establishments, they took the time to look at some of the window displays. The men's apparel store exhibited the latest fashions for the well-dressed gentleman, the milliner's showed women's bonnets and gowns, a barber's shop had curtained windows, and a general emporium offered work pants, teapots, and a coal scuttle. At last, Sarah spied the costumer's. "There it is," she said, tugging Lindsay's sleeve.

Once inside, Lindsay followed Sarah to a counter display of beards and mustaches fashioned from real hair. After closely examining each, Lindsay pointed to a beard-and-mustache combination that was a shade darker than Sarah's coppery brown tresses. "That looks like a good match. Why don't you try it on?"

Sarah picked up the item as the shopkeeper, a short, thin man, approached. She held the hair to her face and gazed into a mirror. The shopkeeper stopped next to her, clasped his hands, and bowed slightly.

"Hello, ladies. I'm Mr. Hennig, at your service." He nodded to Sarah. "That suits you perfectly, miss. Are you acting the part of a man in an upcoming performance?"

"Something like that." Sarah's eyes shone and a smile played at her lips. "I've never used a false beard before. How do I keep it on?"

"I'd be delighted to show you." The man went behind the counter, where he opened a drawer and removed a bottle and a rag. He unscrewed the top from the bottle and poured about a teaspoonful of sticky gel onto the rag. "This is spirit gum. It acts just like glue." He dabbed a little of the gum onto the back of another hairpiece, attached the piece to his own face, and pushed at it with his fingers. "As long as nothing scrapes hard against it, it will stay in place. And it comes off easily." He gave a sharp tug on one edge and peeled it off.

Lindsay's deep blue eyes squinted in puzzlement. "Doesn't the gum irritate your skin? And how do you get the residue off your face?"

The shopkeeper beamed and teetered up and down on his tiptoes. "It's not difficult to remove." He lifted a different bottle from the drawer, poured liquid from it onto the same rag, and swished it across his face. He wiped it away with a clean rag and performed the same act on the back of the hairpiece. After he laid the rags on the countertop, he closed the bottle and turned it around to display the label. "Just plain alcohol melts the gum away. And as for irritation," he said, setting down the bottle and rubbing his chin, "maybe if someone has sensitive skin and wears the piece for long periods of time, I suppose it could irritate the skin. But just wearing it for the usual three or four hours during a performance probably won't hurt."

"I'll take this one." Sarah handed over the beard-and-mustache combination Lindsay had suggested. "And two bottles each of spirit gum and alcohol."

"You probably won't need so much," the man said. "I wouldn't feel right if you were to purchase more than you can use. A little bit goes a long way."

Sarah laughed. "This little bit is going to go a very long way." In fact, she thought, probably over a big portion of Virginia. But she didn't answer the man's quizzical expression, and he didn't ask her to elaborate. She paid for the purchases, accepted the paper bag in which they were placed, and walked with Lindsay back out into the sunshine.

"Do you have everything you need now?" Lindsay asked as they headed toward the train station.

"I think so." Sarah tucked the package under her arm and ticked her fingers up one at a time. "Shirts, trousers, shoes, belts, drawers—"

"Drawers?" Lindsay covered her mouth to squelch a giggle.

"Of course! Those rough trousers would rub my skin raw." She resumed itemizing her list. "A canteen, weapons—"

"Weapons? What kind of weapons? Wouldn't they be given to you?"

"I'd rather have my own and be confident that they work. I'm not using any from the house, though. I bought what I'm taking with me." She started flicking out her fingers again. "A Remington revolver and holster, the newest Springfield repeating rifle, and the proper cartridges for each of them."

Lindsay tilted her head to look up into her sister-in-law's gleaming eyes. "Do you know how to use them?"

"Yes, of course. Father began teaching Scott and me to shoot when we were six years old." Sarah slowed her strides as she realized Lindsay was struggling to keep up with her fast pace. "Of all the things I bought, I had the most trouble finding a kepi."

"A kepi?" Lindsay's giggle bubbled again. "I'm beginning to feel like a talking parrot. What's a kepi?"

"It's that little cap both the Union and Rebel soldiers wear. The Union one is blue, and the Rebel one is gray, of course. You know, the one with the round, flat top." She raised her hand above her head and moved one finger in a circle. "It looks like a hill of mashed beans that someone sat on. It's also called a forage cap, and some call it a bummer."

"Are you taking Redfire?"

"I've ridden Redfire all over this state. I'm not about to go without him." The women arrived at the railway station, bought their return tickets, and sat down to wait for the train.

Lindsay plucked at part of her skirt that had folded under her when she sat. She looked askance at Sarah. "I suppose you know your brother won't like what you're planning."

14

Sarah gazed off into the distance before answering. She thought Scott too cautious by far. He missed a lot of life by never braving the unknown or reaching out for adventure. "You're right, he probably won't, but his disapproval hasn't stopped me yet."

"And what about Phillip?" Lindsay stood, straightened her skirt, and settled back down. "He won't be too happy that his sweetheart wants to join the army. They'll both think it's a foolhardy action."

"Sweetheart?" Sarah poked her elbow into Lindsay's side. "Now I'm the parrot. You of all people know I don't consider myself Phillip's sweetheart."

Phillip Showell, who now was Captain Phillip Showell of the Union Army, grew up with the Coulter twins and gradually fell in love with Sarah. He had proposed marriage a number of times, but Sarah continued to insist she didn't return his feelings.

Her face screwed into a grimace. "I know he cares for me, and I love him dearly, but I've never been in love with him. And probably never will be." Sarah sometimes wondered whether she would ever marry. Even when she felt lonely, the idea of marriage didn't hold any appeal. She couldn't imagine herself performing wifely duties for anyone.

"But you know he'll be upset."

"I don't care!" Sarah's temper flared, and she slapped a hand against the top of her thigh. "Well, I do care, but I'm going anyway." After a moment, she calmed down and spoke in a more even tone. "I think Theo might be more understanding than his brother. He'll see I can be of enormous help to the Union, and he's too dedicated to let his personal feelings get in the way." She turned to face Lindsay and shrugged. "That's why I haven't said anything to Scott or Phillip yet. I'm waiting for Theo to come home on leave. I hope to persuade him of my intentions, so he can convince the other two. I'm sure they'll listen to him."

"Colonel Theodore Showell. That sounds so dignified, doesn't it?" Lindsay clasped her gloved hands together and smiled.

Sarah nodded. Theo always had been dignified. And much more practical than his younger brother. She was counting on that. She intended to go ahead with her plan whether or not Theo approved, but its execution certainly would be a lot easier if she had him as an ally. A sigh escaped her, and Lindsay frowned.

"Are you having second thoughts?"

"Never."

"Sarah, are you sure you want to do this?"

"Yes, I'm sure." She hesitated for a moment. Then she rose and paced back and forth, fiddling with a pearl button on one of her white cotton gloves. "I need some kind of focus to my life. You have a husband and son. Scott and little Pres are your focus."

"You're part of my focus, too." Lindsay's gaze never left the agitated woman. "And you could have a husband in a minute."

Sarah stopped pacing and smiled at her sister-in-law. "Being a wife suits you, Lindsay, but I haven't found my perfect mate. Not yet, anyway. And I'm not even sure what I want to do with my life. Being a wife may suit me, too, one day, but I want some adventure and excitement first."

Lindsay's cheeks dimpled. "I think your announcement will raise some excitement."

The train pulled into the station, and Lindsay stood. Sarah picked up her package, and they moved toward the train. "That sigh, by the way, was over having to wait to deliver my news. Phillip told me Theo's not expected home until Wednesday."

"The day after tomorrow?" Lindsay's voice rose. "Why don't you invite them to join us for dinner Thursday night? You can tell everyone then."

"That's a good idea." A rush of excitement filled Sarah, and she hugged Lindsay with her free arm. "Now that I have everything I need, I can hardly wait to get started."

Lindsay slipped an arm around Sarah's waist and gave her a quick hug in return. They climbed aboard the train to head for home.

So far, so good, Sarah thought. But she hadn't yet made her announcement. Theo and Phillip had joined the Coulters for dinner, as planned. Now, Lindsay and Sarah finished cleaning up while the men settled into the drawing room. Sarah put away the last of the dried dishes while Lindsay went to check on her baby, Prescott Coulter III. She soon rushed back into the kitchen and hurried to the ice chest.

Sarah raised her eyebrows at the unusual activity. "Is Pres all right?"

Lindsay made a face and shook her head. "He awoke as soon as I opened the bedroom door, and he's really cranky from that new tooth he's cutting. I'm going to put a little chunk of ice in a piece of cloth and let him suck on it. Maybe that will soothe him." As she spoke, she grabbed an ice pick, opened the door to the bottom section of the ice chest, and chopped a piece from the foot-square block of ice setting there. To help, Sarah pulled a cotton dishcloth from the linen drawer and took it to her.

"Thank you." Lindsay pushed the chest door closed and straightened up. "I'm afraid I'm going to miss your announcement. I'd like to get Pres back to sleep." She put the ice in the cloth and formed it into a finger shape for the baby to suck on. "I wanted to be there in case you needed some help."

Sarah touched her shoulder. "Just knowing you're on my side is enough." She looked around the kitchen, saw that everything was in order, and followed Lindsay into the hall.

"Good luck." Lindsay reached back and squeezed Sarah's forearm. She was surprised when Sarah continued up the stairs behind her. "You're not going into the drawing room?"

With a wry grin, Sarah shook her head. "Not yet. I'm going to my room and bolster my courage a bit first."

"You know what you want, Sarah. Go after it." Lindsay returned the grin. "I'm behind you one hundred percent."

They parted at the top of the stairs, and Sarah continued toward her own quarters, a little unsettled by what she was about to do, but abuzz with the thrill of anticipation. She sat down at the vanity table in her bedroom, and her luminous amber eyes stared into the mirror. She separated out some strands of her hair, gathered the rest together, and used the loose strands to tie the dark mass into a tail. Her gaze shifted downward as she reached into a drawer and lifted out the bottle of spirit gum, followed by the false beard and mustache. After dabbing a few spots of the gum onto the back of the hairpiece, she placed it on her face and returned her gaze to the mirror. Her eyes widened at the change in her appearance. The closely trimmed beard and mustache looked genuine. She removed the Confederate forage cap from atop one of the posts supporting the mirror and tried it on. After several poses, she settled the kepi straight on her head and tugged on its short brim to pull it tight. The round top of the hat tipped forward as though eager to get on its way.

She tapped a finger against the nose in the reflection and addressed herself with a satisfied smirk, "With the beard on your face and the cap on your head, you look the perfect man, Sarah-Bren Coulter. Or should I call you 'Bren Cordell'?" Her teeth showed in a full grin as she spoke the seldom-heard part of her name, which she planned to use in her masquerade. She settled the hat back onto the post and removed the disguise. As the shopkeeper had demonstrated, she used alcohol to clean the spirit gum from her skin and the false hair and returned the items to the drawer.

From another drawer, she lifted a leather-bound book, empty of writing except for a few words on the cover. Sarah traced her fingers along the engraved letters: *Personal Journal of Bren Cordell.* I'll write in this journal as often as possible, she promised herself. I can keep track of my adventures and illustrate them with my own drawings. This could become a family keepsake. Someday, it might even be published. Sarah beamed at the bold thought and slipped the journal back into the drawer. Drumming the pads of her fingers on the vanity table, she sat for a moment, then told herself she needed to get moving.

She released her hair from its tail and lifted a silver-backed brush from its place on the vanity top, next to a matching hand mirror and comb. As she viewed her actions in the larger mirror, she ran the brush through the dark copper strands and made a face at her image. "Well, my girl, you'll have to use the scissors on this mane. Men wear their hair much shorter than this."

At last, she could think of no more excuses to delay joining the others in the drawing room. A slight fluttering in her stomach reminded her of the nervousness that had brought her upstairs in the first place. She expected all three men to be astonished at her idea, but she had confidence she could persuade Theo that her masquerade would benefit the Union cause.

Sarah replaced the brush on the vanity, gave herself one last stern look to put some steel in her spine, and started back downstairs. It was time for the grand announcement.

Colonel Theodore Showell stood next to the Coulter drawing room fireplace, his elbow resting on the polished surface of the stone mantel. It's good to be here with family and friends, he mused, flicking a glance at Phillip and the Coulter twins. These peaceful surroundings are a welcome respite from the pressures of war, even if I can't escape the reality.

His earlier remarks about the recent battle nearby at Cheat Mountain Summit had given rise to a lively discussion about the war in general. Unconsciously imitating his brother, Captain Phillip Showell stood at the other end of the fireplace, also leaning one elbow against the cool stone. Scott Coulter sprawled comfortably in an overstuffed chair near the fire, a brandy snifter in his hand, while

Sarah sat on one end of the sofa, her fingers tapping noiselessly against its arm. Theo had noticed Sarah's silence during most of the discussion. She wasn't usually so reserved in tendering her opinions, he reflected.

"From what I read in the *Wheeling Intelligencer*," Scott was saying, "that Rebel Jackson has been causing havoc all over eastern Virginia while McClellan is fiddling around at Yorktown. The man is too cautious. It's no wonder President Lincoln replaced him as supreme commander."

Theo stood a little straighter. "Thank goodness Grant's been successful. He's chased the Confederates clean out of Kentucky. But you're right about Jackson. He's a wily one. He makes up his own rules of engagement. It would help a lot if we knew where his army would hit next."

"Trouble is, we need more reliable information about the Rebel troop movements," Phillip said.

Sarah jumped to her feet. "This whole situation is ridiculous!" Her cheeks reddened, and the vehemence of her tone commanded everyone's attention. She strode across the drawing room's carpeted floor, her legs thrusting against the long, black skirt that hindered them. As she fetched up against an ebony desk and swung around, her hair swirled like a cape across her angular face. Abruptly, she tossed her head, clearing her face and bringing her eyes to bear on her audience.

The men struggled to face her anger without shifting away, but they remained mute. Theo sighed to himself. Here they were, surrounded by dainty Victorian furniture and portrait-covered walls that radiated peace and tranquility, and Sarah managed to shatter that ambience with one remark.

Her expression demanded a reaction, and Theo finally broke the silence. "Perhaps you could explain your indignation, Sarah? I don't believe we understand what in particular is disturbing you." His glance touched the other two men. Phillip looked similarly confused. Scott grinned wryly, bowed his head, and raised a hand to shield his eyes as though expecting a blow.

Uh-oh, Theo thought as he riffled stubby fingers through his sandy hair. At thirty-two, he was eight years older than the others in the room, and well aware that he was the shortest. The Coulter twins, both taller than average at 5'9", surpassed him by three inches, and Phillip at 6'2" towered over them all. Theo had watched the other three grow up as close friends and noted, sometimes with

19

consternation, that Sarah was the leader of this pack. Though he admired and respected her intelligence, resourcefulness, and abilities, he wished Phillip would allow some of his own to show. Instead, he followed Sarah around like a lovesick puppy. Scott was the only one with any great influence over his twin, but even he had his limits. Whenever Sarah was adamant about having her way, he yielded to her wishes.

Now Sarah led the conversation. "Phillip is right. The Union Army does need better intelligence about troop movements. And I've been trying to help with that." She scowled with impatience. "But I need to be more active. Why should only the men get a chance to serve in the military?" Her tone brooked no response. "All of you know I can ride and shoot just as well as you can. And I'm more familiar with the terrain in large areas of Virginia than almost anyone. During the summers that we stayed with Mother at Red Oak Manor, I rode for hundreds of miles around."

Everyone in the room recognized the truth of her statements. Mrs. Coulter had often complained to anyone within earshot about her inability to cope with her daughter's strength of will. Instead of the young lady she hoped to form into a genteel member of Southern society, she had a daughter who insisted on being left to her own devices, which included donning trousers instead of dresses and camping out alone for days at a time. It didn't help that her husband admired and encouraged Sarah's independent spirit. Mrs. Coulter eventually gave in, deciding it was easier to grant the girl permission to wander about the wilderness than continually be faced with punishing her. Indeed, Sarah never came to any harm. If anything, her travels helped calm her restlessness.

Scott sipped his drink and raised the glass, slightly tilting it toward his sister in a silent toast. "Sarah, you are serving the Union. As a cultured woman traveling between here and our parents' home, you've been able to cross back and forth through the lines without being questioned. Passing along tidbits of information you glean at the social affairs you attend has been helpful, I'm sure."

Sarah shook her head in frustration. "I'm wasting my time dashing hither and yon, picking up meager and unreliable gossip about the movements of the Confederate Army." She crossed her arms and stared at each of them in turn. "The best way to make a real contribution would be to travel along with the Rebels, while spying for the Union." She hesitated, but no one ventured a response. "I've given this a lot of thought, and I've decided to do just that. I'm going to hire on as a scout, or maybe a courier, and work for the enemy."

The suggestion startled Theo, but he noticed Phillip and Scott seemed to take it in stride. Perhaps they didn't place much credence in Sarah's remarks.

"Of course, the best way to gather information would be to travel as a member of the army," Phillip conceded, followed by a snort of amusement. "But a woman can't do that."

Sarah turned her gaze toward him. Her chin thrust up and her eyes shone with gold highlights. "What if the woman were a man?" she asked, as she set her hands on her hips.

Phillip frowned as though trying to make sense of this remark. He professed admiration for everything about Sarah, including her beauty, her generosity, and her daring, but the workings of her mind often perplexed him.

Scott gave him a withering look. "Please, Phillip, don't give her any more wild ideas." He nodded toward his sister. "She's quite capable of coming up with them on her own."

"Joke if you must, Scott," Sarah said with a sardonic grin, "but I'm completely sincere about this. I've collected my disguise, and with my height and a false beard and mustache, I'll make a passable man." The announcement quieted the men as she continued. "I can fit right in. After spending so many summers in the South, I can speak with a drawl that sounds genuine." A vigorous nod conveyed her confidence and underscored her intentions. "With or without your blessing, I expect to leave within the next few days."

"Sarah, be sensible." Apparently, Phillip finally understood that Sarah actually meant to do what she was threatening. "Don't go running off pretending to be a man. You want something to do? Marry me. Stay here and make a home for us."

"Phillip!" Sarah shook her head. "I'm not at all interested in marriage. How can you suggest something so ordinary while our future hangs on the outcome of this war?"

Phillip lifted both hands in supplication and looked toward her brother.

Scott set his drink down on a side table and sat forward in his chair. "Sarah, you can't be serious. I know you've never been overly concerned about your safety, but this cockeyed plan will put you in terrible danger." He paused a moment, and his argument took a different tack. "Of course, I know the idea of danger intrigues you, but what will Mother and Father say when they hear of it? What will our friends think?"

"I don't need permission from our parents, nor do I intend to ask for it," Sarah said sharply. "I know they wouldn't understand, and I don't want anyone telling them. Battles are being fought very near them, but the last time I visited Red Oak Manor, Mother and Father sat on the verandah, looked out over the gardens, and pretended there was no war. And why would I say anything to anyone else?" she demanded. "My involvement needs to be kept completely confidential, or I could truly be in danger. You can tell people I went to stay with our parents, if you wish."

Obviously still agitated, she plunged ahead with more of her argument. "You know, Scott, this fighting has been going on for more than a year, and every family on this street has sent someone to serve. All except us." A wisp of disappointment crossed Scott's face and settled in his eyes.

Sarah's demeanor softened. "Look, Scott, I realize the government requested that you stay to run the foundry. Making cannons and ammunition is essential to the war effort. But I don't have to be here." Her hands formed into fists and her voice grew harsh. "I don't have to be anywhere. I'm not making any difference in this war, and I want to. I need to. I'm sick of sitting back and doing so little."

"I think your idea has a lot of merit," Scott said, "but I just can't consent to your going into such danger. Mainly because of the fighting, of course, but there's also danger in hanging about with men who are away from the civilizing influence of home and loved ones. Things can happen to a woman, things worse than being wounded in battle."

Such reasoning obviously made no impression at all on Sarah, and Scott changed tactics again. "Stay here and run the business, and I'll join the army. I've shared everything I ever learned about the foundry with you. You know Father made me the manager only because I'm the son."

They were all aware of this arrangement. On the twins' twenty-first birthday, their father turned over the management of Coulter Foundry to Scott and the supervision of the office work to Sarah, stipulating that the twins would share equally in the profits. Simultaneously, Prescott Coulter and his wife Cynthia, who insisted the Southern way of life was superior to the Northern, retired to Red Oak Manor, the Virginia plantation Cynthia had inherited and which the Coulter family had used for years as their summer home. Regardless of Prescott and her children being Yankees, Cynthia refused to budge from her home when the war began between the states.

"You can run the company as well as I can," Scott said as he warmed to this argument, "maybe even better. As long as the business provides enough income for all of us to live on, and for Father and Mother to enjoy their retirement, everyone will be satisfied. You and Lindsay already take care of the office. She can handle those duties while you manage the production of the cannons and ammunition. You take charge of the company, and I'll do the spying."

Sarah's eyes were saying no even before she shook her head. "You don't know the area half as well as I do. While you were abroad learning the foundry business, I was camping all over those hills and valleys. That knowledge alone makes me the better choice. Besides, with my disguise, no one will know I'm a woman. The newspapers have reported that other women have secretly enlisted as soldiers. They say the physical examinations are a mere formality. If you can see, walk, and breathe, you're accepted. Or I could hire on as an independent scout as some people have done."

Before Scott could formulate a response, Sarah turned to Theo. "We need to make arrangements for me to report to you. Information I discover could be too sensitive to telegraph, and I'll have to hand-deliver it. Since my password has already been recorded by sentries along the picket lines, perhaps I should continue to use Lady Blue?"

Everyone started talking at once, and there was a long and heated discussion, but Sarah was unbending. She would become a spy and travel with the Confederate Army.

Theo knew Sarah-Bren Coulter would go forward with her intentions no matter what anyone said. She might as well do it with his endorsement. He could be her contact. With a sigh, he gave in. At least that way, he could keep in touch with her and perhaps have some chance of ensuring her safety.

CHAPTER ONE

1864—BEHIND CONFEDERATE LINES

Redfire cantered swiftly among the trees as Bren Cordell rode the sorrel stallion toward the battlefield. At times, Bren could hardly remember the softer, sweeter life she led just two years ago before becoming a scout-courier for the Confederate Army. Days like today pushed thoughts of those times into the realm of nostalgic dreams. How naïve she had been. That other woman, Sarah-Bren Coulter, had no idea of the hardships her alter ego would have to endure and little comprehension of the deadly business of war.

As thickened branches slapped against her arms, she rolled down her upturned sleeves. The simple action reminded her how much her arms had changed. Constant riding while contending with rough terrain had hardened her muscles, and exposure to the elements had tanned her creamy skin. She acknowledged other changes, too. The rigors of war and the constant companionship of death had toughened a headstrong and sometimes impulsive Sarah-Bren Coulter into the focused, disciplined, and self-controlled Bren Cordell. A crooked smile tugged her lips upward. Living in constant jeopardy had a way of sharpening one's concentration.

Bren's thoughts returned to her current mission, bringing a tinge of remorse. You chose this way, now walk it, she rebuked herself. Even at this distance, she could hear sporadic gunfire from the main battle. A Minie ball screeched against a tree trunk, and Redfire nearly shied, but Bren tightened her hands on the reins and steadied the stallion. Wincing, she leaned her body closer to the animal's neck and patted it, affording some comfort to them both.

"Neither one of us will ever get used to being fired at, will we, boy?"

When a meadow opened out in front of her, she slowed her mount and guided him cautiously along its edge, keeping to the cover of the woods. Distant crackles and booms confirmed that the battle had moved farther away. Just two hours earlier, this very spot provided the stage for the beginning of a deadly conflict. Confederate troops had advanced into a well-prepared ambush, largely because of the false orders Bren had carried to them. Assaulted from both sides by a cannon fusillade, the Rebels surged forward in an effort to outdistance the attack. But as they followed the meadow in its turn to the right, they ran headlong into Union infantry, poised to slaughter the enemy. Sorely crippled even before the blue-clad infantry joined the fray, the Confederate forces nevertheless returned fire. That the battle still raged was testimony to the courage and tenacity of the betrayed Southerners.

Well to the rear of the ongoing skirmish, bodies lay strewn across the field. Some were uniformed in blue, and a few wore civilian clothing, but the majority were garbed in gray or butternut. While an occasional corpse appeared to be sleeping, most lay at unnatural angles, and Bren grimaced at the sight of torsos and limbs with severed parts. Some of the wounded men emitted sporadic moans, and a few women moved among them, tending to their injuries. Even the ground bore scars. Ruts from caisson wheels crisscrossed hoof prints of the animals that had pulled cannons and ammunition carriages into and out of the battle. Hundreds of feet had trampled the grass, and cannonballs had left pits like broad postholes dug in repetitive rows.

Bren hunched her shoulders to ward off the depression that dragged at her as she sought to ignore her contribution to this bloodbath. Her somber eyes roved across the carnage, looking for familiar insignia. Finally, she reined in, bringing Redfire to a halt behind an oak tree. Hoping that the oak's broad trunk afforded some protection, she dismounted and wrapped the sorrel's reins loosely around a branch tattered by earlier gunfire. Her brown wool trousers, ankle-high black boots, and green calico shirt blended into the forest background. After straightening the holster belted at her hips, Bren flipped open the cover, pulled out the .44-caliber Remington to make sure it hadn't jammed into the holster, and replaced it. Satisfied the revolver could be drawn smoothly, she loosened a cord at her chin and removed her wide-brimmed trail hat. She rummaged within a saddlebag, traded the trail hat for a gray Confederate kepi, and settled it atop her tied-back hair.

Heavy smoke, the remnant of cannon and small arms fire, partially obscured the open area before her and filtered into the surrounding thickets. Bren blinked her eyes rapidly, which did little to ease the stinging itch caused by the acrid pall. The smoke and stench of battle so irritated her nose that she longed to willfully quash her sense of smell. With her hand resting on the holster, she peered from behind the oak, examining each of the bodies spread across the nearest part of the meadow.

Heavy artillery pounded in the distance, still close enough that the cannonade reverberated through Bren's booted feet. Continuing up her legs, the vibrations thrummed through broad shoulders and down long arms. Irregular splats of bullets colliding with nearby tree trunks warned that the battle may have moved on for the living, but danger still lingered for those foolhardy enough to travel across this field of the dead and dying.

As Bren searched for the easiest path to her goal, her fingers scratched by habit at her bearded face. The spirit gum mildly irritated her skin. Fortunately, her duties usually took her out of camp, providing the opportunity to remove the false hair often enough to prevent a rash. For safety's sake, she cleaned it only at night, giving her skin and the hairpiece a thorough scrub with alcohol.

Her eyes narrowed as they lit on the object of her search, and her lips turned down in a grim smile. In a stroke of good fortune, her target lay just thirty feet away, sprawled on the churned and reddened grass. From this distance, the officer's bare head looked hauntingly festive. Blood bloomed on it like a scarlet rose, and a matching ribbon draped across his cheek and neck before disappearing into the hair below his ear.

Bren rubbed Redfire's forelock and muttered soothing sounds into the stallion's ear. Next, she tugged the Rebel cap tighter, dropped to her belly, and crawled from behind the sheltering tree. Threading her way through the men who had fallen near their commander, she forced herself to ignore the moans and cries of the wounded. She reached the captain's side and looked into his staring face. Her gut wrenched as she acknowledged that this soldier—a boy, really—lay in death's arms because of her violation of his trust. Just one more betrayal added to a growing list that burdened her heavily.

Two years ago, when she first demonstrated her knowledge of the area to the Confederate officers in charge, Bren was hired as a scout-courier, just as she had planned. As the Southerners' confidence in her grew, they entrusted her with dispatches of increasingly greater sensitivity. This allowed her the opportunity to pass important information to the Union forces, enhancing her value. But she hadn't foreseen how she would be affected by the terrible loss of life brought about by her successful missions. As a direct result of her actions, hundreds of men on both sides were killed or injured. Others were maimed for life.

With heavy heart, she lifted her head and once more looked across the field at the destruction for which she felt responsible. She shivered and worked at convincing herself that the war was responsible, and she was only trying to help the Union win. The sooner they won, the sooner the dying would stop. For two years now, she had clutched this reasoning to her like a suit of armor. But during long and lonely nights, its protection failed her, and nightmares often slipped past conscious thought.

Thick brown hair threatened to come loose from its rawhide tie as Bren gave her head a hard shake, forcing her focus back to the task at hand. She turned the captain's body onto its side, grabbed the strap of a leather dispatch pouch from his shoulder, and lifted it over his head and off his body. Half-sitting, she slipped the strap over her own head, pushed her arm through it, and draped the pouch over her hip.

Click. The slight sound from behind sent a chill through her. Slowly, she looked around and gritted her teeth to stifle a gasp. Just a body length away, the round, black hole of a musket barrel was aimed directly at her.

Careful now, Bren, she warned herself. Don't startle him with any quick moves.

Curled on his side, the soldier clutched the musket in his hands with one arm braced against the ground and the other jammed against his body. Blood oozed through holes in the midsection of his jacket, and pain distorted his features. His slow drawl was little more than a whisper. "What are you doing?" Small and dark-complected, he was already developing the ashen hue of approaching death. "Are you robbing the dead, you spineless vulture?"

"No," she answered in a rush, before trying to project a calm demeanor in spite of her thudding heart. Although in imminent danger, Bren admired that this man summoned his last ounce of strength to continue fighting for his cause. "I was sent to retrieve the captain's battle orders so the bluebellies wouldn't get hold of them."

She forced herself to breathe normally—a difficult task while looking into the death-hole of a musket barrel.

"You could be a bluebelly. Only gray is the cap." He stopped long enough to drag in a ragged breath. "Could've stolen that."

"That's true." Bren nodded. "But I'm a hired scout, not regulation, so I don't wear a uniform. I have written orders. I'll show you."

"No." The soldier labored through another intake of air. "Going to shoot you."

Adrenaline surged and cold sweat oozed as Bren's muscles tensed. Her eyes quickly measured the distance to the musket's barrel. There was no way she could push it aside before he got off a shot. Poised for action, her body jerked when he spoke again.

"Draw."

Confusion muddled Bren's mind for a brief moment, but self-preservation quickly cut through. If he was going to give her a fighting chance, by God, she was going to take it. And if he felt a little better killing someone in the act of trying to shoot him, that was all right, too. At least she'd go down fighting. I can do this, her mind screamed silently.

Bren's every movement registered in excruciating detail as her fingers popped open the holster cover. Her hand hit the revolver butt with a welcome thud. In one continuous motion, she drew the weapon, thumbed back the hammer, and fired. Flame and smoke spurted more than a foot from the Remington's barrel. She winced as the recoil jerked painfully at her wrist. The bullet struck the soldier's right eye, thrusting his head backward. Bright red blood gushed from the wound, and his musket dropped to the ground. As her racing mind slowed to normal speed, Bren realized she was unharmed. The soldier hadn't fired. Instantly, she questioned the ghastly little smile she'd glimpsed on his lips just before she pulled the trigger.

She holstered her pistol and crawled close enough to grab the barrel of the fallen musket. She pulled it nearer to examine it. One of the newer rifled muskets, the weapon was empty. Bren laid her head down against her quivering arms, and tears squeezed out as she fought a bitter mixture of understanding and anger.

He wanted me to kill him. He knew he was dying and didn't want to lie here for hours in agony. But shooting a man face-to-face . . . ending his life with my own hand. That's a heavier burden than carrying messages back and forth and letting others do the killing. Or is it? I bear blame for that, too. God, I hate this war!

When her shaking stopped, she placed the empty musket next to its owner's body, rubbed her eyes against her sleeve, and crawled away. Most of the moans and cries had died out.

I had such lofty dreams of defending the Union cause, she thought. Now all I feel is guilt. I didn't give Death his due. In war, he's the one who makes the difference. He's the only one who wins.

As happened occasionally, the dispatch satchel held information Bren dared not telegraph from Confederate-held territory. But delivering it to Theo, her Union contact, meant a four-day journey on horseback. She watered Redfire at a nearby stream and fed him a bag of oats scrounged from a camp sutler a few days earlier. Afterward, she filled her canteen and checked her stock of beef jerky. Most of it was in her saddlebags, but she had learned to keep a daily ration in the pockets of her trousers. As a scout, she could never be certain when she'd be separated from horse or provisions or where she would find her next meal. Although food and water were available in towns along most of the trails, carrying her own supply saved time. Preparations finished, she started her journey.

Bren felt comfortable in the forest. One of the attractions of being a scout was the chance to spend so much time there. Even as a child, she had felt an affinity for trees. Their wide branches offered warmth and shelter without asking anything from the traveler. Trees and bushes provided nuts and berries to eat in season. Leaves, bark, and roots could be gathered and steeped for refreshing and medicinal teas. Stalwart and noble, trees afforded a stability that soothed her— an especially welcome occurrence now that her world sorely lacked any permanence.

After more than two days of sleepless travel, she decided she and Redfire needed rest. The town of Cranston was near, so she headed there and stopped at the livery stable on its outskirts. Once she had arranged for the care of her horse, she unhooked the saddlebags, which held the dispatch satchel. With the bags slung over her shoulder, she walked to the Brass Rail Tavern. She stepped into a smoke-filled room where oil lamps glowed along the rim of a wagon-wheel chandelier hanging from a heavy chain in the center of the ceiling. A jumble of voices came from men clustered around a few tables, mostly Confederate soldiers with an occasional woman mixed among them. Opposite the door, other soldiers congregated at a long bar fronted by a brass foot rail with spittoons placed along it. To the left of the bar, a stairway rose to the floor above.

"Hey, Cordell!" The loud voice jarred Bren from her weariness. A gray-clad soldier standing next to a table waved an arm. "C'mon over here!" The man pushed out a chair next to him. "I ain't seen you in ages. Where you been?"

"Sparks." Bren hung her saddlebags on the back of the offered chair and nodded at the speaker. "Good to see you."

Two other men at the table watched the exchange. Sparks waved a hand toward them. "These are a couple of my friends, Taggert and Smoot. Cordell here is a sort of itinerant scout." He lifted a glass of beer from the tray carried by a woman serving the table and sat down. "He's an expert on the terrain around here and goes anywhere he's needed."

Bren dropped onto the wooden seat and ordered a sandwich and a beer from the woman server before answering the soldier. "I just came from Burchfield. Captain Holt gave me a few days off." She lowered her voice. "I heard there was a real slaughter."

"Someone came through about an hour ago with the same news," Taggert said. "He said the damn Yankees knew we was coming up that very trail at that very time. He said even the foot soldiers didn't know where they was going or when, so how did the Yanks find out?"

Smoot turned an accusing look on the newcomer. "You're a scout. How come you didn't see the Yanks was ready and waiting?"

"I told you. I just came from Burchfield. Someone else was scouting for Holt that day. Wish I'd been there. I might have made a difference." The four people at the table sat a few moments in silent contemplation. "There has to be a spy, maybe a turncoat officer," Bren said. She dug a coin from her pocket for the server and began gobbling the chicken and cheese sandwich, washing it down with intermittent gulps of tepid beer.

"Wish I could git my hands on him," Smoot said. "I'd castrate the bastard."

Bren choked, and Sparks pounded on her back. "Slow down there, Cordell. You don't want to be strangling yourself before you git a chance at tonight's fun. We got something on the way that will take your mind off this damn war for a while."

Bren got her gagging under control and questioned him with a raised eyebrow.

31

"This place has some interesting choices of repast," Sparks continued, bringing chuckles from the other men. He waggled a finger for the server's attention and whispered in the woman's ear. She nodded, whispered back, and held out her hand, which made the soldier lean closer to Bren. "There's some willing women here," he said. "We made arrangements for their services for the night and are waiting for the word to go ahead upstairs. Kate here says they can rustle up one for you, too." Sparks grinned wolfishly and again banged the flat of his hand on Bren's back. "If you got a dollar, you got a woman. For the whole night."

Had there been any food in her mouth, Bren would have choked again. "Uh, I don't think so, Sparks. I'm just looking for a good night's sleep. Been on the trail for two days, and I'm really worn out. I'm not up to it."

"I never heard of a soldier being too tired for a little hay-rolling. Besides, these women are good. They'll make sure you're up as much as you need to be." Sparks guffawed. He pulled a silver dollar from his pocket and handed it to the server. "I'll even treat you."

Bren glanced around the table. There was no way Sparks was going to let her off the hook. She would have to take her chances that she could convince the woman she only wanted to rest. After all, the woman might be happy to be paid for doing nothing. Bren forced what she hoped was a lecherous smile and clapped Sparks on the back as hard as she could, grinning inwardly at the mighty huff that sounded forth. "All right, then. Who could turn down such an offer?"

Bren knocked on the upstairs door that the server Kate indicated. As Sparks passed by, he elbowed Bren in the side, winked, and followed Kate down the hall. When the door opened, Bren removed her cap as a pretty, slightly overweight woman near her own age appeared. The young woman wore a garish yellow robe that matched her hair, and she looked up at the tall soldier, widening her hazel eyes in an apparent attempt to seem welcoming.

"Hello, there. Come on in." She closed and locked the door, got rid of Bren's cap by tossing it on the bureau, and hung the saddlebags on the door hook. Bren removed her holster belt and hung it above the saddlebags.

"What's your name, soldier?" Taking Bren by the arm, she led her to the turned-down bed.

A kerosene lamp on a circular table near the bed lit the room dimly, but Bren could see it looked clean and neat. A double bed, a bureau, two chairs, and the table made up the bare furnishings. A multicolored throw rug rested on the hardwood floor next to the bed.

"Bren," she muttered, finding the situation totally embarrassing. Blast that idiot Sparks.

"Glad to meet you, Bren. My name's Leah. Why don't you sit here on the bed?" When Bren didn't respond, Leah reached for the rawhide tie at the top of Bren's shirt. "Or maybe you'd rather we start standing up."

Bren pulled the tie away and a blush rose as she thought about what this woman was expecting from her. "Look," she said weakly and cleared her throat for a stronger try. "No offense, miss, but I'm not here for what you think. One of my friends pushed me into this. I just want to get a good night's rest. I'm so tired I can barely stand, and I surely can't do anything else."

Leah dropped her hands and stepped back, peering at what Bren hoped she saw as an exhausted man. "Am I hearing what I think I'm hearing?" Putting her hands on her ample hips, she tilted her head to one side and grinned. "This has got to be a first. A soldier who is too tired to—" Bren could feel herself blushing furiously. "Ah, I understand! You've never been with a woman, have you?"

"I, uh, no. I've never been with anybody," Bren stammered. "I never much wanted to." She hadn't been drawn to the flirtatious games played between the two sexes. In fact, she couldn't relate to their mutual attraction at all. There had been times when men sought her favors, but she was affronted by their attempts to turn a friendly kiss into permission to explore her body. A few sharp words or an occasional slap prevented any further familiarity. Though vague hungers sometimes plagued her, she usually managed to repress them and considered her sexual desires to be nearly nonexistent.

"Well, maybe you just need a little warming up first, honey." Leah's grin broadened into a smile, and she put her dimpled hand on Bren's chest. Bren grabbed the hand and backed away as fast as her feet could move, but Leah came right along with her, until after only four steps, they halted against the wall. At that point, Leah reached out her other hand and clutched the triangle between Bren's legs.

"Stop it!" No one had ever touched Bren there, even through trousers. In spite of the exhaustion that flowed through her like a sluggish river, she was rattled. She grabbed Leah's shoulders and clumsily pushed her away. "Stop it," she protested again. "I told you, I just want to sleep."

A puzzled look replaced Leah's smile. Before Bren could react, she quickly ran her hands across the soldier's shirtfront, encountering the constricted but telltale shapes beneath. "You're a woman!"

Alarmed, Bren sucked in a sharp breath.

Leah grabbed one of Bren's hands and pulled on it. "Honey, I think we both need to sit down." She followed her own advice and drew a shaky Bren down to a seat next to her on the bed. "You want to tell me what's going on?"

What can I say? Bren wondered. At first disconcerted by Leah's touch but now distracted by the woman's discovery of her gender, she groaned inwardly. I surely can't tell her I need to masquerade as a man so I can spy for the Union. I'll tell her I wanted to serve the Confederacy and hope that convinces her.

"The Confederate Army won't let women be soldiers, but I wanted to fight. So I decided to dress like a man." The potential jeopardy suddenly occurred to her. "Please, don't give me away. I could get into a lot of trouble."

"I won't give you away," Leah promised. "Soldiering has to be a hard life for a woman."

"Yes, it is. Harder than I ever imagined."

Leah cocked her head. "But you could leave whenever you want."

"I'm not a quitter. The men are having a hard time, too. They risk their lives for the cause. I can't see me doing any less."

"I guess we each have to do our part in our own way. Me, I just try to keep the troops happy. But in your case, my usual methods aren't going to work." Leah winked. "You sure look like a man. Of course, the beard's false, too. And here I was thinking how handsome you were compared to those other three, and how lucky I was to get you."

"I'm sorry." Bren truly was sympathetic, and she hoped it showed. "But do you mind if I just go to sleep? I really am terribly tired." As if on cue, she yawned, closed her eyes, and struggled to reopen them.

"Hey, you paid the dollar, sweetie. You can do all the sleeping you want. I sure like the idea of getting a rest myself." Leah placed a hand on her back. "But look, you'll be here all night. Why don't you take off that beard and those bindings and truly relax. They can't be all that comfortable."

"That sounds good to me." Bren suppressed the unease she had felt at Leah's touch, just as she had tried to suppress all her emotions for the past two years. Now she stood and shuffled over to look in a mirror atop the bureau. She removed the rawhide tie from her shoulder-length hair and slipped it in a pocket. Then she peeled the beard from her face and laid it carefully on the bureau, her movements hampered by exhaustion. Almost constant wearing of the false hair had protected the lower part of her face from the sun, allowing only a light tanning of her cheeks and chin. As a result, she seemed to be wearing a brown mask wrapped around liquid amber eyes. Her arm shook as she lifted the pink-flowered pitcher resting on the bureau and barely managed to pour some water into the matching bowl.

"Wait, let me do that," Leah said. "Might as well earn my money some way."

Bren nodded. "I do appreciate your offer, but first I have to wash off this spirit gum. It takes alcohol to do that." She went to her saddlebags and got a silver flask and a cloth. Almost by rote, she poured some of the liquid onto the cloth and cleaned her face and the beard she had removed.

As she finished putting the cleaning materials away, Leah came over to her and picked up a washcloth. After dipping it into the water, she washed Bren's face, grabbed a towel, and dried it. "I really should give you a bath," she teased.

"I sure could use one, but I'm used to going without, and I'm too tired to wait for the water to be heated." Bren ventured a lopsided grin. "Maybe you could make that offer again tomorrow." She enjoyed the woman's ministrations. After two years of trail roughness, it felt good to be coddled.

"I just might do that. Now, get your boots off, and then we'll undo those bindings." Like a good soldier following orders, Bren complied. Leah grasped the hem of Bren's shirt and started to lift it, but Bren shook her head and pulled the shirt back down. Leah grinned. "Shy, huh?"

"I guess I'm just not used to undressing in front of someone else."

"Even another woman?" Leah didn't wait for an answer. "How did you manage with all those men around? Didn't they ever jump in a river to wash, or take their shirts off from the heat and expect you to do the same?"

"Actually, I'm a scout and I travel a lot. I'm not around soldiers all of the time, so I've been able to keep my secret. And with so many streams around, I can stay cleaner, too. Lice are a real problem in the camps." Bren grinned as Leah wrinkled her nose and scratched at her head. "Body lice, too. Most soldiers neglect to wash and rarely change clothes for weeks at a time. When I ride toward a camp, I can smell it before I see it." Reaching under her shirt, Bren worked one end of the binding loose and placed it in Leah's waiting hand. She lifted her arms and slowly turned in circles as Leah unwound the cloth, folded it, and laid it on the bureau.

When finished, Bren sat on the edge of the bed and tightened her arms across her chest. Grimacing at the painful tingling as feeling returned, she closed her eyes and fought the moan that was trying to escape. The ache doubled her over for a couple of minutes while Leah looked on sympathetically.

"I could give you a massage," the woman offered.

Bren smiled as the short-lived pain receded and she straightened up. "Some other time, maybe, though it does sound really tempting. Right now, I just have to get some rest." Turning her body, she swung her legs up onto the bed, laid her head down, and immediately fell asleep.

Leah smiled and shook her head. None of the other women would believe her if she told them the truth about this night. But she had given her word, and she wouldn't betray the soldier's trust. Hell, this was the easiest money she had ever earned. She covered Bren with a brown wool blanket, crawled in next to her, and gradually drifted off.

As dawn arrived, fingers of light reached into the room, touched Bren's eyelids, and stirred her from her dreams of war. Flat on her back, she took a few moments to remember where she was. She felt the warmth of a nearby body, and for a brief moment, unfamiliar sensations stirred through her. She tilted her head and saw Leah curled next to her. How sweet and childlike she looks, Bren mused. She inhaled the perfume that rose from the yellow hair, grateful to have it supplant the memories of battlefield odors. Closing her eyes, she went back to sleep.

Several hours later, she woke with a start, alone in the bed. It was time to get up and get moving. She couldn't tarry now for a bath or massage. Even if Leah's offer had been serious, she had already wasted enough time. For the same reason, she decided today's rations would be beef jerky that she could eat as she rode. Although Bren's work with the army gave her a lot of freedom to move around, if anyone noticed she had been missing for better than a week, it might be hard to explain. With a groan, she got up and locked the door. Using the pitcher of water, bowl, and linens on the bureau, she washed her hands and face. That done, she replaced the binding on her chest and reapplied the false beard and mustache. She pulled the rawhide string from her pocket, ran her fingers through her hair, and tied it into a tail.

After claiming her holster belt from the door hook, Bren notched the leather tight around her hips. Then she lifted the saddlebags and laid them on the bureau. She pulled out the dispatch pouch and checked to make sure the papers were still inside. Next, she returned everything to the saddlebags, threw them across her shoulder, and went into the hall. Daylight showed above a door at the far end of the passage, so she headed in that direction. When she pulled the door, it opened onto a three-foot-square wooden porch with stairs to the street level. She was pleasantly surprised to see Leah sitting on a step near the bottom.

The woman turned at the sound of the door opening. She gave Bren a big smile and motioned her forward. "Come on, soldier. Have a seat for a few minutes." Bren clambered down the stairs and sat on the step just below her, bringing them nearly to eye level. "How about some breakfast?"

"Thanks, but I really have to get moving. I have some jerky I can eat." She tapped the saddlebags she had laid on the next step.

"I guess you don't have time for that bath either, huh?" Leah's smile turned wicked as she leaned toward Bren and lowered her voice. "I could probably find a man or two to help us out." Her smile turned to laughter as she saw Bren's face redden, and she gave her shoulder a friendly squeeze. "Stick with me for a while, friend, I'll get you over that shyness."

Before Bren could respond, a little girl with blonde hair and hazel eyes appeared at the bottom of the steps. She held an old metal serving platter on which sat a couple of dented tin cups and several cakes formed from mud. "Mama, look! I made lunch. Do you—" She lifted her eyes and, at the sight of Bren, stopped speaking. Adjusting to the stranger's presence, the girl lifted the tray toward her. "Want some?"

"I surely do," Bren drawled and flashed a broad smile. "If you'll tell me your name."

"Amy," the child answered, returning Bren's smile with one of her own.

Picking up a mudcake, Bren brought it toward her mouth, pretending to bite and chew it. "Mmm, this is really good. May I have some coffee, too?"

"Please do," Amy answered with a tiny curtsy, bringing a chuckle this time.

Bren lifted one of the tin cups and gurgled as though drinking from it. Amy giggled and held the tray out to her mother. Leah went through the motions of eating and drinking, then made a choking sound when she heard Bren belch. She clapped a hand over her mouth as Bren said, "That was really good."

Amy giggled out loud. "I better go make some more for my other friends." She disappeared back behind the staircase.

"You and Amy live here?"

"Yep." Leah pointed a thumb over her shoulder. "My rooms are through that door back there."

"You can't deny she's yours. She looks just like you." Bren met Leah's smiling eyes. "Hey, I have to get going." She jumped upright and reached for her saddlebags. "It's been good meeting you, Leah. And Amy." Bren held out her hand, and Leah rose and gave it a squeeze.

"I enjoyed meeting you, too. Next time you come this way, let me know and I'll see you get the right partner." She winked as Bren blushed again, then she stood on tiptoe and kissed her cheek. Bren waved and walked off toward the stables to reclaim Redfire. She reached in her pocket for a piece of jerky, chiding herself for not getting up in time to have a decent breakfast. But she needed to get the Rebel dispatch into Theo's hands.

CHAPTER TWO

Several hours after leaving Cranston, Bren took off the Rebel cap, stuck it in a saddlebag, and replaced it with the beat-up, wide-brimmed trail hat similar to the ones worn by recruits on both sides of the conflict. For the greater part of the next two days, she moved northwest, keeping away from known trails. Dense undergrowth littered the spaces between the trees, making the trip longer and more difficult, but traversing it increased the likelihood she would arrive at the regional Union headquarters unopposed.

While she journeyed, the brief interlude with Leah kept nudging into her thoughts. *I enjoyed having a warm body close for a while. I wonder if that's part of the appeal of marriage. Would Phillip make me feel warm and affectionate? Maybe I should think more seriously about his proposal.* That thought brought a grin. *I mean his proposals, plural.* She swished a hand in front of her face as though to brush away her muddled thoughts. *Feelings are too damn confusing. I'll think about marriage when this hell is over.*

As she drew closer to the Union lines, she moved onto the established trail, holding Redfire to a slow pace. She was expecting a hail from the picket line of sentries guarding the Union headquarters.

"Halt!" The word came from the vegetation along the trail, though no one was visible. "Identify yourself."

Bren raised both hands. "I'm Lady Blue."

"Come forward, Lady Blue, and be recognized." A click of Bren's tongue moved Redfire ahead, and a soldier appeared next to the path. He stepped closer and squinted up at her as evening's rapid approach left just enough light to make out her features. He nodded, raised a hand, and waved a signal. "Pass, Lady Blue." Because the sentry recognized her, the hand signal was relayed along the picket line, assuring no others would slow her progress.

Now that she was secure in Union territory, Bren urged Redfire along the trail more quickly, hampered only by the descending darkness. Headquarters was in a town that had sprung up near a railroad station. Several coal mines in the area provided work for the townspeople. Houses, stores, a church, a school, and even a hotel helped the town lay claim to being middle-sized.

Bren intended to exchange news with the officer in charge, who she assumed was still Theo, get a room, and—could she possibly hope?—a bath. Her hat shifted as she slipped the fingers of one hand under it and scratched her scalp. The prospect of running a brush through clean hair brought a groan of anticipation. Too bad she overslept at the tavern and had to turn down Leah's offer of a bath. She smiled at the memory of the friendly woman and the little girl who was the image of her mother. Those moments stolen from the clutches of war had been brief but delightful.

The trail broadened and joined one end of the town's main street. Redfire cantered toward the group of lights that indicated some of the town's central stores and offices were still open. Bren knee-guided the horse to a hitching rail, dismounted, and tied the reins to the rail. After removing the dispatch pouch from her saddlebags, she laid the strap across her shoulder and again gave her password to a guard at the building that housed the commander's office.

With the formalities taken care of, the guard smiled at Bren in recognition. "Hey, Blue, you sure don't look like any lady I ever seen. Didn't your ma ever teach you to shave?" He gave a hearty laugh at his recurring joke before turning to knock on the door behind him. At a sound of acknowledgment from within, he opened the door, stepped in, and saluted. "Lady Blue is here, sir."

"Very well, Sergeant. Show him in. And order some victuals for us."

The sergeant, still fighting a smile at the incongruity of calling a man "Lady," held the door wider and gestured for Bren to enter, then saluted and left the room.

Bren tossed her hat on a nearby table as Theo rose from behind his desk. He strode toward her and grasped both her hands in his. "Sarah, it's good to see that you're safe." Still holding her hands, he stepped back and let his searching blue eyes survey her from top to toe, shook his head, and grinned. "You sure do make a fine-looking man." He released her and slung an arm over shoulders that were a little higher than his, leading her to a seat by his desk. "But I have to tell you, you make an even finer-looking woman. I'll be glad when this war is finished and things get back to normal."

Sarah-Bren slumped into the chair and rubbed a hand across her eyes. The sleep with Leah had helped, but being awake for the last thirty hours was catching up to her. "You think we'll ever get back to normal, Theo?" As she finished speaking, she removed the dispatch pouch from her shoulder and laid it on the desk.

Theo sat back against the edge of the desk. "You're certainly doing your part to help things along. That information you gave us last month about the movement of Rebel troops was right on target. We had a regiment in place this past week and whipped the hell out of them."

"I know. I was there." Her expression dimmed for a moment, but she didn't explain. Instead, her hand flicked toward the desk. "There's the dispatch pouch from the captain of that force. It mentions the possibility of an attack on a railroad junction that's close to Confederate lines."

Theo reached inside the pouch and lifted out the papers. After a quick perusal, he raised his head. "They obviously had some information about—" A knock at the door stopped him. "Enter," he said. Two soldiers brought in mugs, sugar, cream, a tin pot of coffee, and a platter of sandwiches. They saluted and pulled the door shut as they departed.

Theo didn't finish his sentence. Instead, he waved the papers and said, "We'll be sure to be prepared for them. Many thanks, Sarah." He set the papers on the desk and rested his hands on his knees. "I have a surprise for you. Guess what?"

"Oh, Theo." Almost too tired to care, Sarah leaned against the chair's high back and stretched her arms above her head. She lowered them and made a desultory attempt to cover a yawn that pulled her bearded cheeks out of shape. "I'm not in the mood for guessing games. What is it?"

Instead of answering, he raised his voice. "Come on in, gentlemen."

Sarah let her head roll sideways toward the room's other door. As soon as her eyes lit on the first figure entering, she jumped to her feet. "Scott!" She hurled herself at her twin. He met her with open arms, flung them around his sister's waist, and lifted her off the floor, spinning in circles. Meanwhile, Sarah wrapped her arms around Scott's neck and squeezed. When he stopped whirling her around and set her down, she kissed his cheek and pulled him to her once more. "Oh, my God, Scott, I sometimes wondered whether we would ever see each other again."

"I wish I never had to let you go." Scott's arms tightened and his voice roughened. "When I think of you facing the dangers of battle, I get sick to my stomach." After a moment, he pushed away from Sarah, and she could see tears seeping from the corners of his eyes. "I swear, Sarah-Bren Coulter, you have more hair on your face than I have on mine." Sarah's fingers wiped the tears from her brother's smooth-shaven cheeks, and he grinned wryly. "Why am I always the one who cries?"

Tears sprang into Sarah's eyes, too, and she wiped them with her sleeve as she choked out an answer. "Because you're the one with the softer heart."

"What a sight." Another voice broke into their absorption in each other. "First, two men who look almost exactly alike are kissing each other, and now they're crying like babies." A big, blond-haired man in a captain's uniform grinned at the twins.

"Phillip!" Sarah gave her brother's arm a squeeze and turned to greet the speaker. "Would you like to kiss a man, too?" she asked with a laugh. "In fact, while I'm dressed as a man, you all better call me Bren."

"Try to stop me." Phillip stepped forward to Bren, and the two embraced and kissed. "You look and taste a lot better when you don't have hair on your face." His voice lowered. "But I'll take a kiss from you anytime I can get one."

Unsettled by Phillip's dogged persistence, Sarah flushed and stepped away. "What are you two doing here?" she asked in a rush, looking from Phillip to her brother. "And where's Lindsay? Did she come?"

"No." Scott shook his head. "Someone had to keep an eye on Pres, as well as the foundry. She was really disappointed that she couldn't come, and she sends her love."

"It would have been wonderful to see her." Sarah made a face. "Especially since I'm usually surrounded by dirty, sweaty men."

Theo rubbed his chin and cleared his throat. "Men aren't the only ones who can be dirty and sweaty."

The other two men snorted as Sarah blushed and laughed. "All right, I guess I deserved that. Be assured I'll get you back for it, Theo." Her tone sobered. "But tell me what this meeting means."

"First, come sit down and eat something," Theo said. "We might as well get comfortable while we discuss this." He sat behind his desk and waved the three to the chairs in front of him. He poured four cups of coffee, handed them around, and pushed the cream, sugar, and spoons within reach of his companions. After each person had taken a sandwich, he continued. "Go ahead, Scott. Your family's foundry is involved in this, so you might as well start. My little brother can fill in his part when you're done." Since Phillip was a good eight inches taller than Theo, the colonel's use of "little" was a familiar brotherly jest.

"Coulter Foundry and Davely Armory are combining to ship a huge supply of munitions by rail," Scott said. "It's designated for the troops in northern Virginia, so it will be transferred at the rail junction in Hadley's Run."

Tired as she was, Sarah's brain raced faster than a team of horses. "Rail's the quickest, but it's also the most dangerous. Part of the rail lines run close to Rebel territory, and that particular junction is within striking distance for them." Sounds like that's what the dispatch was about, she thought. "You'll need extra guards. On the train and on the ground."

"That's where I come in," Phillip said. "I'll have a detachment of troops on the first train, and some others will be lying in wait at the junction. If there's no trouble at the transfer point, after the second train is loaded, the troops will change over to it. Once we get past the transfer area, the remainder should be an easy trip."

Sarah cocked her head toward Phillip. "The munitions and troops are being changed to a second train? Why aren't the cars just being uncoupled and switched to another engine?"

Scott answered instead of Phillip. "We have another shipment going out within the week. We'll need the cars back for that one."

Sarah nodded as she assimilated this information.

"Maybe you can help us . . . Bren." Theo pointed to the papers on the desk. "That information you just brought tells us the Rebs know about the shipment. If you can feed them false information about which trains are involved, or even which day, we can set a trap, clear out the opposition, and send the real trains on their way."

"Good idea." Sarah said. "Maybe you can make up a phony dispatch, and I can claim to have stolen it from a Union courier." She shifted in her chair and stretched her neck. "I don't want you all to think I don't appreciate seeing you, but I'm absolutely worn out. I need to get a bath and grab some sleep. You settle the details and decide what messages need to be delivered, and I'll catch up on everybody's news in the morning." She stood, and the men rose, too.

Theo smiled and offered some welcome information. "I already have a room reserved for you at the Midtown Hotel, with a connecting bath. While we're headquartered here, it's a permanent reservation for whenever you have a chance to stay overnight. It's in the name of Brendan Coulter."

My grandfather, Sarah mused. "Bless you, Theo." She kissed each of the men good night and plodded out the door. Her heart was singing from the unexpected visit with Scott and Phillip, but her body just wanted to drop on the spot and never move.

At the hotel, Sarah arranged to have hot water and towels brought for her bath and dragged herself upstairs to her room. She rooted in her saddlebag for a nightshirt, tossed it on the bed, and dumped the bag in a corner. Not wanting to dirty the bedclothes, she dropped into a chair and watched as a gray-haired man brought buckets of steaming water to fill the metal tub in the adjoining room. When he finished and left a stack of towels, she locked the door and tore off her shirt, exposing her cloth-bound upper body. She quickly unwrapped the cloth, sighing with relief as she freed her breasts from imprisonment. As she ran her hands up and down her chest, the pain of returning sensation brought remembrance of Leah's proposed massage, and a smile broke through despite the discomfort.

Now this damn beard and mustache, she thought with a groan. Watching in the mirror atop the bureau, she removed the disguise from her cheeks and the area above her lips. As she scrutinized her two-tone skin, she addressed her image. "You might look like Grandfather Brendan with the beard on, but you sure don't look like Grandmother Sarah without it." Wonder what they would think of their namesake now? Sarah-Bren Coulter, betrayer of hundreds. Has anyone any idea of how many deaths I'm responsible for? Can I ever atone for that? Sarah quickly suppressed the haunting question, as she always did.

With a helpless shrug for perhaps never finding a suitable answer, she skinned off her boots and the rest of her clothing. Grateful to be free of the sweaty garments, she headed into the next room. She bypassed a chair that held several white towels, tested the bath water with her fingertips, and stepped into the tub. She sat down slowly, prolonging the pleasure of her body meeting the water as she sank into it up to her armpits. For more than ten minutes, she luxuriated in the rare delight of a warm bath, moving occasionally just to feel the water lap over her shoulders and stir against her body. Then, with the realization that the warmth was fleeting, she washed her body and her hair.

She reached for one of the towels piled on the chair and emerged from the tub, enjoying more moments of sensory pleasure as she stroked the soft towel over her body. She watched, amazed, as her hands transformed into Leah's and the tingling of her body took on another dimension. *What is going on with you, Sarah? Yes, a massage would have been nice, but Leah was half-joking. Are you so tired you can't think straight?* She shook her head and brought her wayward thoughts and feelings under control. Quickly, she moved the towel to her head and concentrated on the task of rubbing her scalp and drying her hair.

Back in the bedroom, Sarah slipped on the thigh-length nightshirt, dug a brush from her kit, and sat on the edge of the bed. Starting at the bottom of her hair, she worked the brush slowly through her tangled tresses, fighting to stay awake to complete the delightfully familiar, but now rare, ritual. Using her fingers, she helped the bristles pry the knots loose. When all the snarls were gone, she brushed her hair a hundred strokes, raising shimmering bronze highlights within its brown hue. At last, she put the brush away, lifted the covers, and slid between the sheets. A moment later, she fell asleep with a tentative smile on her lips, hoping for at least one peaceful dream before the staring eyes of a fallen boy-soldier and his small, dark-complected comrade haunted her.

The next morning, Sarah wrapped her bosom and applied the fake beard with fresh spirit gum. Since these townspeople weren't engaged in the actual fighting, she felt she was not in any danger of being recognized as a Rebel scout. Still, she didn't want to draw any attention to herself by appearing in their midst as a woman dressed like a man.

As she entered the hotel's dining area, she saw Scott and Phillip in the far corner of the otherwise empty room and walked over to them. Phillip started to rise, but Scott's hand on his arm stopped him. "I don't think captains rise to greet scouts. Good morning, Sarah. We've finished breakfast, but join us while we have our coffee."

Phillip resettled in his seat. "And I don't know any men named Sarah," he said in a quiet tone, reminding Scott of the name change. "Good morning, Bren."

"Good morning. I'm grateful we're alone at the moment, or my disguise would be compromised. You each get a point for being correct. And a point gets subtracted for also being incorrect." Sarah pulled out a chair and sat as she favored two of the dearest men in her life with a tender look. While they taunted each other like schoolboys for their mistakes, she was reminded of the day in the Coulter drawing room when she first had spoken to them about becoming a spy. *They haven't changed much,* she thought, *but I have.*

"And what are you smiling about?" Scott asked his sister when the men finally ended their verbal jousting.

"I was just thinking about the day I told you I had decided to masquerade as a man. Remember?"

"I remember being totally against it," Scott answered. "But that obviously didn't deter you."

Phillip's lips tightened, and he blurted, "You should have forbidden her! The army is no place for a woman."

Both Scott and Sarah turned to look at him, and Sarah's words were as chill as a winter wind. "You're sorely mistaken if you think that anyone is in a position to forbid me to do anything."

Scott lifted an eyebrow. "You heard her, Phillip. You know Bren's never let me or anyone else order her around. I don't even make the attempt anymore. I'm not happy with her decision, and I'm constantly worried, but I don't have the right to stop her."

"Well, I'm not happy with it either." Phillip's expression showed his disapproval. "I won't be happy until you quit."

"Oh, hush, Phillip. I'm not about to quit. The information I've carried back and forth has helped in a number of battles. I've been there to see it, and I'm none the worse for it. You do agree I'm serving a useful purpose, don't you?" Without waiting for an answer, Sarah lifted her plate from the table and carried it across the spacious room to the food-laden sideboard.

"Your sister is the most hardheaded woman I know," Phillip complained.

Scott gave a short laugh. "You say that like you just figured it out. You grew up with her, same as I did, so the idea is not a new one." He took a sip of his warm coffee. "Maybe you're lucky she keeps turning you down." He had teased his friend for years about

Sarah's lack of commitment to him, but today for some reason, it made Phillip flush.

He ran a finger under his collar, as though it were too tight against his skin, and his gaze followed the object of his affections as she made several selections from the available food. "Do you think she'll ever have me, Scott?" he said in a low voice. "She knows how I feel about her."

Scott watched Phillip watching his sister. "Sarah told you a long time ago she's not the marrying kind. My sister is too independent." He smiled at Phillip to soften his words. "As far as I can recall, she's never mentioned being attracted to anyone. I know she cares a lot for you, though, if that's any consolation."

Phillip grimaced as Sarah made her way back to their table. "I guess it will have to be, for now."

Theo forged a dispatch that included a false date and time for the munitions shipment Coulter Foundry was preparing. The real shipment would go a day earlier. When Bren was satisfied the dispatch looked authentic, she stuffed it into her saddlebag and made her way back to Confederate territory. She knew the area so well, she was able to slip past the Rebel pickets without detection. Scouts always had passwords, but she avoided using hers whenever possible. There was added risk if they became aware of how often she passed through the lines.

She estimated the distance the remnants of Holt's infantry had retreated after their defeat and guided Redfire through the hills and valleys until she found the tattered force. She went directly to the headquarters tent, which displayed the regiment's flag just below that of the Confederacy.

"Hey, Cordell," the soldier posted at the entrance said and nodded.

"Beecher." Bren nodded in return. "I have a dispatch for Captain Holt."

Beecher shook his head. "Where've you been? Captain Holt got killed in the last battle. We got us a Captain Lockman now."

Bren feigned a look of shock. "Damn shame. Holt was a good man. I did hear you took the worst of it."

"We surely did. Lost nearly half our men." The soldier stuck his head through the tent flap and spoke some words. He ducked back out and motioned for Bren to enter. "Captain said to send you in."

Captain Lockman sat at a carved-wood desk that held papers stacked in several piles. "Good to meet you, Cordell." Lockman's voice held the soft drawl of the deep South. "I've come across your name in Captain Holt's papers. He had a high opinion of your abilities."

"Thank you, sir." Bren set her saddlebags on the floor and reached into one. "I have something here that I think may prove important." She pulled out the false dispatch and handed it to Lockman, who read it immediately.

The captain gave a low whistle and raised his eyes. "This information could be very significant. How did you get this?"

Bren pitched her voice lower. "I know this land well, sir. When I was returning from my leave, I crept near the Yankee lines to see whether I could find out anything worthwhile. I was just in the right place at the right time and came across a courier carrying that dispatch. He and I had a little *discussion* about it, and he lost." She hesitated a moment for emphasis. "I hid his body in a cave. When I saw what the message was, I rode here as fast as I could. I figured since your troops are near the railroad junction in question, maybe you would be able to do something to stop the shipment."

"Good work, Cordell. I'll see that this gets into the proper hands. Maybe we'll be lucky enough to play a part in that action." Lockman laid the dispatch on his desk. "You go on and get some rest. I might have some work for you later today."

"Yes, sir. I'll be on the north edge of camp." *Upwind.*

Bren hoisted her saddlebags over her shoulder and left the tent. Leading Redfire by the reins, she walked to the outskirts of the encampment. As soon as she picked a spot to settle, she tied the end of one rein to a tree limb, allowing Redfire enough slack to nibble at the grass. While he fed, Sarah relieved him of saddlebags and saddle, set them on the ground, and used the saddle as a backrest.

She had missed the noon mess, and although she had some food in a sack she kept in a saddlebag, she decided to rely on her supply of beef jerky. She pulled a piece from a pocket, tore off a chunk with her teeth, and chewed the hard substance while her mind went over the plan about the ammunition shipment.

She nodded to herself, satisfied that the ruse concerning the false shipment was working. Now, all she had to do was keep her eyes and ears open for the next few days to be sure that whichever troops were assigned to stop the train would arrive there at least twenty-four hours too late.

Bren hauled her saddlebags closer, pulled out her journal, and removed a nibbed pen and a stoppered bottle of ink from a protective pouch. Fixing the bottle comfortably within reach, she propped the journal against her knees and began writing. For most of the afternoon, she wrote what she could of the past week of her daily activities without divulging her masquerade. When she finished her recording, she drew a camp scene of the men within her current field of vision.

Around suppertime, she grabbed her tin bowl and spoon and selected a couple of potatoes, two apples, and a hunk of cornbread from the sack in her saddlebags. With the food as an offering, she hunted up a group of soldiers who had a "don't-ask-what's-in-it" soup pot going. She had learned early that these thrown-together meals beat the standard mess rations by far. Her potatoes got chopped into the pot, her apples and two pears from another soldier were sliced for dessert, and she got one chunk of bread back for dipping. For all that, Bren received two bowls of one of the best soups she had ever tasted. It was a good day.

Bren didn't have to go anywhere as courier that evening, but at first light the next morning the captain summoned her to take a message to an adjoining regiment, a day's ride away. As soon as she was out of sight of the camp, she pulled Redfire off the trail and inspected the message she was carrying. Captain Lockman was passing on the information she had delivered to him yesterday and asking advice and orders from Colonel Arborough, the ranking officer of the neighboring troops.

Thinking to slow any preparations for attack that reception of the dispatch could set in motion, Bren took her time delivering the missive. When Colonel Arborough received the information, he had Bren wait for his answer to Captain Lockman. He finally handed Bren his response, and she quickly mounted Redfire and left the campsite. After she had traveled a safe distance, she stopped near a stream and dismounted. While the sorrel drank his fill, she read the newly written message. Once she got past the usual flowery greeting and read the text, she gasped. She reread it, but of course, the words had not changed:

We have an informant who sent us a report of this shipment two weeks ago. I, indeed, sent Captain Holt a message notifying him of the shipment, thinking we could mount a combined attack and perhaps capture the arms and ammunition for our own use. Last week, I received a second dispatch from our informant, advising that the shipment would be heavily guarded, both on the train and at the transfer point in Hadley's Run, resulting in a useless loss of many troops. The term "useless" was chosen because it is the informant's belief that any attempt at securing the shipment would likely result in its destruction before the enemy would allow it to be seized.

This probability has given rise to an alternate plan. The informant will ride on the train, hide incendiary devices amid the munitions, and cause them to detonate at Hadley's Run, thus ridding the area of as many of our enemy as possible. In addition, the destruction of the munitions will prevent their use against our own men.

I call to your attention that the message you have forwarded to me names the date of the shipment as one day later than the actual shipping time. This discrepancy will cause no problem, even if your message proves to be more accurate. Our informant will be at the site of departure and will be on the train regardless of the date.

Your troops and mine need not take part in this action. I will soon be informing you of your next assignment.

Colonel Arborough

Bren's hand shook at the implications of this message. She thrust the dispatch back into the pouch, climbed onto Redfire, and kicked her heels into his flanks to urge him forward. As the horse bolted through the trees, she fought against the numbness that threatened to shut down her brain.

This is not the time for panic, she thought. Scott and Phillip will be on that train. They and hundreds of others will be in jeopardy. I have to warn them.

She realized the odds were against her. She was now three days away from the endangered junction, three days away from the nearest Union telegraph office, and the time of shipment was three days away, too. Her best hope was to intercept the train before it arrived at the junction. Redfire just had to get her there in time.

CHAPTER THREE

S cott Coulter twisted his shoulders to ease the discomfort caused by hours of riding on the train. The stretching was pure reflex. The possibility of an enemy assault was what preoccupied his mind. As he sat at the back of the passenger car full of armed soldiers, his gaze continuously surveyed the passing scenery, searching for suspicious movement. He chided himself for allowing the situation to exert such a magnetic effect on his eyes. He had an irrational feeling that if he stayed constantly alert, nothing would happen; but if his vigilance faltered, disaster would overtake them. At one point, he stood, lifted the window beside him, and stuck out his head, careful to immediately turn his face away from the cinders flying out of the engine smokestack.

As the train slowed and traversed a curve around a finger of water, Scott had a good view of each car. His was immediately behind the coal car. Another one full of soldiers rolled directly after his, with two boxcars loaded with rifles, cartridges, and dynamite from Davely Armory next in line. Two flat cars carrying cannons and crates of ammunition concealed by tarpaulins followed, with another passenger car of soldiers and civilian representatives from Coulter and Davely connected to it. A caboose brought up the rear. Satisfied that all looked in order, Scott withdrew his head from the window and sat down. He glanced self-consciously at Phillip, seated facing him. "I hate this uncertainty."

"It's better than the reality of battle," Phillip said. "But let the guards worry about it."

Soldiers had been posted at strategic points inside the passenger cars, and even on the roofs of the boxcars, but Scott noticed that

Phillip occasionally became restless, too. With little other activity available to them, Phillip periodically moved from car to car, checking in with the guards and the other soldiers. Each time, he returned to his seat and met Scott's questioning gaze with the same words. "Relax. Everything's fine."

Scott's fingers played with the fob on the chain that lay against his vest until finally he couldn't resist pulling out his pocket watch. "About twenty more minutes." Then what? his inner voice asked.

Bren pounded through the forest on Redfire, riding low against the animal's neck to avoid the springy branches that slapped at her face and arms. She was too focused to bother rolling down her sleeves, though a few broken branches had gouged her arms. Grateful for her mount's sure-footed response to her urgency, she spoke words of praise and encouragement to him, to which he responded with even greater effort.

Filled with horror by the possibility of losing Scott or Phillip— maybe both of them—she drove Redfire to the very edge of his endurance before stopping to give the animal needed rest. During these brief delays, Bren tried to relax, but the gravity of her mission made that difficult. Several times, she fell asleep from sheer exhaustion, only to jolt awake after a short rest and hasten on her way, carefully skirting picket lines of both armies.

When at last she topped the final mountain ridge, a clear spot allowed her to search the valley below and she could see Hadley's Run, at least two miles away by horseback. Beyond the town, a string of smoke puffs billowed into the air from a train slowly approaching the junction. At such a distance, Bren couldn't tell what the flat cars carried, but dread that it might be the munitions train hammered through her.

She sent Redfire pell-mell straight down the mountainside. "Faster, boy, faster."

Nervous excitement shivered through Scott as they neared the junction. He pulled a linen handkerchief from the inside pocket of his frock coat and pressed it to the slight depression above his upper lip to soak up the perspiration gathered there. As he returned the cloth to his pocket, his friend glanced at him with a slight smile.

Phillip's eyes mirrored Scott's tension as the big man stood up and said, "So far, so good." He stepped into the aisle and spoke to the soldier in the next seat. "Lieutenant Murray, tell those in charge in the other cars to stay alert and be prepared to disembark as soon as we stop. I'll order the transfer of the material immediately afterward." As Murray left, Phillip raised his voice to the other soldiers. "Men, we're almost at our exchange point. Keep your eyes open for anything suspicious. Be ready to leave the train and form up at the nearest freight car as quickly as you can."

Scott rose and teetered a moment before grabbing the top of the nearest backrest to catch his balance. With his other hand, he lifted his derby hat from the seat next to him, placed it on his head, and turned toward Phillip. "The train has slowed enough. I'll jump off and check to make sure the wagons are ready for transferring the shipment to the other train. Maybe I can hurry things up. I'd like to get clear of this junction as soon as possible."

"I agree." Phillip stepped aside, allowing Scott to pass him toward the door of the car. "We have plenty of protection, but sitting here without moving is an invitation to attack." He watched Scott reach for a handrail and disappear through the doorway. As he turned back toward his troops, the men stood and gathered their gear. From a seat, Phillip picked up his sheathed sword, removed earlier for the sake of comfort. He belted the scabbard around his middle and donned the dark blue slouch hat that had rested next to the weapon.

Suddenly, the sound of an explosion burst against his ears. The car shifted as though shaken by a giant hand. Soldiers stumbled and cursed, some falling to their knees. Phillip pushed frantically to the door. He wrenched it open and leaped through. A second explosion slammed him to the ground. Dazed, he looked up and saw a dark shape hurtling toward him. "Oh, God!" he cried aloud, and his world went black.

Still nervous as he emerged from the network of tracks that met at the junction, Scott glanced back across the yard at the train. He saw and heard the first explosion just as he was knocked off his feet. His hat went flying, lifted by the wind from the blast. Moving on instinct, he crawled behind a railroad equipment box sitting near the station building. When he tried to peer around it, a second explosion sent pieces of shrapnel whizzing by. One nicked his cheek as he jerked back. Rolling into a ball, he protected his head while bits of metal and

53

wood rained down around him. He grimaced as explosion after explosion shook the air and rocked the ground. When the blasts stopped, he cautiously poked his head past the side of the box and froze in horror at the sight.

Bren was about a mile and a half from the junction when huge clouds of smoke sprouted into the sky like ugly black blossoms streaked with white. Almost immediately, the sounds of multiple explosions rippled toward her. Please, no. Please, no. She urged her horse across the seemingly endless valley. For several seconds, her brain operated more swiftly than her body traveled, and she saw herself and Redfire slogging across the ground in slow motion. She shook herself back to real time, desperate to reach the train.

She swept to the north, turning a lathered Redfire toward the outskirts of town where the rail tracks met. Passing through hordes of people streaming toward the site of the explosions, she saw others already there, trying to rescue victims of the destruction. Frantic to find Scott and Phillip, Bren dismounted. She wrapped Redfire's reins around her hand, and pulled the uneasy animal through the chaos. The scene was as bad as any battlefield she had seen. The engine lay on its side, knocked off its wheels. The cars behind it were twisted into misshapen clumps of metal, as if huge chunks of grotesque sculpture had erupted from the bowels of the earth. Heat pulsed from everything like a physical presence. Almost by reflex, Bren rolled down her sleeves to protect her scratched arms.

The roar of flames, screams of injured, and calls of rescuers pummeled her ears like an erratic thunderstorm. Fear gnawed her stomach. She tugged Redfire through pieces of building material, body parts, and wreckage strewn amid the injured and dying. Flames spurted and smoke billowed above and around her. She choked on the noxious, cinder-filled air. Her nose and eyes burned from the fumes, and Redfire tossed his head and snuffled. She wiped her sleeve against the tears and sweat oozing onto her face. Most of it ran into her beard.

As she searched the ground, she saw the back of a blond-haired soldier wearing a captain's insignia. He lay sprawled facedown against a shattered ammunition crate, impaled on a piece of its wood. Sarah ran toward him, tripped on a rail, and stumbled. Her hold on Redfire's reins helped keep her balance. When she reached the man, she dropped to her knees. She grabbed his shoulder and yanked him onto his back. It wasn't Phillip.

Bren closed her eyes and swallowed several times, trying to settle her stomach. She felt sorrow for the unfamiliar soldier, but fresh tears of thankfulness seeped from her eyes. It's not Phillip. But where is he? And Scott? She wiped again at her wet face and staggered up to continue searching.

Off to one side, townspeople removed debris so soldiers could place dead bodies in rows, one next to the other. Almost as quickly as workers cleared a space, another body filled it. With a sinking heart, Bren threaded her way through the first of the rows, holding a nervous Redfire at her shoulder. When she looked toward the train, she saw a dark-haired man kneeling next to the first of the overturned cars. She blinked several times. Something about the man's bearing was familiar enough to lift her heart. She mounted Redfire and guided him in that direction, allowing the stallion to pick his way through the rescuers and the debris. Most of the cars were aflame. Billows of black smoke diminished Bren's vision even further, but she thought she saw someone lying on the ground next to the man's knee.

Why are they still by the train? The fire's all around them. Her heart thudded harder as she got closer to the car, and she rode Redfire as near as she could without the flames further spooking the animal.

She dismounted and hung Redfire's reins over a flimsy sticker bush apparently denuded of leaves by the explosion. As she hurried toward the two figures, the heat became stifling. The roar and crackling of the flames grew louder. She squatted next to the kneeling man and saw that he truly was her brother. He opened his mouth. His lips contorted, moving soundlessly.

"Scott." She gave his arm a quick squeeze. "Thank goodness you're all right." Her burning eyes immediately went to the person lying on the ground. She sucked in a sharp breath. Phillip. He looked perfect except for one horrible situation. The top corner of the fallen boxcar had crushed everything about six inches below his right knee. Her words were hoarse. "Oh, my God, Phillip. Your leg!"

Phillip's eyes opened. Smiling at Bren through his pain, he tried to speak. With the noise of the fire crashing around them, she had to bend close to hear him. "I'm in a mess," he struggled to say, "and Scott's reluctant to do the job." He blinked and sighed. "But here you come to the rescue." Then he slipped into unconsciousness.

Bren lifted her head. She told herself to forget it was Phillip. Put his leg out of your mind. He needs help. Think! Her eyes raked the area and she saw immediately that there was nothing available to raise the car from Phillip's leg. Fire shot up into the sky. Her body overheated as flames worked toward them, inching ever nearer. "We have to do something. Fast!"

She turned to Scott. He squinted against the tainted air, tears coursing rivulets down his dirty cheeks. She couldn't tell whether the tears were due to the cinders or due to fear for his friend. He held a hunting knife, and as their eyes met, he spoke. "I tried to find a medic. But with so many people badly hurt, I couldn't get one."

Without hesitation, Bren leaned forward until her lips were next to his ear. Gently she said, "I'll do it, Scott." She placed her hand over his. Her fingers joined his on the hilt of the knife, and she yanked at it.

Scott locked his grip on the knife and spoke thickly. "I'll do it."

"No, I've seen worse. I'm better prepared for this." *How could I ever be prepared for this?* The thought surged through Bren's mind, unsummoned. *But it's either cut off his leg or let him die, so there really is no choice. I can't let Scott carry the burden of crippling his best friend. That would cripple him, too.*

And what of me? She knew it would affect her also, but she dismissed the idea as a distraction from the task at hand. She gave her brother a fierce look. "We don't have time to argue. Give me the damn knife."

Even in a daze, he seemed to recognize the determination on her face, gave a nod of surrender, and released the knife without any further struggle.

Bren slashed off Phillip's pant leg and exposed his knee, allowing a quick glance to determine where and how she should begin. She touched her finger to a spot on his leg. "Take off his belt and tie it tight right here." She turned back her cuffs and rolled up her sleeves. Scott tied the belt and looked back at her. "Okay. Now get my blanket roll from Redfire. We can use it to pull Phillip to safety when I've got him free."

Scott reached over and squeezed his sister's arm. "I'll be right back."

"Thanks," Bren whispered and swallowed hard. She blinked her eyes several times before shutting them tight while she offered up a quick prayer. "I can do this," she muttered, calling up her favorite phrase, which always seemed to fortify her.

She bent down, locked her grasp on Phillip's leg below his knee, and made the first incision near the edge of the crushed tissue. At times, she grabbed the hilt with both hands to power the blade through jagged bone. Blood ran down her hands and across her arms. She barely noticed how it stung the cuts that had been gouged in her skin during her frantic journey. Scott returned with the blanket and held Phillip's body steady for her. A few more hard thrusts and he was free.

They hurried to get Phillip onto the blanket and pulled with all their strength to drag him away from the flames. They hauled him a hundred feet, zigzagging through debris, and nearly ran over a medic. Scott stumbled to the ground and gasped for air. When the medic saw Phillip, he yelled for help, and men came with a stretcher.

As the men took Phillip away, Scott went with them. Bren dashed to Redfire, mounted, and caught up to the group. Would Phillip be all right? She clenched her teeth together so hard that she reckoned her jaw would be sore for several days. She wondered if her heart would ever recover.

Scott and Bren sat at Phillip's bedside in the army's makeshift field hospital. Bren dropped her hat on the floor by her feet and glanced around at the other patients, some with visitors. She pitched her voice low enough for only Scott to hear. "I want to hear everything that happened to you and Phillip, but it's important that you remember to call me Bren."

Her brother quietly explained how he and Phillip escaped death, finishing with the aftermath of the explosions. He nodded toward Phillip. Their friend was still asleep from the chloroform given him before the surgeon cauterized the stump of his leg.

"I found Phillip pinned and he begged me to—" Scott hesitated, unable to put the facts into words. Instead, he just waved his hand. "Then you appeared, like a guardian angel." He gave his sister a grateful look. "You saved us both."

"Listen, Scott." Bren reached up, pulled the rawhide tie from her hair, and stuck it in a pocket. She thrust her fingers through the loosened strands and bowed her head, her fingers still splayed across the crown. "I'm not anyone's guardian angel. I tried my damnedest to get here in time to warn you, but I didn't make it." She jerked as realization struck her like a blow. If she hadn't purposely dallied on her way to deliver the dispatch to Colonel Arborough, she could have saved everyone. "I used some bad judgment, and a lot of people are dead because of it."

"Why do you insist on blaming yourself?" Scott gently chided. "You didn't set off those explosions. The saboteurs who did that are the real culprits. The authorities need to find out who they are."

"You're right." Bren removed her fingers from her hair and sat up straighter, making an effort to ignore her distress. "The dispatch from Colonel Arborough mentioned an informant. In all the turmoil, I forgot about that." Her whole being became more alert. She had always been good at analyzing situations. Her brain seemed to get right to the crux of any problem and systematically examine every possible solution. Scott exhibited the same talent, but his found fruition mainly in the business world. Bren had no such limitations. She thought out loud. "One man could do it. He wouldn't need to smuggle explosives aboard with the train carrying all that ammunition. He would only need to set up some fuses ahead of time and light them at the proper moment. By using several different lengths, he could light the fuses from one or two spots. He also had to have been riding on the train to the junction, but he wouldn't want to be on it when it blew up." Bren rubbed the back of her neck, a habit that seemed to help her concentrate. "Did you see anyone leave the train when you did?" She focused her gaze on her brother.

"Now that you mention it, I think there was someone else who got out of a car farther down from me. I was in such a hurry to make sure the wagons were ready, I didn't pay much attention to him."

"Are you certain he got out of a car? Or could he have been emerging from between cars?"

Scott's brow furrowed as he tried to picture those few moments. He answered slowly, the words measured, "He was down by the two boxcars, so he could have been coming from between them."

"Was he a soldier?"

"No, I think he was a civilian. Yes, that's right. He was wearing a dark brown suit. And I sensed he was hurrying away from the train just as I was. But he went in the opposite direction."

"You need to give that information to the authorities. Tell them about the informant, but do it without implicating me. I have to get back and figure out some way to excuse my absence." Bren picked up her hat and settled it on her head. She stood and put a hand on Scott's shoulder to keep him from rising.

Her brother placed his hand over hers and spoke quietly. "Stay here. You've done more than your share. Aren't you tired of this masquerade?"

"Yes, I'm tired, but of the war, not of the masquerade. And I've been instrumental in changing the tide of battle more than once." Bren sat down heavily in the chair and rested her palms on her thighs. "Did you hear any details about the battle at Hainesville?"

"Some. I heard the Rebs were making a great advance, but one reserve group failed to move forward, and the advance failed. After that, our forces drove them back."

"That's right." Bren nodded and her eyes flashed. "And that group didn't move forward because it received the wrong orders. From me."

Scott's eyebrows lifted. "How did you manage that?"

"I walked right in among General Torlynn's troops. I had met his courier before, so I found him and just hung around him, in case I could cause some mischief. There was so much going on during the advance that the general didn't even write down the orders for the reserve regiment. He had one of his aides deliver it to the courier verbally." Bren looked down at her hands. "I heard every word. So I followed the man, put him out of commission, and delivered the wrong orders. Then I just disappeared."

"Put him out of commission?"

Bren closed her eyes for a moment. She opened them and stared at her brother. "I killed him, Scott. He saw me. There wasn't any other way."

"You killed him?" Scott put a hand to his chest and turned pale. "You always were strong, but the war has made you ruthless. I'm not sure I know you anymore."

Bren stood again, but Scott made no move to rise, though he knew she was leaving. His condemnation had hurt, but she would never admit it to him. In rebuke, she spoke harshly. "Yes, it has made me ruthless. Ruthless enough to save Phillip's life by cutting off his leg, when you were too damn scared to do it." Bren regretted the words as soon as she spoke them, but she couldn't apologize.

Her reproach seemed to hit Scott like a blow to his belly. His body bent and his shoulders hunched in reaction. "I don't appreciate your accusation. Yes, I was scared, but I could have done it," he said. "I would have done it. You think I would have let Phillip die?"

Sarcasm pulled Bren's lips awry. "We'll never really know the answer to that, will we? But let's forget about that." Pushing the unpleasant moment out of her mind, she bent down and kissed Phillip's cheek. "Tell Phillip I'm sorry I had to leave before he woke." She straightened up. "You'd better wire Lindsay that you're both all right. She'll be worried sick about you when she hears of the explosion. Let Theo know, too."

Scott got up and walked his sister to the entrance. "I will. Thank you for reminding me." Bren knew both she and Scott had been hurt by the harsh words between them, but she chose to ignore that. She lifted her arms to her brother. As they hugged goodbye, he said, "Thank you for getting here in time. Phillip and I will be forever grateful. God be with you."

"With you, too, Scott." She whispered in his ear, "I love you."

Scott's voice also dropped so Bren alone could hear. "You know I love you, Sarah. We all do."

Bren pulled away and gave her brother a sidelong look. "I know that's not always such an easy task." Bitter thoughts tore at her. *Deceiver, betrayer, killer—if they really knew me, would anyone love me?* "Goodbye, Scott."

THE WAR BETWEEN THE HEARTS

CHAPTER FOUR

"These dispatches are damn late, Cordell," Captain Lockman said. "What's your explanation?"

Bren fingered the gray cap she held in her hands and shifted her weight from foot to foot in a pretext of nervousness. She dragged her answer out in a slow drawl, as though each word struggled to pull the next one along after it. Each hesitation between sentences seemed a necessary pause to regain her breath. "My blasted horse stumbled, sir. Threw me off, and I banged up against a tree. I don't know how long I was unconscious, maybe a day or even two. I just know I woke up mighty full of pain and mighty hungry." Bren circled the cap once more through her fingers. "I broke several ribs and banged my head real bad. I couldn't move for most of a week except to get my canteen. Good thing I always carry jerky in my pocket, or I would have been near starved."

She removed one hand from the cap and rubbed her stomach. "Finally, a soldier came along the trail, and I got a piece of cloth from him." She pulled the bottom of her shirt out of her trousers and lifted it to show the edge of the cloth bound around her. "Once I got this on, I could pull myself onto my horse, but riding fast was out of the question. I had to walk Redfire most all the way back here. Colonel Arborough didn't indicate that the dispatch was urgent, and I surely hope it wasn't." She raised her head and looked earnestly at the officer. "I've never been this derelict before, sir. I hope that counts in my favor."

"Well, yes. All right. I've had good reports about you, Cordell. I suppose we can overlook this instance since it was unavoidable. In fact, you'd better have some more time off for those ribs to heal properly. We need you to be able to ride. I'll have one of the regulars substitute for you. Report back to me in two weeks."

"Thank you, sir." Bren turned and left the room. Two weeks, she repeated to herself. Hallelujah! That will give me time to check on Mother and Father. My being in this war has played havoc with keeping in touch with them.

During the three-day ride to Paramalin, Virginia, Bren twice bypassed Confederate encampments, giving them a wide berth. Now, as she guided Redfire along the approach to Red Oak Manor, her parents' home, a feeling of nostalgia spread through her. Anxious to see her parents after a prolonged absence, she clucked the sorrel into a trot along the tree-lined entry.

At one time, the manor had been a vast plantation, but when Cynthia Coulter inherited it, she followed her husband Prescott's urging and sold most of the land and slaves. Cynthia and her young twins had spent many summers there with Prescott joining them during his vacations from Coulter Foundry. When cries for emancipation began to spread, Cynthia and Prescott freed the remaining slaves and offered homes and wages to the few who stayed to care for the house and what remained of the grounds, setting an example frowned upon by many of their neighbors.

Smiling as a few childhood escapades played through her mind, Bren was jolted from her reverie by a chilling scream. She spurred her mount into a gallop. A shot rang out, and her heart leaped. What could be happening? No battles were being waged in this area. Still, it paid to be cautious. Near the end of the lane, still out of sight of the house, she reined Redfire in and threw herself off him. Peering through the trees, she saw a disturbing scene. About a hundred feet away, Matthias, the family butler, lay on the ground with a shotgun nearby. His wife Pearl knelt next to him, using the edge of her skirt to try to staunch the red stain spreading on the front of his white jacket.

Bren gasped in anguish. The rest of the scene nearly stopped her breathing. Just beyond Matthias, four men struggled to push Bren's father beneath a tree limb that had a rope thrown over it. Prescott's arms were bound behind his back. One end of the waiting rope was fashioned into a noose. Her mother had grabbed one man's arm and was digging her heels into the ground to try to stop their progress.

With no hesitation, Bren flew into Redfire's saddle and drew her revolver. Shrieking, "Yiyiyiyi," she charged the sorrel toward the scuffling group just as the man threw her mother down. He turned toward Bren and pulled a pistol from the belt at his stomach. Bren fired. The shot hit the man square in the chest, knocking him to the earth. A second man released Prescott, drew a revolver, and stepped away. He spread his feet, lifted the sidearm with two hands, and sighted along the barrel, swinging it to aim directly at her. Bren's second shot hit him in the neck just before his finger tightened on the trigger. As he was flung onto his back, his bullet went harmlessly into the air.

The other two men shoved Prescott away. Her father stumbled to the ground, rolled over, and came to a stop facing the action. "By God, it's Scott!" he yelled.

Bren kept Redfire going at full gallop. The two men separated, grabbed their weapons, and aimed at her. At this close range, she was in great jeopardy. She shut her mind to the danger and focused on the man to her left. Aiming her pistol along the side of Redfire's neck, she fired and ducked to the right. But her quick maneuver wasn't needed. Just as she switched her aim, a shotgun roared behind her. The man on the right went down with half his face gone. She pulled Redfire hard to the right and swung her arm toward the new shooter. Her heart leaped in astonishment when she saw who was dropping the shotgun to the ground. Mother!

With her mind still engaged by the fighting, she dragged her gaze away. As she reined in her horse, she looked to make sure she had hit her last target. The man was gut shot. He twitched and fell still. All the attackers were down and most likely dead or dying. She holstered her pistol and slid from the saddle.

Unconcerned about dropping Redfire's reins to the ground, Bren ran to her father. "Are you all right?" His face had a few red scrapes on it, but she didn't see any other signs of injury.

"Now that you're here, I'm fine."

Bren pulled a knife from its sheath on her belt, cut the rope binding Prescott's hands, and helped him to his feet. They grabbed each other in a mighty hug. She felt another pair of arms encircle them.

"Scott, oh, Scott," Cynthia cried. "I always knew you were courageous. Thank goodness, you got here in time."

At first, her mother's words surprised her, then Bren realized it was natural to be taken for Scott, though he had never worn a beard. They did look remarkably alike. And with her voice pitched a tone lower, they even sounded alike, except for the pronounced drawl she affected around other people. She decided to wait and enlighten her parents privately, to avoid needlessly giving away her masquerade.

"Let's check on Matthias," she reminded them, pulling away from the embrace and dashing toward the fallen man. She knelt next to him and looked at Pearl.

"It's not as bad as it looks, Mr. Scott. Praise the Lord you showed up to help us," Pearl said. "The bullet skipped off a rib. Don't even need a doctor. He just got a lot a blood on him, and a mighty sore side."

"Wonderful news, Pearl." Bren smiled down at Matthias. "You just stay there, my friend. We'll get a couple of boys to help you into the house." Cynthia stood behind Bren and nodded her agreement. Prescott had moved away from them to check on the fallen attackers.

Matthias reached for Pearl's arm, and she helped him sit up. "No need, no need. I was just dizzy for a spell. That bullet clean knocked the breath out of me. I'm all right now. Just need a mite more rest." He gazed around, then peered a little more closely at Bren. "Why you riding Miss Sarah's Redfire? Something wrong with your Blackstar?"

"Nothing serious." Bren winked and took his arm. "Come on, I'll help you into the house."

Pearl shook her head. "Never you mind, Mr. Scott. I'll see to him. You take care of your mama and papa."

"I'll do that." Bren stood and turned toward her mother.

Prescott had just rejoined her. He slapped his hands together as if cleaning dirt from them. "They're all dead. That was some shooting."

"Mother certainly helped," Bren said with sincere gratitude. She noticed her mother looked paler than usual and was not her talkative self. "Why were they trying to hang you? Who were those people?"

Her father said, "We'll tell you all about it. First, let's go inside and get Lettie to break out some brandy. I think we're all a little wobble-legged. At least, I know I am." Prescott smiled as Cynthia slipped an arm around his waist to give him a quick hug.

"What about the bodies?" Bren pointed a thumb over her shoulder.

Pearl spoke up. "I can send a couple of boys into town for the sheriff." With a move of her chin, she indicated a few older boys who were peeking from behind the outbuildings. "Let the law worry about those heathens. And I'll get one of the boys to care for Redfire, too."

Prescott reached down and touched her shoulder. "Thank you, Pearl. I would appreciate that." He beckoned to Bren. "Come on, now, let's go inside and chew over all this."

"Where is everyone else?" Bren was perplexed. Several families lived on the grounds, yet only a few of the older children were visible. "All this commotion and no one heard it?"

Cynthia released Prescott and threaded her arm through Bren's as they headed into the house. "Today's market day, and nearly everyone's in town with Lettie's grocery orders. Her arthritis kept her home, as usual, but you know she doesn't hear all that well." She tugged against Bren's arm. "It's so wonderful to see you, Scott. With this godless war, we didn't expect to see any family for a while. And we hardly ever receive mail from the north."

They entered the home and settled in the parlor. Cynthia rang for Lettie and asked her to bring some iced drinks. "Do you want something to eat now, dear? Dinner won't be served for another two hours."

"No, thank you, Mother. I can wait. But I do have a question for you." She waited until both parents were looking at her. "That was an incredible shot! When did you learn to fire a shotgun?"

"When the war started in earnest, your father insisted I learn to shoot. My eyesight has failed a bit, but I can still see well enough at a distance. He tied straw into a target next to the barn, and I practiced each day until I hit it every time." She pursed her lips and gave a little shiver. "Though I never really expected to have to shoot at another human being."

Prescott rubbed his hands together. "Your mother was a real quick learner, too. Good feel for it. She took to it naturally." He raised his brows at the look Cynthia threw him. "Well, it's true."

"Mother, how did you know to shoot the man on the right?"

Cynthia's cheeks colored. "He was the one closer to me."

Bren laughed out loud as she looked at her father and gestured toward her mother. "What a great strategist. Who would have guessed?" She rose and walked over to stand in front of Cynthia. A smile crooked up one side of her face. "I guess you know you probably saved my life."

"Oh, my dear Scott," Cynthia said as she stood and put her arms around Bren "you have a life eminently worth saving." She leaned back and looked into Bren's eyes, which were quickly filling with tears. She seemed puzzled for a moment before realization dawned.

"You're Sarah!" She held her daughter at arm's length and repeated herself. "You're Sarah."

Sarah forced words through her suddenly constricting throat. "Am I still eminently worth saving?"

"Always," Cynthia choked in return and clutched her daughter to her. After several moments, they parted and Cynthia looked at Prescott. "You knew," she said with a short laugh, and he nodded. "But how?" She looked back at Sarah. "In those men's clothes, you look just like a thinner Scott. Scott with a beard, that is."

Prescott stood, put his arm over Sarah's shoulders, and smiled at her. "I recognized that distinctive get-the-hell-out-of-my-way-or-I'm coming-through-you attitude." He gave his daughter's shoulders a squeeze. "Now let's all sit down, and you can start explaining why you're dressed like a man and how you got here. Then you can give us all the latest news from Scott and Lindsay."

After they returned to their seats, Sarah swept her arm in a wide circle. "First, you must tell me what this attack was all about. Why were they trying to hang you?"

"It's been going on for a while now." Prescott's hand lifted unconsciously to his neck. "This pack of rats has been terrorizing everyone around here. They've already killed four other landowners. When word gets out that you've stopped them, the whole area will be relieved."

"Why didn't you have guards out?"

"Like whom? All the able-bodied men are in the war. I hoped Matthias and I could protect our women and children. That bunch was smarter than I reckoned, and they caught me alone."

"What was their purpose? Was it related to the war?"

"I don't think so. They were just taking advantage of the unsettled times and trying to fill their pockets. They'd kill an owner and steal everything movable worth taking. The killing must have satisfied some bloodlust and greed they had. No real reason for it."

Cynthia interrupted. "Sarah-Bren, I cannot stand it any longer. Please take off that beard. You don't look like yourself at all."

Sarah turned to her mother, knowing that she would see the "sour stomach" look on her face. Sure enough. She turned back to her father and rolled her eyes. Prescott put his fingers to his lips to suppress his smile.

"Mother, I'm not supposed to look like me. It's a disguise."

Cynthia frowned in confusion. "Why on earth do you need a disguise?"

Oh, Lord, Sarah thought, do I dare tell her I'm spying for the Union? "I wanted to be a soldier. The only way I could do that was to masquerade as a man. So I did."

"You're a soldier? You fight in the war?" Cynthia's eyes were wide pools of astonishment. "I wondered why your visits had stopped. I thought it was because of the war, but I never . . ." The sentence died away.

"Actually, I hardly ever fight. I'm a scout. That's why I'm not wearing a uniform."

Shock seemed to still Cynthia's breath, but only for a moment. "Sarah-Bren Coulter, sometimes I just don't understand you. Why can't you act like most other women?"

"Because, Mother," Sarah said in a sharp voice, "I'm not like most other women." She was immediately sorry. She knew her mother had never understood her. Why would today be any different? In some ways, Sarah didn't understand her mother, either. But they loved each other, and bickering only hurt them both. "I apologize for sounding so rude. Please, will you just accept me as I am, and let it go at that?"

"Let it go? How can you think I could let it go? My only daughter is dressing up like a man and pretending to be a soldier. How can I ever hold my head up among my friends when they hear about this?"

"Mother, I'm not about to change." Her mother didn't seem to realize that Southern society as she knew it would never be the same. The Union, with its vast resources and unending supply of soldiers, would win this war, and Southern gentility would lose most of what they held dear. But Sarah couldn't tell her mother that. Instead, she said, "Let's not fight. I just saved your life, and you just saved mine. Let's call a truce and be thankful we still have each other."

Cynthia looked and sounded defeated. "I'll try." With an obvious attempt to change the subject, she said, "Tell us about Scott and Lindsay and the baby. How are they?"

Relieved, Sarah passed along whatever information she could, including the attack on the munitions train and the injury to Phillip. She downplayed her part in the incident, focusing instead on the severity of Phillip's wounds.

"The train carried ammunition for the Union. What were you doing there?" Cynthia surprised Sarah with the speed of her insight.

"I was trying to warn them. I work for the Union, Mother, not the Confederacy." Sarah let this information drop into a pool of silence.

Prescott broke the stillness. "That makes sense to me. Your mother and I both favor the strength of a united country, although we don't say that too loudly around here."

Cynthia didn't remark on that. "It's good you reached them in time to save Phillip's life."

"Scott would have done it if I hadn't been there."

"Do you think so?" Cynthia looked at her daughter rather speculatively. "I'm not so sure about that. He could have saved Phillip before you arrived, couldn't he?"

"I suppose so. But Phillip is his best friend, Mother. That had to make him hesitate."

"Phillip is your friend, too, yet you didn't hesitate for one second. And today," Cynthia said as her voice lifted, "I don't think Scott could have done what you did. Like me, he's too cautious. You have your father's daring streak and his courage." She nodded as if agreeing with herself. "I've never really given you credit for that, and I should have. I'll never be reconciled to your being a soldier, but you're a very courageous young woman."

Sarah could feel herself glowing even as threatening tears stung her eyes. She couldn't remember the last time her mother had paid her a compliment. Usually, Cynthia was too busy doing mother-type things like telling her to stand straight, sit and walk in a more ladylike manner, or ride sidesaddle. Her mother had to know that most of her admonitions to Sarah were a waste of breath, but still she kept trying, perhaps hoping that some would bear fruit. And a few had, but not the ones meant to turn Sarah into a Southern belle.

Today was notable because Sarah saved her father's life. But it also was notable because her mother showed her some acceptance. That long-awaited step in the right direction lifted Sarah's heart with pure pleasure. She didn't care to question how long that pleasure would last.

Sarah spent two days at her parents' home, allowing everyone else to believe she was Scott. She was amused at the thought that her brother had "become a soldier," and a Rebel at that. Though in this part of Virginia, she knew a person had better be a Confederate. A Union soldier would be in grave peril.

With nine days left of her leave, she said goodbye and headed north. She was homesick to see Scott, Lindsay, and little Prescott, and anxious about Phillip's recovery.

The weather stayed dry and mild for the greater part of the journey, and she made good time. As soon as she entered Union territory, she sent Scott and Lindsay a telegram, so they would be expecting her. She told them she had two days to visit and signed it "Bren Cordell."

"Sarah!" Scott pulled his sister through the doorway with barely enough time to drop her knapsack before he engulfed her in an embrace. Lindsay followed his example, then Sarah knelt on the hallway floor and held out her arms to Pres, who toddled toward her. Her nephew hesitated for a moment before he chose to dart behind his mother's skirt. Sarah made a rueful face and rose, laughing.

"He doesn't know you in that disguise," Lindsay said. "He'll recognize Aunt Sarah when you take off the beard and let your hair down."

"I'll take it off around the house, but I'll need to use it if we go out in public. I have only half a tan on my face, and the differences in skin color might be hard for Sarah Coulter to account for. If need be, you can introduce me as a distant cousin."

Scott snorted and shook his head. "I'll be damn glad when I get my sister back." Sarah rolled her eyes, and Scott made a beeline for the door. "I'll go get Phillip. I promised to let him know as soon as you arrived."

"Scott, for heaven's sake, give me time to get cleaned up first." Sarah saw a hand wave as he hustled out the door, and she shook her head and snorted in perfect duplication of her brother's reaction.

Lindsay laughed and grabbed Sarah's arm. "It's easy to see you two are twins." Sarah snatched up her knapsack and hooked its strap over her shoulder as Lindsay led her toward the stairs, with Pres still holding on to his mother's skirt. "Go ahead and get cleaned up, and we can talk in comfort later. I put several pitchers of water on your dresser for you and set out some towels."

"Thank you." Sarah gave her a wide smile and a pat on the arm as Lindsay let go. "I have missed you all so much." She ran up the steps two at a time.

Just as she finished donning a clean shirt and trousers after washing up, she heard Scott and Phillip arrive. She yanked on clean socks and her boots, ran a comb through her loosened hair, and hurried downstairs to the drawing room. Phillip had heard her coming, and he stood waiting for her. Sarah entered the room and hesitated for just a split second as Phillip's crutches and shortened trouser leg slammed her senses. She hastened to embrace and kiss him. "Hello," she said hoarsely, affected by the thought of her friend's narrow escape from death. "It's wonderful to see you."

"You, too, Sarah." He looked down at her and grinned. "At least, I think you're Sarah. Your face is two different shades. And you're still dressed like a man."

As she pulled away, she wrinkled her nose at him in answer. Truthfully, she was so used to wearing a shirt and trousers that choosing a dress hadn't even occurred to her. She waved a hand toward the crutches. "So, how are you doing? Can you get around all right?"

"I've gotten used to the crutches, though balance was tricky at first," Phillip answered. He took several steps to show how well he could maneuver. "The stump is still tender, so I can't get an artificial leg yet. The government is providing them for soldiers." His voice deepened. "I hate losing a leg, but that's a helluva lot better than losing my life. You saved me, Sarah, and I'll never forget that. I owe you."

A pink flush came and went in the white part of Sarah's face. "You would have done the same for me, so let's just forget about owing anyone anything."

Lindsay came in at just that moment. "Why don't you all sit down, and I'll bring us some coffee."

They followed her suggestion and got comfortable on the stuffed chairs and sofa. Scott pointed to a newspaper lying on an end table. "The Confederates almost got to Washington. General Wallace and part of the Sixth Corps held the Rebs up at the Monocacy River near Frederick. Our men were defeated, but it gave Grant time to send the rest of the corps to reinforce the city."

"Really? I hadn't heard that," Sarah said.

Scott picked up the paper and handed it to her. "It happened last week."

"April ninth," she murmured as she skimmed the article. She finished and laid the paper down. "General Grant has been as tenacious as a dog chasing a bone. I like that in him."

"I do, too," Phillip said. "Even his setbacks don't stop him."

Sarah nodded. "Yes, and he's not giving Lee a chance to rest. Gradually, the Confederacy is running out of men and material, and the men are starting to realize it." She reflected a moment. "The lack of success at Gettysburg took a lot out of the whole South, not just the ones who fought there."

Phillip looked grim. "The Union is winning a step at a time. Let's hope it ends soon and all the killing stops. Our country has lost enough of its young men."

"Amen to that," Lindsay said as she brought in the coffee and set it on the low table in front of the sofa. As they each served themselves, Sarah gave them her news.

"Mother and Father had a little excitement at their place." She recounted the incident. "I'm sure you'll get Mother's version in the mail before too long, if a letter can still get through."

Lindsay set her empty cup on the table. "So Mother Coulter mistook you for Scott? How amusing."

Scott bristled. "I can't even join the army, and my sister is a war hero. I don't find that particularly amusing." He reached for the cut-glass decanter on the table, lifted two glasses from the tray next to it, and poured some liquor into them. First pushing one toward Phillip, Scott grabbed the other glass and tossed the whiskey down in a single gulp. "I should have been the one to help them," he muttered.

Sarah's eyes narrowed as she looked at her brother, but Lindsay forestalled her reply by patting her sister-in-law's arm. "Well, you couldn't be there, Scott, and I for one am delighted that Sarah was. Your parents could have been killed. We owe Sarah a debt of thanks."

"By all means." Scott poured more whiskey and lifted his glass toward his sister. "Thank you, dear sister, for upholding the family honor. Again. You always seem to be in the right place at the right time."

His voice had a resentful edge to it, and Sarah could sense the others' embarrassment. But she wasn't embarrassed. At first, she was angry. Then she was sad.

She took a glass from the tray and poured two fingers of whiskey into it. She lifted it toward Scott then brought it to her lips, her eyes challenging her brother to object, though she knew he wouldn't dare. He might as well get used to the idea that the niceties of the drawing room were lost on her. Soldiers are not ladies.

Obviously recognizing the tinderbox of emotional byplay, Lindsay turned the subject to Coulter Foundry's recovery from their loss at the train tragedy. "Inventory can be replaced," she said during the discussion. "In fact, the government had already paid for the munitions before their destruction, so we were fortunate. But lost lives can never be replaced."

Sarah nodded her head in sympathy. "Has anyone figured out how the explosions started?"

"I'm on the army's investigating team," Phillip answered. "We think he must have had a couple of fuses secreted within the ammunition boxcars. He could have pretended to be inspecting the cars, lit the fuses, and jumped off the train. At that point, all eyes were on the perimeter, expecting trouble from outside, not inside. All he needed was about thirty seconds to get away. But we won't know for sure until we catch him."

Sarah leaned forward with interest. "Has there been any progress in identifying him?"

"Not yet," Phillip admitted. "We've been working from a list of people we knew were on the train. Most of them died, and many of the bodies were impossible to identify, so it's been a difficult task." He struck a fist against the arm of the chair. "But I won't stop until I find him."

Scott eyed his emotional friend. "What will you do when you find him?"

Phillip's face darkened as his fist opened and closed. "I know what I'd like to do with him, but I think of myself as a civilized man. I'll turn him in to the authorities."

Sarah's thoughts fumed white-hot. You should kill the bastard. Immediately, the strength of her hate sickened her. Her eyes turned toward Scott, who was looking straight at her. She saw a shadow flicker across his face and a nearly imperceptible shake move his head. Good grief, he's reading my mind. This had happened more than once between the twins, and it worked both ways. But it was rare enough to still be surprising.

"I hope you find him, Phillip." Sarah's voice reflected her anger but not her spike of fervor for vengeance. "I'll keep my ears open, too. He might feel a need to brag about his success, and that would be more likely to happen in Rebel territories."

Phillip said, "That's a good idea. But I wish you would give up your masquerade. War is no place for a woman."

Sarah lifted one eyebrow. "War is no place for a man, either, I think. No mother's child should be blown to bits like some I've seen." She heard Lindsay's indrawn breath. "But I'm driven to help put an end to it, so save your words, Phillip. I'm not changing my mind."

"You know I'll keep trying." Phillip grinned wryly. "I'm driven to protect you."

Struggling to reach a lighter plane, Sarah winked. "I know that. You want to be my knight in shining armor, but this damsel isn't in distress. I think you need to find one who is."

"Speaking of damsels in distress," Scott said, "how about a game of Charades? Men against the women." He cast a sly smile at Sarah and rubbed his chin. "Or is that men against a woman and a half?"

Sarah laughed out loud. "I'll show you who's half a woman. Come on, Lindsay, let's give them their comeuppance." The group all joined in the laughter and fun, thriving on the camaraderie. Knowing she had only one more day to spend with her family made the time even more enjoyable for Sarah, and the lighthearted competition was a welcome respite from the darkness of the war hanging over them. A war she would soon rejoin.

CHAPTER FIVE

G usts of damp, blustery wind warned of a storm's impending arrival. Leaves fluttered and flapped, the tops of the trees leaned to the left, and the smell of the air changed. Bren halted Redfire to pull an oilskin poncho from a saddlebag and put it on. The draped oilskin hung down far enough to cover her thighs and calves, protecting her from the elements. She turned down the brim of her hat so rain could run off it freely and resumed her journey.

Soon, the daylight dimmed to murky gray, and rain started as a soft patter. It strengthened into a steady rhythm, eventually coming down in blowing sheets as water poured onto the trees. Rivulets ran down the branches, and drips turned into streams accompanied by a chorus of gushing noises. The porous earth beneath the trees sopped up most of the downpour, but Bren couldn't be sure of Redfire's footing, so she slowed the sorrel from the usual trot to a steady walk.

The trail Bren traversed wound gradually up a mountainside, then steepened, and the trees and underbrush thinned. As Redfire picked and slid his way to the summit, Bren thought she heard muskets firing and tilted her head to listen. As the sorrel topped the treeless rise, she stared at the meadow in the valley below. She could see a wall-like division where the rain ended and the sun shone, partway up the valley. Under a bright sky, the Confederate infantry engaged the Union troops. It was a new battle, with the pall of blue smoke just beginning to build.

The creaks, clanks, and rumbles of soldiers on the move intermingled with the crack of muskets and the cries of the wounded. From the Union lines, fife and drum, barely heard amid the din, urged the men onward.

Sarah guessed about a hundred yards separated the opposing forces. Foot soldiers in the front rows of each group fired their muskets. They knelt to reload while the row behind them fired and moved forward. As dead and wounded men dropped, the ranks stepped over them to continue their firing rotation and the lines advanced.

Flag bearers on both sides kept pace with their front lines. Red and white stripes streaming beside a starred blue field proudly led the Union troops forward. Bren noted that the Rebel flag, a red banner crisscrossed with star-encrusted blue bars, was being driven back. The Confederate ranks slowly gave ground as the Union Army moved against them.

I have nothing to do with this battle, Bren told herself. It's good to be up here and well out of range. In fact, she thought bleakly, I'm often running away from friendly bullets, while people I know are being slain. She wrenched her thoughts away from that track.

While she watched, the rain drifted past her and the sun broke through, making her too warm under the oilskin. She removed her hat with one hand and pulled the oilskin over her head with the other, taking care not to dislodge her beard.

She replaced her hat and observed the battle for a few more minutes, saddened by its useless pageantry. After shaking out the oilskin, she folded it, stuck it back into a saddlebag, and turned Redfire away. She recognized she was near Cranston and thought she might get something to eat and stop to visit Leah. Memory of the pleasant blonde lightened her gloomy thoughts. She wondered how Leah could stay so cheerful with the life she led.

As soon as trees enveloped her descent, she headed for Cranston, about half an hour's ride on the other side of the mountain. She knew she might run into a picket line of sentries, especially with a battle going on close by, so she slowed the sorrel as she neared the town.

Without warning, someone opened fire. Bren swerved her mount away and drew her pistol. Immediately, she faced a second threat. A Rebel stepped from behind a tree to take aim. He jumped to get out of Redfire's way and fired erratically, just a fraction later than Bren. Her bullet hit him in the chest. His caught her in the bone of her lower left leg. Redfire leaped over the fallen man as Bren gasped at the pain. With her unscathed leg, she spurred the horse to greater speed. More firing broke out behind her.

Riding low against the sorrel's neck, Bren felt dizzy and nauseous. She struggled to keep her thoughts focused, knowing she needed to take some precautions. She removed the rawhide cord from her hair, fumbled with one hand, and tried to tie the cord around her leg. Finally, she reined to a stop to fasten the tourniquet. Listening, she heard no pursuit. Clumsy from lightheadedness, she groped behind her for a saddlebag. She managed to pull out a length of rope, looped it around her body, and tied it to a grommet hole in her army saddle.

"Think!" she urged herself in a low voice. With painful precision, she knotted the very ends of the reins around her left wrist. This would give Redfire enough slack to have his head if the reins slipped from her hands. To complete her safety measures, she took off the trail hat, replaced it with the Confederate cap, and fastened the strap under her chin.

If she made it to Cranston without falling, perhaps she could find some help there, maybe from Leah. Her thigh throbbed with pain as though her leg had been chopped off below the knee. My God, is this how Phillip felt? She attempted to move her foot and fainted from the agony, but the rope held her in the saddle. She didn't regain consciousness, and without direction, Redfire stayed in place for several hours. At last, hunger urged him to feed on the sparse grass. As he moved from patch to patch, he gradually drew closer to the town. When the forest gave way to cleared land, the horse stopped near the edge of the trees and lowered his head to continue munching.

Faith Pruitt opened the back door of her house and stepped into the yard. A slight breeze stirred her red curls, obscuring her vision, so she set down the metal buckets she carried and pulled a ribbon from her apron pocket. As she tied the ribbon around her hair, she frowned at the sounds of battle coming over the mountain. The muskets crackled like a hundred breaking twigs, and the heavy cannons boomed like pealing thunder. For two days, the fighting had disturbed the countryside, and Faith wondered whether Cranston was in danger of being seized by the Yankees.

She turned around and looked fondly at her home. It sat at the very end of the gravel road, eight blocks east of the town's center. Behind it and to one side stretched open fields and forest. The town council had provided the white building for the hired schoolmaster, her husband Nathan. They had lived in it together for seven years, and their son Benjamin had been born there. Two years earlier, in the seventh year of their marriage, Nathan was seduced by the fervor of states' rights. With the town council's agreement, Faith took over his teaching responsibilities so he could join the Army of the Confederacy. He died in battle before completing his first year of service. As a result, Faith was still teaching.

Lifting her face to the pleasant breeze, she stood for a moment. She didn't want to think of death or war, but the nearness of the battle led her thoughts in that direction. Nathan died for his belief in states' rights, but to her, staying in the Union made more sense. Surely, states united under one government formed a stronger alliance. When the slavery issue raised its head, her Union sympathies strengthened, but she kept her political views to herself. She knew speaking out would serve no useful purpose. It could only jeopardize her life and Benjamin's. With a slight shake of her head, she abandoned her troubling thoughts and picked up the buckets just as Benjamin came through the door.

"Mama, can I play outside now?" He tossed his head as the breeze blew dark brown curls into his eyes.

She was happy for her son's sake that he had his father's complexion. Brown eyes and tan skin coped with the sun better than her own green eyes and freckles. But at eight years of age, Benjamin showed obvious signs of having inherited her sturdiness. His father had been short and slight, almost womanish, while she was 5'6" tall and large boned, bigger than most women and many men. She turned her head, listening.

"Do you hear the muskets and the cannons?"

"Yes, ma'am."

Yesterday, Faith hadn't allowed Benjamin out at all, but the battle didn't sound any nearer. It had to be a mile or two away on the other side of the mountain, so it seemed safe to let him play outside. "You stay in the yard, and if the sounds get any louder, you come inside and let me know, all right?"

"All right, Mama. Do you need any help with the water?" When Faith smiled and shook her head, the boy darted away.

Faith took the buckets to a rain barrel sitting at one corner of the house. Rainwater was directed to the site by boards nailed against the lip of the roof to form crude gutters. Wooden barrels, on the ground at each side, caught the runoff and provided an extra source of water. Faith used well water for drinking and cooking, and the rain barrels took care of most other needs. She dipped the buckets into the barrel, filled them, and carried them into the house.

Benjamin spied a piece of wood he could use for a musket. He picked it up, lodged it against his shoulder, and sighted down its length. Now he would search for the enemy. He lifted his gaze across the field stretching behind his yard and spotted a horse near the forest. Although it stood in shadow next to the trees, it didn't look dark enough to be their horse, and a glance at their corral confirmed Nightglow was still there. Forgetting his mother's admonition, he dropped the stick-musket and loped toward the strange horse to investigate. He slowed to a walk when he got close. A rider lay against the horse's neck.

Crusted blood formed a trail from a hole in the person's pant leg down to and along a black boot. Flies buzzed around and covered the blood's path. The horse didn't move as Benjamin edged up to it. He saw the ends of the reins were wrapped tightly around the rider's hand. Speaking softly and moving slowly, as his mother had taught him, he took hold of the bridle and led horse and rider to his home.

He tied the horse with a length of rope that dangled from a rail of the corral and ran into the house, calling his mother. A moment later, the two came back out.

"See, Mama, he doesn't have any uniform, just the gray cap. But he's hurt."

"You're right, Benjamin. It looks like he's been shot." She brushed away the flies and carefully lifted the foot of the bloody left leg from the stirrup. "Many soldiers don't have full uniforms, but he's wearing the cap, so let's figure that he is one. We know he needs help." Benjamin nodded and stood still until Faith gave him directions. "Hold on to his leg. It's all right to let it move, but make sure it doesn't bang into anything. We have to lift him down from this side so as not to spook the horse. Be careful now, it looks pretty bad. And watch out for that piece of rawhide tied below his knee. Don't loosen it."

While the youngster grasped the wounded leg, Faith released the reins from the rider's hand and untied the rope attached to the saddle. The man mumbled something unintelligible, and Faith wondered how conscious he was. "We're trying to help you, and we need to get you off your horse. Can you put your arms around my neck as I slide you down?"

"No," the soldier said, appearing to revive a bit. Faith paused, wondering whether he would say more. He spoke quietly, but clearly, and she heard the pain in his voice. "I'm too heavy. Hold on to my injured leg, and I'll bring the other one over." He stopped and took some extra breaths. "Maybe you can balance me as I slide down. First, give me a minute."

Faith waited until the soldier felt ready. When he moved his good leg, she put a hand against his waist to steady him. As his leg swung over the horse's back, the soldier began to slide and he clutched at the saddle to slow his momentum. Faith put both hands on his waist to support him, and from the corner of her eye, watched Benjamin. He was allowing the injured leg to move, but keeping it lifted as the rider's good foot met the soil. Pleased with her son's actions, Faith raised her hands to the soldier's armpits and helped lower his slumping form to the ground.

Once the rider was down, Faith helped settle his wounded leg, handling it gently. "Good work, Benjamin. Now run get Doc Schafer." The soldier's foot had flopped a bit, suggesting the leg might be broken. Faith's father had been a doctor, and she had often assisted him. But her knowledge of healing didn't extend to gunshot wounds, and she possessed no strong painkillers or the proper instruments to deal with such trauma.

The soldier hadn't said a word since being helped to dismount. Perhaps the exertion had caused a loss of consciousness. Faith took scissors from a pocket in her apron and cut along the seams of the damaged pant leg and the drawers beneath it, being careful not to displace the tourniquet. The leg was swollen from the knee down, and there was a hole about four inches above the short boot, next to the outside edge of the shinbone.

She went into the house and brought back two blankets and a jug of water. She folded one blanket and placed it under the soldier's head. The other she meant to use as a cover. But first, she wanted to check whether there were any other injuries. She felt down the arm nearest her, and when she got to the hand, it turned and clasped her wrist.

"Stop," the soldier whispered, and the closed eyes flew open. His voice was weak and hoarse. "Who are you?"

For the first time, Faith noticed the dark-haired soldier was quite good-looking. He had strong features and light brown eyes that seemed to shine with a golden light. She thought he must be in distress and wondered how much he was aware of.

"I'm Faith Pruitt. My son found you and brought you here to our house. He's gone to get Dr. Schafer, the surgeon." Faith held the jug of water to his lips, and the soldier emptied it without stopping. When he finished, Faith returned the question. "And who are you?"

The muscles around his eyes were tense with pain. "Bren Cordell. I'm a scout with the army. I was coming into Cranston when some damn-fool sentries opened fire on me. The idiots didn't give me a chance to identify myself."

Faith's eyes widened. "That sounds like terribly bad luck to me. I guess with the fighting so near, everyone is nervous and overreacting." She looked at Bren's hand. The scout released the wrist, and Faith winced as she rubbed it. "I was only checking whether you have any wounds besides the one in your leg."

"No, that's it. Tell the doc to tend my leg and leave the rest of me alone. I don't take kindly to being poked and prodded." The soldier's voice had strengthened a bit. He spoke with a thick drawl, but in a no-nonsense tone, and Faith looked toward the holstered pistol. Maybe she should have taken the weapon, just to be on the safe side. Bren's glance followed hers, and Faith realized her expressive face betrayed her thoughts. "Don't even think that, ma'am. No one takes my sidearm." The man paused for a ragged breath. "But don't worry. I'm not about to shoot my angel of mercy. Not as long as you abide by my wishes, anyway."

The soldier's warnings sounded ominous, and he had a pistol to back up his words. Good heavens, Faith thought. I offer help, and I get threatened in return? He must realize he needs my assistance. She fought to keep her quick temper in check and decided to concentrate on the soldier's wounds. She looked up as Dr. Schafer arrived on foot, followed by Benjamin.

"Hello, Doc. This soldier dropped practically on my doorstep. He's in a lot of pain, so I thought we might tend him here before moving him inside." She made a quick decision about a thorough examination. "Will you examine his leg? As far as I can tell, it's the only wound he has." Faith knew Dr. Schafer well. A thin, middle-aged man with black chin whiskers, he had started as an assistant to Faith's late father, Dr. Pruitt, and occasionally he called on her when he needed help.

He knelt on the ground next to her. "You were lucky Benjamin caught me. A rider just came in asking me to treat some of the wounded from the battle in the next valley. With two days' worth of casualties, the medical staff's overloaded. They've set up a field hospital, and I'm on my way there."

Faith glanced toward Benjamin, whose eyes were glued to the soldier. Watching the treatment of the soldier's wounds would be a harsh lesson in reality, but with the war so close, he might see far worse. She decided he could stay.

Dr. Schafer did a quick examination of Bren's wound, using a metal probe and not reacting to Bren's gasps of pain. "This is a nasty one, soldier. Looks like a musket shot hit the edge of the bone, broke it, and embedded itself in part of it. It's a good thing it wasn't a Minie ball, or the leg bone would have been shattered." He met Bren's worried gaze. "Infection has already started. I can scrape the damaged tissue out and set the bone, but I can tell you from experience we would just be prolonging the agony. Battle infections like these are virtually impossible to treat. Best thing is to take the leg off right now, or it will probably kill you."

Benjamin gasped, and the doctor's last words hung in the air for a moment before the soldier reacted. "No!" The voice came loud and forceful. "No one's taking my leg off."

Faith's face went white as the doctor uttered his prognosis. She felt a connection to this soldier. For some reason, fate had brought him to her house, and she would do her best to help him. "Doc, why don't you clean the wound and set the bone the best you can. I'll tend to it and keep a close watch on it. Maybe the leg can be saved."

"Yes, Mama, please take care of it," Benjamin urged, his voice full of hope.

"All right, Faith," Schafer said. "Heaven knows you've worked some healing miracles before." He bent to the task of removing the musket shot and took pains to pick out shreds of trouser material embedded in the wound. Faith reached for Bren's hand and nearly had her own mangled as the soldier's grip intensified with the pain. Finally, Schafer finished the cleaning and debridement of the damaged tissue and flushed the wound with whiskey from a flask kept in his bag. Bren groaned and the doctor passed the flask to his patient, who took a lusty drink.

Dr. Schafer dusted morphine powder into the wound to numb some of the pain, filled the hole with scraped and softened linen, and wound a bandage around it. Moving beyond Bren's feet, the doctor grasped the wounded leg's foot and gave it a firm jerk. When the leg seemed straight, he took two hickory splints from his bag and bound them along the broken area, taking care to leave access to the wound. He removed the tourniquet and laid it on the ground. Next, he cut open the boot that was compressing the swollen foot, slipped it off, and snipped away the blood-soaked stocking.

Benjamin made a hissing sound.

Faith reached out and touched her son's sleeve. "It's all right."

She watched muscles tense along the soldier's clenched jaw and heard him droning over and over, "I can do this. I can do this," punctuated with strangled grunts. His dogged persistence in the midst of agonizing pain impressed her.

At last, the surgeon finished. He and Faith rose, and she put a hand on his arm. "Before you go, please help me get our patient into the house." Dr. Schafer lifted Bren's shoulders, Faith and Benjamin each supported a leg, and the three managed to move the soldier inside. Faith led them to her bedroom, yanked down the covers with one hand, and they laid their burden on the bed.

"Benjamin, you can put the horse in the barn now," she said. "Give him some hay and water and brush him down."

"Yes, ma'am." He backed away from the bed, staring as though unable to take his gaze from the man lying there.

"Go," his mother ordered. He turned and tore out of the house.

The doctor removed Bren's other boot and stocking, and Faith pulled the covers over the patient. She left the bound leg sticking out to keep the weight of the covers from pushing against the soldier's foot. Afterward, she moved to her bureau, took some bills from a drawer, and tried to pay the doctor his fee.

"No. This isn't your responsibility, Faith. I can't take your money." She thanked him, put the bills away, and walked with him through the sitting room to the door. The surgeon paused a moment, rubbing his chin. "Maybe he should be moved to my infirmary. You're a widow woman and the schoolteacher. Some of the townspeople, especially the Yankee sympathizers, might frown on you tending a Confederate soldier in your home."

"Perhaps that is a concern, Doc, but he's going to need vigilant care, and you said you were called to the battlefield. You're the only one who's seen that he's here, and I know I can rely on your discretion."

"Yes, you can. I'm staying neutral in this war. Oh, I almost forgot to give you some supplies. Do you have sufficient bandaging material?" When Faith nodded, he opened his bag and handed her paper packets of morphine and some opium tablets. "Dust the wound with morphine when you change the dressings. That should ease some of the pain. And you can give him a tablet or two of opium when it becomes unbearable." He closed the bag and touched Faith's arm. "Remember, if the infection gets out of hand, send Benjamin after me. I'm helping the army out today, but I'll be back tomorrow. I have patients here who need me." He lowered his voice. "Though I doubt if I could be much help to your soldier at that point. The leg should come off now. If the infection isn't stopped, he'll die."

"I'll watch it closely. Maybe a constant change of dressing will prevent it from worsening. I have to try." Faith walked out with the doctor and watched him walk away. She picked up the soldier's sliced boot, bloody sock, and tourniquet and put them in the trash can and went back inside.

With a jug of water and an earthenware cup, she returned to the bedroom. The soldier had lost blood and would need plenty of liquid to replenish it. His eyes were closed, but as water gurgled into the cup, he opened them. He appeared to have recovered some energy, but still seemed weak, so Faith held the cup while he emptied it.

When he finished, she watched as his eyes roved around the room before resting on hers. There wasn't much of note about the room, though Faith believed its soft, warm colors added to its comfort. Next to the dark walnut bedstead sat a matching side table, with a bureau along one wall. A rocking chair and a straight-backed chair completed the furniture. Several articles in the room matched the dark brown, deep red, and yellow in the bed's quilt—a woven brown and yellow rug, red cushions on the rocking chair, and yellow drapes at the two white-curtained windows. The only other color in the quilt was a rich green that almost exactly matched Faith's eyes.

Faith waited, giving Bren a chance to speak, but he remained silent, staring at her as though mesmerized. "Is there something you need, Mr. Cordell?" She poured more water in the cup and held it out.

"No, I, um . . ." He stumbled for a moment, seemingly flustered, then cleared his throat. "Please, call me Bren. I don't stand much on formality. But I must apologize, ma'am, for being so rude. I thank you for your care of me and for accommodating me in your home."

Faith acknowledged the words with a nod. "You can thank my son Benjamin for that. He's the one who found you and brought you here." She lifted the cup to his lips. The second cupful disappeared as quickly as the first.

"I'd like to thank him." Bren lifted a hand to cover a yawn, and Faith realized the effort the soldier was putting forth to remain alert. His life force needed rest to restore itself. She set the cup back on the bedside table.

"He's tending to your horse. He'll put him in the barn."

"Redfire. His name is Redfire." The words drifted slowly from Bren's lips, then his eyes closed and he slept.

While Faith's hands automatically smoothed covers that weren't yet wrinkled, she gazed at the person occupying her bed. His face looked drawn and tired, but that could be the result of his wounds. She wondered whether scouts could leave a battle whenever they pleased, or had he deserted in the face of the enemy? Or had his horse just wandered in this direction after he got shot? And had it really been a sentry who shot him? Whatever the answers, Faith could tell that her protective instincts were rising to the fore, and she laughed at herself. Like this soldier needs my protection. I might need protection from him as he recovers. Though, as slim as he is, I could probably outfight him. She snorted softly. And I know for sure I can outrun him.

The possibility of his death struck her with a pang of sadness. But she was determined not to let that happen. She made a silent vow to do whatever was in her power to save his life. And his leg.

She placed her hand on his forehead and noticed he burned with fever. When his eyelids flickered, she quickly removed her hand, lest she wake him. We're about to embark on a tough journey, Bren Cordell, she thought. Her eyes lit with purpose as she recalled the words he had fortified himself with: "I can do this." This time, she promised silently, you have an ally. We can do this together.

A day later, on Sunday morning, Bren still hadn't returned to consciousness. Faith knew the soldier needed constant attention, so she sent Benjamin off to church services with a note to the parson's wife.

Dear Mrs. Hebert,

Unforeseen circumstances have arisen, and I beg you to have the kindness to assume my teaching responsibilities at school for this week. I'm sorry to have to ask such a favor in the first week of the school year, but I have no choice. Benjamin will be absent from school for several days as well. Thank you in advance for what I pray will be your agreement to my request.

With sincere gratitude,
Mrs. Faith Pruitt

Faith decided Benjamin should stay at home because the excitement of having a soldier in their home might be more than her son could keep to himself. She hoped a few days away from school would give her the chance to ensure his silence about them boarding a man. The situation was innocent enough, but as the schoolteacher, Faith hoped to avoid any hint of indiscretion.

While Benjamin was on his errand, Faith made preparations to bathe Bren. First, she pushed against the soldier's arm to make sure he wouldn't awaken and threaten her again. When there was no response, she unbuckled and removed the gun belt, tucked it around the holstered pistol, and laid the bundle in a bureau drawer. She carried the buckets outside and dipped water from one of the rain barrels. After hauling the pails into the kitchen, she hung them on hooks at the top of the fireplace to heat over the fire.

Faith went out to the barn where Bren's saddlebags hung on a peg and pulled the contents out onto a worktable. Two outfits of clean clothes, including drawers and stockings, were wrapped together next to a roll of white cotton cloth. She set aside clothes identical to those Bren was wearing and placed the other set back in the saddlebags, along with the cotton cloth. A great believer in a person's right to privacy, she avoided snooping through the other articles. Her beliefs were sorely tempted, however, when a journal fell from the table and flipped open, revealing pages filled with strong handwriting and detailed drawings. Intrigued, she riffled through the pages and saw that the drawings depicted battle scenes, weapons, an occasional single figure or face, and what appeared to be maps. Chiding herself for prying, she quickly stuffed the journal back into the saddlebag.

After returning to the house with the clothes, she collected linen towels, washcloths, and a square of soap from the washroom shelf and carried everything into the bedroom. It would take some time to remove the soldier's clothes, and by then, the buckets of water should be comfortably warm. She pulled the cover from atop Bren and left it at the foot of the bed. After unlacing the cord at the neck of the pullover shirt, she unbuckled the trouser belt and worked the shirttail loose. She pulled the tail toward Bren's shoulders and stopped, surprised by the appearance of white cotton wrapping. *What's this? Does he have broken ribs he didn't mention? That can't be. Surely, he would have said something to Doc Schafer about it.*

Uncertain now, Faith pondered her next move as she finished removing the shirt. She decided there was only one answer. If Bren had another injury, the bandage still needed to be changed to a clean one. She took her scissors out of her apron pocket and cut along the side of the binding. When she finished cutting all the way to the top, she lifted the loose strands to move them aside and promptly released them. She dropped into the chair next to the bed, hardly believing her eyes. Glory be! My soldier is a woman.

The discovery was so unexpected that Faith sat in the chair for several minutes just getting used to the idea. Gradually, her common sense took over. Woman or man, Bren still needed a bath. Faith carefully finished undressing her patient, sliding both the wide trouser leg and drawers leg past the splints. She pulled the cover back over the woman and went after the buckets of water.

Faith finished bathing and dressing Bren before Benjamin returned. Thinking it might be better if Benjamin continued to believe the soldier was a man, she left the beard on and washed around it. She folded the clean trousers and stockings and laid them on the bureau, having decided the drawers by themselves would be more comfortable, and the shirt was long enough to act as a tunic. On the injured leg, she had to cut the drawers leg to allow access to the wound and the splints. Now, she reminded herself, my soldier has one pair of trousers and two pairs of drawers that need mended. I can do this, she thought, and smiled, knowing she had repeated Bren's words. She wasn't trivializing them. She was giving the words her blessing. Indeed, she admired the woman's strength of purpose.

She put clean linens on the bed and covered Bren with an extra quilt while she opened the windows wide to air out the sweaty odor. She debated whether to rewrap Bren's torso and pretend the masquerade hadn't been discovered. On one hand, Bren would be more comfortable without the wrapping, and if the infection was stopped, she would be recuperating for weeks. She couldn't expect Faith to be kept in the dark for that length of time. On the other hand, it might be better for Bren if she were unmasked slowly. With her mind made up, Faith retrieved the clean cotton wrapping from the saddlebag. She put the bindings back on and pulled the clean shirt over them. As she settled in the rocking chair, she pushed the discovery of Bren's gender from her mind and contemplated the most serious aspect of the situation—the wound.

Bren's wounded limb would need the bandage changed every twelve hours. After thinking about that reality for a while, Faith got up and exchanged the wraparound bandage for one straight up-and-down, allowing better access to the wound without the necessity of removing the splints. Since yesterday, the infection in Bren's leg had spread and festered until the swollen limb looked like an overripe melon ready to burst. A dark brown, heart-shaped mole on the skin adjoining the wound had originally been the size of a pea and now was as wide as a coat button.

Faith had to admit she needed help. As soon as Benjamin got home from church, she sent him to see if Doc Schafer had returned from the field hospital.

The surgeon came and brought a pair of crutches with him. "Keep these crutches, Faith, and let's hope our patient lives long enough to use them." He handed them to her, and she set them in a corner of the bedroom. When he examined the wound, however, he raised his hands in resignation. "We can't save this leg."

Faith saw Bren's eyelids move and heard her groan. The soldier's good leg flailed out and caught her in the stomach, bringing an "Oof" as the breath spurted from her body.

"Damn your hide, soldier!" Doc Schafer bellowed. "She's trying to help you."

Bren took some heavy breaths and gasped, "Sorry. It pains. It pains."

"Don't worry." Faith's firm hand touched for a moment to Bren's forehead. "You didn't hurt me. Here, I have something that will help ease the pain." She drew two opium tablets from the pocket of her apron and reached for the jug on the side table. She poured some water into the earthenware cup. Bren grimaced and reached for the cup handle, but her arm dropped weakly back to the bed.

Faith put an arm under Bren's neck and shoulders to support her head. Holding the cup to her lips, Faith watched the patient attempt to gulp the whole cupful. Quickly, she pulled it back. "Take the pills first, then you can have more water." She poked the tablets one at a time between Bren's shaking lips and allowed her to finish off the water. "They should start working in a few moments," she said encouragingly. She refilled the cup several times until Bren was satisfied, then called to Benjamin to fetch more water. He brought the jug in and set it on the bedside table. Faith sympathized when she saw his nose wrinkle, probably from the sickening-sweet odor of the wound. She assumed he would leave and didn't notice when he stayed, hovering quietly in the background.

She tried not to show she was terribly worried about the condition of Bren's leg as well as the fever burning through her. Her heart had sunk when Doc Schafer removed the bandage and she saw how much worse the infection had become.

Flies buzzed annoyingly around her face, and she brushed at them. When her hand came in contact with one of the insects, the touch sent an exciting message to her brain. "Doc!" she said with such force that he turned to her with a look of surprise. "Do you remember that strange theory another doctor told Father a couple of years ago? The one about maggots cleaning out wounds?"

Dr. Schafer wrinkled his brow. "I can't say as I do. Can you explain it to me?"

Faith flushed, partly from tension and partly from excitement. "About a month before he died, Father told me he met with a colleague who professed that some surgeons were using live maggots to clean infected tissue out of wounds. Father laughed about it and said he wondered how you trained maggots to eat the bad parts and leave the good. But he did say he might investigate it some day." Faith waved a hand at Bren's leg. "What better time to investigate it? We can put some maggots in this wound and see what happens."

Bren's eyes went wide. "Now wait a minute—"

"Look, soldier," Doc Schafer interrupted, "you're out of choices. I told you before that the chances of saving your leg were not good. Now the infection is even worse, and unless something stops the poison from spreading, you'll lose the leg for sure—and your life, too." The creases in the doctor's forehead deepened, and his voice roughened. "We don't have any cure. Do you want to give this maggot idea one last try, or should I just cut off your leg right now?"

"That's pretty damn blunt," Bren said in a hoarse drawl. Her hands trembled and her face blanched, and neither the doctor nor Faith said another word. They waited for the answer as they watched Bren collect her control. Finally, she nodded. "All right, let's try it."

Faith headed for the door. "Benjamin and I will get some maggots from the compost pile out back." Her eyebrows raised in surprise when she saw her son was still in the room, and she motioned to him to accompany her.

"Fine," the doctor said. "I'll get this bandage off." He bent to his task.

Bren watched Faith and Benjamin leave. She struggled to keep her voice from wavering. "Do you think this will work, Doc?" She had visions of going through life with part of her left leg missing. She and Phillip would make a great pair as mirror images of each other. A shiver went through her, and she blinked her eyes in an attempt to banish that mental picture.

"I don't know, soldier. I just know if it were my leg, I would surely try it." The doctor raised sympathetic eyes. "If this maggot theory works, other soldiers can be saved, too. Hell, I'll go back to that field hospital and put maggots in some of those wounds just in case it does work. There sure aren't any alternative solutions."

Faith reentered the room with her son following. Benjamin's hands encircled a bowl of writhing, wriggling, white maggots, and his eyes were big and round and scared looking.

Bren looked from Benjamin's pale face to the pile of squirming larvae, and her stomach lurched, but she wanted to calm the boy's fears. She winked at him and drawled in a weakened voice, "Thank the Almighty, I don't have to eat the blasted things."

Overcome by a combination of opium, fever, and pain, Bren lapsed into semiconsciousness. For three days, fever wracked her body. She was vaguely aware of Faith applying wet compresses to her forehead, tending to her wounded leg, and coaxing opium tablets and water down her throat. Finally, the fever broke and she woke, soaked in perspiration. An early-morning sun shone a golden path across the bed, and as Bren's eyes followed it, she saw Faith asleep in the rocking chair. Clothed in a dark brown dress with a beige apron, she looked appealingly doll-like with her legs stretched out in front of her and her head tilted to one side. Tendrils of curls touched softly against her cheeks, and Bren felt a strange ache in her chest as she gazed at her.

The sun's rays reflected from Faith's red hair, forming a halo around her head. A lopsided grin pulled against Bren's lips. How appropriate. I do believe this angel has saved my life. And my leg. The ache in Bren's chest intensified, and she attributed it to gratitude. Then a puff of laughter escaped her. Maggots. A truly outlandish idea, but Faith had the courage to propose it. Bren struggled to a sitting position for a better view of the lovely picture across from her.

As though Faith could feel someone looking at her, she opened her eyes and answered Bren's grin with a slow one of her own. Suddenly, she jumped up and crossed to the bedside. "You're awake," she said, obviously pleased. "And sitting up!" Her eyes sparkled as she quickly felt Bren's forehead. "I can hardly believe it. Your fever has disappeared. The maggots are working."

"Are working?" Bren swallowed. "You mean they're still in my leg?" Faith smiled and nodded as she poured some water into the cup and held it for her patient. Bren lifted her arm to help and dropped it back with pretended weakness. While Faith once again supported her shoulders and held the cup to her lips, Bren took a good, close look at her savior. This woman had invested a lot of time and effort in saving her leg. Her eyes softened as warm feelings of gratitude washed over her.

Faith glanced up from the cup directly into those grateful amber eyes. For a long moment, both women paused. Faith broke the spell. Quickly, she pulled the cup back, set it on the table, and moved toward the lower part of the bed to examine Bren's leg. The wound had been left open to the air, so as not to suffocate the maggots as they did their lifesaving work. Several of the worms had managed to crawl away onto the sheet, and Faith made short work of picking them up and discarding them into a slop jar under the bed.

"I think perhaps we can remove all but a very few of the little creatures now," she remarked. "The wound looks almost clean." She finally raised her eyes and observed Bren. "Speaking of clean . . ."

"Yes," Bren hastened to agree. "I have other clothes in my saddlebags if Benjamin can bring the bags in for me." She fingered her beard, which was straggly from perspiration. "And maybe you could lend me a pair of scissors and a comb to smooth out this mess."

Faith nodded. "You'll need a bath first. I'll warm some water for you, and I can give you a hand."

"No!" Bren was adamant, then softened her tone. "No, thank you. I can take care of my own bathing, ma'am. Just bring me the proper necessities—soap, water, linens—if you please, and allow me some privacy."

"You're too weak to hold a cup, but not too weak to wash yourself?" Faith's eyes twinkled, but she had the grace not to laugh when Bren's face reddened.

"I'm getting stronger by the minute," Bren protested, then grinned wryly, acknowledging her earlier deception. She didn't even know why she had pretended to be weak. The reaction had been impulsive. Admit it, you laggard, you like having this woman tend to you. Obviously, her attempted ruse hadn't fooled Faith, who now had a hand over her mouth smothering a laugh as Bren blushed a deeper red. At that moment, fortunately, Benjamin knocked on the side of the doorjamb and waited until Bren invited him in.

"I heard you talking," he said shyly. "Are you feeling better?"

"Yes, I am, Benjamin. It's kind of you to ask. I feel much better. I'm wondering if you can do me a favor?"

The youngster practically ran to the side of the bed. "I'll do whatever you want, sir."

"Now that's the kind of enthusiasm I like," Bren drawled. "You would make a fine soldier." Benjamin's face gleamed with pleasure at the praise. "Your ma and I agree that I need to get washed up. But my extra clothes are in my saddlebags. Can you bring the bags in from the barn?"

"Yes, sir. I'll do that right away, sir." When Bren gave him an abbreviated salute, the boy stood at attention, returned it, and ran to perform his task.

"You've won over at least one person in this household," Faith remarked. Bren cocked a questioning eyebrow. "Well," Faith said, counting on her fingers, "you cussed me, you kicked me, you cussed me some more, and you tricked me into waiting on you." She wiggled the four fingers. "Not exactly an auspicious beginning."

Bren was annoyed with herself for the telltale blushing she had difficulty controlling. "Well, ma'am, the cussing I don't remember, but I apologize for it. And the kick was purely accidental, but I apologize for that, too." She rubbed the back of her neck. "As for the trickery . . ." She grimaced comically before continuing, "I have to confess I would do it all over again if I thought I could get away with it. Having you wait on me certainly is more pleasant than having to do everything for myself, like I do out on the trail. For that, I thank you."

A soft laugh bubbled out of Faith. "You're quite welcome. Except for Benjamin, I haven't had anyone to take care of for a long time. I'm enjoying the opportunity." She waved a hand toward the kitchen. "I'll go warm some water for you. And I'll bet you're hungry, too."

Bren let her body relax into the bed. "To tell the truth, ma'am, I think I need a nap before I bathe. But if you could bring me something to eat—a piece of bread would do—I'd be grateful. I'm so hungry that even if the food had some of those maggots all over it, I'd just brush them aside and take my turn."

Faith smiled at the answer just as Benjamin came in with the saddlebags, drawing their attention. She pointed to the bed. "Put them there, close enough so Mr. Cordell can reach them without any trouble."

Bren nodded. "Thank you for getting them, Benjamin."

"You're welcome, sir." With a nod in return, the youngster set the bags on the bed. Faith put a hand on his shoulder and steered him toward the door.

"I'll be back in a moment with some bread and cheese," she promised as the two left the room.

Bren tried to stay awake, but exhaustion overcame her, and she drifted off to sleep before Faith returned.

When Faith brought the bread and cheese, she quietly set it on the side table next to the water jug, within Bren's reach. She turned to tiptoe from the room when a low moan arrested her movement. Returning to the side of the bed, she gazed for a moment at her patient. The soldier looked gaunt and pale, and her body twitched several times, accompanied by more moaning. Faith could only imagine what terrible scenes Bren might be reliving. But at least the woman was alive. She pulled the covers up close to Bren's chin, offered a prayer of thanksgiving, and left the room.

As she entered the kitchen and picked up the buckets to get water, she grew thoughtful. *Who would guess that my soldier would turn out to be a woman? A woman who looks, talks, and acts like a man.* Faith found the situation strangely intriguing and the woman surprisingly attractive. *Bren Cordell and I need to have a discussion soon. She's been too sick to notice yet, but she'll suspect something's amiss as soon as she realizes her trousers are missing. As well as her pistol.*

For the first time since being wounded, Bren woke with a good feeling—hunger. Her leg merely ached, her body felt cool, and her head was clear. She lay still for a minute, savoring her near-miraculous recovery, before she turned to reach for the cheese on the table next to the bed. Her hand stayed midair, however, when the action made her aware that her belt, pistol, and holster were gone. She moved her good leg and realized she also no longer wore trousers. Glancing at the door to make sure it was closed, she flipped the cover partway off her body. Her long shirt reached down to the middle of her thighs, but sure enough, no trousers encased her legs. She put the cover back in place, raised herself on one elbow and searched the room with her eyes. She didn't see the pistol, but she did spot folded trousers lying on the bureau.

Damn it. I'll bet the woman took my trousers and washed them. I wonder just how far she undressed me? So much for being cool and clearheaded. The idea that she might have been unmasked shook Bren, and a knock on the door made her insides jump. She tensed in anticipation of confrontation.

"Come in." She nearly sighed with relief when Benjamin entered.

His words tumbled out in a rush. "Hi, Mr. Cordell. Mama sent me to see if you were awake, and how do you feel, and would you like some vegetable soup?" A smile lit his face, and his eyebrows lifted. "Mama killed a chicken and put it in the soup." He leaned a little closer to Bren as though imparting a secret. "And she's saving me the wishbone."

"Is that so?" Bren relaxed even more. *Maybe the situation was all right. It didn't sound threatening.* The youngster's whole attitude drew a friendly smile from her. "And what are you going to wish for?"

Benjamin straightened up and said soberly, "I'm going to wish for you to get all better."

Bren's voice stuck in her throat for a second until she cleared it. "Thank you, Benjamin. I really appreciate that." She blinked and took a deep breath. "Tell your mama I'm feeling much better, and I would dearly love to have a bowl of vegetable soup."

"Yes, sir."

"When I finish eating, maybe you would come visit with me for a while. All right?"

The boy's grin spread across his face. "I'd like that. I'll ask Mama."

Bren watched him leave. *What a sweet youngster. He seems quite grown up for his age. Maybe a ten-year-old?*

Hunger pushed any further thoughts away. She reached for the cheese and tore a chunk out with her teeth. She ate it and the bread before Faith entered, carrying a wooden tray that had sides and legs. The bowl of soup, a spoon, and another chunk of bread rested on the tray, and a folded linen napkin lay next to a vase containing a single yellow rosebud. The rosebud completed Bren's relief. It seemed she was being treated like a guest.

"I'm happy to see that you're feeling better." Faith placed the tray on the bedside table. "Do you think you can sit up and manage this yourself?" Her eyes sparkled as she looked at Bren. "Or would you rather I feed it to you?"

"Not a good question, ma'am, if you're looking to save yourself some work. But I'm feeling a lot stronger. I think I can take care of it." She sat up and pushed against the mattress to maneuver herself toward the bed's headboard. Faith picked up the pillow and positioned it behind her back. As Faith set the tray across her thighs, Bren said, "Thank you for the food. And the flower."

Faith turned toward the door. "You're very welcome. I'll leave you in peace while you eat."

"No, please." Bren stopped with a spoonful of soup on its way toward her mouth. "Stay and talk with me if you have time. Have you heard any news about the fighting nearby?" She returned to eating, and Faith settled in the rocking chair and pushed her feet against the wood floor.

Red curls bounced as Faith shook her head. "I haven't seen anyone to get any news. When I'm outside, the noise of battle does sound stronger, like it's getting closer. The fighting seems to go on in fits and starts, though. For several days, there were no sounds at all."

"That could be because of reinforcements each side is getting." Bren tore off a piece of bread, dipped it into the soup, and stuffed it into her mouth. Too late, she noticed Faith was watching her eat. She swallowed the bread as she wiped her dripping chin with the napkin. "Please excuse my rough manner of eating. I don't get much opportunity to share a meal with a lady."

Faith brushed away the excuse with a wave of her hand. "I would guess that good manners are one of the first casualties of army life. One can't politely try to exterminate one's enemy." Faith stopped rocking and leaned forward, lacing her fingers together and supporting her forearms in her lap. "In fact, army life must be rough for everyone concerned."

Bren silently finished eating and replaced the spoon on the tray.

At that, Faith rose and moved the tray to the side table. Bren assumed she was leaving, but she returned to the rocker. "I'm sure you would agree, wouldn't you, that army life is hard on a man and perhaps even harder on a woman?"

A premonition of trouble guttered through Bren. She tilted her head back overtop the pillow until she felt the headboard, then she brought it forward again, straightening her neck. "You bathed me while I was unconscious."

"Yes, I did."

"And changed my clothes."

"Yes."

"All of them."

"Yes, including the bandage around your chest."

Bren looked down at her hands, which were twisting the covers. She grimaced as she raised her head and met Faith's eyes again. Her shoulders tensed and her drawl thickened. "Are you going to tell anyone?"

"I must admit that was my first inclination." Faith's expression showed concern and uncertainty. "I've been pondering it for the last several days, while you very nearly died from your wound. If I turn you in, you can go home and be safe. You won't be in danger anymore."

Going from embarrassed to outraged in a heartbeat, Bren leaned forward. "Danger's part of my job. I accepted that when I decided to hire out to the army."

"But it doesn't have to be. You've already done your share." Faith pulled a sheet of paper from her apron pocket. "Look at this. Here's an article I read in a journal called the *Sibyl*. It tells of a woman masquerading as a soldier. Her true identity was discovered when she was wounded, and the authorities didn't do her any harm. They just mustered her out and sent her home, away from the fighting."

Bren sneered at Faith's words. "That's overprotective drivel. I want to keep doing what I contracted to do, not get flung away like useless baggage."

"You won't be flung away. You'll just be relieved of any further duties, and you'll be safe. I believe I shall report you."

Muscles rippled across Bren's jaw as her teeth clenched. "I'm a grown woman. What makes you think you have the right to choose my life for me?"

"I saved that life, remember?" Faith's cheeks flushed. "I hate to think that effort was wasted, that you'll just go right back to putting yourself at risk."

"And why not?" Bren's voice grew quieter, somehow making the soft drawl in her words sound more passionate. "If I were a man, I would do the same thing, and you wouldn't threaten me or chastise me about it. In fact, you would expect it. Maybe even admire it."

Faith stomped a foot against the floor, jerking the rocker. Her hands tightened on the arms of the chair. "No, I wouldn't. I would feel . . ." She hesitated as a flicker of doubt crossed her face. After a long moment, she continued. "Maybe your gender is coloring my thinking, but that doesn't make your masquerade right."

Bren snorted in disgust and threw off the covers. Leaning forward to grasp her splinted limb, she swung both legs over the side of the bed. With some discomfort, she pushed herself to sit upright.

Faith jumped to her feet and dropped a hand onto Bren's shoulder. "What do you think you're doing?"

"What's it look like I'm doing? I'm getting the hell out of here before you betray me." She tried to stand, but Faith easily held her down. Bren yanked the hand from her shoulder, grabbed Faith's arm, and pulled herself up to stand on one leg, holding on to Faith for balance.

The action startled Faith. "You're tall," she said pointlessly. "And hardheaded."

"So are you," Bren retorted. Faith was only a few inches shorter than she was and, she guessed, about thirty pounds heavier than her own scrawny frame. She frowned and her drawling tone deepened. "Either hand me those crutches from the corner, or move out of my way."

"Surely you can't be that determined to stay in the army after nearly dying."

"I *am* determined." Bren's gaze turned even fiercer, and her hand squeezed Faith's arm, causing a wince. "I will keep doing my best to help my cause, no matter what you think." Still holding on to Faith, Bren took one hop toward the crutches. She let go and immediately swayed.

Faith grabbed Bren's upper arm and steadied her. "Sit back down. Please. If you have your mind so firmly set, I won't stand in your way." She sighed. "I don't agree with your choice, but you're right. It's not up to me to decide how you live. Or how you die."

Bren turned her head to measure Faith eye to eye and nodded. "All right. I'll trust your word on it." Leaning on Faith, Bren hopped back to the bed and sat, short of breath. Heh, she jeered at herself. Me and my brave talk about leaving. I wouldn't have had enough energy to get dressed, let alone make it to the barn or saddle Redfire.

"I suppose," Faith said, "as long as you don't interfere with anyone else's rights, you can do as you please." She helped Bren raise her wounded leg onto the bed and pulled the covers up, then she sat again in the rocker and leaned her head to the side. "I am curious, though. You're obviously an educated woman. Just why did you want to take part in the war?"

"I wanted to do something to make a difference in the world." Bren recalled her initial longing. "Families in my town were sending men and boys to fight for their cause, and I didn't see why I shouldn't go, too. I can ride and shoot as well as they can, and I'm bigger than most of them. I didn't see why my gender should keep me from helping." Such innocence of purpose, she thought. I wonder when that became a casualty of war?

Faith's lips quirked. "I was bigger than my husband, and I have to admit that I probably would have made a stronger soldier. But the idea of joining up never entered my mind. Maybe because I had to take care of Benjamin. Speaking of which—" She nodded her head toward the door. "I think it might be better for Benjamin's sake to remain silent about your gender. This war has been difficult enough for him to understand, without confusing him further."

"I have no intentions of telling anyone. In a day or two, I'll be out of here, and you won't have to be concerned about it." Speaking aloud about leaving saddened Bren, though she was at a loss to explain why.

"Oh, no, you won't." Faith's expression had begun to lighten, but now it turned stern, and Bren got a dose of her schoolmarm attitude. "You're not going anywhere until that open wound is healed. I didn't struggle to save your leg so you could go out and get it reinfected." She nodded toward the crutches Bren had tried to reach. They were fashioned simply, each a long pole with a curved piece of wood attached to the top. "Tomorrow, we'll find out whether you can manage those crutches and get up and around a bit. Until then, you stay right in that bed."

"Yes, ma'am." So she doesn't like losing an argument, Bren thought. But I do owe her some consideration. She saluted in mock obedience, granting Faith the opportunity to save face. "But may I at least use the slop jar again when necessary? I found it under the bed a little earlier."

Faith's cheeks turned pink. "Of course, you may. I'll see to emptying it for you." She stood up. "Benjamin said you invited him to visit you after you finished eating."

"Yes, I did. He's a fine boy. You should be proud of him."

"Thank you. And thank you for showing him such kindness. He's very excited about your being here. I'll send him right in. Do you need anything?"

"Not really, but I have a question. Isn't the *Sibyl* a journal for women?"

"Yes." Faith bent down and busied herself with removing the covered slop jar from beneath the bed. "Are you familiar with it?"

"Indeed, I am." Bren scratched her head above her ear. "I believe they support a woman's right to be whatever she pleases. Even to having equality with men."

"Look." Faith stood up with the jar in her hands and starch in her words. "You won your point. Just don't go getting overbearing about it."

A tiny smile appeared on Bren's face. "Yes, ma'am," she said again, drawing the words out in exaggeration.

With a flounce, Faith departed, closing the door behind her.

The smile broadened as Bren let relief wash over her. *So she reads the Sibyl. I like a woman with some fire in her veins. This is becoming an interesting recuperation.*

She was still smiling when a knock sounded. "Come in," she called, and Benjamin entered with a cloth bag in his hand. "What's that you have, Benjamin?"

The boy came over to the bed and opened the bag. He grabbed its edges, pulled them apart, and held the bag out for Bren to see inside. "My pa gave me these. They're soldiers."

Bren pushed down the top edge of the bag with her finger and looked in. She slapped the mattress beside her. "Good! Dump them on the bed, and let's take a closer look at them."

Benjamin turned the bag over and about two dozen painted lead figures tumbled out into a pile. Dressed in uniforms of the Revolutionary War, the figures in blue represented the patriots, and those in red, the British. Some figures wielded swords, some aimed muskets, and some were on horseback. Two drummer boys, two soldiers carrying their respective flags, and four cannons mounted on caissons rounded out the assemblage.

They sorted out the two colors, putting a group on one side of Bren and the other on the opposite side. When they finished, Benjamin pointed to the red-clad figures.

"I call the red ones our soldiers, and the blue are the Yankees."

"That sounds good to me. Do you want to fight against each other, or both be on the same side?"

Dark brown eyes widened. "Mama always fights against me. Are we allowed to both fight on the same side?"

"Hmm." Bren pressed her lips together and nodded. "I don't see why not. We're both fighting for the Confederacy, aren't we?"

"Yes, sir." A broad smile lit the boy's face. "You and me on the same side. I like that."

"How old are you, Benjamin?"

"I'm eight, sir."

"Eight? I thought you were at least ten. You're tall, like your mother." Bren picked up a horse-mounted figure dressed in a red uniform and bounced the rider along the mattress. "For now, you're eighteen and we're going to capture us some bluebellies. Get your horse, soldier, and let's scout them out."

"Yes, sir." Benjamin saluted, grabbed one of the mounted soldiers and followed along behind Bren. She brought her figure to a halt and waited for the boy to catch up, and they resumed their mission, side by side.

A while later, Faith peeked in the doorway, smiled at the two dark-haired soldiers engrossed in their activity, and returned to her tasks, still wishing Bren weren't going back to the war.

CHAPTER SIX

The following morning, Bren enjoyed a breakfast of hotcakes drenched in butter and syrup and finished it with a cup of tea. Faith came into the bedroom, set the breakfast tray aside, and handed Bren the folded trousers from the bureau.

"Ready to get up out of bed?" she asked. She gathered the crutches from their corner and set them against the near wall.

Bren's face lit up at the idea. "Yes, I am." With Faith's help, she dressed, took the offered crutch, and managed to stand. Faith steadied her while passing her the other crutch, and Bren fit the armrests against her armpits. "These feel like they were made for a shorter person," she said as their height forced her to slump at an uncomfortable angle.

"This is a pair Doc Schafer keeps around for anyone's use." Faith let go of her and stayed alongside as Bren tried out a few steps. "I would suggest you use them sparingly, or your back will complain about it."

Bren moved to and fro across the room until she caught on to the rhythm of walking with the crutches. "Speaking of backs, I'm truly happy to be able to get off of mine for a change. Lying abed for so long has sapped my strength." Indeed, she already felt drops of perspiration sprouting along her hairline.

Faith beckoned with one hand. "Let me show you the parlor and the kitchen. You might want to rest a bit before walking any farther than that." Gaining confidence, Bren followed her through the doorway into the next room.

About thirty feet long and fifteen feet wide, the parlor's random-planked floor ran the full width of the house. A green sofa and two

101

brown, stuffed chairs formed a sitting area in front of a stone fireplace. Above the fireplace, a mantel held a daguerreotype of a Confederate soldier. Bren recognized the origin of Benjamin's dark complexion and brown eyes, even before Faith followed her gaze and remarked, "That's my late husband, Benjamin's father." On the wall above the mantel, a musket and a saber rested in the hooks of a rack. The far end of the room contained an office area, complete with desk, chair, and wooden filing cabinets. A framed piece of corkboard on the wall behind the desk served as a bulletin board and contained odd-sized pieces of paper as well as a child's drawings. Halfway along the room's wall, a very steep staircase, little more than an expanded ladder, led to a door set into the ceiling. Again, Faith followed Bren's eyes. "That's the loft. Two bedrooms are up there—one is Benjamin's, and the other is mine at the moment."

Bren returned her gaze to Faith. "I'm sorry I've displaced you from your bedroom. Now that I can get around, let me move into the loft so you can have your bed back."

"No, no," Faith said. "There's no way you should make that climb. I'm comfortable enough up there." She moved past Bren to the desk area. "Come sit down and rest for a minute. You're not used to those crutches yet."

Though she had been standing for just a few minutes, Bren welcomed the chance to sit. Not only did the crutches hurt her arms and shoulders, but also weakness made her legs quiver, which surprised and annoyed her. This recuperation would take longer than she had hoped. She hobbled to the chair and removed the crutches from beneath her arms. After she leaned them against the desk, she sat in the spindle-backed chair and directed her gaze around the room.

Lifting her splinted leg an inch above the floor and using her unhampered foot, Bren turned the chair to look at the bulletin board on the wall behind her. She skimmed past Faith's notes and examined the drawings that had "Benjamin" carefully printed on each in capital letters. The pictures had been drawn in charcoal and colored in with crayon pencils. Although simply fashioned, each figure displayed a developing talent. Bren tapped a finger against a sketch of a robin on a tree limb. "He's good," she said and turned back to Faith. "I do some drawing, too. Maybe I could give him a few lessons while I'm here."

"Thank you." Faith's green eyes shone with pride in her son. "That's a generous offer. I'm sure Benjamin would appreciate your help. He loves to draw. He'll spend hours on one picture until he gets it just the way he wants it. Some of them never suit him, and he won't even show them to me."

Bren smiled. "I was the same way. When my mother came across something I had finished, she put it on the drawing room mantel for display. I went behind her and took down the ones I wasn't satisfied with." Her smile turned wistful. "Of course, being my mother, she thought they all were wonderful. I think my drawing was the one thing I did that she approved of."

"Really?" Faith cocked her head. "What does she think of your being in the war?"

Rolling her shoulders to stretch the muscles, Bren looked down and hesitated before answering. Her fingers beat a slow tattoo on the desktop. She stopped her motions and raised her gaze to meet Faith's.

"At first, I wouldn't let anyone tell my parents. They retired to Paramalin, Virginia, a place near Gordonsville. I'd always kept in touch with them through the mail, such as it is, but I would send my letters to my brother. He would send them on so it appeared as if I were still at home." Bren's gaze flicked away. "But I missed them and worried about them with the war so close to where they live. I stopped a while ago to see them and showed up as a scout. My father accepted my decision, but my mother reacted by wringing her hands, telling me she doesn't recognize the woman I've grown into, and denying any responsibility for the foolish things I do."

"And you don't care what she thinks?"

"Of course I do." Bren puffed a breath through her nose. "But I can't help what my mother thinks." With a shove against the desk, she shifted the chair back. She bent to lift her leg away from the kneehole. "I don't care to discuss this any further."

Faith grasped one of the crutches and reached out a hand to help Bren stand. "I'm sorry. I shouldn't have asked such a personal question. I was just thinking that, as a mother, I would be really upset if Benjamin chose to fight in a war when he didn't have to."

Bren accepted the hand up and placed the crutches beneath her arms. "Would you try to stop him if his principles were involved?" She moved toward the bedroom with Faith accompanying her.

"I would probably try to talk him out of it, but I can see that the decision would be his. I apologize for arguing against your having the same privilege. That was wrong of me. And rude."

Back in the bedroom, Bren sat on the edge of the bed. She leaned the crutches against the wall and looked up at Faith. "No apology is necessary. Even a hardhead like me can recognize when a suggestion is meant to be in my best interests." When Faith raised her eyebrows, Bren chuckled. "All right, so it may take me a while to figure out some things. I get there eventually." She reached down to lift her leg onto the bed, and Faith helped her. "By the way, where is Benjamin? Has school started?"

"He's out picking apples right now. School has started, but I'm keeping him home for a few days. He's too excited to concentrate on schoolwork right now."

"Won't the schoolteacher wonder why he's not there?"

"Not really," Faith answered with a twinkle in her eye. "I'm the schoolteacher. The parson's wife is taking my place this week."

"Because of me?" Damn. I hadn't considered that, Bren thought. "I'm sorry."

"Now you're apologizing when there's no need to." Faith shook her head, jiggling red curls and bouncing out a few tendrils that always seemed ready to fall loose. "You didn't ask to be shot. Nor to fall practically on my doorstep. To tell the truth, I find it exciting to have a wounded soldier to tend. You may consider it my little part in helping the war."

"I was lucky to fall onto your doorstep. I'm sure I would have died otherwise." Bren reflected a moment. "Your 'little part in helping the war' saved my life, and I'm grateful." Without warning, she yawned. "Pardon me. I think I need to take a nap, if you don't mind."

She lay down and Faith pulled the covers over her. "You might want to keep covered while you sleep. We can't have you catching a chill on top of everything else." She folded the top of the cover and smoothed it across Bren's waist. "And if you take your nap like a good little soldier, you might get a piece of apple pie for lunch."

"Mmm. Apple pie sounds wonderful." Bren's drawl trailed away as she closed her eyes and fell quickly to sleep. Against the canvas of her mind, a slow-motion kaleidoscope intertwined wispy projections of red curls, green eyes, and apple pie, blocking out blood-soaked nightmares and bringing a rare smile to her slumbering face.

Faith stood still a minute, watching Bren's deep, even breathing. She leaned down as if to kiss Bren's forehead. Instead, with a rueful smile, she tiptoed out of the room.

Over the following three weeks, good food and plenty of rest strengthened Bren until she finally could be up and about all day without feeling drained. To add to her comfort, she had dispensed with the bindings on her chest. Faith had agreed that, with a little caution, her loose tunic would keep Benjamin unaware of her gender, and no one else would be likely to see her.

The open wound on her leg had nearly healed, and it had left a slight depression, covered with an ugly scar. Faith told her it could be another month before the broken bone finished mending. The awkward splints had to stay in place for a while longer.

At first, Bren had been anxious to get on her way, but as the days went by, she found she cherished the feeling of family she found with Faith and Benjamin. The mother and son had a deep love and mutual respect for each other, but beyond that, there was a sense of warmth and caring between the two that had rarely been evident between Bren and her own mother. Faith, in her generosity, extended that same warmth and caring to Bren. A part of Bren was learning to respond to that, and she knew she would sorely miss the Pruitts when she left. In fact, even the thought of leaving brought on feelings of loss.

Benjamin joined her every day for drawing lessons or for military games with the lead soldiers. One evening, after supper, the two of them sat side by side at the kitchen table completing an earlier art project.

Faith finished cleaning the dishes and walked over to stand behind her son. "Why, Benjamin, you're doing that drawing in perspective," she said, marveling at his work.

"Yes," Bren said, "and I only showed him how to do that yesterday." Reaching over, she ruffled his brown curls. "You learn quickly, Benjamin. I'm very pleased with your progress."

The grinning youngster put the last stroke on the picture and held it up for a better look. After he had examined it thoroughly and nodded in satisfaction, his mother lifted it from his fingers and placed it upright against the wall on a shelf. Benjamin looked from his picture to Bren. "Do you have any drawings you can show us, Mr. Cordell?"

"Yes, yes I do." Bren slowed her drawl and dragged out the answer, her eyes twinkling as she teased the eager youngster. "If you'll bring me my saddlebags from my bedroom, I have some in there I can show you." The boy rushed out to get the bags. Faith's gaze returned to the picture her son had just completed, and Bren said, "I think Benjamin might have a future in art. His pictures show a lively spirit and a good eye for line and color."

"I'll try to pay more attention to his drawing. With your help, he's already progressed beyond my capabilities." Faith shot Bren a sideways glance and smiled. "Maybe I'll be taking lessons from him. Thank you for your encouragement."

Benjamin came back with the saddlebags and set them on the table. Bren opened one and brought out the leather-bound book. "This is a journal of my travels and experiences since I started working for the army." Benjamin sat down next to her at the table, with Faith just beyond him. Bren opened the journal and paged through it, showing them sketches accompanied by strong, precise writing. "Some of these are general scenes of battles or the land I traveled through." She stopped at one particular page and pointed to three drawings of single figures situated among the written words. "Others, like these, are individuals I happened to meet."

"Look, Mama, there's a drummer boy." Benjamin pointed to a youngster who looked about twelve years old. Dressed in a gray uniform, he carried a drum cross-belted over his shoulders and hanging near his waist. He held two sticks above the drumhead as though ready to strike it. "Did you know him, Mr. Cordell?"

"Yes, I did." Bren touched a finger to another portrait that showed the head and shoulders of an officer. "This is his father, who was a captain in one of the regiments I worked with. He was—"

"Who's the woman?" Faith said. When Bren looked at her and raised one eyebrow, Faith hurried to apologize. "Please pardon me for interrupting you. I'm just very curious about what the woman has to do with the war."

Bren brought her gaze back to the picture in question. The woman wore a long-skirted work dress covered with a soiled apron. She knelt on the ground holding a piece of cloth in one hand and a pair of scissors in the other. "Some of the men had wives and sweethearts who followed after them. I suppose at first they just wanted to be near their men, but when the army engaged in a battle, the women went into the field and tended to the wounded. It was an amazing sight to see them out there, sometimes even while shooting was still going on. I've heard that a few were actually wounded. Some may have been killed, though I'm not sure of that."

"I've read about it in the newspapers," Faith said. "But your drawing brings it to life. This is the first time it has really made an impression on me. They must be very brave."

"Maybe they believe in their men and support the cause they fight for. That would make the risks seem worthwhile." Faith lifted her eyebrows, and Bren continued. "To them, anyway."

"What's the drummer boy's name?" Benjamin's question stopped the word battle that was forming between Bren and Faith.

"I don't think I ever heard his real name. All the men called him Sticks."

Benjamin smiled at that. "Is he still with the regiment?" The youngster, engrossed in the picture, didn't see the anguished look Bren quickly fought down, but a trace of it remained in the gaze she flicked toward Faith. The drummer's fate was imprinted forever in Bren's mind. Closing her eyes, she remembered the day clearly.

Strong resistance from the top of the ridge had stalled the Confederate assault. The Union cannoneers laid down a barrage interspersed with musket fire that seemed impossible to penetrate. Bren dismounted and delivered the dispatch to the Rebel captain. She quickly remounted Redfire to leave, knowing she had changed the colonel's message. The superior officer had commanded a retreat, but Bren's substituted words now ordered the captain to push the regiment forward at all costs.

"Stay here," the captain said. "I might have an answer to send." The officer read the piece of paper and called to his son, and the boy hurried to his father's side. The captain pulled a quill pen and bottle of ink from a pouch, scribbled some words on the dispatch, and handed it up to Bren. "Take this back to the colonel." The officer turned to the drummer boy. "Send them the charge, son."

Bren started away as the beating drum signaled the soldiers to renew the assault. Slowed by the men streaming by, she looked toward the first wave of troops. The drum cadence beat an accompaniment to the booming of cannon fire, the creaking and squeaking of gear, the shouts and pounding feet of the foot soldiers that filled the air. Even in such tumult, her ears picked out the whine of a particular shot of canister. In a split-second tableau of horror, a hundred chunks of metal pierced father and son together, and a mushroom of blood gushed into the air, blotting them from sight.

Shaking with grief and guilt, Bren spurred Redfire away, in utter disregard of the soldiers shunted aside by the big animal's momentum. The horse thundered through the troops and burst into the woods. Small animals and insects scurried away, and birds darted into the sky in black clouds as the horse tore among the trees. Bren repeatedly gulped in huge lungfuls of air and finally pulled Redfire to a halt. Calming herself enough to take time to refocus, she took the dispatch from its pouch and read: "We fulfill our duty as ordered, and we trust in Almighty God to reward us in this life or the next, as He sees fit."

"Oh, God," Bren whispered as tears ran from her eyes, "have mercy on us all."

"Mr. Cordell?" Benjamin shook her arm. "Did you hear me? I was wondering if they're both still with the regiment?"

Bren opened her mouth to answer Benjamin, but her constricted throat betrayed her. During the day, she usually managed to push the memory away, hoping to thrust it into the dark pit reserved for such horrors, but this one recurred at night in bloodstained nightmares that seared her soul. Seeing her distress, Faith answered for her as she pointed to a date written below the picture.

"Look, Benjamin. Mr. Cordell drew this in March 1863, nearly a year and a half ago. He might not have seen the boy after that." She looked up at Bren. "Have you?"

With a nod of gratitude, Bren finally found her voice. "No, I haven't. Armies move all over, so there's no telling where that regiment might be by now."

Benjamin looked disappointed, but he soon perked up at another thought. "Will you read us some of your journal?"

"Not tonight, Benjamin." Faith shook her head. "It's your bedtime."

"Aww, Mama. Just one story, please?"

Bren closed the journal with a light thud and answered in Faith's stead. "Maybe another time. Your mama said it's your bedtime, and good soldiers follow orders. The book will still be here tomorrow evening."

"All right, sir," Benjamin said with little enthusiasm. He gathered up his drawing materials, put them away, and went outside for a visit to the outhouse. After watching him leave, Bren turned to face the question she knew Faith would ask.

"What happened to the boy?" Bren's mouth twitched, and again, she found it hard to answer. The drummer boy's face and Benjamin's kept changing places in her mind. Faith waited a moment, searching Bren's expression. "He didn't live, did he?"

Bren shook her head slowly, until she could talk. "No, he didn't. He and his father were both—" Bren stopped as Benjamin came back inside and kissed his mother good night. Bren tossed him a quick salute, which he returned with a grin before he clambered up the ladder to the loft.

Faith softened her voice so her son wouldn't hear. "What happened to them?"

Bren swallowed hard and answered in a voice so low that Faith could barely make out the slow drawl. "I saw them both die."

"Were they shot?"

"You might call it that." The scene reappeared in all its horror, and Bren's mind clenched with pain all over again. *My God, they were shredded!* Her hands quivered, and she clasped them together to hide it. "Terrible things happen in war. Some are too dreadful to ever speak about. You have to harden your heart to survive them."

"I'm sorry." Faith reached over and laid her hand on top of Bren's while giving her a look of concern. "I suspect maybe yours isn't as hard as you'd like to think it is."

Bren couldn't argue with that. Her usual way of coping with emotional turmoil was to turn her mind from it as quickly as possible, or bury it. But this time, Faith's touch soothed her. Warmth spread through her body, quieting her grieving heart. She didn't question why the touch helped her. She was just grateful that it did.

Several days later, on a Sunday morning, Bren awoke to the thumping of many feet and the unmistakable creaking of gear. She sat up and looked toward the window, but soon realized the sound came from the dirt road in front of the house. With a caution that had become second nature, she pulled out the drawer in the side table and lifted the false beard and spirit gum from it. Hurriedly, she attached the beard. She replaced the gum and shut the drawer. Yanking on her trousers, she had to jiggle the pant leg that tried to catch on the splints. With a crutch stuck under one arm, she hobbled into the front room.

Faith stood at the window, peering out. The sun had risen just enough to reflect softly from the white cotton shift she wore, and Bren felt a rush of heat as she admired the way the rays burnished Faith's russet curls. She was feeling these rushes often and recognized she was growing overly fond of her hostess. In the midst of a war was no time to get emotionally attached to anyone, and especially not a woman who favored the Confederate cause. No one had ever aroused such feelings in Bren before. That a woman had this effect on her took some getting used to. But she would worry about that later.

Glancing back, Faith grimaced toward Bren, who moved up behind her. "The Union seems to have taken over our town."

Bren leaned over Faith's shoulder to look out and study the troops. The redhead smelled fresh and clean, tinged with a hint of roses new-bloomed on a spring morning. The mix of scents filled Bren with longing. She wanted to put her arms around Faith and pull her close.

"You smell good. Like roses," Bren surprised herself by saying. Embarrassed by her outspokenness, she fought to direct her focus back to the marching men. She rested a hand on Faith's shoulder for balance and felt her tremble. It has to be disturbing to see the enemy come into your town, she thought. The soldiers marched four abreast, and she could see the end of the column. Her drawl deepened even further. "Assuming that the beginning of the column woke us up, it looks like they're few in number, maybe a couple of hundred or so. But I don't hear any resistance."

Faith's response suggested she was more disturbed than she would ever admit. Her voice started out as a strangled whisper and gradually grew stronger. "The only thing here of any importance to the military is the telegraph office. But the lines to that were cut so many times, they finally abandoned repair attempts." She lifted her hands into the air and let them drop. "That's hardly worth fighting for. Most of the Confederate soldiers come here on leave, looking for food and relaxation. Any who were here are probably scurrying back to their regiments."

Relaxation? An image of Leah pulsed through Bren's mind, and she turned her head away to hide her grin. It dawned on her that soldiering had broadened her acceptance of people's differences. In polite circles, Leah would be considered a fallen woman, not worthy of respect. But she was kind to me, and she didn't betray my secret, Bren mused. Faith's voice interrupted her thoughts.

"I had no idea they would bother taking over the town. I thought the fighting was passing us by. You could be in danger."

Hunched over the crutch, Bren turned her head to meet Faith's eyes. "You could be in danger, too. For harboring a Confederate soldier."

Faith's eyes widened. "That thought never occurred to me." She looked back out at the blue-clad troops, her expression turning anxious. "Please keep well out of sight."

"Don't worry, I've been very careful about that. And I won't stay any longer. My wound is healed well enough that I can slip away tonight, after dark. Once I get on Redfire, the splinted bone shouldn't hinder me."

Faith swung around toward Bren and looked up with her lips parted. Bren's body turned of its own accord, and a surge of desire washed over her. She could almost swear that Faith's eyes were filled with desire, too. But the moment ended when noise came from the loft above. Benjamin had awakened.

As Faith's tongue peeked out to moisten her lips, Bren sucked in a breath. Faith spoke, and her voice held a slight catch. "I hoped you could stay until the bone knit all the way, but perhaps it's best that you go."

"No!" Benjamin came scrambling down the ladder from the loft, still in his nightshirt. "I don't want Mr. Cordell to leave." He ran to Bren's side and grabbed her shirttail. "Please don't leave."

Bren placed her hand on his shoulder and squeezed gently. "I have to go, Benjamin. We don't want those bluebellies catching me here. Besides," she said with a smile, "how are we going to win this war if I'm not there to help?" A pang struck her heart. She had lowered her defenses enough to begin to feel like a part of this family. The arrival of the Union troops, however, brought home the unpleasant fact that Faith and Benjamin were on the opposite side of the war.

"Yes, sir," Benjamin answered reluctantly as Bren released his shoulder and put her hand back on the crutch.

"Since we're all awake," Faith said, "I might as well fix breakfast. I'll stoke the stove so it can warm up while we change." Faith moved away from the window and touched her son's cheek. "Put your good clothes on, Benjamin. We'll be going to the Sunday service as usual. Especially today." She tilted her head and met Bren's inquiring gaze. "A lot of people come to church and mingle afterward. It's a great place to get all the news. Maybe I can find out where the soldiers will be billeted."

"That's a good idea." Bren realized she needed to ask for the information that a Rebel would want. "See if you can learn where the others are camped outside of town. That's an area I'll want to avoid."

"I'll do that," Faith said. "Now, let's get ready for breakfast."

While Faith and Benjamin were attending the Sunday service, Bren sat at Faith's desk, adding another drawing to her journal. She paused to look out the window beside her. The sun shone brightly, a gentle warmth filled the air, and a mild breeze was just kicking up. Bren sniffed the air and frowned. What should have been a remarkably beautiful day was tainted with the odor of the men and beasts that had passed by earlier. Thankfully, the breeze should carry the smells away and let nature's pleasanter scents revive. Her face contorted briefly, as if from pain. The Pruitts had helped her forget the war for a while, but now it had come to fetch her back. Breathing a sigh of resigned acceptance, she resumed her drawing.

The picture she worked on portrayed her, Faith, and Benjamin, sitting at this same desk, looking at this same journal. She placed the final stroke and smiled, satisfied with her rendition. When she heard a noise just outside the front door, she assumed it was the two returning home. She knew Faith had locked the door, but Bren hadn't bolted it from within, so she didn't need to get up.

Suddenly, something hit the outside of the door with a loud thump, bursting it open. Three Union soldiers charged into the room and leveled their muskets at Bren. "So the redhead was telling the truth," the biggest soldier said. "There is a Johnny Reb here. Put your hands in the air." He motioned upward with the musket.

Startled into submission, Bren laid down her pen and raised her hands. Her body tensed for action. But her common sense took over. She would just quietly go along with the soldiers. After all, she was Lady Blue. Once she gave that information to the officer in charge, and he made inquiries, she had no doubt the authorities would release her. But a torrent of other thoughts tumbled through her brain. A redhead told them. Faith gave me up. She turned me in. No, she wouldn't do that. But maybe she did it to protect her home and to protect Benjamin. No, I can't believe she would think she needed to do that. But no one else knew I was here. Only the doc, and he wouldn't have any reason to betray me. She did it! She must have.

Bren felt battered by the betrayal. Dark anguish seeped into her heart. In the short time she had been there, Faith and Benjamin had treated her like family, and she had begun to love them. And the strength of what she felt for Faith confused her. She hurt more from the woman's betrayal than from any danger to herself.

"Get up, and get over here," the soldier commanded. The men tensed as Bren reached for the crutches, but she merely slid the curved tops under her arms and moved forward, inspecting the soldiers as she went. The big man wore a sergeant's triple chevron on his sleeves, obviously giving him charge over the two wearing no insignia. Her brain automatically took inventory of their physical appearance. Two had brown hair, brown eyes, and dark beards. The third and youngest one had black hair, blue eyes, and only the patchy beginnings of a beard. The slim young soldier and the burly sergeant stood nearly her height, while the other man was a head shorter.

Bren stopped in front of the sergeant. "I want to see your commanding officer." The man swung his rifle butt around and smacked the side of it against her face, knocking her to the hardwood floor as the crutches tumbled away. The blow slammed her cheek against her teeth, splitting the inside skin. Though momentarily dazed, she tasted blood crossing her tongue.

"You'll speak when you're spoken to, you swine," the sergeant snarled.

Bren shook her head, trying to clear it. She retrieved one of the crutches and attempted to rise. The soldier knocked her back with a hard slap across the face, spurting blood from her mouth and dislodging the fake beard.

"What the hell?" He reached down and yanked on the loosened bit of hair, and the whole piece came free in his hand. The man squinted at the hair and back at Bren. "Why the hell are you wearing a false beard?"

Lying on one side, Bren stayed on the floor. She swallowed some of the blood that pooled in her mouth while most dribbled out the corner. "I'm working for the Union. Take me to your commanding officer, and I can prove it." Her tongue flicked at the split in her lip, softening it. "And keep you out of trouble."

The man snorted and looked at his companions. "He must think we never heard that one before, huh?" He laughed, and the two joined him. He kicked Bren's shoulder, flopping her over onto her back. The movement pulled her shirt tight against her body, outlining the curves of her breasts. "By God, you're a woman!" At once, his whole demeanor changed. "A woman pretending to be a man—that's blasphemy." He looked again at his men. "Do you know what we have here, boys? A whore. She figures dressing like a man will give her a chance to mix with the Johnny Rebs and make herself a pot of money." He turned back to Bren. "Well, bitch, if you want to be a whore, we'll treat you like one." He motioned toward her. "Pick her up and follow me. We just found ourselves a free plaything. We can use the woods out back of here to give us some cover."

The men hesitated, and the sergeant barked at them. "What are you waiting for? Do what I say, damn it. I'm in charge here."

The younger man spoke up. "But Sergeant Angston, we're just supposed to round up the Rebs and take them to the jail."

The other soldier nodded. "Hager's right, Sergeant. We could get in trouble."

"Shut up, Wertz. I'll worry about that. You'll get in worse trouble if you don't do what I tell you."

The soldiers glanced at each other, and Wertz shrugged. They slung their rifles onto their backs and reached for Bren. She tried to fight them, but Sergeant Angston slammed her in the head with the rifle butt, knocking her unconscious. The men kicked the crutches out of the way, pulled her up, and drew her arms across their shoulders. With Bren's head lolling and her bare feet dragging behind them, they followed Angston down the hallway and out the back door of the house.

Faith and Benjamin strolled across the fields, using a shortcut to return from church. As they neared home, Faith was talking to her son about some chores that needed done. Benjamin interrupted her and pointed to the house.

"Mama, look!" A soldier held the back door open, and two more men came outside, hauling Bren between them. Her head was down, and her hair fell forward, obscuring her face, but if there had been any doubt about her identity, the splinted leg dispersed it. "It's Mr. Cordell," Benjamin said. "They're taking him away! We have to help." Benjamin tried to bolt toward the soldiers, but Faith grabbed his sleeve.

"No, Benjamin. Stay here. We can't do anything for Mr. Cordell." Her free hand flew up to cover her mouth. She watched, and her heart hammered against her chest.

"But where are they taking him, Mama? Mr. Cordell is their enemy. They'll probably put him in prison."

Faith pulled her son into an embrace and buried his head against her, shutting the scene from his vision. Bren won't have to suffer those consequences, she thought. As past newspaper articles had indicated, when they discover Bren is a woman, she will merely be sent home. When she heard her son crying, she hugged him closer.

"Bad things happen in wartime, Benjamin. Soldiers know they run the risk of being captured, or even killed. At least Mr. Cordell is alive." And out of danger, thank goodness, she told herself. She kissed the top of Benjamin's head. "He's a strong person. He'll be all right." As the group passed the corral, Faith saw the sergeant lift a rope from a post and slip his arm through the coils. A perplexed look crossed her face when the soldiers took Bren into the forest. She wondered if the army had set up a stockade in the woods.

Faith could have cried, too. From the moment she had discovered Bren was a woman, she had been intrigued by her. During the several weeks of recuperation, that interest had confounded her by gradually turning into a physical and emotional attraction. She tried to deny it, but the fact had been amply demonstrated by several subtle occurrences. The one that convinced her she had fallen in love was her body's reaction to Bren's proximity when they watched the Union troops enter town. When Bren had come up behind her and leaned over her shoulder, Faith's knees had gone weak. She had shivered with the heat of the passion lit by Bren's innocent touch on her shoulder. She wanted more.

Indeed, she had always been attracted to women, even more so than to men, but she had never met one she cared for enough to love. Now she had met a woman who captured her heart, and she had no way of knowing if she would ever see Bren again. Or even whether Bren felt any attraction for her. Although, for that brief moment in the parlor, she seemed to. But so what if Bren did care? They would never have met if it hadn't been for the war, and now the war had come between them, making any intimacy virtually impossible. She silently cried at the unfairness of it all.

CHAPTER SEVEN

B ren stirred and groggily came to, her head pounding. The soldier who had attacked her at Faith's cabin stepped forward. He kicked her hard in the bad leg. She cried out as the pain roused her to full consciousness. The sergeant stood over her, and there was no mistaking his intent. He unbuttoned his pants.

Her whole body jerked to bring her arms and legs up to fight him off, but she could barely move them. She raised her head to see that ropes and pegs held her spread-eagled to the ground. And she was naked. Oh God, oh God. Not this. Help me! Terror flooded her brain and pounded against her throbbing head.

"Stop him!" she called as her eyes flicked to the other soldiers, but they looked away. Within seconds, she realized the futility of seeking anyone's help. She was about to be violated, and she could do nothing to prevent it. Nothing physical, that is. Terror changed to a rage that laid cold, black slabs of hate in her heart, constructing a wall that she vowed would not be breached by whatever happened to her today. A wall she would carry with her until she had her revenge.

Angston fell on top of her, his hands groping her. He reeked of sweat, filth, and alcohol. She looked straight into his eyes. "You are a dead man," she said in a flat voice, with her teeth grinding together.

He laughed. "Girlie, you're going to find out I'm not as dead as you say." He moved against Bren's body, and every thrust laid another slab in the wall of hate. She forced her humiliation and disgust behind the barrier, and true to her vow, blocked out all other sensation. I can do this.

Angston finished, and with little prodding, Wertz was next. Bren gave him the same flat warning. He drew back for a moment, but obviously his urges overcame any qualms he might have had. When he was finished, he dropped to a seat under one of the trees and hung his head.

"Your turn, Hager," Angston said.

"No." The young soldier shook his head.

"What do you mean, no?" Angston jumped up from where he had been sitting.

Hager looked down at the ground. "I don't want to force a woman. I don't believe in it."

"A woman? She's a whore. She don't deserve no respect." Angston grabbed his musket. "You thinking of going back to camp and reporting us?" Hager just continued to look down, and Angston took a step toward him. "You better get on over there and take your turn, or I'll put a bullet in you. I'm not letting no whiney boy turn me in." He pointed the weapon at Hager. "You stupid kid, you ought to be happy to have this chance. I bet you never even had a woman before. I'll give you to the count of three, and you better be servicing that bitch or I'll blow your balls off. One . . ."

Slowly, Hager rose. He walked over to Bren and knelt between her legs. "I'm sorry," he whispered. "I'm truly sorry."

"Get to it, Hager, or I'll unbutton your pants with my knife, and you'll never be able to have another woman."

Hager fumbled with his buttons and visibly cringed when Bren's husky voice struck his ear. "You are a dead man."

In spite of his statements of remorse, he completed the act Angston had forced on him. He cried afterward, mumbling, "I'm sorry. Please forgive me."

The soldier's tears wet her face, but Bren had no forgiveness to offer him. Hatred burned away any hope of that as soon as the first soldier violated her.

Hager rose and buttoned his pants. Angston brought the soldier's musket over and handed it to him. "You took so damn long, we have to get back to camp right away. Shoot the bitch."

Wertz's head snapped up, and Hager's jaw dropped. "Sh-shoot her? But why?" The young soldier took a step back. "Can't we just leave her here?"

"Use your head, stupid. What do you think she'll do as soon as she's loose?" Angston spat toward her. "She'll run squealing to the camp, and we'll have a pack of trouble. Shoot her." He raised his own rifle and pointed it again at Hager. "Either you shoot her, or I shoot you. Then she gets shot anyway. Suit yourself."

Hager swallowed hard and nodded. "I'll do it. Can I have a minute alone? I want to pray for her first."

Angston snorted and gave a toss of his head for Wertz to follow him. They moved about forty feet away, looking into the forest as they waited.

Hager approached Bren. "I guess you heard. I've been ordered to shoot you." He wiped at the tears that trickled down his cheeks again. "Oh, God, forgive me." He mumbled another prayer as he put the musket barrel against Bren's forehead.

He hesitated and looked back toward the other two soldiers just as Angston glanced toward him. Hager turned and met Bren's gaze. She looked up at him with empty eyes. She had repressed her emotions so thoroughly that she didn't feel any grief, just a morbid curiosity.

So this is the end, she thought. I wonder what price I'll have to pay for all the dead I sent ahead of me? Maybe they'll be waiting for me. Her mouth curled up on one side.

"Do it," she said and watched Hager's finger squeeze the trigger. The explosion slammed against her head, and her world disappeared.

The bright flash that erupted from the musket barrel forced Hager to close his eyes. When he opened them, he saw blood running from one side of the woman's forehead. His breath caught. The red stream moved across burnt skin and slid down above her ear to cover the smoldering area where hair once grew. The smell of blood, scorched skin, and burning hair nearly overwhelmed him. Staggering for a moment, he fought off queasiness. He leaned down and turned Bren's head toward where the sergeant stood with Wertz. He circled her, kicked the pegs out of the ground, and untied her. Next, he straightened her arms and legs and partially covered her torso with her ripped shirt, muttering another prayer as he did so. Afterward, he joined the other soldiers.

"She dead?" Angston looked toward Bren as he asked.

Hager nodded dumbly and showed his bloodied hand. He had to clear his throat to answer. "I made sure."

"Okay, let's get back. Here's our story. We chased a Reb into the woods and hunted for him, but he got away." Angston gestured at each of them with his musket. "I don't want to hear nothing else about this, you hear? We're all in it together." The men trotted back to town in silence, while Hager's tears ran unchecked.

From a deep, dark hole, Bren fought to awaken. For the first glorious moments, her body felt nothing until a deluge of pain swept over her. She had never experienced the kind of storm now assaulting her head, seeming to thrust her brain so hard against the inside of her skull that both brain and skull felt crushed. She smelled burnt flesh. But she didn't want to think yet about the fiery sensation that spiked one corner of her eye and covered part of her face like a hot blanket. The eye was swollen shut. A lava stream of anger erupted through her, and she fought to control it. Those scum ravaged me!

Stifling the aches as best she could, she slowly worked her way to a sitting position. She rested briefly, but her mind screamed: Who am I now? I'm someone else. Someone I don't know. I'll make them sorry for the day they created me. Driven beyond the pain, she threw her head back and glared with one good eye toward the sky, lifting her arms high as though beseeching God for an answer. Who am I?

As she lowered her arms, she raged at the power of the soldiers' evil deeds to make her feel this way. Her locked-in fury reinforced the wall of hate she had built, a wall she refused to let shatter. It would fend off all distractions while she sought revenge. She moved an arm to swish away the flies that gathered to feast on her blood, and her head thudded in even greater agony. She groaned as a new source of pain revealed itself. The three bastards had used her body roughly, and she was bruised inside and out, body and soul.

The honey-colored shirt, sliced open from top to bottom, had fallen into her lap when she sat up. As she picked it up, she only now absorbed the fact that her hands and feet had been untied, and the shirt had been draped over her. Did Hager really try to kill me? she wondered. Or did he just pretend to? Either way, I'll find them all, no matter how long it takes, and they'll pay for what they've done to me. I swear it.

Bren slipped the shirt on backward, affording her a bit of modesty. She crawled to where her trousers had been thrown. Every movement of her legs sent rivers of agony to meet the aches swirling around her head. She decided to forgo the drawers. Just donning the trousers would be a struggle. Her mending leg was swollen from the kick the sergeant had delivered. By God, it hurt enough to be rebroken. She was astonished that she could isolate one pain from another.

It took a long time to pull on her trousers, and her breath came in gasps by the time she finished. She gazed around slowly, and her look fell on the splints that had been cut away. She managed to collect them and use strips torn from the drawers to tie them back into place. The rest of the garment she tucked into her waistband, knowing it would be useful for cleaning herself. A further search of the ground nearby turned up a fallen branch that could serve as a crude crutch.

Using the branch and a tree to push against for balance, Bren struggled to her feet, waited for her initial dizziness to diminish, and took stock of the terrain. From her earlier travels to Cranston, she remembered a stream just south of this area. She also remembered the tavern where Leah worked was at the south end of town. Leah might be willing to help her. It was worth a try. She muttered her mantra, "I can do this," calling upon reserves of strength as she hobbled painfully toward the stream to wash herself. She could barely hear her own words. Her right eardrum must have been damaged by the musket blast.

At the bank of the stream, she sank to her knees and took a good look at her reflection. Bile rose in her throat, and she gagged. Quickly, she tore a swatch of cloth from the drawers, folded it, and slapped it into the water, dispersing the damaged likeness. She bent over the stream and laid the cloth against the burned area of her head and face. Moaning with the pain, she held the cloth still, and eventually its coolness provided a measure of relief. After a while, she lifted it away, dipped it back into the water, and washed the blood from her forehead. She wanted to clean her whole body to rid it of the filth from what they had done. She removed her shirt and laid it beside her. Her hands shook as she unbuttoned her trousers. With a weak push, she worked them down to her knees and washed as well as she could. When she finished and re-dressed, she sat beside the stream, clasped her arms tightly around her body, and cried. At last, she forced herself to accept a stark reality. Sarah-Bren Coulter would never be or look the same again.

Those soldiers would answer for that.

Amy knew she was supposed to stay inside after dark, but Mama was taking a nap, and she didn't want to wake her. It would take only a minute to run outside and get her dolly Ree-Ree. Amy felt bad about leaving Ree-Ree outside, especially because her dolly was afraid of the dark. She pulled a kitchen chair over to the door, climbed up on it, and lifted the latch. After pushing the chair back into place, she opened the street-level door and looked back and forth. She didn't see anyone moving in the alley beyond the door, so she slipped out, leaving the door ajar. She knew exactly where she had left Ree-Ree. The spot was only a few steps away, and she moved toward it. Sure enough, the doll was there, and Amy picked her up and hugged her to her chest.

"Amy."

The little girl jumped at the whisper of her name, and her gaze flitted toward the sound. She backed toward the door, holding Ree-Ree even more tightly.

"Don't be afraid, honey. It's Bren, the soldier. Remember you gave me some pretend food a long while ago when I was sitting on the steps with your mama? Go get her, please. Tell her I need her."

Amy remembered the big soldier who had played "breakfast" with her, and she took a step forward.

"No, Amy," the voice continued. "I'm hurt. Please, just go get your mama."

"Oh." Amy drew in a quick breath. "All right." She turned and ran through the open door.

A few moments later, Leah came out, straightening the waist of the blue calico dress she wore. Amy followed until Leah stopped her and sent her back into the house.

"Bren?" Leah squinted into the shadows, raking her gaze along the alley. "Where are you?"

"Over here. I'm injured. I need help."

One of the shadows grew taller, and Leah saw someone lurching toward her. She hurried to Bren's side, slipped Bren's arm over her own shoulder, and helped her toward the door. Bren leaned on her heavily while using a branch to balance some of the weight. They stumbled as far as the kitchen, and Leah eased Bren into one of the chairs, took the branch from her, and leaned it against a counter.

Bren placed an elbow on the table and rested one side of her head against her palm. Her hair had fallen forward and partly obscured her face, but now she lifted her chin, and Leah looked at her.

One hand flew to Leah's mouth, and she gasped. The woman in front of her looked hideous. An inch-long wound, still seeping blood, was evident on the right side of her forehead. Her skin was burned and blistered from the top curve of her forehead, down along the very edge of her eye to the bottom of her earlobe. Her right eyebrow and eyelashes were gone, and only charred stubble remained of the hair bordering the burned skin. Bren wore her shirt backward, and Leah realized that was because the front of it had been sliced open. There must be something wrong with her leg, too, since she had such trouble walking.

Leah sat down beside Bren and rested a hand on her arm. "My God, what happened to you? You need a doctor."

"No. No doctor. Please. No one can know I'm here." Bren's arm slipped, and she barely caught herself before her head hit the table.

Leah rose and hurried to grab her. "You poor thing, you're exhausted. Let me help you over to the bed. You can tell me everything after you get rested up." She handed Bren the branch, helped her rise, and led her to a narrow bed in a small room off the kitchen. She sat Bren on the edge of the bed and noticed for the first time that she wore no shoes and one foot was swollen. "Let Amy get you a nightshirt. You need to sleep, and we can clean you up in the morning."

As soon as Leah said "nightshirt," Amy ran from the room and returned with one. Leah hugged the child and sent her out of the room. She removed Bren's torn shirt and replaced it with the nightshirt. Gently, she pushed Bren back onto the mattress and lifted her legs up into the bed. Before she removed the trousers that Bren wore, she noticed one seam was cut, and she lifted the cloth to examine the leg. The movement revealed roughly bound splints, with evidence of a recent wound. Leah saw that the whole lower leg was swollen, not just the foot. Sure looks like she has a broken bone, Leah thought. Guess that's why it's splinted.

She took off the trousers, being careful not to jar the injured limb. Bren had already fallen asleep. Leah put a light cover over her, went to one of the kitchen cupboards, and hunted up some burn ointment. She lightly dabbed the ointment on the burned area of Bren's head and face, hardly disturbing her, and left her to rest. But Leah's curiosity was piqued. What story would Bren have to tell?

Bren woke at dawn the next morning with the same terrible headache that had plagued her since her brush with death the day before. The long rest had improved her vitality, but the aches in her head, body, and leg—and innermost self—almost made her wish for a return to her original numbness. She groaned aloud. A blonde head popped up next to the bed, and Bren shuddered.

"It's all right." Leah touched her arm. "It's just me. I put some quilts on the floor next to the bed and slept here." She stood up and pointed to garments lying on a chair. "I got together some clothes and shoes for you. Just dresses, I'm afraid. But I think it's better for now to give up your disguise, anyway." She tilted her head. "You'll need some makeup to blend the tan skin with the light."

Bren's voice was raspy. "Don't worry about my looks."

"Oh, honey, you'll look lots better when you heal. But don't think about that right now. You must be hungry. I'll fix you an early breakfast. Amy's likely to sleep late this morning. She was too excited to go to sleep at her usual hour. We'll go ahead and eat, then you can tell me what happened to you."

Bren swallowed and waved a hand. "That sounds good. I need to use the . . ."

"Sure," Leah said and pointed. "It's over there behind the curtain. There's a wash jar with a basin, too. Do you need help getting to it?"

"No. I can manage as long as there's no rush to get back and forth."

"Well, I have to wash and change before I cook. So you have plenty of time."

"Thank you, Leah." One side of Bren's mouth quirked up, though her eyes looked sad and troubled. "Thank you for coming to my rescue."

"I'm happy to help." Leah touched Bren's shoulder. "I'll come get you when breakfast is ready."

"To be tied down like that," Bren said, and her chest heaved, "and to have my life tossed away as though it were nothing . . ." Her voice failed, and she sat back in the chair at the table, with her chin resting on her chest.

"Oh, Bren." Leah clutched a hand to her bosom. "My heart hurts for you. I'm so sorry this happened. I've had a few awful experiences myself, but nothing this bad. I know you have to be feeling a lot of hate right now."

Bren looked up. "Hate?" She spat out the word. "That doesn't even come near to describing what I feel. I want to take them apart, piece by piece. I want to tear off their—" Bren shook her head as the words couldn't get past her closed throat.

Leah switched to a chair alongside her. "This might sound odd, coming from me, but most men are pretty decent sorts. Please don't let those three turn you against them all."

"You're right." Bren struggled to calm herself. "But I haven't turned against all men. Believe me, I'm focused on the demon spawn who did this. They will pay." Her face changed to an unreadable expression, while her tone grew icy. "And it was a woman who betrayed me. So, you see, my loathing is not reserved just for men."

Leah shivered. "This woman meant something to you?"

"I trusted her. I cared about her." Bren looked down again, and pain roughened her voice. "She treated me like one of her family. She even saved my life." She raised her head and winced at the anguish squeezing her heart. "I never imagined she would give me away. I guess she was afraid, and maybe for good reason, but I was going to leave anyway. I just don't understand it."

"I suspect the only one who understands it is the woman herself. We can't get inside other people's minds." Leah stood up as Amy entered the kitchen, rubbing sleep from her eyes. "Hi, darlin'. Mama made some pancakes. Go wash up and come eat."

Amy plucked at her nightshirt, pulling it from where it was stuck against her body. She walked over to Bren and stopped beside her. A smile pulled Bren's lips up the uninjured side of her face. Amy studied her, tilting her head several times. "Something hurted you."

"Yes. I got too close to a fire, and it burned me."

Amy's mouth formed a circle. "Oh." She drew out the word. "But Mama will make it all better. She fixes hurts good." Her face screwed up, and she frowned. "Are you a girl today, like Mama?"

Bren nodded. "Yes, I am."

Amy smiled and stamped her foot. "Good. You make a really pretty girl."

Tears welled in Bren's eyes as she reached out, gathered Amy close, and gave her a hug. The last thing Bren felt was pretty, in any way, shape, or form. But Amy's innocent remark found its way through the blackness engulfing her, and a tiny spark lit the darkness for a moment. "Thank you, Amy," she said hoarsely.

When the hug was finished, Leah tapped Amy on the shoulder. "Go get washed, sweetie." As though sensing Bren was troubled, Amy patted her on the thigh and scampered away.

"She thinks I'm pretty."

"You are, you know." Leah took hold of Bren's chin and turned her full-face toward her. "This will heal, and you probably will have some scarring, but your natural good looks will offset that." She released the chin and playfully tapped Bren's nose. "Don't go getting vain on me."

Bren's grin was sad. "Don't worry about that. I never put much stock in looks. At least not in my own." Her gaze lightened for a split second as the vision of a sun-haloed redhead with laughing eyes slipped past her defenses. But she quickly pushed the memory away, replacing it with recollections of her betrayal. Darkness crowded in on her again, and she rose from the table. "I'm still a bit tired. Do you mind if I take a nap? When I wake up, maybe I can figure out what to do. I can't stay here forever."

"You *will* stay here until that burn heals. You'll be my cousin from Kentucky. No one will bother you. By the way, my last name is Overton. Guess you better know that." Leah dished up a pancake for her daughter. "Amy, come eat," she called. She turned to Bren. "I go back to work tomorrow night. You can stay here and watch Amy for me and save me a few dollars. How does that sound?"

"Too generous, by far. But I'll leap at the offer." She used the branch to hobble to the bed and lay down. For once, she hoped she did dream of battles. Anything would be better than reliving the nightmare of the attack. She flung her arm across her eyes, then quickly jerked it back. The burn would hurt for quite a while. She sighed, placed both hands on her stomach, and went to sleep.

During the three months that Bren stayed with Leah and Amy, she pestered Leah to get the full names, army billets, and personal information about the men who had assaulted her. Leah seemed reluctant to do so, and Bren couldn't understand why. She needed those details so she could make them pay, not only for their heinous violation of her body but also for the horrible damage they had done to her face.

The broken bone in her leg mended poorly, and whenever Bren grew too tired to ignore the constant pain, it caused a slight limp. The burn on the right side of her head healed after weeks of painful washings, debridements of rotten tissue, and ointment applications. Leah had gleaned the treatment information from the doctor without Bren having to see him. Scar tissue covered the area, making ripples in the skin and pinching at the edge of Bren's eye, giving her a just-about-to-wink look that Leah assured her was quite attractive. Bren, being Bren, received this information with a snort. The burnt hair stubble fell away with the washings, and the new hair from above her ear to the top of her brow came in snow white. Injury from the loud blast of the musket shot caused some hearing loss in her right ear.

Bren resumed the name of Sarah and tried to readjust to life as a woman, which was not an easy task. It was, however, a necessary one. That had become apparent soon after her arrival at Leah's, when she threw up on an empty stomach for three mornings.

Leah had sat down next to Sarah at the kitchen table. "You've been sick three days in a row now."

"Do you think maybe I'm coming down with something? I seem to be all right the rest of the day." It surprised her when Leah moved the chair nearer to her and took hold of her hand.

"Look at me, Sarah."

Their eyes met and Sarah frowned. "You look so serious. What's wrong?"

"I think you're pregnant."

"What?" Sarah practically tossed Leah's hand out of hers. She stared hard at her friend, but Leah's gaze never wavered. The reality of the words sank in, and Sarah turned away, burying her head in her hands. "Oh, God, no." Tears welled in her eyes and overflowed against her fingers. The salty drops washed into the ointment, stinging the healing burns on her face. No, no, no, no, no, her mind kept demanding

"I'm sorry," Leah murmured. She laid her hand on Sarah's back and rubbed comfortingly. "So sorry." When Sarah at last calmed a bit, Leah continued, "You don't have to carry this baby, if you don't want to. I know someone who can get rid of it for you."

Sarah sat up straight, and Leah handed her a cotton napkin to dry her eyes and blow her nose. She took her time, letting Leah's words clang around in her head. She balled up the soiled napkin and used her fingers to wipe away a few last tears. "I can't do that. I certainly don't want a child, but I can't punish it for someone else's evil deed. Besides, I've seen too much of death already."

Leah nodded. "I was terribly upset and scared when I got pregnant with Amy. But I couldn't get rid of her, either, and I've always been glad I didn't. Someday, you'll look at your child and you'll be glad, too."

"I didn't say I'll raise it. Only that I can't kill it."

"What will you do? Give your own child away?"

Sarah took a deep breath and let it whoosh out. "I don't know what I'll do then. I need to decide what to do right now." She rested her arms on the table and drummed her fingers against its wooden surface.

"Well, for right now, you're staying here until your wounds are healed. You can worry about where to go when you're in better condition to leave."

She sounded adamant, and Sarah was too worn out to argue. What Leah said made good sense, anyway. So Sarah had stayed. She wrote home to let them know she had been wounded, but was being well taken care of, and she wired Theo that Lady Blue would be out of action for the foreseeable future. She didn't tell anyone of the true severity of her wounds.

Later, when she finally was well enough to travel, she plotted with Leah to retrieve Redfire from Faith's barn. But when Leah investigated, the sorrel was nowhere to be found.

"Have you decided where you will go, Sarah?" Leah asked. "Do you have to have a horse? I might be able to buy one for you."

"No, never mind. I want to go to my mother's. I can take a train from here to there. I'll just need a pass. As a civilian, I shouldn't have much trouble getting one."

"I thought you and your mother didn't get along too well?"

Sarah sighed. "We haven't in the past, but one can always hope. Actually, the last time I saw her, she seemed to have mellowed toward me." A short burst of laughter tempered her statement. "At least for that moment." She quickly grew pensive. "I always found my mother's attempts to direct my life annoying, but I think now is one of those times when her attention is just what I need."

"I have to agree with you there. Wish I'd had a mother to go home to."

Sarah touched Leah's hand. "If you need anyone ever again, come to me. I mean that, Leah, with all my heart."

Sarah acquired the train pass, and on her day of departure, Leah and Amy accompanied her to the railroad station. They sat down to wait, and Sarah looked around the area. "The last time I was at a station, a munitions train had just been blown up."

"What?" Leah looked astonished. "Tell me about it."

While they waited for the train's arrival, Sarah described the havoc she had witnessed at Hadley's Run, including the part Scott and Phillip had in it. Leah listened, rapt with attention, and when Sarah finished, Leah grabbed her arm.

"A man came through here not too long ago who got drunk and said he was the one who done that attack. He couldn't stop bragging about it."

Sarah sat stunned for a moment. "My God, Leah, I wish you'd spoken of this sooner."

"I would've if I'd known you were mixed up in it." Leah let go of Sarah's arm. "What can I do now?"

"I'll get in touch with Phillip, the friend who lost his leg. I'm sure he'll want to talk to you and possibly pick up the man's trail. Do you remember his name?"

"Well, no, but I doubt if he gave me his real name, anyway. He stayed at the hotel, but he probably lied there, too." She looked up the tracks as the train pulled in.

"Phillip's last name is Showell. He might even come in person, since Cranston is in Union hands now. He's a big, blond man and might have an artificial leg by now."

"I'll wait for news from him."

The train was about to leave, and they said their goodbyes. "Please, Leah, see if you can get the information about those soldiers for me. I'll be looking for them as soon as I get the opportunity."

"Oh, Sarah, forget about them for now. I'll get all that later and mail it to you. You need to take care of yourself first." She gave the taller woman a tight hug. "I'll miss you. I hope we meet again."

"Me, too. You've been a true friend, and I'll never forget what you did for me. Remember what I said about if you ever need me." She released Leah and picked up Amy. "I'll never forget you, either, sweetheart. I love you dearly." She clasped the child to her, kissed her cheek, and set her back down.

"Will you come and see us again soon, Aunt Sarah?" Amy's wistful expression touched Sarah's heart, and when she saw the same look on Leah's face, she sniffed and wiped at her cheeks.

"I can't promise that, Amy, but someday, maybe you'll see me again. No one knows for sure what might happen." The full meaning of the words struck Sarah as she turned to board the train. She couldn't have predicted the misfortunes that had befallen her, and knowing that the future could be just as disastrous was a little scary. She straightened up and sucked in a sharp breath. But I can do this. After mounting the steps, she entered the carriage and waved to Leah and Amy through the window as the train pulled away.

She sat down, leaned back, and closed her eyes. The noisy clack-clack-clack of the wheels underscored the intensity of her thoughts.

I'm going to my parents' home. I'll have this baby. Then I'll go after those bastards. They won't escape my vengeance.

CHAPTER EIGHT

Prescott Coulter met Lindsay and little Prescott at the railroad station. Her father-in-law looked just as Lindsay knew Scott would at his age, handsome and dignified. Bundled in hat, overcoat, and gloves, he smiled with cheeks glowing from the trip to the station in the sunny, but cold, December weather. They exchanged happy greetings, and Lindsay gave thanks that the train trip had ended. Little Pres had been generally well behaved but was beginning to show signs of tiring. Prescott loaded the bags into the buggy and helped her and Pres into the seat. He unhitched the reins, climbed in beside them, and started home.

"How is Sarah?" Lindsay asked. "She had written that she was wounded in the leg, but she didn't give us any details. As soon as we received Mother Coulter's letter that she was here, I had to come."

"I think you'd better prepare yourself for a shock, my dear." His answer raised the fine hairs on the back of Lindsay's neck. "The leg wound gives her some trouble, and I think she has more pain than she admits. Sometimes she limps." He took a ragged breath. "But she suffered a head wound that's much worse. She has a gouge on the side of her forehead. And her face was burned." His jaw worked, but no words came.

Lindsay held little Pres on her lap, but she freed one arm and slipped it through her father-in-law's.

He continued in a controlled voice. "The top half of one side of her face is badly scarred, and the hair next to it was burned away and has grown back completely white." He glanced down at the tears on Lindsay's cheeks. "It's better to get your tears out of the way now. You know Sarah won't stand for anyone feeling sorry for her."

Nodding, Lindsay sniffled. She released Prescott's arm to get a handkerchief from her pocket and dab at her face.

Prescott's voice got lower and hoarser. "There's more."

His stern expression made Lindsay scrunch the handkerchief in her hand. "More?"

"Those men who shot her also violated her." Lindsay's sharp intake of breath hissed in the chill air. Prescott rapidly blinked against the tears evident in his eyes. "And she's with child."

Lindsay was too stunned to speak. Every piece of information she had just received struck a blow to her heart, each harder than the one before. My God, she thought, this is overwhelming to me, and I'm only hearing it. Sarah has lived through it. Is now living through it, she amended. She's an incredibly strong woman, but is she strong enough to cope with so much, and all at once?

They rode in silence for a while. Apparently, even little Pres was affected by the somber atmosphere. He curled against his mother and fell asleep.

When Prescott spoke again, Lindsay started. "Sarah has changed, Lindsay, and not for the better."

She needed a moment to gather her thoughts and refocus her attention, but the ominous words hung in the air like buzzards, ready to tear at her flesh. She spoke with trepidation. "How, Father?"

"It's understandable that she's bitter. She's had a lot to handle. But there's a moodiness about her, a blackness. Sometimes she's fine. Other times, she acts as though she has closed down a part of herself. The better part, I'm afraid. I'm hoping you can help her with that."

"I'll do my best. Maybe having Pres around will help, too. Sarah's always loved children." But Lindsay wondered how Sarah felt about the one she was carrying.

Sarah glanced down as Lindsay took her arm and urged her toward the kitchen table. "Everyone's outside, Sarah. Sit down and talk to me."

Am I ready for this? Sarah wondered. She pulled back, but Lindsay sat in a chair and dragged her down into the next one.

A hint of amusement flickered across Sarah's face as Lindsay immediately jumped up. She spooned some tea leaves into a china teapot and poured hot water over them from a kettle that simmered constantly on the back of the cast iron woodstove. Next, she put the pot and a sieve on the table. After she gathered cups, saucers, and spoons from the cupboard and a covered stoneware bowl from the ice chest, she added them to the table and resettled in her chair. She propped her elbow on the table and rested her chin in her hand. "Sarah, I know you're hurting. Please talk to me about it."

Sarah leaned forward and set her arms on the table. She cocked her head toward Lindsay, glad to have her undamaged profile on the side next to her companion. Her fingertips drummed softly against the tabletop, but she became aware of it and stilled them. She lifted one shoulder. "You've heard all the details, and you can see the results."

"I'm not talking about what I've heard or what I can see. I want to know what you feel. How you feel."

Though Sarah's eyes took on a guarded expression, her voice burned with passion. "I want to make them pay." She struggled to rein in her emotion. "Until I can go after them, I'm trying not to let myself feel much of anything. Not that I'm succeeding all that well."

"Go after them? Why? You can't undo what's happened."

"Weren't you listening? I want to make them pay."

"But what about the baby?" Lindsay picked up the sieve, grasped the teapot's handle, and poured tea through the sieve into their cups. She uncovered the bowl, revealing a chunk of honeycomb dripping with honey. With a spoon, she pushed pieces of beeswax out of the honey pooled around the comb. She put a dollop of the golden syrup in Sarah's cup and one in her own.

The women stirred their tea while Sarah continued to ponder. She knew her answer would upset Lindsay, and she delayed as long as possible. She lifted her cup and took a sip. As she lowered it to the saucer, she sneered at herself for being concerned about Lindsay's displeasure. Whatever happened to the headstrong Sarah Coulter who made her own way no matter what others thought? Had she lost her spine along with her virginity in that forest clearing? No, she still would make her own way, but her focus had changed. Helping the Union cause had given way to her determination to hunt down the men who had attacked her. Every bone in her body ached to bring them to justice, and she was the only one who could do that. And nothing, or no one, could be allowed to get in her way.

"I'm not keeping the baby."

"What?" Lindsay had just taken a drink of tea, and the teacup clattered against the saucer as she hurriedly set it down. "You can't be serious. What will you do with the child?" The reproach hit Sarah's good ear like a slap.

"Put him up for adoption, I suppose."

133

"You can't do that. He's a Coulter."

"He's a bastard." Sarah saw Lindsay flinch. "Well, he is," she said in a flat voice.

"He's part of you. Your blood. You can't just ignore that."

"My blood and the blood of one of those demons who forced themselves on me. Don't you think I would relive that horror every time I looked at him? And come to hate him for being a constant reminder of it?" One side of her lip lifted. "You weren't there. You can't imagine how terrible it was. And who's to say he wouldn't inherit the evil he came from?" She curled her hand into a fist and tapped it several times against the tabletop. "I'm adamant about this. I will not keep him." She glared at Lindsay, challenging her to disagree.

But Lindsay was silent. She picked up her spoon and stirred her now lukewarm tea, while watching the circular motion. Sarah could almost see her thinking. Lindsay put the teaspoon down, sat up straighter, and met Sarah's gaze.

"Scott and I will take the baby."

Sarah's jaw dropped. In all of her wrenching thoughts and decisions about the child, that possibility never occurred to her. Her teeth clicked together as she closed her jaw. "No. He'd still be a constant reminder to me."

"You're a grown woman. You can learn to deal with that," Lindsay said with some severity. "It's better than giving a member of our family away to strangers. You know we all would have trouble accepting that. This is the perfect answer. Scott and I can raise him as our own," she went on, gaining enthusiasm. "I'll be away from home long enough that people will believe I could have had a child. That way he won't be labeled a bastard."

Sarah's fingers started drumming again. She could tell Lindsay's mind was as determined as her own had been. She had to admit that it sounded like a workable idea. It would free her to search for the three attackers, and when she got back home, if seeing the child bothered her too much, she could make a point of staying away from him.

"Sarah, please say yes. I know Scott will agree." At last, Sarah answered with a nod, delighting Lindsay. "Wonderful. It's settled." She tilted her head and touched Sarah's fingers, quieting their drumming. "Father said you had a leg wound. How did that happen?"

Sarah told her the whole story. As it ended, her voice grew passionate, and she fidgeted with anger. "Faith turned me in. I still don't understand how she could."

"It truly doesn't make much sense that she would save your life and then betray you. Why would she do that?"

"She wanted me out of the war," Sarah practically shouted, "and I told her I wouldn't leave it. She must have figured that was the only way to get me out. She broke my trust."

"She must have meant well. It sounds like she cared a lot for you. And you cared for her, didn't you?"

"Cared?" Sarah fumed. "Of course, I cared. I lo—" Sarah stopped and threw her hands up to cover her face, which quickly turned red. "Oh, my God," she whispered and quietly began to cry.

Lindsay scooted her chair closer and put an arm over Sarah's slumped shoulders. "You fell in love with her. I could tell from the first time you spoke her name. You lit up like a sunbeam." She didn't say anything more, just sat in silence, squeezing Sarah's shoulders.

At last, Sarah stopped crying, pulled a handkerchief from her pocket, and dried her tears. "I can't believe I'm in love with Faith. I had no idea." Giving words to her confused emotions so astonished her that her whole body thrummed. She leaned into Lindsay's embrace and touched heads with her, accepting her solace. After a few moments, a grimace tilted one side of Sarah's lips. "You don't seem to have a problem with my discovery that I love a woman."

Lindsay released Sarah's shoulders and leaned back. "That's because I'm not exactly surprised. Look at all the eligible men I had Scott bring around, and you never showed the slightest interest in any of them." She tapped Sarah's forearm. "Not to mention how you never gave the eminently eligible Phillip Showell a chance."

Sarah took some time to digest those remarks as she got up and limped to the stove. She brought the iron kettle and tea leaves to the table and prepared fresh tea in the china pot. After she replaced the kettle, she sat back down.

"You don't think I'm some kind of perverted person?"

Lindsay gave her a warm glance. "Do you think you're perverted?"

Sarah scowled. "I know a lot of people would say I am." The frown smoothed out and her expression calmed. "But, no, I don't feel perverted. I feel a little strange, but the more I think about it, the more right it seems for me." In a quick change of mood, her face darkened again. "But why did I have to fall in love with a woman I can't trust? A woman who betrayed me? I won't ever be able to believe in her again."

"Do you think she fell in love with you?"

"Good Lord, no. She was married before and has a son."

"That doesn't mean anything," Lindsay said. "I have this cousin who was married for fifteen years before she admitted her own feelings."

Sarah's sister-in-law proceeded to give her an earful of information about another woman who discovered she loved women. When she heard the story, Sarah searched through the time she had spent with the Pruitts, looking for clues to Faith's feelings for her. The only time she remembered thinking that Faith might have been attracted to her was the morning the Union troops had entered Cranston. But that was the same day Faith betrayed her. Sarah gave up her quest in disgust.

Later, Lindsay wrote a letter to Scott, sharing the news about Sarah's condition. She told him of her plan that they would take on the responsibility of raising Sarah's child as their own, and she asked for his agreement. Scott's answer came back quickly. He wrote a long letter to Sarah and another to Lindsay, each including an unconditional yes to the plan.

The time of Sarah's pregnancy passed slowly for her. Being heavy with the baby during the Virginia spring was the easy part. Her enforced inaction was what tried her patience. She kept up with the news of the war, all the while resenting that her part in it had been curtailed. By the beginning of 1865, as she had already supposed, severe shortages of food and supplies had Confederate soldiers deserting in droves. General Grant pursued General Lee relentlessly, and after Richmond, the capital of the Confederacy, fell in early April, the decimated Rebel forces soon surrendered.

At last, the baby came on May 10.

To the family's delight, the child was a girl, and Lindsay and Scott had already picked a name. They called her Jessica, after Lindsay's mother. Upon the birth of the new daughter, the whole household became one big nursery, lightening some of the gloom brought on by Sarah's ill fortunes. Sarah wanted a wet nurse, but since the slaves had been freed, none was available. She was forced to nurse little Jessica herself for the first four months of the baby's life.

Jessica had Coulter features but different coloring. Her straight black hair and pale blue eyes told Sarah which of her attackers had fathered the child—the apologetic Hager. Thank God, it hadn't been Angston.

Throughout the whole time, Lindsay was a rock, providing needed support while buffering the loving but often quarrelsome relationship between Sarah and her mother. Sarah was happy to give her sister-in-law the news that neither Angston's nor Wertz's blood tainted the baby. She saw no need to add that she still intended to kill the father.

Sarah stood on the verandah at Red Oak Manor looking out over the peaceful scene while thinking of the war. Thank goodness, Sheridan's army had marched down the valley on the other side of the Blue Ridge Mountains. Her parents were fortunate. The Union Army had cut a destructive path through the Shenandoah Valley, taking what it needed from the land and destroying the rest. After the baby's birth, Sarah had ridden out to survey the damage, and she returned heavy-hearted to her parents' home, knowing that so many who hadn't fought in the war—perhaps had not even believed in it—had lost so much. A noise turned her from her survey of the landscape, and she looked toward the door as Matthias came out of the house.

"Got some mail for you, Miss Sarah." He handed her a long envelope with unfamiliar writing on it. "Looks like today'll be another hot one. Would you want something to drink, child?"

Sarah took the letter and affectionately squeezed the hand of the elderly, dark-skinned man. "No, thank you, Matthias. But you better get back inside where it's cooler. No sense in you staying out in this heat when there's no need to."

"Now you sound like my Pearl," he grumbled good-naturedly. "What's a man to do when the womenfolk boss him around all the time?" He waggled a finger and answered his own question. "I know, I know, just do what they say." Sarah smiled and nodded as Matthias reentered the house.

Turning her attention to the letter, she tore it open, anticipation burning her stomach. She skipped immediately to the signature, and her heart jumped. It was the long-awaited news from Leah about the scum she was itching to hunt down. At least, that's what she hoped it was. She put a hand to her chest as if to quiet the pounding of her heart and sat at one of the verandah tables to read.

Dear Sarah,

I hope this finds you well. There was so many soldiers coming threw here it was hard to get what you want but I hope I got enuff now to help you tho I worry about you and what you might do that will put you back in danger.

The one named George Wertz is dead. He was killed in a battle and I hope his soul rots in hell for what he done to you.

I could not find much about Hager except his first name is Perry and he came from Cleeveland Ohio so maybe he will go back there if he is still alive.

The sargent is named Willard Angston and he is still in these parts. He has something to do with the mustering out of soldiers or maybe prisoners I am not sure which.

Captain Phillip Showell has been writing to me about the man who said he blew up that train. First the captain wrote his health kept him from making the trip here but now he wants to see me but wants you here so you can draw a pitcher of the man I saw. You two can just come on by when it suits you. Amy asks about you all the time and sends her love as I do to. Please be carefull and do not get hurt no more.

Your friend,
Leah

Sarah folded the letter and stuffed it in her skirt pocket, her heart still racing. Phillip had written her several times, too, enthused about the possibility that Leah could give him a lead on the saboteur. He had been anxious to go to Cranston right away but was delayed by an infection in the stump of his leg. Sarah hoped it was healed now.

This idea about drawing the likeness of the man seemed promising, if Leah could give her a good enough description. The potential of putting a face to the man excited Sarah enough to make her eager to get to Cranston. But the likelihood of finding Angston positively exhilarated her, and she hurried into the house to begin preparations for the journey.

In her bedroom, she pulled a valise from under the bed and placed it on the green chintz bedspread. On an earlier trip to town, she had purchased replacements for the clothing, disguise, and pistol left behind at Faith's, and now she removed them from the bureau drawers and packed them. She had purchased another Remington revolver, but in place of the covered military holster, she chose the open western style with rawhide thongs to strap it closely to her leg. This holster was more suited to the quick draw she had perfected. She had prepared herself well for the chase.

The possibility of seeing Faith leaped to her mind, but the thought that she should be chasing her down, too, quickly burst a rising bubble of joy. Disturbed, Sarah buried the idea of vengeance against Faith and continued packing.

"Are you going somewhere?" Lindsay's question interrupted Sarah, and she looked toward the doorway, answering her sister-in-law with a nod. Lindsay had baby Jessica in her arms, and she walked over next to Sarah and held her out. "First, Jessie wants a hug from her favorite aunt."

Sarah raised an eyebrow. "Favorite aunt? I'm her only aunt." She grabbed Jessie under her arms and hugged the baby to her chest, then held her away and gazed at her. By sheer coincidence, Jessica had Lindsay's coloring, but she definitely had Coulter features. Especially our stubborn chin, Sarah thought, though she believed she was far more stubborn than Scott would ever be.

Lindsay lowered her voice and stage-whispered, "You would be her favorite aunt even if she had twenty others." She reached for the baby and took her from Sarah. "But I do think you need some baby-holding lessons, even after four months of nursing her. You act like she would break if you squeezed her too hard."

"Well, wouldn't she?" Sarah returned to her packing. This was not a new conversation. Lindsay often tormented Sarah about her discomfort around the child and kept thrusting Jessie on her in an attempt to cure that.

Lindsay elbowed her in the side, eliciting a grunt. "So, why are you packing as though the devil were after you?"

"You've got that backward. I'm going after the devil. Two of them, at least."

"You've heard from Leah!" Lindsay laid Jessica on the bed and sat down on the edge, patting the cooing child.

"Yes." In the past months, Lindsay had pried nearly every bit of information about Sarah's ordeal from her, though Sarah had difficulty speaking about most of it. She wouldn't have been able to confide in anyone else, but she and her sister-in-law had a bond of trust in each other that augmented their friendship. They each knew the other would never betray a confidence. "She sent me the information I've been waiting for. One man's dead, and she found out where the youngest one's home is." Sarah's face twisted with hate. "The head devil's still in Cranston. So that's where I'm going."

"Sarah." Lindsay shifted her hand from the baby to Sarah's arm, halting the taller woman's movement. "Are you certain you want to do this? What they did to you was horrible beyond words, but you're no killer."

Lifting her arm away from Lindsay's touch, Sarah moved to the bureau. She picked out some more clothes and brought them to the bedside. In a hard voice, she said, "You don't seem to grasp that I've already killed hundreds of people." She thrust the clothes into the valise and shoved them down. "What difference will two more make?"

"Oh, Sarah." Lindsay's deep blue eyes darkened with emotion. "That was war. You shouldn't take those deaths so personally."

"Maybe. But Angston and Hager made war on Sarah-Bren Coulter, and I take that very personally." She lifted a hand to touch her scarred face, pausing at the pinched corner of her eye. Her fingers brushed the dent in her forehead and pushed back through the broad white streak of hair. "They owe me a debt, and I aim to collect it. So save your breath. As soon as I telegraph Phillip to meet me in Cranston, I'm leaving."

"Faith lives in Cranston, too, doesn't she?"

Sarah frowned and her lips tightened. "She turned me in, remember?" She stomped back to the bureau and yanked some more clothes into her arms.

"Maybe you should look her up and ask her about that day."

Sarah dumped the armload of clothes on the bed, startling the baby. Jessie let out a cry, and Lindsay picked her up and soothed her.

"Sorry," Sarah muttered. She looked into Lindsay's eyes and glanced away. "You know how I feel about Faith. That just makes her betrayal all the harder to forgive."

"Are you absolutely sure it was Faith? What about her son? Couldn't he have been the one?"

Sarah's expression softened, and she shook her head. "Not Benjamin. He's a sweetheart. In the short time I was there, he and I formed a bond. Besides, his father was a Confederate soldier. He would never have turned me in to the Union."

Leaning Jessie against her shoulder, Lindsay stroked the baby's back as she fell asleep. With a tilt of her head, she looked up at Sarah. "You and Faith formed a bond, too."

"No." Sarah stopped dead and stared at her sister-in-law. "Not Faith, just me." She raised one shoulder and lowered it. "The woman saved my life. But I hate that she turned me in. I trusted her. Hell, I fell in love with her. I've never been so wrong about anyone in my life, and I hate that, too. Do I hate her?" Sarah's fist slammed into her opposite palm with a loud pop, and Lindsay jerked reflexively. "I come damn close to it."

Jessie whimpered and gnawed at Lindsay's shoulder. "I think our little lady is telling us she's hungry. Time to hunt for some milk and pap." She stood up, and Sarah reached out a hand to cup the back of the baby's head.

The silky softness of the child's hair emphasized the baby's vulnerability and brought a lump to Sarah's throat. "She's lucky to be young enough to have missed this war. Don't ever tell her my part in it."

"I won't promise you that." Lindsay shook her head. "Sarah-Bren Coulter is one of my heroes. I want Jessie to know about your service—and Pres, too."

Sarah gave a wry look. "And they call me the stubborn one." Folding her arms around Lindsay and the baby, she hugged them quickly. "I'll finish packing while you feed Jessie. I want to leave as soon as possible."

"All right. I'll see you downstairs."

Sarah put her hands on her hips and looked around the room, ostensibly checking to see if she had thought of everything she wanted to take. In truth, Lindsay's earlier words echoed through her mind. *You and Faith formed a bond, too.* Had Faith felt anything for her? If she did, she had a strange way of showing it. Sarah snorted at the impossibility even though her heart thudded painfully as she resumed packing.

CHAPTER NINE

Sarah checked into Cranston's only hotel, washed up after the sooty train ride, and put some of her belongings away.

Before leaving for the telegraph office to check for a message from Phillip, she took a last look in the mirror, something she usually avoided. She and Phillip hadn't seen each other since she had been attacked. He didn't know the whole story of the assault or anything about Jessie being her baby, and Sarah didn't plan to tell him those details. Her parents' household, Leah, and Scott and Lindsay knew, of course, but Phillip heard only that she had been severely wounded.

She recalled her own reaction to Phillip's injury. While Phillip wanted the saboteur brought to justice, she wanted to kill the bastard. How would Phillip feel about the ones who had damaged her? She knew the wounding had upset him, but she hoped to keep his focus on the person guilty of treason. She'd take care of justice for the other scum herself.

The telegraph office occupied a corner of the train station, and its lone occupant apparently served as both telegrapher and ticket taker. Sarah's inquiry resulted in her being handed a telegram from Phillip that announced his arrival on the late afternoon train. Deciding she had time to greet Leah, who was expecting her, Sarah folded the message and put it in the pocket of her dark brown dress. She left the station and headed up the sidewalk toward the Brass Rail Tavern, several blocks away on the same street.

Sarah's gaze swept the whole area, and she felt restless. She suddenly realized she was searching for a glimpse of red hair and green eyes. Faith's image jumped to mind, and the intensity of her reaction jarred her. She ducked quickly into the alley near Leah's

143

rooms. Fighting to suppress the memory and to slow her racing heartbeat, she cursed herself for letting those stray thoughts affect her. She made her way around and behind the wooden steps that led to the tavern's upper floor and knocked on the familiar door.

The door swung open, and Leah pulled Sarah into a strong embrace. When Leah released her, she took hold of Sarah's hands and gave them a squeeze before letting them go. "I can't believe it. You look like a different person. Your cheeks are all rosy, and I see you finally got some meat on your bones."

"You look great, too, Leah. Being at Mother's was good for me, in spite of our differences. She decided if she couldn't change my attitude, she could at least change my skinny ass." Both women chuckled, and Leah motioned toward the kitchen table, which held two cups and saucers and the necessities for tea.

"Have a seat. I have tea already made." Leah lifted a teakettle from the iron stove and held a sieve over each cup to catch the steeped leaves as she poured. "Amy's up the street playing with a friend. She was so excited you were coming, I had to send her out before she exploded. She's crazy about her Aunt Sarah." Leah replaced the pot and joined Sarah at the table.

"You look good, Sarah. The best I ever seen you." Sarah's hand went to her scarred face, and Leah reached out and pushed her hand down. "Never you mind that. I know you won't believe me, but the marks on your face and that white slice of hair look kind of attractive. Mysterious like."

"That's what you said the last time." Sarah barked a derisive laugh. "You still haven't convinced me."

"So, how are you?"

Sarah had written to Leah about the baby and Lindsay's offer to raise Jessica secretly as her own, so she knew Leah already had that news. "Physically, I'm in great shape." Sarah's expression hardened and her voice pitched lower. "But I'm so focused on catching those bastards that it's almost all I can think of."

"What will you do when you catch up with them? Kill them?"

Sarah's forearms rested on the table on either side of her teacup. Her long fingers curled tightly into fists. "That was my first impulse, but now I think a quick death would be too easy for them. What they did will affect me for the rest of my life. They should suffer awhile for that."

Leah rubbed the goose bumps suddenly covering her arms. "So Lindsay wasn't able to convince you that vengeance wasn't the answer." Her words were a statement, not a question, and Sarah didn't reply. "I'm glad she came to help you out. From what you wrote of her, she sounds like a good person."

Sarah's expression softened, and her fists loosened. "She's one of the best people I've ever known. I couldn't have asked for a closer sister."

"Will you go back to live with her and Scott and the children when you've finished this mission you're on?"

"I haven't thought that far ahead." A crooked grin pulled at Sarah's full lips. "But that's a good question. I'm not sure I'd be happy there after all I've experienced in the war. Fitting back into that life doesn't appeal to me at all." Sarah suspected that the events of one horrific day had changed her more than all the other parts of the war she had been through. "I'm a different person now."

Leah nodded just as a train whistle wailed nearby. Sarah cocked her head toward the sound.

"I have to meet that train. Phillip should be on it." The women stood up. "Is it all right if Phillip and I come by tomorrow to work on the picture of the man you saw? Would after lunch suit you?"

"That's fine. I'm looking forward to meeting Phillip." She walked Sarah to the door and along the alley to the main street. "Amy will be sorry she missed you. If you're still here when she gets out of school tomorrow, maybe she can see you then."

"I'd like that." Sarah gave Leah a hug and walked back to the hotel. This time she forced herself not to scrutinize the street.

Faith stepped out onto the wooden walk and closed the door to the doctor's office. Shifting a medical bag to her other hand, she looked up the gravel street. A few blocks away, she saw one of the women from the tavern just releasing a much taller woman from an embrace. She watched as the tall woman walked away. Long dark hair, not covered by the customary bonnet, swung about as the woman turned to cross the street. Faith had just a glimpse of the woman's profile, and the combination of height, dark brown hair, and straight features jogged a wrenching memory. She scoffed at her imaginings, knowing there was little likelihood that the woman was Bren Cordell. She wondered if she would even recognize Bren in a dress. And without a beard.

As she hurried along the sidewalk, Faith thought back to the events following Bren's capture. The picture of the soldiers dragging

145

Bren away still upset her when it came to mind, and occasionally it even intruded on her dreams. The fate that had brought the two women together in such unexpected circumstances had treated neither of them well. Bren undoubtedly had been unmasked and probably sent home against her wishes, and unfair as it might be, Faith had paid dearly for helping the Rebel scout.

After Cranston had been in Union hands for several months, some influential townspeople questioned the advisability of keeping Faith as the schoolteacher. They pointed out that not only had she housed a Rebel soldier in her home, but also her husband had served in the Rebel army. After due consideration, the town council revoked Faith's contract, removing her from her teaching position and evicting her from the home included in the original agreement.

Disgusted by the town's decision, Doc Schafer offered her a position as his assistant and provided two bedrooms and a modest sitting room in his home for her and Benjamin. When the war ended, Faith knew her days with the doctor were limited. After most of the soldiers had been mustered out and went back to their homes, he wouldn't need her help. What would she do when that happened? Life could be hard for a widowed mother. She decided to worry about that when the time drew nearer.

For a long while after Bren's arrest, Faith hoped she might return, if only to retrieve Redfire and her belongings, including her journal. But wishing for a return for any reason had been in vain. She put Bren's clothes and journal in one of the saddlebags and stored them in a closet. When she lost the house, she sold her own horse and rented a stall for Redfire in one of the livery stables.

Recollection of Redfire brought Faith back to the present, and some questions crossed her mind. She couldn't understand why Bren never came for him. Maybe she went back home and circumstances kept her from returning. She wondered what would become of Redfire when she couldn't afford to board the horse anymore. She might have to sell him.

And would she ever see Bren Cordell again? She acknowledged that a connection had formed between them in the short time the woman had stayed with her. Something about Bren had touched Faith's heart, and the spurt of yearning that accompanied any thought of her continued to plague Faith at odd times. Could she possibly be lovesick over a woman? Although she had been attracted to women before, she had never acted on it. Nor had she ever fallen in love with a woman. Now she chided herself for having feelings that Bren hadn't shown any sign of reciprocating. Except—unless it was pure imagination on her part—something had passed between them on the morning the Union troops had arrived in town. If only they'd had more time.

Faith knocked on the door of her patient's home. As she waited for the knock to be answered, she pushed a feeling of regret deep into the back of her mind. Not much chance they would ever meet again, anyway. She'd best put such nonsense out of her head once and for all and spend more time figuring how to manage a safe future for Benjamin and herself.

Sarah stood on the wooden platform of the train station waiting for Phillip to disembark. The clatter and squealing from the train wheels ended when the train came to a stop, but the boiler still hissed and moaned, driving dark soot-laden puffs from the engine's smokestack. Several other people, mostly businessmen judging from their attire, either greeted arriving passengers or waited to board the train themselves. People stepped down from the passenger cars, and Sarah saw Phillip's blond head rising above the person in front of him. As she hurried toward him, she saw he was standing on two legs and wasn't using crutches.

Phillip spied her, dropped his valise next to his good leg, and held open his arms. Even in her joy at seeing him, Sarah noticed his look of delight momentarily wavered as she neared him and he saw the scars on her face. But nothing was held back in his hug. She stepped toward him, and he pulled her into his arms and kissed her. Sarah's stomach got queasy, and she had to fight her inclination to turn away from him. She recognized that her unexpected distaste stemmed from her violation at the hands of the soldiers, and she wondered if she could ever kiss someone without being reminded of that horror.

After the kiss, Phillip held on to her shoulders as she stepped back. "No fire for me yet, Sarah?"

"The fire of loyal friendship, Phillip," Sarah bantered back, "as always." She said no more, watching Phillip's eyes as he scrutinized her face.

He lifted one hand from her shoulder and gently traced over the scars with his fingertips, blinking back tears as he did so. With a sniff, he pulled her to him again and pressed his cheek to hers. Sarah could hear his heavy breathing as he fought for control of his emotions. Finally, he mumbled something, straightened up, and released her.

Sarah pointed to the side of her head. "I don't hear too well in this ear. What did you say?"

"Oh, Sarah . . ." Phillip pulled a handkerchief from his jacket pocket, wiped his face, and blew his nose. "I said, 'Thank God, you're still alive.'" He tucked the handkerchief away. "You could have been killed."

"Are you getting soft-hearted in your old age?" Sarah slapped playfully at his jacket sleeve. "No 'I told you so'?"

Her gambit to lighten the atmosphere worked, and Phillip smiled. "I have plenty of those to hit you with. Just thought I'd take it easy on you for a while, since we haven't seen each other for so long."

Sarah smiled up at him, too, noticing, not for the first time, that he was one of the few people taller than she was. "It has been a long time, hasn't it." She stuck her arm through Phillip's, and he picked up his valise. "I see you're walking well with your new leg. Scott wrote that you had one."

"Yes, the government kept its word and issued them to amputees. I had to wait about nine months for the stump to heal, but as soon as I got the leg, I learned pretty quickly how to use it." He grimaced. "That blasted infection slowed me down. I have to take the leg off once in a while and use the crutches. The stump's still a bit tender, and that makes walking more difficult."

As they strolled from the platform toward the hotel, Sarah said, "Let's spend the rest of the day just catching up on each other's news. Tomorrow, I'll introduce you to Leah, and we'll get started on the drawing of the man who stole your leg."

Phillip brought them both to a stop and looked down at her in surprise. "He did a lot more than steal my leg. He killed hundreds of people."

"I know that, and I hate him for it." Sarah's expression hardened. "But I remember it as the day you lost your leg, and that makes it more personal to me. I hate him even more because of that."

They resumed walking. Phillip was silent for a moment before he shook his head. "It was war, Sarah. In war, people kill people."

"But he wasn't fighting like a regular soldier, face-to-face. He sneaked around and betrayed the people who trusted him."

"Is it so very different from what you were doing?"

This time Sarah pulled them to a halt. "Phillip," she said, her words forced between stiff lips, "I'll always carry a load of guilt about my part in the war. I can only hope the soldiers I saved are more plentiful than those who died." She shrugged. "But I was working within the military and following orders. According to what I read in a dispatch, this piece of slime was a civilian."

Phillip raised a hand and dropped it. "Let's put the hate behind us. Don't let it poison you. I'll be happy just to catch whoever it is and have him brought to trial."

"Apparently, I'm not as charitable as you." She fingered the scars on her face. "I hate the person who crippled you, and I hate the ones who did this to me. You exact your justice for your enemy, and I'll exact my justice for mine."

The hoarseness of Sarah's voice emphasized her determination, and she saw Phillip shiver. "A dedicated focus on your target has always been one of your strengths, Sarah. This time it could burn your soul."

Sarah sneered and suddenly strode forward, nearly yanking Phillip off balance. "First, I'll deal with the ones who burned my face, then I'll worry about my soul."

After lunch the next day, Sarah took Phillip to Leah's rooms and introduced them. Following the social niceties of tea and a chat, they stayed at the kitchen table, and from a bag she had brought, Sarah withdrew her drawing pad, some charcoal pencils, and a soft gum eraser.

"Let's start with a general description of the man you saw, Leah. What was the basic shape of his head? Round like a pumpkin? Oval like an egg?" She drew examples as she spoke. "Rectangular like this table, or square like a box?" Sarah held the pencil poised above the pad, waiting as Leah considered her answer. "Don't hesitate to make suggestions. We can always erase."

With Phillip helping to jog specific descriptions from Leah's memory, the three spent several hours working on the portrayal. When the face on the pad took on more detail, Phillip said, "He's beginning to look vaguely familiar."

Sarah sat up, lifted the pad, and held it away from her to study the portrait. "By God!" She pulled the pad close and bent over it. She quickly added about twenty more bold strokes and held it back up.

149

"That's him!" Leah pointed to the pad. "That's the man who said he done it."

"I can't believe it." Phillip sounded tired. "Virgil Stegner." He looked at Sarah, and she nodded. His fingers curled into a fist and he tapped his knuckles softly against the tabletop. "That man grew up with us, went to the same school, played the same games." His obvious distress slowed his words, and the women remained silent as they waited for him to continue. "But he had trouble with whiskey from early on. Drank himself out of a job. Scott took pity on his family and hired him. We thought he died in the explosion." He tightened the fist and banged it against the table. "That son of a bitch must have done it for money. God knows he never had any principles to speak of." Loathing threatened Phillip's voice and disbelief colored his tone. "He literally blew people into little pieces. People he knew."

Leah touched his arm. "Now you know who he is, you can turn him in and make him pay for that."

Sarah made an unearthly sound, and the other two looked quickly toward her. Her face twisted into an ugly mask. "A slap on the wrist won't bring anyone back to life or give Phillip back his leg. He should be shot on sight."

"You ask for too much, Sarah." Phillip reached for her hand and enclosed it in his. "We have to go on from where we are. No one can go back and change anything." He rubbed his thumb along the back of her hand. "I have to cope with an artificial leg, and you have to live with your scars, but we're both alive. I'm thankful for that."

Sarah took deep breaths to calm her anger. Giving Phillip's hand a squeeze, she echoed his words. "I'm thankful for that, too."

"And me three!" Leah's response brought a smile from both of them just as a knock sounded at the door. "Here's Amy home from school." She jumped up, unlocked the door, and opened it.

When Amy spied Sarah, the little girl dashed across the kitchen and threw herself into Sarah's arms. "Aunt Sarah! Hello, hello!"

"Hello, Amy, darlin'." Sarah swooped the child up onto her lap and gave her a big hug and a kiss. "I have someone I want you to meet." She turned Amy so she could see Phillip. "This is Mr. Phillip Showell, one of my dearest friends."

Phillip stood, stepped somewhat awkwardly toward Amy, and took her hand. He bowed low and kissed the back of her hand while she giggled. "I am pleased to meet you, Miss Amy," he said very seriously. The giggles won him over, and he laughed as he stepped back and resumed his seat. "Your Aunt Sarah told me all about you. I hope she didn't tell you all about me."

Amy's giggles subsided. "She told me you are a very nice man and lots of fun to grow up with." She pointed to Phillip's leg. "But she didn't tell me you had a funny leg."

"Amy! That's not polite," Leah said, but Phillip waved his hand in a shushing motion.

"That's all right, Leah. It is a funny leg." He looked directly into Amy's eyes. "I was in a bad accident, and your Aunt Sarah saved my life. But the accident took away part of my leg, and the doctors gave me a new one to take its place. The foot on it doesn't work too well, but it helps me walk."

Amy frowned in thought. "Aunt Sarah saved your life?"

"Yes, she did."

"Mama said that when someone saves your life, they are . . . what's the rest, Mama?"

"They are responsible for you forever and ever," Leah finished for her.

"Really?" Phillip grinned and lifted his gaze to meet Sarah's matching grin. "I'd like that."

Sarah's grin turned sly, and she quirked an eyebrow as she shook her head. "Oh, no you wouldn't." Then a picture of Faith ministering to her wounded leg flitted across her mind, and her smile disappeared. Forget Faith! she told herself. Admittedly, she saved my life, but she also threw it away. Not what I would call "feeling responsible."

"Look, Mama." Amy drew everyone's attention to the portrait lying on the table, "It's a picture of Mr. Walker."

The three adults stared at her, astonished. Sarah recovered first. "You've seen that man?"

"Uh-huh." Amy nodded. "He was helping Mr. Bullens at the stable. But I haven't seen him for a long time."

Phillip clapped his hands. "Sounds like a good lead has fallen right into our laps."

"You mean right into my lap." Sarah squeezed Amy, who giggled again and returned Sarah's hug. She jumped down from her perch when Leah told her to change into play clothes. "And please don't say anything to anyone about Mr. Walker," Sarah called as the youngster left the room.

Phillip said, "Looks like I'll set up headquarters here in Cranston for the time being."

Leah shook her head. "He's probably long gone."

"But it's a starting point," Phillip said.

"What about you, Sarah?" Leah leaned against a counter and crossed her arms in front of her. "Are you staying for a while?"

"That all depends on Sergeant Angston. Have you heard anything more about him or Hager?"

Leah shook her head. "Haven't heard nothing recently. Far as I know, Angston's still at the army post just outside of town. Never did find Hager."

"All right. I'll investigate the post first," Sarah said as she rose. She tore Stegner's likeness from the pad, rolled it up, and handed it to Phillip. She gathered her drawing pencils and eraser and dropped everything into her bag. "Leah, thank you so much for your help."

Phillip stood, too. "Yes, indeed. I'm quite in your debt. This is the first solid lead I've had." He tapped the roll of paper. "I'll check the livery stable, and if Stegner has left town, this picture will make it easier to track him."

The women hugged and Phillip shook Leah's hand. Sarah called from the doorway, "Tell Amy we said goodbye."

Leah nodded. "You two come back whenever you want. Tell me what's going on, will you?"

"We'll do that," Phillip said.

But Sarah just waved and went out.

The next morning, Sarah finished dressing just moments before Phillip knocked on the door to escort her to breakfast. Their rooms were on the second floor of the hotel, so they took the stairs down to the first-floor dining room. Sarah flew down the steps with only a little pain in her bad leg. She turned and watched Phillip as he descended more slowly.

"Ladies are supposed to walk sedately, Sarah," he said, only half-teasing.

"Right." Sarah stretched the word sarcastically. Phillip knew she didn't aspire to being ladylike. She waved her hand toward him. "You're doing very well with your leg. I would think steps can be difficult."

"Just walking was hard in the beginning. You don't realize how much balance your foot gives you until it's gone. But things could be worse. I'm grateful I still have a knee." He completed his descent, and they walked down the hallway and into the dining room. "I limped badly at first, but I finally learned to compensate and rid myself of most of it."

"Yes, it's barely noticeable. I was shot in the leg, and when I get tired, or sore, I limp a little, too." They sat at a table and, with a quick look at the menu, gave their orders to a server.

"You got shot in the leg? Just how many wounds did you suffer that I haven't heard about?"

Sarah swallowed, stalling to get her voice just right. "Only two major ones—my leg and my head. I got them within a month of each other. A musket ball broke a bone in my lower leg, and it never healed properly. But the head wound was the one that ended Bren Cordell's army service."

Phillip braced his arms against the edge of the table and leaned forward. "When Scott got the letter from your mother about you getting captured and shot as a Rebel, I was hard hit by the news. We all were. But I have to admit I was glad you were out of the war. And I'm thankful the fighting ended before you recuperated sufficiently to get back into it. With your stubborn streak, I know you would have."

Sarah sat back and folded her arms. "Well, Phillip, I still have a little more fighting to do."

He frowned. "What's that supposed to mean? Are you talking about Stegner?"

"No." Sarah shook her head. "I'm talking about the Union soldiers who captured me. They were supposed to take me to their commanding officer. I could have revealed my identity to him and been released. Instead, they shot me and left me for dead. I'm going to get them for that."

Sarah fell silent, and Phillip sat up straighter as the server brought their food. "I don't understand your thirst for vengeance, Sarah. You've developed a dark side I've never seen before."

"My thirst isn't for vengeance. It's for justice." Sarah spread a napkin on her lap, lifted her fork, and chopped at a piece of sausage on her plate. "As soon as we finish eating, I'm going looking for the sergeant who was in charge of them."

"And?" Phillip poked a piece of toast into the yolk of his egg. "What happens when you find him?"

Sarah's eyes met Phillip's all the while she chewed the sausage. She swallowed and said, "You don't want to know."

"Perhaps not." Phillip ate a bite of toast. "And I can't talk you out of it?" His voice seemed calm, but the toast quivered in his grip as he dunked it back into the egg yolk.

Sarah pushed the sausage around without spearing any. "My dear friend," she said, and her lips curved into a smile, "have you ever been able to talk me out of anything?"

"No, damn it!" The words burst from Phillip's mouth. He picked up a second piece of toast and tore it in two. "Not *into* anything, either."

Sarah laughed out loud, and Phillip finally grinned wryly. She reached over and patted his arm. "Let's finish eating. I'm anxious to get on my way."

Sarah walked across the army yard and passed through the gate of the wooden fortifications on her way back into town. Her masquerade as Private Hager's cousin had succeeded perfectly. The sergeant at the post's office had been quickly accommodating when she asked him for information concerning her "cousin." Feigning a nasty cold, she maneuvered a plain, white handkerchief to screen her nose and mouth from his view. A brown bonnet pulled tight to the edges of her eyes concealed her scars and slash of white hair, and she shrunk into herself and affected a pronounced stoop to reduce her height.

The soldier riffled through some files and informed her Hager had mustered out months earlier. When Sarah suggested his friend, Sergeant Angston, might have information about his whereabouts, the soldier agreed and readily told her Angston was on leave, presumably in town. Sarah thanked him and left.

A few yards from the post walls, she stepped onto the town's boardwalk and hurried the two blocks to her hotel. She went to her room, stripped and packed the clothes she wore, and donned the clothes and beard she had worn as Bren Cordell. As she tied her hair back, she noted that the change of clothes also caused a change in her demeanor. Almost instantly, she became more focused, harder minded, more like her old self. But that old self was not Bren Cordell, who no longer existed. She was Sarah Coulter no matter how she dressed.

She lifted the holstered Remington from its resting place and strapped on the belt. Two pieces of rawhide hung down, and she wrapped them around her thigh and tied them tight, anchoring the holster to her leg. Her fingers curved around the butt of the gun, and she slid the revolver out and checked its load. Anxious to get moving, she pushed the piece back into the holster and forced herself to finish packing her belongings methodically into the valise.

Sarah searched the drawers and closet. Satisfied she had left nothing behind, she tossed her saddlebags over her left shoulder, slapped a slouch hat on her head, hefted the valise, and walked out the door. Downstairs, she checked the valise in Sarah Coulter's name. The obviously confused clerk opened his mouth, but the look Sarah gave him squelched any questions. With a curt nod, she turned away and headed for the livery stable.

When she had taken but a few steps into the dim, pungent atmosphere, a horse whickered nearly in her ear, bringing her head around in a hurry. Redfire! It was indeed Redfire, hanging his head over a stall gate. Bren flung her arms around the stallion's russet neck and hid her face against him to conceal the tears of joy filling her eyes. She heard footsteps approaching and struggled to compose her features.

A nasal, but friendly, voice inquired, "You know that horse?"

Sarah took an off-balance step back as Redfire kept nuzzling her. With a lame chuckle, she replied, "He seems to think he knows me. Reminds me of one I used to have." She looked toward the man, whose sweat-stained and straw-sprinkled clothes proclaimed him the livery stable keeper. Mr. Bullens, no doubt. Phillip would be following up with him. A chaw of tobacco swelled one side of his jaw. "Are you the owner?"

"Of the stable, yep. Bullens is my name. Of the horse, nah." The man lifted a hand to the area between Redfire's ears and scratched the animal's tuft of mane. "Lady name of Mizzus Pruitt boards him here. Sold her other one, but kept this one. Said he belongs to a friend. She has him up for hire if yer just looking for a temporary ride."

The thought tempted Sarah. She could hire Redfire and never bring him back. She wondered if she could be arrested for stealing her own horse. But the man's next words cancelled that notion.

"Her boy comes here nigh every day and takes this one out. Calls him Redfire. You ever seen two that belong together like eggs and grits, it's those two. Hell, that young'un don't even use a saddle. Just puts the bridle on, grabs a bit of mane, and flops up bareback."

Sarah figured Benjamin must be a head taller now if he could mount bareback. She smiled at the picture in her mind, even as she denied the yearning in her heart.

Bullens spat tobacco juice onto the dirt floor and eyed Sarah speculatively. "I sure hope that friend ain't in no big hurry to come back for his horse. Be a damn shame to deprive the boy of an animal he cares so much about."

"I'd have to agree with that." Sarah lightly punched Redfire's shoulder and rubbed the spot with the palm of her hand as the horse butted her with his head. She turned her back for a moment and swallowed the pain of knowing she had to walk away from an animal that was family to her. Someday she would have him back. Someday. She pulled herself together and turned back to the hostler. "I need to buy one. Tack, too. Do you have any for sale?"

"I got three. Best is a nice broad-shouldered chestnut. Tack comes with him."

Sarah examined the horses and decided on the chestnut. He was a powerfully built horse and looked like he could run forever. She paid the fees, saddled and mounted the horse, and rode up the street to the nearest saloon, not allowing herself to look back. She noticed right away that the chestnut put his hooves down with a heavier thud than Redfire did, like a drumbeat. Drummer. She would call him Drummer. She dismounted, gave his shoulder a hard pat, and hitched him to a rail.

First yanking her hat low over her eyes, she pushed through the swinging doors and entered the saloon. She made her way slowly toward the bar, which formed a thirty-foot half oval against the far wall. Her eyes roved over the patrons as she went, only a few at this early hour of the day. Her heart punched heavily against the inside of her chest when she recognized Angston just rising from a seat at one of the round tables scattered about the room.

The day has just turned luckier, Sarah thought. Angston headed toward a side door that probably led to an alley. She did an about-face and ambled back out through the swinging doors. As soon as her feet touched the boardwalk, she hurried to the edge of the building and looked around the corner. Sure enough, Angston was in the alley, his back to Sarah, standing in the unmistakable pose of a man relieving himself.

A glance around told her the street was empty. She slipped into the alley, pulled out her pistol, and quietly made her way up behind Angston. She let him finish buttoning his fly before she sapped him behind the ear with the butt of the revolver. He slumped to the ground without a sound. She took the soldier's sidearm from his holster and tucked it into her belt. A quick search for other weapons revealed only a sheathed knife, which she also removed.

After hurrying back to the front of the building, she placed the knife and gun in Drummer's saddlebags, untied the horse, and led him into the alley, where she laid a rock on the ends of the reins to keep him still. She pulled some rope and a blanket from the saddlebags. With a muffled grunt, she hefted Angston across Drummer's rump behind the saddle and tied the soldier's hands to his feet under the horse. Thankful that Drummer didn't shy at the unaccustomed arrangement, she covered Angston's form with the blanket and tucked it in around him, concealing him completely.

With her cargo secure, Sarah retrieved the reins, mounted Drummer, and steered him slowly through the main part of town. The few people walking about paid her little notice. Once past the center of town, she cantered down a side street and into the woods. The exact spot where the soldiers had forced themselves on her was burned into Sarah's memory, and she took Angston there.

She dismounted and tethered Drummer to a tree beside the clearing. Checking first to make sure Angston hadn't regained consciousness, she untied him and dropped him on the ground. She looped the rope over her shoulder before searching the saddlebag for the four good-sized wooden pegs she had brought for this specific purpose. She pounded them into the ground with the handle of the knife she carried in a sheath at her belt. When finished, she removed the rope from her shoulder and cut it into four pieces, laying one piece near each peg.

Angston stirred, so Sarah walked over to him. The sergeant grabbed the side of his head with one hand and sat up. "What the h—"

Sarah clobbered him on the other side of his head with her gun barrel and watched with satisfaction as he fell heavily against the sparse grass. She moved to his feet, turned her back and lifted each foot, removing his boots. She turned again, cut Angston's suspenders with her knife, and pulled off his pants and drawers. She stowed the knife back in its sheath. With her bare hands, she grabbed Angston's shirttails and ripped open his shirt, her lip curling at the popping sound made by the metal buttons. After she yanked off the shirt and undershirt, she dragged the nude man to the center of the pegs and tied his arms and legs to them, spread-eagled. She sat cross-legged next to him and waited for him to waken.

In a short time, his eyes flickered open. He tried to move. Though there was a little give in the ropes, he quickly realized he was tied down. Sarah relished the look of fear that flitted across his face and played back across his features when he looked down and saw he was naked. His gaze jumped around like a treed squirrel until it lit on her.

"Who the hell are you?" he demanded. "What's going on?"

Sarah stood and loomed above his head so he could see her better. "Take a good look, Angston. See if you remember me." With intentional deliberation, she lifted off her hat and laid it upside down on the ground. She peeled off the false beard and set it in the hat. Next, she untied her hair and let it fall around her face as she looked down at him. "Now do you remember me? Do you remember this clearing?"

Angston's brows came together in a frown, and he stared hard. As recognition dawned, his face paled and his jaw went slack. "It can't be. It can't be. You're dead. I saw Hager shoot you."

"Damn right, he shot me." Sarah slammed a kick into Angston's side with her booted toe and ran her hand over her face and hair. "That's where I got these scars. But he didn't kill me. You should have been more thorough, Sergeant. You should have checked."

Angston's gaze flashed around erratically, obviously looking for help, knowing that none would arrive. He wailed, "What're you doing?" He seemed to shrink into himself as Sarah stood silent, staring at him like a stone statue. His wail turned into a whine. "You going to kill me?"

Unhurried, she let him squirm for a while as he waited for her answer. "If you remember, that's what I promised. But first, you're going to suffer, just as I did." She took a calculated step across one of Angston's legs and stood between his spread limbs, facing him. "Of course, I'm not about to force myself on you, but I can make you hurt just the same." She curled her hands into fists, drew back her foot, and kicked him between the legs. The impact was hard enough to cause extreme pain, but not enough to kill him. She didn't want him to die too soon.

Angston shrieked and writhed for a good two minutes. When he quieted, Sarah drew back her foot again. She held it there for a long moment. Tears streamed down Angston's cheeks, but he couldn't take his eyes from her foot. She faked a kick several times. When he stopped flinching, she kicked him again. It took longer for him to calm himself this time. His body heaved as he struggled to gulp in air. Sarah lifted her foot again. A nasty smile spread across her face as the tethered man begged for mercy.

"I'll show you as much mercy as you showed me." He flinched and whimpered with each movement as she merely jabbed at him with her toe. Finally, she drew back her foot and kicked him for the third time. "That's one kick for each of you, you bastard."

As Angston's howls continued, Sarah stepped over his leg and walked away. Such murderous blackness filled her that she hardly recognized herself. She paced back and forth across the clearing, trying to rein in her fury. She had wreaked her vengeance, at least part of it, but she didn't feel any better for it. Angston deserved to die. He had been the instigator. But no court would punish him for his crime. Sarah had no evidence. And shouldn't the punishment fit the crime? Well, she had seen to that. He had suffered as he should. Now it was time to finish with him. Sarah pulled her revolver and strode over to the pitiful heap of a man.

Angston's eyes were pinched shut, his face contorted in pain. He heard her approach and barely cracked open his eyes. He saw the gun in her hand and groaned as he closed his eyes again. They reopened when he heard the cock of the hammer. His voice came out as a hoarse whisper, a mere remnant of his usual bluster. "Please don't kill me."

Without hesitation, Sarah put the open end of the gun barrel against his forehead. "You have about five seconds to make peace with your Creator." Her words sounded as flat and metallic as a clapper thumping against a broken bell. But should she kill him, which he surely deserved? Or should she wound him the same as she was wounded, and let him go through life seeing the scars every time he looked in the mirror? Seeing them every time he looked into a woman's eyes. Should she, or shouldn't she? Sarah thought about it as the realization of his imminent death grew in Angston's eyes. She made her decision. Baring her teeth in feral triumph, she pulled the trigger.

Sarah stopped at Leah's just long enough to let her know she was leaving town. Too agitated for visiting, she didn't even step inside when Leah came to the door. By way of greeting, she said, "I'll be going after Hager now."

"Wait." Leah raised a hand to shade her eyes as she looked up at Sarah. "You found Angston?" Sarah's head jerked in a short nod. "What happened? Did you kill him?"

Sarah pulled her gaze away from Leah's piercing look and stared off into the distance, her face set. Leah waited a moment, then laid a hand on Sarah's arm and squeezed. "All right, but Hager could be anywhere, you know? You might never find him."

"You may be right." Sarah jerked another nod. "I have to try. I'm heading to Cleveland. I'll see what I can find out there."

Leah opened her arms and Sarah stepped into her embrace. "You take care of yourself, Bren Cordell, or Sarah Coulter, or whoever you are. You both take care of yourselves."

"You, too." Sarah gave her an extra squeeze, kissed her on the cheek, and stepped back. "I'll keep in touch." She turned and walked away.

When she got back to the hotel, Phillip wasn't there. She gathered hotel stationery, pen, and ink and wrote him a letter of goodbye, directing that any mail for her could be sent in care of General Delivery in Cleveland. Afterward, she gave the clerk her home address and left some money for him to ship her belongings there. For this portion of her search, she would continue to use Bren Cordell as her identity, but she would forgo the now-unnecessary beard and mustache. Her scars gave her ready credibility as a wounded veteran.

With her business in Cranston taken care of, she left the hotel, the town, and the state, on her way to Ohio. To find Hager.

Sarah sat on the edge of the hotel bed, fingering the letter she had just read. She frowned and swore under her breath. She had been traveling all over Ohio and parts of Kentucky during the winter and most of spring, following leads about Hager's whereabouts. His family hoped he would return to settle down in Cleveland, but he always seemed to be somewhere else. Now she had received a letter from Lindsay asking her to return home for a visit that would coincide with Jessica's first birthday. A frustrating interruption to her frustrating search.

Her gaze lifted to the calendar hanging on the opposite wall. On May 10, two weeks from now, Jessica would be a year old.

From the start of this part of her quest, Sarah had forced herself to concentrate solely on finding Hager. She refused to allow any thoughts about the baby to deflect her from her goal. The letter weakened her resolve, and buried memories swirled to the surface, bringing the image of her daughter into sharp focus.

My daughter? She's not my daughter anymore, Sarah reminded herself. I gave her away to Lindsay and Scott. Memories of the weight of Jessie in her arms, the warmth of the baby against her body, and the pull of that tiny mouth suckling at her breast overwhelmed her unexpectedly. She could almost smell the baby's freshness and feel the soft smoothness of her skin. A bolt of yearning shot through her, and she fought to push it away.

Because she had been apprehensive of the growing bond that nursing induced, Sarah had purposely refused to hold her child except for feedings. She threw reproachful looks at Lindsay whenever her sister-in-law tried to hand the baby to her. She knew without question that she was unable to get past the fact that the child came from the seed of a man who had violated her and agreed to kill her. In truth, she didn't want to get past it. She craved locating him. All his tears and pleas for her forgiveness back then hadn't stopped him from going through with the heinous act Angston ordered. And it wouldn't stop her actions when she found him.

But she owed it to Lindsay and Scott to go home for a visit, if that was what they wanted. She folded the letter and slipped it back into the envelope. She rose and walked over to her saddlebags, which lay on the floor next to the bureau. Squatting down, she slipped the letter into one side of the bags, stood, and grabbed a pencil from on top of the bureau. After moving the couple of steps to the wall calendar, she circled May 10 and sighed. I can do this.

CHAPTER TEN

Sarah let go of the mixer handle and straightened up. "I'm sure the ice cream will be hard enough," she called to Lindsay from the back porch. "I can barely turn the crank." In the bucket, a combination of rock salt and ice surrounded the steel cylinder full of vanilla-flavored dessert. The ice would keep the treat cold until they were ready to eat it. She heaped some more salt-ice mixture over the crank mechanism, covered everything with a piece of burlap, and entered the kitchen through the screen door.

Lindsay handed her a tray stacked with plates and forks for the birthday cake and spoons for the ice cream, which would be scooped straight from the mixer into individual bowls and topped with sugared strawberries.

"I invited Theo and Phillip to join us for the celebration," Lindsay said.

"Phillip has come home?" Sarah had intended to take the tray into the dining room, but she stopped and half turned toward Lindsay. "This is news. I thought he was still in Cranston, looking for that snake Stegner."

"I'm sorry." Lindsay waved a couple of linen napkins she had just picked up. "I meant to tell you earlier, but with all the party preparations, it slipped my mind. Scott saw Theo this morning and he said Phillip got home last night. With an announcement."

Sarah turned full face to Lindsay and leaned a shoulder against the wall, bracing the tray against her hip. For some reason, her leg pained her today more than usual. "What kind of announcement?"

"Theo wouldn't say." Lindsay's dark curls danced as she shook her head. "I guess Phillip wants to surprise us with something."

Sarah moved away from the wall and pushed the door with an elbow. She heard Scott's voice raised in greeting. The opening door gave her a clear view through the dining room and drawing room and into the foyer. What she saw made her gasp, and she abruptly turned back toward Lindsay. Her whole body sagged. Lindsay grabbed the platter from her hands just as Sarah's slack fingers lost their grasp.

"What's wrong?" Concern colored Lindsay's face as all the blood left Sarah's. She had to brace herself against the doorjamb. Lindsay set the platter on the table and took hold of Sarah's arm, offering support as she led her to a chair. "Are you feeling ill?"

"It's her," Sarah whispered at last. Shock had jolted through her, causing momentary paralysis and interfering with her power of speech. She struggled with turbulent thoughts. *Faith! Why is she here? What is she doing with Phillip?*

"Who?" Lindsay's voice broke through to her muddled brain. "Who is it, Sarah?" She leaned closer to hear.

"Faith Pruitt . . . the woman who betrayed me. She just came through the front door."

Lindsay's eyes grew wide. She moved to the door and pulled it softly closed before hurrying back to sit at Sarah's side. "That must be Phillip's surprise. But why would she be with him? Does he know who she is? I mean, in relation to you."

Sarah's head jerked. "No. I told him only a simple outline of being wounded and very little about my recovery. Even Theo knows only the bare facts. I guess Phillip could always tell I didn't want to talk about it. He never pressed me for details." She laid the heel of one hand against the table and began tapping all four fingers against the surface. "I can't go in there."

"You have to, Sarah, if only to greet Phillip. You can't just ignore him." She touched Sarah's arm. "Please don't let this question upset you, but would she even connect you with the Rebel soldier she treated? You're a Northerner, you've gained weight since then, your hair is longer, and you aren't speaking with the drawl you used." She grinned wryly. "Not to mention that now you actually look like a woman."

Sarah considered what Lindsay said and recovered some of her calm. "She never saw me without my beard and mustache either. Or with a scarred face. You could be right about her not recognizing me. But that's only part of the reason I'm troubled." Her drumming fingers stopped and she made a fist. "Damn it! I trusted the woman, and she turned me in to soldiers she thought of as my enemy." That thought pulled another right behind it. "What's Phillip doing with a Rebel sympathizer, anyway?"

As the shock of seeing Faith wore off, Sarah's heart thudded for a very different reason. She recognized that Lindsay's assessment months back had been correct. She had an emotional connection with Faith. But was she really in love with her? She didn't know how else to interpret the yearning she felt. Would seeing Faith strengthen that yearning or help her get over feelings that weren't entirely welcome? How could she reconcile her desires with the terrible cloud of rejection Faith's betrayal had cast over her?

"How do you know she's a Rebel?"

"She was married to one." Realizing what she had said, Sarah chided herself. Faith had been married. Sarah thought that in itself should be proof that her own desires were misplaced. She had pounded that into her head a thousand times, but with frustrating stubbornness, her heart refused to listen to reason.

The door opened, and Scott stuck his head into the kitchen. "What's the holdup, ladies? Our guests are here. All except Theo, that is. He was called away."

"We'll be right out, dear." Lindsay smiled at him. "Are the children behaving?"

"Jessie is still sound asleep in the crib, but Pres is getting a bit anxious. Try to hurry, will you? Phillip has something he's dying to tell you both."

"Give us a clue?" Lindsay coaxed.

"No." Scott's gaze flicked from his wife to his sister and back. "Not on your life. Or rather, mine. Phillip would kill me."

Lindsay stood and offered Scott the tray she had taken from Sarah earlier. "Set this on the table, please. We'll bring the cake and get Phillip's news. As soon as Jessie wakes, we can serve the ice cream."

"All right." Scott stepped forward and took the tray from his wife. "Hurry, please," he said again as he returned to the dining room.

Lindsay touched Sarah's shoulder. "Are you ready?"

Sarah sighed. "No. But waiting won't make it any easier."

Lindsay lifted the cake from the table, and Sarah followed her out, pausing while Lindsay set the cake on the dining-room table. Sarah stepped to Lindsay's side, and they proceeded into the drawing room.

Phillip spied the women right away and came toward them with arms outstretched. He hugged Sarah and kissed her cheek, repeating the greeting with Lindsay. "Hello! I've missed you," he said and continued without hesitation. "I've brought some people I want you to meet."

Sarah glimpsed Faith seated off to her right and was chagrined that Faith would see the scarred side of her face first. That reaction disturbed her. Why should it matter? She didn't mean anything to Faith. Another figure entered her peripheral vision and lightened her dark mood a little. Benjamin stood next to his mother. Seeing the youngster brought a flood of warmth. He must be nearly ten, she mused. He's grown several inches taller.

"This way, please." Phillip put an arm around each woman and steered them over toward Faith, then he stepped off to the side. "Ladies, I want you to meet my fiancée, Mrs. Faith Pruitt. Faith, this is Scott's wife, Lindsay, and his sister, Sarah."

Sarah stiffened at the word "fiancée," and she knew Lindsay was conscious of it. The "how do you do" coming from her own lips sounded clipped and cold even to her, but Lindsay's greeting was warm.

"Welcome to our home, Mrs. Pruitt. We're delighted to meet you."

"Thank you, Mrs. Coulter. I'm delighted to be here. But please, call me Faith."

"Only if you call me Lindsay." She glanced at Sarah, who remained silent.

Faith turned aside. "This is my son, Benjamin."

Benjamin bowed slightly as the two women smiled at him.

"Welcome, Benjamin," Lindsay said. "Do you like ice cream?"

"Yes, ma'am." His smile would have been answer enough.

Lindsay gestured toward Sarah. "Perhaps you would like to help Miss Coulter get the ice cream from the mixer?"

Benjamin smiled and nodded.

"Come with me, then. It's out on the porch," Sarah said, silently blessing Lindsay for her quick thinking. Coming face-to-face with Faith disturbed her even more than she'd expected, affirming that she needed more time to adapt. With a hand on Benjamin's elbow, she directed him into the kitchen.

Sarah let go and gathered a heavy scoop and two spoons from a drawer. She nodded toward the table. "Please wash your hands and bring those bowls. We can fill them with ice cream and set them on the table. Mrs. Coulter mixed some sugared strawberries to put on top of each bowl. How does that sound?"

"Good," Benjamin said with a shy smile. He washed and dried his hands, picked up the bowls, and followed Sarah outside. The roofed porch was encircled by a white fence rail, supported by matching slats. Otherwise open to the air, it wrapped around two sides of the house, with short steps giving access to it at front and back. Sarah set the utensils on the wooden table and watched Benjamin survey his surroundings. The boy blinked in the bright sunshine as his gaze swept the view of the grassy yard and surrounding trees. A slight breeze lifted the front of his hair like invisible fingers clearing his brow. She smiled at him when his gaze moved back to the porch and ended on the oaken, bucket-sized tub sitting on one of six straight-backed chairs placed around the table. A tan burlap bag lay across the top of the tub.

"Before we do anything else, I think you better take off that good-looking jacket and hang it on the back of one of the chairs." Sarah waited as he obeyed her suggestion, and she nodded as he rolled up his shirtsleeves.

With the boy hovering next to her, she lifted the burlap bag and laid it on the porch floor. She grabbed the side of the wooden tub with one hand and tipped it. As she scooped out some ice-and-rock-salt mixture packed around a metal cylinder in the center of the tub, she directed the sodden mess onto the burlap bag. Setting the tub straight again, she asked, "Have you ever seen an ice-cream maker?"

"No, ma'am. I had ice cream at some parties, but I never saw anyone make it."

Pointing to a crank handle protruding from a metal apparatus connected across the top of the tub, Sarah said, "Try to give that a turn. Use both hands." He grasped the handle and grunted as he tried to turn it, but it barely moved. Sarah grinned. "That's good. It means the ice cream is firm enough to eat."

"How does this make ice cream?"

"You see the cylinder in the middle?" Benjamin nodded, his face red from his exertion. Sarah unhooked the crank apparatus and lifted it back across the top of the tub on its hinges, freeing the cylinder. A short metal rod poked through the top of the cylinder cap, which she unscrewed. "There are several different recipes, but this is a rather plain one. You pour measured amounts of cream, sugar, and vanilla flavoring into this cylinder, which also contains a dasher." The cap came off, and Benjamin leaned forward and grinned at sight of the ice cream.

"You put the top back on and hook the crank across so it clamps onto these gears on top of the lid." Sarah pointed to them. "Next, you pack ice and rock salt into the tub all around the cylinder. Then you start cranking. It's easy at first, but as the ice cream thickens, it gets harder. And when the cream is almost solid, like now, you can't turn it anymore, so you just have to eat it."

Benjamin's grin grew wider.

"But the workers get paid first." Sarah flashed a conspiratorial smile. "Remember I said there's a dasher inside the cylinder? Well, that's the piece that trails through the liquid and mixes it as you crank. It keeps the ice cream smooth, too." She worked her fingers down into the cream next to the protruding rod, hooked them around something, and slowly pulled on it. A flat, cast-iron frame, slotted with three narrow panels of swiveled wood on each side, slid from the cylinder, carrying some of the frozen cream with it. Benjamin looked so rapt that Sarah's throat threatened to close. She remembered that same look on his face when he'd finished a difficult piece of drawing. She wanted to hug him but knew she couldn't. He had no idea she was Bren Cordell. What would happen if he found out? Undoubtedly, the revelation would shock him, especially because he thought Bren was a man.

Her voice came out as a whisper, which luckily suited the occasion. "Grab a spoon." She nodded toward the two she had set on the table. "And have a seat." She sat next to him, laying the contraption on a ceramic platter put out for that purpose. "The first taste is ours."

While watching Benjamin attack the frozen dessert on the dasher with gusto and taking a few spoonfuls herself, Sarah regained tenuous control of her emotions. "So, Benjamin, do you have any hobbies?"

His dark head nodded as he finished swallowing. "Yes, ma'am. I like to draw."

"So do I!" Sarah made herself look surprised, but she didn't have to fake her delight that he would tell her about it. "What do you like to draw?"

Benjamin moved one shoulder as shyness crept back. "Just about anything. I'm not real good yet."

"Would you show me some of your drawings? Maybe we can work together and learn from each other." Sarah nipped a bite of ice cream, giving him time to consider her offer. It occurred to her that he probably had left his pictures at home. "Did you bring any with you?"

"We brought just about everything with us. Mama said we're going to live here now."

Sarah struggled to keep her expression pleasant. Why did that remark bring a twinge to her heart, she wondered. But she knew the answer. She was torn between wanting to see more of Faith and accepting that the woman who owned her heart was going to marry one of her best friends. Owned her heart? Yes, she admitted. In spite of what Faith had done to her, Sarah wanted to hold her and kiss her and— She yanked her thoughts up short. Experiencing this consuming desire for a woman confused her. And the passage of time had only strengthened the desire—and the confusion.

She looked over to see Benjamin waiting for her attention. "You'll be happy here. This is a friendly town, and Mr. Showell is a very good man." She smiled. "Have you decided about showing me your drawings?"

"All right. I like when people help me. A soldier stayed with us for a while, and he showed me a lot." Benjamin merely licked at his next spoonful of ice cream, as though he had more to say, so Sarah pretended to eat, too. Finally, he swallowed the spoonful and poured out a rush of words. "He went away in a hurry, and we still have his drawing book. He draws really good. I'll ask Mama if I can show it to you." After the outburst, Sarah handed him the dasher to lick clean, and he concentrated on that diversion.

She was delighted they had preserved her journal, but she kicked herself mentally for not being wiser than to offer to help Benjamin. The boy had a good eye for art. When he saw the drawings side by side, he would know at a glance that hers looked just like Bren Cordell's. But would he make the leap from a bearded male soldier with a heavy drawl to a longer-haired female with no drawl at all? And scars? Probably not, though children could be surprising with their canny perceptions.

Her thoughts continued to dart around like leaves scattered by the wind. Would her current misdirection hold up? Bren Cordell hadn't fooled Faith, but the circumstances played against her then. Why not just tell Faith who she was? Why try to mislead her? Sarah clamped her lips tight, trying to restrain the lip that wanted to lift in a sneer. Because she betrayed me! The answer shouted in her head. She knew if the secret of Bren Cordell came out, she would throw that betrayal in Faith's face and demand an accounting for it. So why not do that now? Why not?

Because of Phillip, Sarah thought with a sigh. If she accused Faith in front of everyone else, people would be forced to make choices. Scott and Lindsay knew everything that had happened and most likely would come down on her side, but Phillip would be caught in the middle. Faith was his bride-to-be. He would be loyal to her, even though his choice might ostracize him from the Coulter family. She just couldn't put him in that position. He was too good a friend, too fine a person. She would keep her silence and pray everything somehow worked out. The distress and uncertainty of the whole situation cast a gray pall over her. On top of everything else, she wondered what had happened to Redfire, but she couldn't ask.

Benjamin had cleaned the dasher of the last traces of ice cream, so Sarah nodded toward it. "You want to put that in the sink and wash your hands again? And give your face a swipe, too." When he finished, he came back to the porch where Sarah was now standing with the scoop in her hand. She gave him a smile and spooned the cream from the cylinder into the bowls.

"Miss Coulter?"

"Yes?"

"I feel like I've known you for a long time. I think we'll be friends."

Sarah's movements froze, and it was a long few seconds later that she forced a laugh. "Indeed. I think we will, too." She turned and winked her good eye at the boy. "You may be a very young man, Benjamin, but you already sound like a grown-up."

"Well, here come the ice-cream servers! We thought you got lost." Scott held Jessie in one arm as he rose and helped Sarah pass along the two bowls she carried. When finished, he handed Jessie toward her. "Here, Aunt Sarah, give Jessie her birthday kiss."

As Jessie reached out for her, Sarah stiffened visibly. She awkwardly took the child into her arms and raised her up to her cheek. Scott stayed nearby, apparently expecting Jessie would be handed back soon.

"She's not going to bite you, Sarah." A light danced in his eyes. "She doesn't know you well enough, yet."

Phillip's laugh brayed out. "Good one, Scott." Sarah turned his way and lifted one eyebrow, causing Phillip to press a napkin to his mouth in an apparent attempt to smother any further expressions of hilarity. He turned red with the effort, which drew smiles from both Lindsay and Faith.

Sarah pitched her voice higher and batted her long lashes. "I do declare, sir. No one's *ever* known me well enough to bite me." This brought more smiles and Phillip's face grew even redder. Unbidden, a suppressed memory of Angston's attack leaped into her mind, and Sarah's voice and expression sobered. "Not without dire consequences."

Scott jumped into the silence that resulted from the rapid change of mood. "Give Jessie back. Let's get this party going before the ice cream melts." Sarah passed Jessie to him just as the youngster began to squirm and call for "Da-Da."

Scott cradled the child in his arms and took her hand. Whirling her around like a dance partner, he moved to the head of the table. Jessie squealed with laughter as the ribbons on her pinafore bow lifted in the air behind her. "Thank you, my dear." Scott seated Jessie in the place of honor and bowed, bringing another laugh from her.

After Benjamin finished setting out the ice cream and strawberries, he donned his suit coat and sat beside his mother. With young Pres' help, Jessie blew out the one fat candle sitting atop the bright yellow icing. Lindsay cut and served the lemon-flavored slices on delicate Haviland cake plates ringed with gold and trimmed with tiny bouquets of blue and pink flowers.

After everyone had eaten, Scott set the birthday gifts in the middle of the drawing-room floor. Jessie and Pres opened them, spurning assistance from their parents, and the children remained there, playing. Benjamin retrieved his bag of lead soldiers from his mother's keeping, and he and Pres fought a vigorous battle. Jessie investigated a new doll, turning it every which way and pulling its arms and legs. The adults returned to the dining room for coffee, all the while keeping an eye on the children through the arched double doorway between the rooms.

"Scott," Faith said, after a lull in conversation while the adults fixed their coffee, "I was wondering if you had been in the war?" She peered at him, a puzzled look on her face. She smiled and shook her head no when Lindsay offered her more cake.

"I wasn't privileged to serve," he answered, disappointment evident in his voice. "Phillip and Theo got a chance to go, but I had to stay and run the family foundry. We made cannons during the war."

"And he'll likely never let us forget he got left out." Phillip accepted another slice of cake from Lindsay. "When we played soldiers as children, Scott was always at least a colonel."

Scott grinned at Phillip's reminiscence. "And Sarah was always the general." He reached for the cake plate handed to him and nodded his thanks to his wife. "I think we spoiled her, always letting her have her way."

Unprepared for Faith's question, Sarah was still a bit off balance and almost forgot to project the expected glare to her childhood playmates.

Phillip snorted, but remained silent as Faith persisted with her questions. "I met a soldier who looked remarkably like you, especially your coloring and your eyes. He was very thin and wore a beard, but he could have passed for your brother. He stayed with us for a short time while he was wounded."

"Sorry." Scott swallowed a forkful of cake. "It couldn't have been me. I might have had some distant cousins who served without my knowing, but I don't have any brothers." He turned and smiled at Sarah, barely winking the eye Faith couldn't see. "Just a sister." He reached for his cup and drank some coffee.

It seemed to Sarah that Faith jumped at the opening, and she could have strangled Scott.

"Sarah? Did you fight in the war?"

Sarah pulled in her chin and sat up to her full height. Still, Faith was tall, too, and Sarah had to tilt her head back to give the impression of looking down her nose. "What a strange question. Do you know any women who fought?"

Faith glanced toward the children and lowered her voice. "The soldier I just spoke of was a woman, though I prefer that my son doesn't know."

Sarah touched her fingers to her scarred face. "Don't tell me she was wounded in the head." She smiled inwardly when she saw Faith not quite succeed in suppressing a wince.

"No." Faith clasped her hands in her lap and leaned forward. "The wound was in her leg."

I can hardly stand this, Sarah thought as her fingers toyed with a coffee spoon. "What happened to her after the wound was healed? Did she go back to fighting?" Her stomach clenched when Faith's red curls bounced as she shook her head. The woman actually managed to look sad.

"No, she was captured by Union soldiers."

The china saucer rang as Sarah dropped her spoon onto it. "By the Union? Are you talking about a Rebel?" She raised her voice. "You dare to think that Scott might have been a Rebel soldier? He would have fought for the Union!"

Phillip cleared his throat. "Sarah, the war's over, remember? We're not Union and Confederate anymore. We're all Americans. We need to make peace with each other."

"Of course we do." Sarcasm painted her words as she looked from Phillip to Faith and back again. "And we can see you've already made your little contribution to that reunification effort." She didn't harbor any ill feeling toward Phillip, she just needed an excuse to leave the group before she exploded. Sitting so close to Faith and conversing with her had roused emotions that flamed from anger to desire to regret. Confused, Sarah struggled to marshal all her defenses, and they were in imminent danger of crumbling.

Phillip's face turned red, but he was too much of a gentleman to join an argument with Sarah at Jessie's party. When Sarah got up, he rose, too, and tossed his napkin on the table, but he didn't say a word.

"If you'll excuse me, I'll begin cleaning up the table." Sarah picked up her china and let her gaze sweep right past Phillip and Faith, barely acknowledging them with a nod. In her peripheral vision, she saw Scott wave Phillip back to his seat as she entered the kitchen.

She set the dishes in the sink and went out onto the porch to give the spring breeze a chance to cool her brow, and maybe her emotions. She paced the wraparound porch, turned at the corner and walked the full distance across the front of the house before retracing her footsteps. After half an hour of such pacing, she stopped at the edge of the porch, leaned her hands against the rail, and gazed unseeing into the distance. For a while, she closed her eyes and just stood there.

Sarah's weaker ear was on the side nearest the screen door that led to the kitchen, and she didn't realize Lindsay had come outside until the smaller woman touched her shoulder. She jumped and turned around, thrusting herself back against the rail. Her arms folded across her chest in a protective gesture.

"I'm sorry," Lindsay said, "I didn't mean to startle you." Her fingers moved to Sarah's arm. "Are you all right?"

Sarah's crossed arms rose high and fell, moved by the deep breath she forced herself to take. "I'm not going back in there." Her voice was flat, devoid of the emotion she had shoved again into its prison. "I can't."

"It's all right, they've gone." Sarah heaved another deep breath, this one of relief. Lindsay tilted her head in the endearing way Sarah couldn't resist. "Does Phillip know you're the one Faith was talking about? Or that she told the Union soldiers where you were?"

"Apparently not." Sarah switched her gaze to the brown-planked porch floor and spoke softly. "She must not have told him my name. I never gave him all the details of my wounds or of my recovery. I made him take an oath never to tell anyone I had been in the war. It's nobody else's business." Her voice took on a sharper edge. "Besides, I didn't want any connection made between me and those bastards I vowed vengeance on."

"Are you going to tell him about Faith—what she did, how you feel about her?"

Should I? Sarah wondered. How could I hurt Phillip when I'm not even sure that Faith cares about me as a person, let alone as a love interest? Her folded arms lifted again, this time in a shrug. "What's the point? He cares enough about the woman to marry her. Why should I raise doubts about his choice?"

She stood up straight, uncrossed her arms, and turned to gaze out across the lawn. With unconscious grace, she lifted her hands and ran her fingers up into her hair, pushing it straight up into a fountain that flowed back down around her shoulders as her fingers passed through. She dropped her arms to her sides just as the setting sun angled its rays beneath the porch roof. The golden light bathed her uplifted face in a warm glow. She turned slightly and raised an eyebrow when she heard Lindsay hiss.

"What a lovely picture you make. The sun brings out the golden depths in your eyes and highlights the copper strands in your hair." Lindsay's hand lifted, and her fingertips touched gently against Sarah's jaw line. "You really are quite beautiful, Sarah Coulter. Inside and out. That woman is a fool."

"Oh, Lindsay." A chuckle started low in Sarah's belly and bubbled to the surface. She threw her arms wide and gathered Lindsay into a hug. "I'm so happy you're my sister-in-law. You are so good for my ego."

Lindsay's arms tightened around Sarah, then she let go and stepped back. "Sarah." The look on her face warned of bad news that brought the lightness of the moment to a halt. "I have to tell you something Scott did, and you're not going to like it."

Sarah's exuberance deflated, and she resumed her pose against the porch rail. Her crossed arms lifted once again as she inhaled deeply and forced her breath back out. "What now?"

Faith was troubled but determined to keep it to herself as Phillip escorted her and Benjamin back to their hotel. Benjamin changed his clothes and took a sketchpad and pencils out onto the balcony, while Phillip settled next to Faith on a sofa in the living-room area.

"Would you like something to drink?" she said and made a face. "All I can offer you is water."

"I'd rather have a kiss." With a smile, Phillip put an arm behind Faith and drew her nearer. Benjamin was sitting just outside the door, so the kiss was short and chaste. "Mmm, you smell good," he murmured. "Is that roses?"

Faith's cheeks grew red as a memory of Bren Cordell saying almost the same words jumped into her thoughts. Funny that Phillip should say it now. Guiltily, she buried her head in his shoulder. "Yes, it's a fragrance in one of the soaps I use."

"You made a great impression on the Coulters." He kissed her hair. "Not that I expected anything less."

"You've talked so much about them, I felt I already knew them." Faith lifted her gaze to him. "And they were just as wonderful and friendly as you portrayed them. All except Sarah. She got along well with Benjamin, but she didn't seem to take to me."

"I noticed that. I hoped it would be different, but it didn't surprise me. Sarah's always been somewhat reserved around strangers. And since her injury, she's even more withdrawn."

"How was she injured? Are those burn scars?"

"Yes, and I don't know how she got them. I went away to war, and when I returned, she had the scars. She's never spoken of them to me, and one doesn't ask Sarah something she doesn't want to talk about. It's a waste of breath." A pained expression appeared on Phillip's face and receded. "But you'll get a better chance to know her now that you'll be staying with the family."

"Wasn't that terribly generous?" Faith's expression lit with pleasure. "I could hardly believe my ears when Scott offered to have Benjamin and me stay there until the wedding." She chuckled. "He obviously hadn't consulted Lindsay, but she took it in stride. Sarah, though, might be a different story." She changed in a flash from animated to pensive. "Maybe I shouldn't have accepted the invitation. I don't want to impose."

"Nonsense. It's only for four weeks, and I know Scott and Lindsay will love having you there. If Sarah gets out of sorts, the house is big enough that she can avoid you, or vice versa. Besides, Benjamin will have more fun there than cooped up in this hotel."

"Yes, that's true, on both counts. But I hope Sarah doesn't choose to avoid me. I'd like to have her for a friend. Especially since you're so close to her and Scott." Faith lifted Phillip's hand from where it rested at her waist. She turned it palm up and traced the calluses on it. A broad, solid, carpenter's hand, she thought, roughened by his home-building business. Again, she felt a guilty twinge as her mind was filled with a picture of a strong, long-fingered hand lying on a bed coverlet while its owner fought to live.

Faith couldn't deny Bren Cordell had made a lasting impression on her or that something inside her yearned to see Bren again. But what were the chances of that ever happening? And even if it did, what would result from it? One couldn't assume things that were never said. No, better to push such useless longings away and settle down with a good and stable man like Phillip. She and Phillip knew they weren't in love in the romantic sense, but they did love each other. He would make a dependable husband and an attentive father for Benjamin. She hadn't been in love with Nathan, either, but that hadn't been a bad marriage.

"Do you still think she'll agree to be my maid of honor? Without anyone I'd care to ask, I thought your suggestion of Sarah would be perfect. Now, I'm not too sure. Perhaps Lindsay would be a better choice?"

"Sarah will come around. Once you get to know her, you and she will be great friends, I'm sure. Besides, with the wedding being private, it's not like she has to appear before a crowd." Phillip pulled Faith to him and kissed her forehead. He released her and stood. "I better get home. I'd hoped for some extra time off to help you get settled, but with Theo away, I need to be available to our customers. It's back to work in the morning."

As he left, Phillip stopped at the balcony arch to tell Benjamin goodbye, and Faith met him at the door. "Scott said by the time I finish work tomorrow, he and Lindsay will have you moved in, so I'll see you there." They kissed once more, and Phillip left.

With her hand still resting on the knob of the closed door, Faith leaned her head against the door panel. *Why do I feel this way?* she wondered. I thought I had gotten over that silly infatuation. In fact, I know I had gotten over it. Until I saw Scott and it all came rushing back. Why does he have to look so much like Bren Cordell? Even Sarah has the same dark hair with copper highlights, the same amber eyes. But that's where the resemblance ends. Bren's low drawl was charming and attractive, and she had a warm dignity about her, not this cold rigidity of Sarah's. Sarah's voice is squeaky in comparison, and she sounds like a royal bitch. Or a spoiled brat. Maybe both. No danger of an attraction there. Maybe Bren is one of those distant Coulter cousins.

She let go of the doorknob and walked back to sit on the sofa. This is ridiculous. I never felt this strong a pull for a woman, or anyone else for that matter. Why do memories of Bren keep turning me inside out? Why do I keep imagining her arms around me, her lips on mine, and . . . even more? She rested her elbow on the stuffed arm of the sofa and put her chin in her hand. I'm going to marry Phillip in four weeks, and I need to focus on that. He deserves my loyalty, not a wife who gets puppy-eyed thinking of a woman she'll never see again.

Faith kept arguing with herself until she'd managed to bring her thoughts under better control. Then one sprung up and knocked her tail over tin cup once again. What if Bren Cordell walked through that door right now and promised herself to me? Would I still choose Phillip? Would I? She knew it couldn't happen. But what if it did? Realizing that she wasn't sure of her answer shook her to the core.

CHAPTER ELEVEN

Lindsay glanced at Scott and smiled. With his hands in the pockets of his brown serge pants, he leaned against the doorjamb of Jessica's bedroom, watching Lindsay dress their daughter for a morning walk with him. A lightweight tan jacket hung loosely over his green tunic.

Without his business suit, he looks about sixteen, she thought, her heart swelling with love. And although his face was broader and his jaw heavier, his slightly turned face looked even more like Sarah's, a resemblance that often struck her.

Sarah. Lindsay felt so frustrated by her sister-in-law's situation. She could readily understand the depth of Sarah's love for Faith, even though the two had known each other for such a short time. She herself had fallen in love with Scott about fifteen minutes after meeting him. Some might say that wasn't time enough to fall seriously in love, but it was time enough for her.

She had been visiting her cousin, Jane, when Scott stopped in to see Jane's brother, William. William introduced Lindsay to Prescott "Scott" Coulter, Jr., and the four young people went into the back yard for a game of croquet. That otherwise insignificant little moment precipitated a year-long courtship that fulfilled every wish a girl could dream.

Lindsay's mind shifted quickly to the present when Jessie slipped away from her and dashed toward Scott.

"Whoa there," Scott said with a laugh. He scooped Jessie high into the air and gave her a toss even higher, as the child squealed in delight. He kissed her cheek and set her back on the floor. "Let Mama finish dressing you, sweetheart, and we can go outside." He gave her a nudge toward Lindsay with a pat on her diapered behind.

"Ousside, Da-Da," Jessie said and toddled back to Lindsay.

"Scott, don't you think you throw her too high? She could get hurt. Or scared." Lindsay buttoned Jessie's calf-length blue dress and sat her on the edge of the low bed. She lifted one matching stocking from the bed, worked her hands back and forth to roll the top down, and slipped it over Jessie's toes.

"Nonsense. Jessie needs to get tough enough that Pres can't boss her around. Besides, she's a born daredevil." A whimsical smile touched his lips as he returned to his position against the doorjamb. "She has Sarah stamped all over her. How are you and I going to keep up with her?"

Lindsay laughed. "We'll just have to fumble our way through. I think Pres is the one who's already getting bossed around." Jessie pushed her mama's hands away and grabbed the top of the stocking, giving it a yank toward her knee. "And so are the rest of us," Lindsay muttered. She lifted the second stocking, went through the same motions, and got the same result.

"Speaking of Sarah . . ." Scott hesitated. "Have you any idea why she's been so miserable to Faith for the past two weeks? I can't for the life of me figure out what she's got against her." He shook his head in puzzlement. "Surely, it can't be jealousy. Sarah's had plenty of chances to marry Phillip."

Lindsay tried to slip a shoe onto Jessica's foot, but she had to take it off and loosen the laces before trying again. As she pushed the shoe all the way onto the wriggling foot, she noticed in amazement that Jessie had picked up the other shoe and was loosening its laces. Surely, she's just mimicking me, Lindsay thought. She turned her attention back to the shod foot and began at the bottom row of laces, pulling each row tight in succession and finally tying a double bow at the top.

Questions danced in her head as she stopped to consider Scott's question, leaving Jessie free to try to fit the second shoe over her stocking foot.

How much should I tell him? Lindsay wondered. Will he even understand Sarah's predicament, or will he turn against her for loving a woman? No, she told herself. He's a kind man, and he loves his sister. Surely, nothing she could do would come between them. Besides, better for him to know now than perhaps find out later and be upset that neither of us said anything to him.

She straightened up and turned toward her husband, giving him her full attention. "Scott, do you remember Sarah telling us that a woman saved her leg?"

"Of course I do." He frowned. "My sister being shot and almost losing her leg isn't something I'm likely to forget."

"Faith is the woman who saved her." Lindsay watched as raised eyebrows erased the ridges of Scott's frown.

"And Faith didn't recognize her? How could that be?" Lindsay just looked at him in silence, and his face relaxed as he answered his own questions. "Because Sarah looks so different. Even without the scars, she's different. Heavier, longer hair." Other possible explanations clicked into place. "And she has no beard and no drawl. Plus, she's obviously not a Rebel sympathizer, not to mention a Rebel soldier." Lindsay nodded as he ticked off each reason.

He looked at his wife and raised only one eyebrow, a habit he and his twin shared. "Why didn't Sarah tell Faith who she was? That first day at Jessie's birthday party would have been a perfect time."

"Think, dear," Lindsay said gently with a sad smile. "The woman who saved her life also betrayed her to the Union soldiers."

"My God, Sarah hates her! She hates the woman Phillip's going to marry." Scott rubbed a hand across the back of his neck. "I can't believe it. Faith doesn't strike me as the untrustworthy type."

"She probably isn't, under ordinary circumstances. People do strange things when they feel endangered, though. Union sympathizers could have made a lot of trouble for Faith for helping a Rebel soldier. And she had Benjamin to worry about, too."

Scott looked into the distance. Lindsay could tell when her husband was piecing his thoughts together like a wooden picture puzzle. His gaze returned, and he said, "I know the betrayal rocked the foundations of Sarah's trust in people. So, perhaps she doesn't want to hurt Phillip by telling him. He might not marry Faith if he knew."

For a moment, Lindsay glanced back toward Jessie and saw she had the shoe over her toes and was engrossed in her attempts to put it all the way on. She turned back toward Scott. "Yes, that's part of it, but it's more involved than that."

"More involved?"

Lindsay nodded. "Sarah stayed with Faith for three weeks. That doesn't sound like very long, but it was enough time for something else to happen to her."

"So stop tormenting me, and tell me what it was!"

She walked over and took one of his hands between hers, an action that caused him to look askance at her. "Sarah fell in love with the woman who saved her. She isn't jealous of Faith. She's jealous of Phillip." She watched Scott's expression go from irritation to perplexity to understanding—then to disbelief and denial.

"No." He tried to extricate his hand, but Lindsay held on. "I don't believe it. Not Sarah. Not my sister."

"And why not?" Lindsay knew Scott was aware that some people preferred to match up with their same gender, but like most people, he discreetly ignored it. She tugged his hand and led him to sit on the end of the bed where she sat between him and Jessie. Too engrossed to pay them much mind, the child had pulled most of the laces loose from her shoe and had her foot halfway in it. When Lindsay reached a hand to help, Jessie frowned and swung her foot farther away.

Shocked, Scott shook his head. "Falling in love with a woman? It's not natural."

Lindsay's glance swung back from Jessie to Scott. "You fell in love with a woman."

"That's different." Scott waved his free hand about in a gesture of frustration. "It's natural for a man to fall in love with a woman."

"Of course it's natural for you, because that's the way your feelings work. But can't you see that someone else's feelings might work differently? Sarah's love for Faith seems just as right to her as your love for me seems to you." Lindsay waited until Scott's eyes met hers. She tilted her head and smiled gently. "Do you remember when you fell in love with me?"

He stared at her for a moment, then gave her hand a quick squeeze. "It started at the croquet game. I had a suspicion right away that you were the girl I'd marry. Within the next few weeks, I was certain."

"Suppose at that point I had done something terrible, something so totally unexpected and crushing to you that marriage seemed impossible. Would you still have loved me?"

"I can't even imagine not loving you. If I couldn't marry you, I would have been in agony. I probably would have wanted to die."

"Well, that's where Sarah is now. Trapped by love for a woman who betrayed her."

"Love for a woman."

Seeing that he still struggled with that concept, Lindsay tried a different approach. "You've told me a million times you couldn't understand why she never accepted Phillip's proposals. Try to imagine yourself married to Phillip."

"That wouldn't happen in a million years." Scott glared at his wife.

A quick spurt of laughter burst from Lindsay. "That's been Sarah's reaction exactly, from his first proposal to his last. Marriage to a man seems just as unnatural to her as it does to you. And no matter what we say or do, we can't change the way she feels." She caressed the hand she held. "We need to accept it."

"Accept it?" Scott winced. Lindsay nodded, and they sat in silence for several moments. He lifted their joined hands and brushed a kiss on his wife's fingers. As he lowered their hands, Lindsay looked from them to his face and saw the corner of his mouth twist to the side. "Some things do make more sense now in light of what you've told me. Sarah never has displayed what most people think of as feminine ways. But this is going to take some getting used to. I'm not sure I can. I'm not sure I even want to."

Jessie said, "Shoe on!" and swung her foot toward her mother. Lindsay picked her up and sat her on her lap. The shoe, with half of its laces pulled out and hanging, was indeed completely on the proper foot.

"Good girl," she said, pointing a finger to draw Scott's attention to Jessie's triumph. She threaded the laces, pulled them snug, and tied the shoe, afterward giving her child a lingering hug and kiss. She loved snuggling against the baby's soft skin and inhaling her sweet scent. Scott nudged her arm, so she handed Jessie to him.

"Jessie, you are so smart." He hugged and kissed her before setting her on the floor. He and Lindsay both rose from the bed, and Jessie immediately raised her arms to Scott.

He reached down and lifted her into his embrace, and Jessie threw her arms around his neck. "Ousside. Ousside, Da-Da."

"That's where we're headed, sweetheart," he said, patting her back and smiling at her enthusiasm. "Children are amazing, aren't they?" He turned his smile toward Lindsay. "She was quiet all the time she was focused on putting on that shoe, but now that it's on, she's on a tear to get outside and play."

He started toward the door, but Lindsay stayed him by placing a hand on his arm. She cupped her hand on the crown of Jessie's head. "Sarah has given us the greatest gift she ever could. She's given us our daughter. The least we can give her in return is acceptance."

Scott's voice rasped through a tight throat. "I'm finding that almost impossible. I think Sarah's injuries have twisted her thinking. What about Faith? Does she feel the same way? Should we say something to Phillip?"

"I can't speak for Faith. Even Sarah doesn't know that answer, and I'm sure it's grieving her. I think we should keep silent. No matter what happens, someone we love will suffer, either Sarah or Phillip. Our only option is to stand by and try to help wherever we're needed."

Scott's words were hesitant. "Surely Sarah won't do anything to hurt Phillip."

"I doubt she would." Lindsay's mournful gaze matched her husband's. "Fate has a way of muddling lives, but Sarah's had more than her share of muddling. I'd love to see something good happen for her, for a change. That possibility, though, looks pretty dim."

"You've pointed out at least one good thing that has come from all her problems." Scott bent his head and nuzzled his daughter's stomach, causing a gurgle of giggling. "Jessie."

"Yes, Jessie." Lindsay patted the baby and Scott one last time, and as they left the room, her eyes teared. Sarah gave away her daughter with absolutely no understanding of what she was losing.

As far as Sarah knew, everyone else had gone out visiting after dinner. The day had been gray and gloomy, and although the sun had shown itself toward dusk, the evening seemed well suited to curling up in bed with a good book. She lit the wall-mounted gaslight above her bed and changed into her nightshift. After choosing a book from the ample supply on the nightstand, she climbed into the high bed to concentrate on the story. At least, she tried to concentrate. Even a good book couldn't pull her thoughts from the awkward situation with Faith. Seeing the woman so often was wrenching, and each day got harder instead of easier. For two weeks, she had avoided Faith whenever possible and had spoken only when common courtesy demanded it.

Two more weeks to go, she thought. Maid of honor? Thank goodness a quiet family wedding is planned. Mr. and Mrs. Phillip Showell. Another twinge shuddered through her, one of many she finally admitted came from jealousy. She set the book on the nightstand and chided herself for her stubborn heart. A strong cup of tea sounded like the perfect prescription for her restlessness. She rose, donned a pair of leather slippers, and headed for the back stairs.

Unlike the ornate winding stairway flanked by a carved balustrade in the front entry of the Coulter home, the back stairway was utilitarian. Straight and narrower overall, the stairs abutted the wall on one side, with their outer edge bordered by a plain oak banister with poker-straight balusters. Because no windows allowed light, the dark steps were constantly lit by gas fixtures at each landing. The flight from the second floor ended in a short hallway on the first floor. An entrance to the kitchen opened immediately to the left, while an outside doorway sat about eight feet to the right, just past a closet.

Sarah noted with relief that the kitchen's gaslight had been left burning. She could see its glimmer spreading into the hallway downstairs. Despite her weakened leg, she made quick time down the dimly lit steps, running from her thoughts as though being chased. As her foot reached the hallway floor, a figure bustled through the kitchen doorway. Their feet tangled, and Sarah fell, thudding against the hardwood floor. She cried out as a heavy wooden tray landed on her leg, its edge striking the site of her old wound. She saw bursting stars before her vision cleared. Faith knelt at her feet, hurrying to lift the tray and set it aside.

"Oh, my God, Sarah, I'm sorry." Her words poured forth in a nervous tumble. "I didn't see you. I was going to put the tray away in the closet. I had no idea you were coming down the stairs. I'm so sorry. Let me see your leg." She reached for the hem of Sarah's nightshift.

"No!" Sarah grabbed a baluster and dragged herself into a sitting position. "Don't touch me. You've done enough damage." She got her good leg under her and pulled herself to a seat on the third step.

"Don't be foolish." Faith moved forward on her knees to bring herself closer. "I'm a trained physician's assistant. Your leg could be broken." She again reached toward Sarah, who tried to shift her leg away. But this time, Faith took hold of a bare ankle. Sarah's attempt to move resulted in a short gasp that she quickly smothered, gritting her teeth.

Ignoring the movement and the sound, Faith lifted the hem of the nightshift and folded it back above Sarah's knee. "You have an old injury here. Judging from this red mark, the tray crashed right onto the scar tissue." Her hands moved along Sarah's leg. "This feels like a poorly mended break. Bothers you, too, I'll bet." She glanced up, but Sarah didn't answer.

Sarah couldn't answer. She had frozen in place as Faith's fingers felt along the scar and two soft hands wrapped around her leg, examining and testing it. But she hadn't frozen from irritation. Faith's touch on her bare skin made her heart thud louder in her ears than any drummer boy's cadence. Torn between the pain in her leg and the pain in her heart, she closed her eyes and said nothing.

"I can't see properly in this dim light," Faith muttered. "Nothing feels broken, but I want to get a clearer look at the point of impact." Holding Sarah's leg immobile, she shifted to allow the light coming from the kitchen to fall on the area she was examining. With her hands one above the other wrapped around the back of Sarah's calf, she bent a little closer to get a better look.

Sarah heard her gasp.

"Oh, my God." Faith gently put Sarah's leg down, sat back on her heels, and dropped her shaking hands into her lap. Sarah's eyes flew open, and the two sat staring at each other. Faith's lips moved, and then she spoke. "You're Bren Cordell. At first, I was struck with how familiar you and Scott both seemed. But you skirted my questions, and I began to think the idea preposterous. It's been a long time, and you look and sound very different from the Bren Cordell I remember. But you're Bren."

"Don't be ridiculous." Sarah struggled to sound haughty, but she was having such a hard time speaking that her voice was raspy. "Just because I have an old leg injury, you think I'm someone you knew?" She reached up to the banister and pulled herself erect.

Faith slowly stood, too. "No, that's not it. I know who you are because you have a heart-shaped mole right next to your old wound. I dreamed about that leg for months. I couldn't possibly forget it."

"All right. I'll not deny it. I'm Bren Cordell. So what?" Sarah's emotions plummeted from fever hot to ice cold in a matter of seconds, and she shivered.

"So what happened to you? I tried for months to find out where the soldiers had taken you. No one knew anything. You could have dropped off the face of the earth."

"In a manner of speaking, I did." Bitterness drenched Sarah's words. "What did you care?"

"I was worried about you."

Sarah limped forward two steps until she stood face-to-face with Faith. Her words slashed out like rapiers. "Maybe you should have thought of that before you betrayed me."

"Betrayed you?" Faith's eyes widened and clouded. "But I didn't—" A stinging slap snapped her head back, and a spot of blood showed on her bottom lip.

"Don't lie to me!" Sarah shook with fury. "The soldiers said it was you."

Faith raised her hands, palms-outward, as if to ward off another blow. "They made a mistake. I never told anyone. I swear it."

"You knew I was there, Benjamin knew, and the doctor knew." Faith flinched as Sarah reached up and grabbed several of her curls. "They said 'the redhead' told them. Which one of you three has red hair?" Sarah winced as she saw resignation come into Faith's face. In her heart, she had hoped she was wrong. This seeming acknowledgement was additional proof of Faith's treachery, and it enraged her.

She let go of the hair and stepped closer, crowding Faith toward the wall. "Do you know what you betrayed me into? Why you couldn't find out anything about me?" Faith took a step back and stopped, but Sarah kept coming. She bumped Faith against the wall with her body as her voice pitched lower and thickened. "Those bastards hauled me into the woods, stripped me naked, and tied me to the ground. Oh, and don't let me forget, their leader kicked my broken leg—the one with the heart-shaped mole—and it has never healed properly." She bumped Faith again, hard. "All three of them forced themselves on me. Forced themselves on me!" She saw Faith's face blanch with shock and tears well in her eyes.

Hoarse now, Sarah breathed hard as her voice hammered at Faith. "You see these scars?" She grabbed Faith's hand and rubbed the palm across the rippled skin on her face. Grimacing, she shoved it up to the depression in the side of her forehead where she had been struck by the bullet. "Feel them? They're also a legacy from you. When they finished with me, the bastards put a musket to my head and shot me. They left me for dead."

When Sarah released her grasp, Faith's hand still rested on her face. Tears ran freely down Faith's cheeks. "Oh, Sarah, I had no idea such terrible things had happened to you. I am so, so sorry. I wouldn't have hurt you for the world." Her hand caressed Sarah's ravaged face, her fingers gently touching the scars.

The chance to voice her torment to the woman responsible had some cathartic value to Sarah, purging some of her bitterness, but not all. She knew Faith hadn't intended for such evil to befall her. That part she could forgive. What she balked at forgiving was the act of betrayal, which robbed her of ever being able to trust Faith again. Eventually, the bitterness would dissolve, but that lack of trust would never disappear.

As her torrent of accusations came to a halt, Sarah suddenly became very conscious that her body was pushed up against Faith's. As though a dam had given way, a strong wave of desire flooded through her. Her knees weakened, and she put her hands on Faith's waist to keep from falling. In the light from the kitchen, she saw Faith's eyes darken and her lips part. Sarah couldn't keep her head from lowering toward such temptation, but she hesitated as a terrible truth shrieked through her mind. She's going to marry Phillip!

Once again, the other woman's response staggered her.

Faith's hand slid from Sarah's temple toward the back of her head. At the same time, Faith lifted her lower arm and encircled Sarah's neck. With a tug, she pulled herself up toward Sarah's descending lips. The movement burned through Sarah's thin nightshift like a tinder strike on dry twigs, setting both women afire.

Sarah wrapped her arms around Faith's waist and splayed her fingers across Faith's hips as their mouths met in a hard, demanding fusion of need. Sarah's arms jerked, slamming their hips together, and both women moaned. Sarah tasted the blood her blow had drawn from Faith's lip, and its presence was like a slap to her own face. She broke off the kiss and looked down at the woman she held in her arms, the woman she had dreamed about for so long with no real hope of ever holding her. The woman who was promised to Phillip. Promised to Phillip. Sarah closed her eyes. She couldn't fight the tears any longer. She let them come.

Faith loosened her arms and ran her fingers up the back of Sarah's head. When Sarah's eyes closed, Faith pulled her head down and kissed the tears from her cheeks. She very gently kissed Sarah's lips . . . again . . . and again, until Sarah responded, and they fell into a sweet, heart-clenching exploration. Emotions unleashed, Sarah couldn't fight any longer. She surrendered to the sensations tumbling through her. Finally, she and Faith ended the kiss and stood there for a while with their arms clasped around one another, each lost in her own thoughts.

Sounds of the front door opening and voices raised in happy chatter alerted them that the others had returned. Sarah took a shuddering breath and let her arms drop. As Faith released her hold, Sarah stepped back and said, "I have to go." She turned to start up the steps.

"We need to talk, Sarah," Faith said in a low voice.

Sarah only heard the word "talk," and she shook her head. "I have to go." She grasped the banister with both hands and pulled herself up the steps, limping heavily. She didn't even glance back.

"We'll talk tomorrow," Faith called in a loud whisper, her words sounding as much like a promise to herself as to Sarah. She watched, heartsick, as Sarah struggled up the stairs and disappeared. *But what can I say to her?* Faith wondered. *I love her like I've never loved anyone else. She's in my bones. But I'm promised to Phillip. Oh, Sarah, don't you see I despaired of ever finding you again? I could only see a lost and lonely life ahead. What's to become of us?*

Faith dried her cheeks and picked up the tray to put it away. Tomorrow would be filled with emotional upheaval, one way or another. She needed to meet with Sarah first thing in the morning and try to work out some answers.

The pain in Sarah's leg flared with every step up the long staircase and through the seemingly endless hallway to her bedroom. But her heart ached even more. How had this happened? Could she trust her own reactions? What about Faith's response? What did that mean? And where did Phillip fit into things? He was her friend—and he had always trusted her.

Even in her agony, she recognized the irony of the situation. *Faith betrayed me so readily in the past—would a promise to Phillip mean anything? The woman might be perfectly willing to abandon him and choose me in his place. Her actions said she wanted me.*

And I want her, more than I've ever wanted anyone or anything. But I'm still not sure whether it's love or just lust. How could I love someone who turned me over to the Union? Besides, when she did that, she dishonored the Confederate cause her husband had died for. Has she no principles?

These turbulent thoughts threatened to overwhelm her, and only Sarah's ingrained self-discipline kept her going. After dressing in drawers, shirt, trousers, and boots, she forced herself to concentrate on packing. She gathered her belongings and stuffed them into two saddlebags, which she slung over her shoulders. As she crept softly down the back stairs, the house seemed quiet. Undetected, she slipped out the door and limped toward the stable, every agonizing step a reminder of the woman who had ministered to her body. And stolen her heart. And betrayed her soul.

Get away. Get away. Get away. Drummer's hoofbeats drilled the words into Sarah's skull. As though sensing her urgency to put distance between herself and heartache, the horse lengthened his stride along the moonlit trail.

She struggled to push away thoughts of Faith, but memories of their meeting streaked through her mind like erratic flashes of lightning. She recalled the flood of desire engulfing her, mirroring itself in Faith's face; cool fingers claiming the back of her neck, immediately burning her skin; Faith's body lifting against hers, arousing excruciating passion.

Sarah's hands tightened on Drummer's reins as she remembered the fullness of strong hips against her palms . . . the burst of flame when they surged together . . . the feeling of completeness when they wrapped their arms around each other and Faith's body imprinted itself on hers. Her tongue moved along her lips as she summoned the taste and feel of their mouths meeting and melting, sending the intensity of her feelings into places she'd never known before, places she yearned to explore.

But couldn't. That realization slammed into her at every turn, darkening every image of Faith, every remembrance of their moments together. Sarah rode for hours with her emotions seesawing relentlessly. First, a rising surge of passion would grip her, seizing control of her mind. A life with Faith seemed possible—no, inevitable—something she couldn't live without. And she would want to turn back to claim her love.

Then reality would hit, shattering her hopes and dreams, banishing any possibility of ever being with the only person she had ever loved. Yes, loved, she finally admitted. Just physical desire couldn't hurt so badly. Faith was promised to Phillip, and Sarah knew she would never interfere with that betrothal. She would have to learn to live with it. But the thought of Faith in someone else's arms filled her with an anguish she knew she could manage only at a distance. So she had run away.

Finally tiring from his mad dash through the forest, Drummer slowed. Sarah dragged her thoughts back to the present. I have to pull myself together. The situation with Faith is impossible. Nothing I can do will change that. I need to concentrate on things I can change.

She knew these few hours were only a precursor of the endless agony yet to come. But she still had a purpose. Hunting down Hager. She concentrated her thoughts on Hager until her mind shifted to that focus. Yes, her most important task right now was to find her third attacker. But first, she would try to retrieve Redfire. Faith hadn't brought the horse with her, and Phillip apparently knew nothing about him. She feared Faith might have sold him. Only one way to find out. She directed Drummer toward Cranston.

CHAPTER TWELVE

Two days later, Sarah arrived in Cranston at midmorning and reined Drummer to a stop in front of the livery stable. After dismounting, she tied the horse to a hitching rail, gave him a pat on the shoulder, and entered the rough-hewn structure. The same stable keeper from her previous visit ambled toward her, tucking his tobacco chaw into his cheek in preparation for talking. What was the stable owner's name? Bullens, she recalled.

"Howdy," he said, squinting up at her as he approached. Sarah touched the brim of her slouch hat in greeting. "You been here before, ain't you?"

"Yes. You have a good memory." Of course, Sarah admitted, her scarred face and white blaze of hair might have given him a clue. "I bought a chestnut from you about eight months ago. Good animal."

"Yeah, I remember now. You look different, though. Younger." His face crinkled in thought, and he raised a finger and waggled it. "You had a beard." When Sarah nodded, he seemed pleased with his recollection. She smiled as he went through what was probably a habitual rite. He spat tobacco juice onto a patch of sawdust littering the dirt floor and wiped a stained sleeve across his chin to catch the dribbles. "What can I do for you?"

Sarah knew that Redfire wasn't in the stable. He would have whinnied when she entered. "I remember you had a sorrel stallion for hire, called Redfire. Is he still here?"

"Nah." Bullens leaned a shoulder against one of the stable posts. "Mizzus Pruitt had to sell him. Just about broke her heart. Her boy loved that horse."

193

Sarah's heartbeat picked up. "Do you know who she sold him to? I'm interested in buying him—" She stopped before saying "back."

"Save yourself some time and trouble, friend." Bullens shook his head. "She got a paper signed by Herman Drucker, the man she sold it to, promising he won't sell the horse to nobody but her."

Sarah quirked an eyebrow. "He bought the horse with the idea of selling it back to her?"

Bullens nodded, and his eyes gleamed.

"Well, now . . ." She recognized he had a tale he was anxious to tell. "That seems like a strange bargain."

Sure enough, words flowed from the stable keeper in an unbroken stream. "Yep, but you see, he did her a favor. She explained she couldn't afford the rental here any longer, and Drucker offered to keep the horse on his farm for free. She said it was only fair that she give him a bill of sale, but she wanted to buy the horse back when she could take care of it. He agreed, and I signed the paper as a witness." He beamed. "Just think. Me a witness! First time I ever heard of doing such a thing, but they both seemed satisfied."

Sarah's hopes plummeted. "Guess that's that. Thanks for the information." She touched her hat brim again and left. Damn, she thought as she mounted Drummer, there's one more frustration. Getting Redfire back seems as unlikely as getting Faith. Wish I'd never met the woman! But a twinge went through her heart, and she knew the wish was a lie.

Maybe Phillip can get Redfire back for me, after he and Faith are . . . Oh, God, I can't even say it, let alone think about it.

She walked Drummer farther up the street and stopped at the tavern where Leah worked. After dismounting and tying off Drummer's reins again, she turned into the alley next to the tavern and tapped on the door to Leah's rooms. She heard some movement inside, but no one answered the door. Leaning closer, she tapped again. "Leah? It's Sarah Coulter. Are you there?" She heard some rustling and waited. As she was just about to knock again, the door opened.

"Amy!" Sarah removed her hat and squatted down. "Do you remember me? Miss Sarah?"

The child nodded, but her face looked sad.

"Where's your mama?" Sarah stood up, wincing as the discomfort in her leg reminded her of the damage done in her collision with Faith.

Tears welled in the little girl's blue eyes. "Mama got hurt."

"Hurt!" Sarah's troubles flew out of her mind as this new worry displaced them. "What happened? Where is she?" Amy motioned with her fingers and turned away. Sarah entered, closed the door, and followed her to Leah's bedroom.

Amy went directly to her mother's bedside. When Sarah's gaze fell on Leah, she hurried the last few steps to her. A mass of bruises covered the woman's face, nearly obscuring her features. Spots of blood seeped from cuts on her lips, and a dark red line marked where more blood had trickled from her nose. The arm that lay outside the quilt cover was also purpling, though not so severely as her face.

"Leah, what happened?" Sarah guessed the answer. Prostitution was a risky business. Anger flared in her at the thought of some man beating on Leah. "Who did this to you?" She wanted to run right out and knock the bastard senseless, but Leah needed help first.

Leah barely opened her lips. "Sssmmm."

"Wait, I'll get you some water and get you cleaned up. Amy, bring me a washcloth and towel, please." Sarah went into the kitchen, grabbed a mug and a bowl from the cupboard, and took them to the sink. She worked the handle of the miniature pump several times until a stream of cool water gushed out. Pumping one more time, she filled the mug and bowl, and took them to the bedroom.

She set the dishes down on a bedside table and gently lifted Leah to a sitting position. While supporting her, she picked up the mug and tipped it so a little water dribbled past swollen lips. Each time Leah swallowed, Sarah tipped a bit more water until she heard the muffled but understandable word, "Thanks."

Sarah took the washcloth Amy handed her and dipped it into the bowl. "Amy, honey, why don't you go play? I'll take care of your mama." Amy went out, and Sarah gently wiped Leah's face and dried it. "Did this happen last night?"

Leah winced, but she was able to nod.

"Let me get some ice on it for you." Sarah laid her down and covered her. She returned to the kitchen, found a dish towel, and filled it with ice she chipped from the block in the icebox. Back in the bedroom, she laid the ice-filled towel over Leah's face and soon heard a groan, which she hoped indicated relief.

Sarah kept replacing the ice as it melted. Several times, she steeped some tea, heaped it with sugar, and spooned it into Leah's mouth. She forgot about lunch, but Amy remembered, and the two shared some bread and cheese. Sarah made some sandwiches and put them in the icebox, and she and Amy ate them later for supper. By evening, the swelling receded enough that Leah could open her eyes a crack, and she could mumble a few words.

Sarah squatted next to the bed. "Just tell me who did this, and I'll make sure the bastard never hits another woman."

"No, let it be." Leah struggled to get the words out.

"Never mind. Don't try to talk. You'll feel a lot better in the morning, and you can tell me all about it then."

Before the sun went down, Sarah lit a kerosene lamp in the bedroom and one in the sitting room to give Amy light to play by for a while after preparing for bed. Later, Sarah tucked the bedcover around Leah, put a fresh ice-filled towel over her face, and joined Amy.

"About ready for some sleep, darlin'?"

"Will Mama be all right?"

The child sounded so forlorn that Sarah leaned down and held out her arms. Amy left the picture she was drawing, ran into the offered embrace, and began crying. Sarah lifted her and walked to the stuffed chair in the corner. She sat and situated Amy on her lap, pulling the small body close.

"Your mama's going to be fine. She's just feeling very sore right now, and it's hard for her to talk." Sarah rubbed Amy's back slowly and rhythmically until the crying stopped. "Don't worry, honey, I'll take care of you and your mama until she feels better." Sarah wrapped her arms tighter around the little girl and leaned her head back against the soft chair. Neither one of them stirred for the rest of the night.

In the morning, Leah refused to tell Sarah the man's name. "Forget it, Sarah. These things happen."

"Not to my friends," Sarah said so coldly that Leah shivered.

Sarah again was squatted next to the bed, and Leah moved carefully to reach out and touch her. "It won't help if you beat on him. He'll just take his anger out another time, on another woman. You can't protect us all." She took a shallow breath. "Please don't do nothing. I need you here."

Sarah's voice was ragged. "All right."

"Promise?"

"I promise." Sarah placed her hand over Leah's. "And I promise to stay with you until you're well."

"You're the best friend I ever had." Tears filled Leah's eyes, and Sarah held her hand until she drifted off to sleep.

Sarah placed Leah's hand back under the bedcover and rose. "You're one of my best friends, too, Leah." She dashed away her own tears as she tiptoed out of the room.

"I don't want to hear one more word about the money. I have enough to help out." Sarah set a bag of food on the table in the kitchen. She cocked her head at Leah, who sat in a rocker between the table and the cylindrical coal stove. After three days of rest, Leah's swollen face was returning to near-normal size, but the bruising looked worse in its healing stages than it did shortly after it was inflicted. "Besides," Sarah continued, "I eat more than the two of you put together."

This earned her a snicker. "Just wait till my jaw stops hurting. I'll put you to shame."

Sarah surprised both of them by leaning down and kissing Leah's cheek. With a blush moving up her face, she quickly emptied the bag of food, put the bread into the breadbox and the fresh green beans and potatoes on the counter next to the sink. The eggs, cheese, and ham went into the icebox. She left the chocolate cookies on the table for a treat when Amy came home from school.

Leah spoke softly. "You know, it ain't . . . it isn't . . . a sin to care about people."

Sarah meticulously folded and creased the empty paper bag and put it in a drawer before flopping into a chair. "No," she said, and her lip curled, "it's only a sin if a woman falls in love with another woman."

"You saying you're in love with me?" Leah fluttered her eyelids and grinned as well as her sore mouth would permit.

Sarah returned a sad smile. "I wish it were you." Within seconds, her face darkened. "Instead of that no-good bitch who handed me over to those fucking animals." Leah blinked, and Sarah's face reddened again. "I apologize for using rough language in your home. I just get so angry—"

Leah waved a hand. "My home is your home, Sarah. It's not like I never heard those words before, just not from you." She hesitated for a moment, and her brows drew together. "Are you really sure you're in love? It's not just a passing fancy?"

"I've asked myself that question a hundred times. Maybe a thousand." She sighed, rubbed her hand across the back of her neck, and grinned wryly. "I wondered if maybe I fell for Faith because she was the first woman I ever had any desire for. So I've spent more than a year checking out every woman I came in contact with, asking myself why I loved Faith and not one of these other women. I even caught on that some were flirting with me, and I sat with a few for an evening or two, talking. But that didn't work. I couldn't imagine kissing one, let alone them kissing me." She took a deep breath. "But as soon as my lips touched Faith's . . ." Emotion forced Sarah's voice to a whisper. "I never wanted to stop."

Leah's eyes widened. "You kissed her?"

Sarah nodded and Leah waited, her expression begging for an explanation. At last, Sarah regained her voice and the whole story fell from her lips. She began with Faith's arrival as Phillip's fiancée and ended with the scene in the downstairs hallway and her subsequent flight. Tears of frustration filled her eyes as she finished.

Leah had to be aching in every part of her body, but she pushed up from the rocking chair and moved to sit at the table. She reached for one of Sarah's long hands and enclosed it in her own. "I know this is tearing your guts out, and I'm very, very sorry that things happened the way they did."

Sarah bent her head and plowed the fingers of her other hand through her hair. "What the hell can I do?" she muttered, not expecting an answer. Her head flew up with Leah's forceful response.

"Go back after her."

"Go back?" Sarah pulled her hand from Leah's, jumped to her feet, and strode to the door, still with a slight limp. Her fingers closed on the handle, and she stopped. Her shoulders slumped, and she leaned her head against the door's dark wood. "I can't do that."

"But why not?"

After a moment, Sarah returned to the table. She settled into the same chair and seemed to take great interest in a dark whorl in the grain of the tabletop. She rubbed it several times with her fingers. "I just can't force her to make a decision between me and Phillip. That's up to her."

"But you left." Leah lifted her hands. "You don't even know what decision she might have made."

"Why would she choose me?" Sarah scrunched lower in the chair and hugged her arms around her body. "Phillip's a loving, generous man, and handsome, too. He'll provide her with a decent home and be a good father for Benjamin. He has his own successful business. She'll be set for life." Her next words jabbed like prods to an open wound. "What can I offer her? A woman with a scarred face and a damaged body and soul? A life where people point at us and whisper behind our backs? At Benjamin, too?" She shook her head. "Faith would be a fool to choose me."

They sat silent for several minutes, Sarah's heavy breathing the only sound. At last, Leah stirred. "If you were Faith . . ." Sarah's dark head lifted, and she turned to listen. "Suppose you were Faith, and you were in love with Sarah Coulter. What would you do?"

Sarah puffed a snort, and her head went back down. "I'd marry Phillip, because I had promised myself to him."

The side of Leah's mouth curled up. "That shouldn't surprise me, I guess. You have too damn much integrity for your own good." She voiced another thought. "The question is, though, how much integrity does Faith have? Would she come with you instead of staying with Phillip?"

Another snort. "She betrayed me. It probably wouldn't bother her one bit to betray Phillip." Sarah sat forward and rested her elbows on the table. "But don't you see? I couldn't live with knowing she betrayed Phillip because of me." She grabbed fistfuls of her hair and pulled. "I don't think I could even live with her, knowing she had turned me in to those enemy soldiers. I'm so damned confused, I don't know what I want or who I want or where I want to be!" She dropped her hands and pounded her fists against the table. "I love her, but I hate her, too. I don't see any way out of this situation. I knew I couldn't stay around, so I ran away."

Leah gave her a sympathetic look and touched her forearm. Silence settled in the room, as soothing as cool air on a fevered brow.

After some time had passed, Leah interrupted the interlude. "Maybe you could go west. I've heard tell there's some places out there where no one cares who or what you are, just so you don't bother anyone." Her voice became wistful. "Some of us gals at the Brass Rail talk about retiring there and finding us a decent man who don't know or don't care how we lived."

"Are you saying there are places that don't mind if a female like me wears trousers, smokes, drinks, and spits on the floor?" Sarah slowly grinned, a sign she had won the hard-fought battle to chain down her roiled emotions.

"For all I know, you might smoke and drink." A giggle bubbled out of Leah. "But darned if I'll ever believe you'd spit on the floor."

Sarah chuckled. "I think you're right. I don't feel any need to foul my own area." She slapped a hand on the table, making Leah jump. "Leah! You and Amy come with me! Let's go west together. We can both start new lives."

For several seconds, Leah could only gape. Then her eyes lit up but just as quickly darkened. "Oh, how I wish we could. But I can't afford it." Her crestfallen look told Sarah volumes.

"Listen to me. I have money from Coulter Foundry. I've established a trust fund for Jessica, and most of my current income will go into that. But I had already saved more than enough to buy a home somewhere. Money won't be a problem for a while."

"But I can't take your money. It's not right when I haven't earned it. Not unless you want me to . . ."

Sarah frowned at Leah's odd expression, then her brow cleared and she laughed out loud. "No, no, no. I'm not looking for a bed partner, thank you." She laughed again at the look of relief on Leah's face. "But I would welcome someone who takes care of all the other wifely chores. You know, cooking, cleaning, washing, ironing, and so forth. I've never taken any interest in those tasks." She wrinkled her nose. "I'd rather be the one who provides the room and board. I've been able to sell some articles and illustrations for good prices, and I know I can make a living at it if I devote more time to it."

At the lack of response, she turned on her most charming smile. "Please, please, please. You'll be doing me a great favor. We can go by train and put Drummer in a boxcar. I'll hire you as my housekeeper, which will give you your own income. And we both can keep Amy abreast of her schooling until we get settled. Let's go west together. Maybe Kansas or Missouri."

Leah covered her face with her hands, and her shoulders shook.

When it dawned on Sarah that her friend was crying, she put an arm around her shoulders and squeezed. "Is that a yes?" she teased, and Leah nodded.

Sarah kissed the side of Leah's head, jumped up, and threw both arms in the air. "Wonderful!" The sadness and frustration of the earlier part of the day made this victory all the sweeter. But she quickly sobered, and her next words dropped between them, as flat and ominous as a black cloud. "First, we have to stop at Cleveland and look again for Hager."

Sarah secured a room for herself and one for Leah and Amy at the Riverside Hotel, separated from the Wayfarer's Tavern by a narrow alley between the buildings. On her first visit to Cleveland, she had learned that the tavern was Hager's chosen drinking place, though she had been unable to find him there at the time.

This morning was the third day she had watched and waited for the ex-soldier. Sitting at a table in the corner of the saloon, she sipped occasionally from a mug of beer. Dressed in men's garb, she went unnoticed by the other customers. Shortly after noon, she almost dropped the mug when Hager walked through the door, took a searching look around the room, and strode to the bar, nodding at the greetings called to him by the two men he joined. The barroom was dim, but there was no mistaking him. No longer a boy, he had grown into his full height of well over six feet. She watched as one of the men he spoke with left, but the other stayed and bought him a beer.

When Hager had first entered the tavern, Sarah's breath had stopped as his glance fell on her, but his gaze continued past her and she could breathe again. Of course, he wouldn't recognize the scarred veteran seated at a corner table. As far as he knew, she was dead. But just the sight of him jolted her. Vivid memories of the last time she had been in his presence leaped to mind, and the rage that had been born then surged within her. Grabbing the edge of the table, she struggled to stop the shaking of her hands.

She fought hard for control. She wanted to jump right in his face and confront him. But that would destroy any chance she had of making him pay for his sins against her. Secrecy had enabled her to avoid arrest or prosecution for her retribution against Angston, and she planned to keep her actions quiet this time, too. Cautioning herself to remain patient, she stayed rooted to her chair while he had two mugs of beer with his friend.

Finally, he left.

Sarah stood and sauntered out the door behind him. He had paused at the edge of the boardwalk, next to the narrow street that ran between the tavern and the hotel. As the tavern door swung shut behind Sarah, he stepped down and turned into the alley. She followed right behind him and glanced about to make sure no one else was in the vicinity. As she approached him, she drew her Remington. Without a horse to hide him on, as she had done with Angston, she couldn't just knock him out in broad daylight. She'd have to hold the pistol on him and march him away from this built-up area.

"Stop!" she said, pitching her voice lower. "I have a gun. Put your hands up and turn around." Hager halted, put his hands shoulder high, and did as ordered. Face-to-face with blue eyes that looked just like Jessica's, Sarah battled to keep her resolve strong.

201

Hager blinked and spoke quietly. "I'm terrible sorry for what we done to you. I been sorry every day since it happened. You got a right to shoot me. Go ahead."

A whisper of warning hissed through Sarah's mind. *He knows who I am. He's not even surprised I'm alive. Something's wrong.* Her intuition proved correct when she heard a harsh voice behind her.

"Yeah, go ahead and shoot the piece of shit. I can take care of you by myself now that he's helped me find you." Sergeant Angston's words froze Sarah for a moment, and she cursed herself for being trapped so easily.

Slowly, she slipped her Remington back into its holster, raised her hands, and turned toward Angston. He was wearing his uniform, and his scarred face and slash of white hair gave her some grim satisfaction. But she was an idiot for untying the scum instead of leaving him for the wild animals to feast on. Her voice so steeped with hate that it sounded warped, she said, "I should have killed you when I had the chance."

Angston brayed an ugly laugh and rubbed his hand across his scars. "You know how many times I said the same about you?" He lifted his chin toward Hager. "This mealy-mouthed worm let you live. It's only fitting he should be the bait for finding you."

It can't end like this. I have to keep him talking. Maybe he'll make a mistake, and I can get out of this mess. Her throat had tightened up, and she had to force the words through. "And how did you manage that?"

"Hmph," Angston grunted. "Took him a long time, but he finally wrote to headquarters to get a copy of his discharge papers. When I found out where he was in Kentucky, I went after him. Showed him what you done to me." His expression turned sly. "I told him we needed to capture you and turn you in, before you did the same to him." He tapped the scarred side of his forehead. "Or killed him. I figured you'd be looking for him here. His hometown's on record. So we came back here to visit his folks. It was just a matter of time."

"We been watching for you." Hager's voice sounded behind her. "We seen you go into the hotel yesterday and into the tavern today. So I went in and let you get a look at me. When I left, we waited for you to make your move."

As he talked, Sarah took a cautious step sideways, keeping her hands raised. She half turned so she could see both men. She paid most attention to Angston, the more dangerous one, though Hager had also drawn a revolver.

Hager switched his gaze from Sarah to Angston. His voice sounded shaky, and even his gun hand wavered. "Let's take her to the sheriff and get this over with."

"Not so fast," Angston answered. He licked his lips and leered at Sarah. "I had a good ride the last time we took this bitch. I'm hankering to give her another try."

"No!" The word exploded from Hager's lips. "We shouldn't a hurt her last time, and we sure ain't going to do it again." His hand, still unsteady, pointed his pistol toward Angston.

"You no-good coward." Angston's Colt swung toward Hager and fire blasted from its barrel a fraction of a second before Hager fired at him.

When Angston's pistol swerved away from her, Sarah dove to the side. She pulled her Remington, thumbed the hammer, and fired at Angston. The shot caught him directly in the chest, toppling him like a felled tree. Pain stabbed through her leg as she twisted in the dirt and swung back toward Hager. He lay sprawled on his back, unmoving, his gun in the dirt beside him.

Sarah managed to stand and cautiously step over to Angston. She pushed him with her booted toe, but he didn't react. A swift kick shoved his pistol away from his limp hand, and she holstered her Remington.

She went to Hager and knelt at his side. People were making tentative steps into the alley, drawn by the gunfire. Hager's eyes fluttered, and pain twisted his features. Sarah sat down, reached an arm beneath his shoulders, and pulled his head onto her lap. Someone's hand clasped her shoulder, but she ignored its owner.

The blood rushing from Hager's stomach told her no one could help him. He was dying. He wrapped his fingers in her shirtsleeve and pulled, so she leaned closer. "Forgive me," he whispered in halting words. "I was too weak to stand up to him."

Sarah remembered that Hager had been reluctant and Angston had threatened to kill him. Hager must have been the one who untied her and draped her tunic over her body. She looked into his familiar blue eyes—duplicates of Jessie's—and the slabs of rage enclosing her heart crumbled. She no longer hated this young man. She almost felt sorry for him. He had fathered a child he would never see. She bent close until her lips were next to his ear, and she whispered to him, "You have a beautiful daughter."

His eyes widened. He blinked several times, and his anguished expression softened. "I'm honored, ma'am," he said quite clearly. Then he closed his eyes and died.

The hand on her shoulder tightened, and Sarah gazed up into Leah's worried eyes. "Are you all right?" Leah asked. When Sarah nodded, Leah sighed. "I heard shots and looked out the window. I near fainted when I seen you lying on the ground. Thank God, you moved right away." Sarah reached up and covered Leah's hand. Leah craned her neck to get a better look at Hager. "He wasn't bad looking."

Several bystanders moved Hager from Sarah's lap, and she stood up. "No, and not really bad at heart either. A different kind of casualty of the war." She looked toward Angston, but the spot was empty. She tensed as her heart chilled. Her hand dropped to her gun.

"It's all right." Leah stopped her arm. "Angston's dead. Some folks carried his body away. You can rest easy now." She cocked her head. "If you think about it, he did you a favor."

"A favor? How do you figure that?"

As the sheriff came their way, Leah stepped a little closer and lowered her voice. "He kept you from killing your baby's father."

Sarah's head jerked back and her lips tightened into a firm line. She nodded. "You're right. I put one over on the bastard again. I hope he sees that from hell." They waited in silence for the law officer to reach them.

After Sheriff Ziegler introduced himself, he wrote Sarah's "Bren Cordell" name and her West Virginia address in his notebook and stuck it in his shirt pocket. "Can you tell me what happened here?"

"Sure can." Sarah looked up and saw Amy with her face plastered to their hotel room window on the second floor. She nudged Leah in the side, pointed up, and waved. "Amy's watching. Maybe you should get back there and tell her everything's all right." Leah waved, too, and hurried off to join her daughter.

Sarah turned back to the sheriff and pointed to where Angston had been. "The soldier who was lying there pulled a gun on me and Mr. Hager. Hager and I pulled ours, too, and everyone fired. The soldier killed Hager, and I killed the soldier."

"Any idea what caused it?"

"Seems he and Hager had some kind of falling-out. I just happened to be here at the wrong time."

"I knew Hager. He got married recently, and his wife's with child." Ziegler frowned. "It's going to be hard to tell her about this."

"That's too bad." Sarah did feel a twinge of pity for the woman.

The sheriff stared at Sarah, searching her face. "That soldier had scars on his face just like yours." He tipped his chin toward her. "And a blaze of white hair."

"I got shot in the war. I guess he did, too. And a lot more soldiers besides."

Ziegler looked thoughtful. He took off his round, black hat and wiped the sweatband with a forefinger. "Was there any connection between you two?"

"None to speak of."

He nodded and replaced the hat. "I guess that's all for now." He tapped his thumb against the notebook sticking from his shirt pocket. "If I need you, I'll contact you." He walked away from Sarah, and she headed toward the hotel.

Any connection between the two of us? she thought. Never again. I'm free of that son of a bitch forever. Free of them all. She rolled her shoulders to relieve her stress. A thought that she didn't want to acknowledge popped up, and though she struggled to resist it, the words seared themselves in deep red letters on her brain. There will always be a connection between Hager and me.

CHAPTER THIRTEEN

After Sarah had escorted Leah and Amy by train as far as Pilot Knob, Missouri, they disembarked and Sarah purchased a horse and wagon. They piled it with Leah's belongings, tied Drummer to the back, and made their way to the first town that caught their fancy. Bonneforte, Missouri, was several miles from Cape Girardeau, a bustling city on the western banks of the Mississippi River. The trio settled in an imposing six-bedroom residence situated on thirty acres of land just beyond Bonneforte. Unable to buy the property because she was a single female, Sarah purchased it through her Coulter Foundry account.

The home suited both women. Not quite too big for Leah to take care of, it afforded the ample space to spread out that Sarah desired. One huge, glassed-in room, located in a separate wing on the southern end of the house, had swayed her into buying. Light and airy, it served perfectly for her writing and drawing studio. Although connected to the main part of the house, the studio wing had its own staircase to Sarah's upstairs bedroom. The kitchen won Leah over. It offered the newest range and icebox, and she announced that she had never had a kitchen that contained so many cupboards.

All the rooms were large. The women had converted the only downstairs bedroom to a combination library and household-business office they shared. Leah's and Amy's bedrooms were upstairs in the central part of the house. Amy was fascinated with hers, which she proclaimed was bigger than all the rooms of their old place put together.

A second wing, with a single, long room downstairs and two more bedrooms above, went off the northern side of the house. That remained closed, since they had no need for the extra space.

In the main house, an entry foyer had its own closet plus doors that opened onto the drawing room and the halls to the two wings. A straight staircase led to the upper floor. The women agreed that a dining room, which sat next to the kitchen, could be used for Amy to play and do her homework in as they didn't expect to use it for quite a while, if ever, for dining. They furnished it with a table, four chairs, a credenza, and a couch. In spite of Leah's objections, Sarah had already begun to fill it with toys and books.

A long, roofed porch with two sets of wicker tables and chairs ran across the width of the main house and spanned the front of each wing. The house sat almost exactly in the middle of one acre of cleared ground, and a neat lawn dotted with trees surrounded it and distanced it from the dirt road that ran in front of the property. Most of the other thirty acres was wooded, and after a quarter mile of flat ground, the forest lifted slowly toward the Ozark Plateau.

"Enjoying the view?" Sarah had finished working for the day, and she sat down next to Leah at one of the porch tables. Amy was playing with her dolls at the table farther down the porch.

Leah glanced sideways at her friend and smiled. "Isn't it unbelievable? I didn't know the outdoors could be so beautiful." She pointed. "Look, you can see an eagle flying over there."

Sarah smiled at the childlike wonder in her voice. "I'm so happy you came with me and got a chance to see all this."

"I'm the one who's happy. Thanks to you, Amy has a chance at a real life, and with you teaching me how to speak and act like a lady, so do I. I'll never be able to repay you."

"You repay me just by being here. You've helped me get through some mighty rough times, when a lot of so-called ladies would have turned their noses up at me." A grin lifted the corners of Sarah's lips. "Besides, I haven't had to do a lick of housework in the three months we've been here. You're taking wonderful care of the place, and that suits me just fine." She rubbed her stomach. "You're even a great cook."

Leah sparkled at the compliment. "Thank you, Sarah. I really appreciate it." She shook her head. "Not that you eat much. You don't relax enough to give your appetite a chance. I'd hoped with those men dead you'd stop driving yourself. But no, now you pour that energy into working too hard. Why can't you take it easy?"

Sarah stared down at her hands, studying them intently. She kept looking at them as she answered. "You know, on the surface of things, I should be satisfied with my life right now. I have a good friend, a beautiful home, and work that I thoroughly enjoy. And I *am* happy about all that." She took a deep breath and let it out. It was almost a sigh.

"But?" Leah's question furrowed Sarah's brow.

"But I'm not satisfied." Sarah jerked to her feet and strode to the porch rail. Wrapping her arm around a post supporting the roof, she leaned against it and stared out over the grounds. Because of the bend in the river, the house had a full view of the hills from the front porch and the side. Every sight of the breathtaking vista pulled at Sarah's artistic soul, but the yearning she felt overshadowed that.

She grimaced. "You know, for years, I never cared a whit about love and its entanglements. I scoffed at women who did. Any hint of sexual desire was foreign territory to me. Then . . ."

"You met Faith."

"I met Faith." Sarah could feel the muscles of her face tightening, trying to squeeze away the pain she felt at every mention of the woman's name.

"You need to find out whether she married Phillip. You won't be happy until you do."

Sarah hit the roof post with her fist. "And just how will knowing that she married Phillip make me happy?"

"You're not sure she married him. But even if she did, you wouldn't be any worse off than you are now. And if she didn't, she doesn't even know how to contact you. Just think, she could be pining after you the same as you are after her."

A bitter bark of a laugh erupted from Sarah. "And maybe she's never given me a second thought. I'm probably daydreaming like a lovesick fool. Why would such a vital, beautiful woman want a broken-down soldier like me, scarred and ugly?"

"Sarah-Bren Coulter, I'm ashamed of you!" Leah got up and went to the railing. Sarah jumped when Leah punched her on the arm. "You act more like a yellow belly than a bluebelly. Your scars don't make you ugly. You're a handsome woman, and if I liked women, I'd be after you like a bear after honey." She raised her voice and spoke so firmly, even Amy turned to look. "So don't be using that as an excuse. Stop hanging out here feeling sorry for yourself. Go take charge of your life."

Sarah's mouth hung open for a moment before she could get her thoughts together. "So what made you so smart all of a sudden?"

"You did." Leah poked Sarah's shoulder. "You made me decide to take charge of my life. Do you think I wasn't scared to leave everything I knew and come out here? You gave me the courage to do that, and it's turned out better than I ever dreamed. Now it's up to you to practice what you preach." She reached for Sarah's arm and gave it a shake. "Go home, Sarah. Go home and find some answers. You won't stand a chance at happiness until you do."

Sarah stared deeply into Leah's eyes. She knew her friend spoke the truth. These past few months she had tried to deny her feelings. She had even tried to pretend she had never met Faith, never fallen in love with her, never knew Faith had promised to marry Phillip. When that didn't work, she reminded herself that Faith had betrayed her. But nothing had satisfied her. She was miserable. She hated going to bed alone and waking alone. Her dreams were full of Faith. Her body ached for her touch, while her mind taunted that Phillip was taking her place.

"You're right, I'm tearing myself apart." She rubbed the back of her neck and made a face. "I'll go."

At Sarah's words, Leah clapped her hands in joy. She grabbed Sarah and squeezed her tight. "I knew you had the guts to do it. At least you'll find some answers."

Sarah returned the hug even as she shivered. What if the answers made things worse?

Sarah had telegraphed ahead, and when she arrived at the Coulter residence in dress and bonnet, Lindsay threw her arms around her.

"How wonderful that you've come, Sarah. We were so happy to hear from you." She stepped back while young Prescott and Jessica hugged her, too. "All right, children, you can talk with Aunt Sarah later. Pres, please take Jessie back into the study and finish your schoolwork." After a few moans from Pres and some shooing by Lindsay, the children departed.

"Lindsay, let me freshen up and change into a clean dress, and I'll join you in the kitchen."

"I'll put the teapot on. Then I want to hear all your news."

When Sarah came back downstairs, Lindsay poured tea and sat near her at the table. "I'm so glad to see you, but I can hardly believe my eyes. When last you were here, your leaving was so unexpected and unannounced we didn't know what to make of it. And we haven't heard a word from you since. We didn't even know where you were until your telegram arrived."

Sarah was a little surprised that Lindsay had jumped right into this discussion. "Surely you had some suspicions? I told you how I felt about Faith. Did you really think I could stay and watch her marry Phillip? The very idea distressed me."

Lindsay stirred the sugar she had just added to her teacup. "But you acted as though you had decided to accept it."

"That was before she kissed me." Sarah's fingers drummed the table.

"What?" Lindsay gasped. She stopped stirring her tea, and her gaze leaped to Sarah's. "She kissed you? When? You never told me that."

"She kissed me that night, while you all were out visiting. That's why I left. It's a long story. But when I realized she cared about me, too, I just couldn't stay." Sarah's eyes filled with tears, and she looked away, blinking to stem their flow. "I couldn't watch her marry Phillip. Even now, thinking about them together tears me apart."

Lindsay's eyes widened. "That's right. You don't know. But, of course, how could you?"

"Don't know what?" Sarah's heart skipped a beat as her fingers stopped drumming and clenched into fists.

Lindsay put her hands over Sarah's fists, and her voice softened. "They didn't get married. They said it was by mutual agreement. But now I suspect Faith backed out and they just wanted to hide the truth. What man would want to admit he was jilted because of another woman?" Lindsay released Sarah's fists and put her hands up to her own cheeks. "My goodness. What a mess this is."

"Where is she?" Sarah blurted the words like a starving woman begging for food. "Where is Faith?"

Lindsay frowned in thought. "She lives in or near town somewhere. I heard she has a temporary teaching position at the school." She picked up her almost forgotten tea and took a sip.

Sarah's thoughts were running wild. Then one struck her and slowed her down considerably. "How is Phillip doing?"

"After hearing your tale, I would think not as well as he pretends." Lindsay touched Sarah's hand again. "I'm guessing he probably told Scott most of the story. I know Scott's made some disparaging remarks about your stealing away in the middle of the night and leaving everything in an uproar."

Sarah bristled. "Don't let them lay this at my doorstep. I didn't do any speaking for Faith, and I'm not responsible for her actions."

"I know that, but I think the men have circled their wagons, and you and Faith are the Indian attackers." Lindsay smiled wanly. "Maybe you should talk to Phillip."

"Yes," Sarah said without enthusiasm, "I know I have to. Poor Phillip. He needs to get better at picking the women he falls for."

"Maybe you should pick a woman for him."

Sarah's lips tightened for a second, but the corners tipped up anyway. "That's not funny, Lindsay."

"I know." Although Lindsay tried to look contrite, she couldn't repress her giggle. "You have to admit, it's rather bizarre. Phillip falls for two women who love women, and those two women just happen to love each other."

A sigh escaped Sarah. "A kiss doesn't promise a lifetime commitment, and that's what I'm looking for. I don't know whether Faith feels the same or not. And I won't find out until I catch up with her." *And she asks my forgiveness*, Sarah added silently.

Uncannily, Lindsay seemed to tune into that feeling. "The last I heard, you weren't able to forgive Faith for betraying you to the Union soldiers. Has that changed?"

Sarah raised one fist, tapped her knuckles against her forehead, then opened her fingers and ran them along the slight depression in the bone. Her fingertips traced the scars that wove a wrinkled path from her forehead nearly to her earlobe.

"I honestly don't know. Do I love her enough to forgive and forget?" Her fingers moved to the back of her neck and stopped there. "I hope my meeting with her will solidify our feelings, one way or another."

"Let me get this straight." Lindsay leaned back in her chair and folded her arms across her breasts. "If you come face-to-face with Faith and suddenly realize you still can't forgive her, what will you do? Run away again?"

Sarah's hand moved from her neck to grab a hank of her own hair and yank on it, pulling her head down with it. Her voice was low and full of pain. "Maybe."

"Let's look at the bright side." Lindsay's voice became lighter. She leaned forward, uncrossed her arms, and patted Sarah's shoulder. "What if she falls into your embrace and promises undying love?"

Sarah's head lifted slowly. "Somehow, I can't believe it will be that easy. This relationship—if you can even call it a relationship—has been on a rocky road from the very beginning." She struggled to force a wry grin from the depths of her pain. "Faith did save my life. I've heard that means she's responsible for me."

Lindsay's tinkling laugh lightened Sarah's somber mood a little. "Good luck on convincing her of that."

"Thanks. I'm sure I'll need it." Sarah pushed her untouched tea away. "But I'll talk to Phillip, first. He deserves at least that consideration from me."

Scott must have told Phillip that Sarah was coming home. His hug was subdued, and he didn't seem surprised to see her.

"Welcome, Sarah. Let me take your coat and bonnet." He hung the clothing in the foyer closet. "Come, sit with me in the drawing room." As he escorted her there, he said, "Would you care for a sherry? Something stronger? Or tea?"

"No, thank you. I've just had tea with Lindsay." For the first time in her life, Sarah felt uncomfortable around Phillip, and she supposed he felt the same, though he seemed surprisingly calm. "You're looking very well, Phillip."

He motioned her to a stuffed chair and sat on one across from her. "I'd like to say you're looking well, too, but I'd be lying. How have you been?"

Sarah decided to get right to essentials. She never had been one for social talk, and Phillip was aware of that. "You knew I was still looking for the scum who shot me?" She touched her forehead, and Phillip nodded. "I found out one was killed in the war, but I finally caught up to the other two."

"And?"

"They're dead."

Phillip sucked in a breath. "You killed them?"

"The sergeant killed the private, and I killed the sergeant." Phillip grimaced, and she quickly said, "It was fair, Phillip. He was aiming at me when I fired."

"So your search for vengeance is over. Do you feel better for it?"

"We've had this discussion before, and I know you'd like me to say no. But they deserved punishment. They meant to kill me, and the law would never get them. If it hadn't been for me, they would have gotten away with their crime." Sarah wouldn't admit it to Phillip, but her vengeance had added another burden to the weight of guilt she carried from the war. So many dead at her hand. She shook her head, determined not to think of that right now. She had other problems more pressing.

"I never have understood your way of thinking, Sarah."

"I know, yet you've always cared about me." Sarah glanced down, and when she looked back up, it pained her to meet Phillip's eyes. "I'm so very, very sorry that Faith and I hurt you. I never meant that to happen."

Phillip tensed. "I wondered if you'd have the nerve to bring that up. But then, you've seldom lacked nerve." His voice turned harsh. "I suppose you two had a good laugh at my expense."

Sarah's jaw dropped. "My God, Phillip. How could you think that of me? I've been in agony over the whole mess. Why on earth do you think I left? You're a dear friend and the sincerest man I know. I would never laugh at you." She ran a shaking hand back through her loose hair, which hung past her shoulders.

Leaning forward, she spoke with increasing intensity. "Please let me explain what happened. Faith truly saved my life when I was wounded in the leg. She let me stay at her home to recuperate, and I fell in love with her." She winced at the look on Phillip's face. "I know you don't understand or approve of that, but a fact is a fact. I hadn't planned to fall in love with a woman. It just happened. I was as astonished as anyone could be. At the time, I had no idea she felt the same. When the Union soldiers marched into Cranston, she betrayed me to them. And I hated her for that. I loved her, but I hated her. It was all very confusing."

Phillip's facial expression was neutral, but his eyes looked interested.

"It wasn't until you brought her here, and she finally recognized me, that we discovered we were attracted to each other. I respected that she was engaged to you, and I left. We haven't seen each other since." Sarah put her hand over her heart. "I swear to you—on our years of friendship—I didn't know the marriage had been called off. When I came home today, Lindsay told me. Please forgive me, Phillip. Forgive us both. Neither of us could have foreseen what happened."

Phillip pushed his hands down against the brown upholstered chair arms and resettled himself. "I think I need more time. I believe you, and I want to be big enough to forgive you, but the wound is too raw right now." Sarah heard his teeth grind together as a lost look passed across his face. "When Faith told me she was in love with you, I was hurt, yes, but I was also embarrassed." He lifted a hand and waved it around while he searched for words. "The idea of a woman being in love with another woman seemed—seems—so unnatural to me, I know I'll have trouble getting used to it. I'm not sure I ever can."

Sarah nodded. At least he wasn't trying to condemn her and Faith. "I'm not able to apologize for that. What seems unnatural to you seems perfectly natural to me. Maybe it will help if you can just think of us as two women friends who aren't interested in men as marriage partners." She blew out a quick breath. "Heh. Listen to me. I don't know whether Faith and I have any future together or not. But I mean to find out. Lindsay said she stayed in town. Do you know where she lives?"

"Yes, I have her address. Let me get it for you." Phillip looked grateful for the excuse to move. He rose and went to his writing desk, which sat in a corner of the drawing room. On top of the desk, a matching cabinet had glass doors decorated with ornate filigrees of carved wood. After opening one door and pulling out a leather-bound address book from the top shelf, he leafed through to find the proper page. He dipped a quill pen into an inkpot, wrote the address on a piece of paper, and blotted it. Then he returned the book to its shelf and took the address to Sarah. "She's on the other side of town," he said as he handed her the paper.

"Are you two still speaking?" Sarah held her breath for the answer, not really understanding why.

Phillip gave one nod. "We're civil to each other. Faith's explanation was very much like yours. She said she needed to be honest with me about her feelings for you. She offered to marry me anyway." His smile was sad and rueful at the same time. "But I couldn't hold her to that. We knew when we agreed to marry that we weren't in love with each other. We were both lonely, she was struggling to keep a home, and she felt Benjamin would be better off." The ruefulness cleared from his smile, leaving just a little sadness. "I'm going to miss being Benjamin's stepfather. He's a great boy."

"He is," Sarah agreed. Though she wondered how he'd like her being the object of his mother's love. The possibility that he might not like it at all bothered her immensely.

215

She was amazed that another friend seemed to read her mind when Phillip said, "This situation between you and his mother might be difficult for him to accept."

Sarah's heart ached as she sighed. "Don't you think I've told myself that a thousand times? You see how long it took me to come back here." She slowly pounded her fist into her palm. "But I can't help loving Faith, and I can't ignore my feelings any longer. If she feels the same, we'll face that problem together and hope for the best."

Phillip sat back down. "Just between you and me, I've suffered quite a bit over this whole predicament, but the irony of it is almost comical. I've loved you and proposed to you for years, but you were never in love with me. You never even pretended to be. I finally met another woman I became very fond of, and when I proposed to her, she accepted. But lo and behold, not only have I cared for two women who love each other, but also I bring them back together again." He shook his head. "Is there something wrong with me?"

Sarah's head tilted as she surveyed him, and one brow lifted. "You just need to get me out of your system. And if finding out that I love a woman doesn't do that, then by God, you do have something wrong with you."

Phillip grinned. Not a full-force Phillip grin, but getting closer. "Ah, Sarah, you've always been an irreverent—"

"Bitch," she supplied, and they both had a small laugh. "On that true note, I'll leave." She stood and walked toward the door, and Phillip collected her coat and bonnet. As he held the coat and Sarah put it on, she said, "I'm glad we had this talk. Thank you for being so understanding." She turned to face him as she donned her bonnet and tied it beneath her chin. His face looked sad.

"I'm really not as understanding as I seem, but I'll work on it."

"That's all I ask." Sarah stood on her tiptoes and kissed him on the cheek.

Phillip hugged and released her. "You might find Scott a harder nut to crack. He was really upset about your leaving without any explanation. In spite of anything I say, he insists on blaming you for the marriage being cancelled."

"Hopefully, I'll leave Scott to Lindsay. I haven't the energy to argue with him right now." She thought of the green-eyed redhead wrapped around her heart and wondered whether she would have sufficient energy to argue successfully with her. "Goodbye, Phillip." She took his hand. "I do love you, you know."

"That sounds too, too familiar," he said as he raised her hand and kissed it. "Goodbye, Sarah. Better luck to us both." He watched from the doorway as she returned to the Coulter home.

Just before entering, Sarah turned and waved, and Phillip waved back. She thought about what a good man her friend was. Hurting him had added another rung to the ladder of black deeds she regretted. At least this talk had eased a portion of her guilt. But would anything ever relieve the rest of it? Why hadn't her final revenge on Angston helped?

Sarah's hopes that a confrontation with Scott could be avoided were dashed when he insisted on speaking with her privately after dinner. She could have refused but thought it better not to. Which meant she couldn't see Faith until tomorrow, after school let out. He chose the office for their discussion, and he sat at the desk while Sarah took a seat across from him.

"Sarah, I want an explanation of your rude behavior on your past visit. You caused quite a stir." Scott sat back and folded his hands across his stomach. He still wore his dark brown business suit, white shirt, and tie, and his hands rested just below a watch chain and fob that crossed his vest.

The cane bottom of her chair pressed against Sarah's rear end, making her conscious of the weight she'd lost in the last few months. It also increased her irritability. "Since when do I have to explain my actions to you, brother dear? I'm a grown woman and may act as I choose."

"Not when you cause the rumpus you did," Scott said sharply. "One sign of maturity is taking responsibility for the consequences of your actions. A wedding was cancelled because of you."

Sarah jumped up, leaned her hands on the desk, and thrust her head forward. Scott flinched, and a hint of a wry smile flashed across Sarah's lips. "The only consequence of my actions would have been the need to replace me in the wedding party. I had nothing to do with the wedding being cancelled."

"That's not exactly true, and you know it." Scott's chin lifted in a gesture of defiance. "Your . . . relationship . . . with Faith had everything to do with it."

Sarah lifted one hand from the desk and rolled it into a fist. She tapped the clenched hand gently, but firmly, on the desktop with each word. "I had no 'relationship' with Faith." She unfurled her fingers

217

and laid her hand back on the desk. "We discovered we were attracted to each other, and that's as far as it went. Why do you think I left? She was promised to Phillip, and I didn't intend to disrupt that. Anything Faith decided was between her and Phillip."

Scott actually sniffed. "Two women being in love with each other is unnatural and unchristian. Why would any decent man want to marry a woman like that?"

"Scott, you look and sound like a pompous ass." Sarah straightened up and folded her arms across her chest. "And that's an unsupported statement. Show me in the Bible where Jesus says two people of the same gender can't love each other, and maybe I'll take your argument seriously." She unfolded her arms. "Meanwhile, I'll act in a way that's perfectly natural to me. Your sister is in love with a woman whether you like it or not."

"There, you see? It's your foolish determination to follow an unacceptable lifestyle that broke up the marriage." Scott seemed to be clutching at straws. "And that stubborn attitude of yours."

Sarah shook her head in frustration. "Phillip and Faith called off the marriage, not me. Can't you at least accept that?"

"Maybe," Scott conceded reluctantly. "But I'll never accept your choice of loving a woman. And I think you owe Phillip an apology."

"You know, it's funny." Sarah sat back down and leaned forward. "I've already talked to Phillip, and he wasn't anywhere near as pigheaded as you are. Nor did he blame me for destroying his wedding plans."

"He's not your blood."

"What's that supposed to mean?" Sarah's eyes narrowed as she contemplated Scott's remark. Something occurred to her that was almost too unthinkable to voice. Was he worried about heredity? She forced the words between her teeth. "Does this have something to do with Jessica?"

"No!" Red suffused Scott's face. His jaw opened and closed twice before he spoke. "How dare you bring her into this. Are you using her to threaten me?"

Well, no, Sarah thought. But maybe I'll just let him worry about that. She stayed silent.

Scott glared at her. He apparently decided to let that thought rest and try another tack. "And speaking of the children, what will they think when they're old enough to understand what you're doing? How will that taint their minds?" Scott's expression turned rather

218

smug, as though he had scored some winning points in a game. "And how about Mother and Father? They'll be appalled."

"I lived half my life more or less following what my parents wanted for me. When I started making my own decisions, twice I nearly died." Sarah slapped the desktop with her open palm. "But by God, I have a right to make my own decisions, and I'll take full responsibility for whatever results from them." Her voice lowered. "I don't have to answer to you, or the children, or our parents. I'm going to live my life the way I see fit."

"That is so typical of you. I should have known it was too much to expect you to consider other people's feelings."

"If that isn't the pot calling the kettle black, brother." Sarah stood up and sneered. "You're more worried about what everyone else might think about me than you are about *my* feelings or desires." Resigned, she moved toward the door but turned as she reached it. "I'm living in Missouri, Scott. No one needs to know my personal business, nor will they be close enough to be 'tainted' by my example." She put a hand on the knob, twisted it, and pulled open the door. "Your children will be just as tolerant and forgiving as you teach them to be. I hope to God that Lindsay has more influence on them than you have with your narrow, self-righteous bigotry." She walked through the door and slammed it shut, tormented by the knowledge that she might have slammed the door on the affection that had always existed between her and her twin.

She yearned for Scott to be more like Lindsay or Phillip. Maybe time would soften his bitterness. Meanwhile, no matter how battered she felt, she still had to face Faith. Tomorrow.

Sarah worried that Scott might continue their argument into the next day, but fortunately, he had a business meeting with a new supplier and left early for the Coulter Foundry. After the war, the foundry had sold off the armament machinery and geared up for peacetime pursuits. Now the company made nails and sheet metal, both in plentiful demand. The office worker who had been hired when Lindsay went to Virginia to attend to Sarah had been kept on, thus leaving Lindsay free to take care of her home and children.

With lunch finished, Lindsay and Sarah lingered at the kitchen table, lazily enjoying cups of tea. The children played almost at their feet. Pres was supervising the building of what he had informed them was a fort, and he pointed to a specific block for Jessica to hand him.

She crawled to the block, picked it up, and stood. With a mischievous glance at Pres, she took off running down the hallway. Pres chased after her, got ahead of her, and herded her back to the kitchen, both children laughing wildly. Jessica set the block exactly where Pres indicated and clapped her hands. The two knelt back down and continued building.

Sarah was beguiled. "That went a lot better than I expected. No yelling, crying, or fighting."

"Yes, but it certainly took a while. No matter what Pres was playing with, Jessie would come along, grab it, and take off. I finally convinced him that she was only teasing, and if he joined in the game and made it fun, she would eventually give back whatever she took." She gazed fondly at both children. "Now, he sometimes grabs stuff she's playing with, and they do the same thing, only he lets her catch him. They have a grand time."

"Jessie's a little on the pushy side, huh?"

"A little?" Lindsay laughed. "Scott and Phillip declare that she takes exactly after her Aunt Sarah."

"Both the children are getting so big. I miss being here to see them grow," Sarah admitted.

"It's too bad you don't live closer. You could move back here, couldn't you?" Lindsay sounded enthusiastic, but soon she groaned. "I guess that would depend on what happens with Faith."

"Scott seems to think that my relationship with Faith—or any woman, for that matter—would taint the children."

Lindsay's face crumpled. "Oh, Sarah. I noticed you both were awfully quiet this morning. Was he impossible?"

"You could call it that." Sarah hesitated. "But I'd rather not discuss it." She stood and looked out the window. "There are children passing by. It's too early for school dismissal, isn't it?"

Lindsay joined her at the window. "Sometimes they have half days. This must be one."

"I guess I'll get a buggy and go see Faith." The livery stable at the corner had buggies for hire, and the Coulters had a standing account.

"Good luck." Lindsay slipped an arm around Sarah's waist and gave a squeeze. "Go get your woman."

Sarah turned and embraced the small woman. She laid her head on Lindsay's dark hair. "I thank God you're my sister-in-law. You're more like a sister to me."

When Sarah let go and stepped back, Lindsay looked up to meet Sarah's eyes. "You will come back and let me know what happens, won't you? No more running away without notice."

"I will," Sarah promised. "But I hope I'm not running away at all."

Sarah walked up three steps and stood on the cement stoop in front of Faith's house. A brass knocker shaped like an upside-down woodpecker loomed before her eyes, awaiting her touch. I can do this. I can do this. The mantra had worked for her in some dire situations, although in none of them had her knees felt more wobbly than they did now. She touched her scarred face and damaged eyelid. True, Faith had kissed her. But no matter what Lindsay said, how long could anyone overlook such devastation? And what about her scarred soul? Still, she wouldn't know until she tried, would she? She squared her shoulders, grabbed the back of the woodpecker's body, and hit the beak solidly against the striker three times.

Without warning, the door immediately opened. And there stood the redheaded, green-eyed vision who had haunted her dreams for months. Sarah wet her lips and cursed inwardly at her throat's tendency to tighten during emotional difficulties, cutting off speech. With her heart pounding, she watched Faith's expression go from curious, to startled, to cold. They stared at each other for several moments.

Sarah's chin lifted up, and she cleared her throat and swallowed. "May I come in?"

Without a word, Faith stepped back and pulled the door farther open. Sarah stepped into the hallway, and Faith closed the door. They were close enough to touch, but a gulf of icy distance loomed between them.

Sarah hadn't brought a handbag, something she left at home whenever possible. It was bad enough that custom demanded she wear a bonnet. But now she wished she had a bag to fiddle with. She stuck her hands into the pockets of the light coat she was wearing. The movement hunched her shoulders, making her feel slightly defensive. She looked down into chilled green eyes, and her stomach spasmed. "I came back."

"So I see." Faith's tone could have frozen a burning log. Silence reigned again until she slightly shook her head. "What do you want from me, Sarah?"

Forgiveness? But the word wouldn't issue from Sarah's throat. She couldn't get past the belief that Faith should ask her for forgiveness, too. "You didn't marry Phillip."

"That's rather obvious." Faith jerked around and walked toward the kitchen. Sarah hesitated, then followed her.

She spoke to Faith's back. "Had I known sooner, I would have returned sooner."

Faith halted near the kitchen table and swung around, forcing Sarah to an abrupt stop. "Why bother? You slap me silly, accuse me of all manner of things I never did, and when I'm stupid enough to give in to my—" She shook her head again. "When I'm stupid enough to kiss you, you run away. You left me all alone to face Phillip's shocked dismay and your brother's anger."

"You didn't have to tell them," Sarah murmured. She hung her head, ashamed of her lack of support for Faith during that time. But she had been shocked, too. That Faith was actually attracted to her hadn't even occurred to her before the kiss.

Faith's mouth snapped shut, and she breathed heavily through her nose. "I was supposed to just go ahead and marry Phillip after that? I needed time to get my feelings straightened out. Damn you! Damn you, Sarah Coulter or Bren Cordell, or whoever the hell you are. You turned my whole life upside down and my son's, too."

Stung, Sarah fought back. "I turned your life upside down? You're still lying about your part in the attack on me. After everything that's happened, you still won't admit what you did." She tore at her bonnet's strings and snatched it off. She thrust the damaged side of her face toward Faith, stopping a fraction away from butting their heads together. Faith drew back, and the corners of Sarah's lips turned down. "Yes, go ahead and pull away. Can't stand to look at me this closely in the daylight, can you? You think this hasn't changed my life? You don't know the half of it."

Now Sarah was breathing heavily, too. She turned to leave, and Faith spoke, her tone still sharp.

"That's it? That's it? You yell at me and run away again? Why did you come back, Sarah? Why?"

Sarah kept silent, but her thoughts clamored to be heard. *Because of the kisses. I came back because of your "stupid" kisses.* She sneered at herself for presuming that the kisses meant anything to Faith beyond a momentary attraction. She strode toward the entryway, slapped the bonnet back on her head, and pulled open the door. "Damned if I know!" she shouted. She stalked out and yanked the door shut so hard the loud bang reverberated up her arm and through her body, providing a lonely note of satisfaction in a chord of misery.

"Sarah," Lindsay said in protest, "you didn't get any information from Faith at all. You haven't cleared up whether she loves you or not." When Sarah had come storming back into the house, she found Lindsay in the drawing room, folding a pile of clean clothes. Lindsay had helped calm her enough to sit on the couch and tell about the meeting with Faith.

Sarah turned glaring eyes on her sister-in-law. "There wasn't any warmth there, Lindsay. Only anger. She didn't give a damn about me. She just cursed me for breaking up her marriage to Phillip and 'turning her life upside down.'"

"I think you're mistaken. She's the one who told Phillip about her feelings for you. He never would have known if she hadn't said something."

Fuming, Sarah said, "That's what I told her!" She grabbed one of Jessica's dresses from the pile of clothes and started folding it in her lap.

"Exactly, so she can't blame that on you. She's probably angry that you ran off without settling anything between the two of you. She saw a door opening up, and you slammed it in her face." She reached to take the dress, but Sarah pulled it away from her. "Sarah, it's no good to squeeze more wrinkles into the cloth than you're smoothing out of it."

Sarah stared at Lindsay as though her words were foreign. She looked down at the mangled frock, frowned, and thrust it into Lindsay's hands. "Sorry."

Lindsay expertly folded the dress, laid it on Jessie's pile, and reached for the last piece, a blue shirt belonging to Pres. "It sounds to me like we have two women in love, and both too proud to be the first one to admit it." She folded the shirt and set it on the proper pile.

"I swallowed my pride long enough to come back for her, and she almost bit my head off." Sarah shrugged. "I'll be leaving on the first train west. If you're right and she wants to see me, you can tell her where to find me. I'll be at the address I gave you."

The news shocked Lindsay. "My goodness, you drop into Faith's life, and you're going to drop right out again? Don't you think you should give her some time to think about it?"

"She's had plenty of time." Sarah's sideways glance met Lindsay's concerned gaze. "Has she ever inquired about how to contact me?"

"We didn't know how to contact you. Even your parents wrote that they hadn't heard from you."

"But Faith didn't know that." Sarah stood.

"That's true, though we haven't really stayed in touch with her. She might have been too embarrassed to ask us." She rose also. "But you can't leave already, you just got here. Stay and visit for a while. It's been ages since we've seen you. Besides," she said as she slipped her arm through Sarah's, "I'd like the children to have more opportunity to get to know their favorite aunt."

Sarah shook her head. "I'm sorry, Lindsay. I don't feel welcome here. Scott seems even angrier than Faith, if that's possible. I think everyone needs a cooling-off period." She gave Lindsay's arm a squeeze. "I'll wait until the children wake from their naps, though. I don't want to miss giving them a hug and kiss goodbye." A tiny jolt of pain at these words surprised her, and she scoffed inwardly. Don't go getting motherly at this late date. You're mixed up enough as it is.

Lindsay let go of her arm and picked up a couple of piles of the folded clothes. "Good. At least that will give you time to help me put these clothes away." She tilted her head and gave a sweet smile with just a hint of tease in it. "Make yourself useful?"

Sarah picked up the other two piles. "Useful instead of a pain in the neck?"

"Right." Lindsay poked her with an elbow.

"Damn!" Sarah stopped dead still.

"What?"

"Faith got me so befuddled, I forgot to ask about Redfire."

"Oh, your poor horse! I'll try to find out for you."

"Thank you. I'd even be willing to buy him from her if that's what she wants. Please write to me as soon as you find out anything, all right?"

"You know I will."

Sarah gave her a big hug. Seeing Lindsay was the brightest spot in this short visit. That, and seeing the children again. Who knew how long it might be until the next visit? She felt a momentary return of anger. Supposing there ever would be a next visit.

After the door slammed behind Sarah, Faith stormed up and down the hallway, her arms hugged against her chest.

Her voice grated into the silence, echoing her last questions to the woman who had spurred her fury. "Why did you come back, Sarah? Why?" She knew the answer she wanted to hear, but those words hadn't been spoken. How many times had she asked herself what the incident between them that night in the Coulter home had meant to Sarah?

Faith's memory had replayed those kisses a thousand times over. She had felt desire surge through them both. And oh, how sweet those kisses were. She had believed that it was a new beginning and that Sarah mirrored her love.

Could I have been so mistaken? Faith shuddered as the memories flowed over her, and she felt her body respond to her desire for Sarah. Surely, she can see my side of this. Maybe if I give her more time, she'll feel calmer and be able to understand how I feel and why I jumped all over her. She chewed on a knuckle, knowing that might never happen. Sarah might just disappear out of her life altogether. She threw herself into a chair and covered her face with her hands, again muttering her woeful lament. "Why, Sarah? Why couldn't you say you came back because you love me?"

Faith was surprised when a courier delivered a note to her door the day after Sarah's appearance. And she was even more astonished at its message.

Dear Faith,

> *Sarah has left, once again.*
> *Please forgive me for intruding into affairs that would appear to be no concern of mine. But I care very much for Sarah, and I know Sarah cares very much for you. She used to be bold and self-sufficient, but her confidence in her worth has been shattered by war experiences terrible beyond belief. Her stay with you and Benjamin is the only reminiscence that brings a smile to her face. What a loss it would be for us all if that smile should disappear forever.*
> *I hope I am not presuming too much when I believe you might be interested to know she is living in Bonneforte, a town south of Cape Girardeau, Missouri.*

With sincere regard and all best wishes, I remain yours truly,

Lindsay Coulter

Yearning filled Faith as she felt the pull of the words, "I know Sarah cares very much for you." Why couldn't Sarah have said that? Surely the answer lay in Lindsay's following words, "Her confidence in her worth has been shattered by war experiences terrible beyond belief."

Faith's hand curled in as her fingers remembered the texture of Sarah's scars. Those scars don't affect my feelings for her, she thought, but they obviously affect Sarah's belief in herself. How awful for her. She bore a constant reminder of the violence she endured—the violence that also took her innocence. Tears brimmed in Faith's eyes and overflowed.

If I am to convince her she's loved, I'll have to do it in person. Faith went to her desk and pulled out paper and pen. Her assignment at the school had been only temporary, and she had been trying to find work. Maybe she could find something near Bonneforte.

CHAPTER FOURTEEN

Sarah bent over her drawing board, focused on one arm of the Rebel soldier she was sketching. A soft knock sounded, then a harder one, demanding her attention. "Come in," she called. The door opened, and Leah brought in a tray holding a cup of coffee, a white cloth napkin, and a cheese and tomato sandwich on a ceramic plate.

Leah's smile was tentative. "I thought you might like some lunch for a change."

Sarah looked up, her face somber. The artist in her noticed Leah wore a dress that almost exactly matched her blonde hair and was dotted with varicolored geometric designs. It made a bright contrast to Sarah's own dark brown trousers and forest green tunic. "I like your dress," she said, and Leah's smile glowed.

"Thank you. I just finished making it yesterday." She placed the tray on a table in front of the cinnamon brown couch that rested in one corner of the gallery. "Are we in a better mood today?"

"Only if you stop that 'we' nonsense."

"You've got a deal." In a wheedling tone, she said, "Come on over here and relax while you eat."

Sarah sighed, put down her pen, and rose from the five-foot-long ebony bench she used when drawing. "I know I've been very poor company, and I apologize." She picked up the sandwich, took a tentative bite, and then gobbled half.

"Please sit down." Leah pointed to the couch cushion next to her.

A half smile quirked one side of Sarah's mouth as she tried to chew and talk at the same time. "Uh-oh, you're being so polite. I must

227

really be in trouble." She sat next to Leah, finished the sandwich, and took a long drink of coffee. She dried her mouth with the linen napkin and laid the cloth back on the tray. "Ahh, that was good. Why do you take such great care of me, even when I'm wretched to you?"

Leah reached over and pinched Sarah's cheek. "You know it's because you're so damn cute I can't resist you." Her lilting tone sobered. "And I figure when you're miserable is when you most need to be taken care of."

Tears sprang to Sarah's eyes, and she dragged her sleeve across her face, catching them before they fell. "I'm sorry," she apologized again. "I think I'm becoming an emotional wreck."

"Do you want to talk about it?"

Sarah looked at her and waited for a moment, a puzzled look on her face. "What did you say?"

"I asked if you want to talk about it." She raised her eyebrows. "You didn't understand what I said?"

Sarah rubbed her hand across her face and touched it to her right ear. "No. I think the hearing in this ear is getting worse. Or maybe I just notice it more now. Anyway, I can't do anything about that." She tapped her fingertips against the depression on her forehead and lowered her hand to her lap. "I guess you want to hear about my trip home."

"Only if you want to tell me."

"I do. Anyway, after putting up with my sulking for the past week, you've earned it. But when I'm done recounting my tale of woe, I want your honest opinion. Tell me whether or not I'm an idiot." Leah nodded, and Sarah related the whole story.

When she finished, she laid her head against the back of the couch and closed her eyes. She waited several moments. "Well?"

"You're an idiot."

Pain distorted Sarah's face. She opened her eyes and sat up, then leaned forward, braced her elbows on her knees, and rested her head in her hands. "I am an idiot. I am. An idiot for thinking Faith loved me. She was right, it was just some stupid kisses." Sarah rocked back and forth. I will not cry, she promised herself.

"That's not why I said you're an idiot. Think, Sarah. Faith told Phillip she was in love with you. She knew her life would turn topsy-turvy, but she told him anyway. She had to mean it."

Sarah dropped her hands and straightened up, confusion written on her face. "Maybe she had just learned for the first time that she was attracted to women. Maybe when she spoke to Phillip she only thought she was in love with me."

"I think she knew a long time ago that she liked you. I mean, where did those kisses come from? If I remember right, you had just smacked the hell out of her." Leah banged the back of her hand against the side of Sarah's trouser leg, and Sarah jumped. "You think that's a good reason to kiss someone? The attraction must have been mighty strong for her to ignore that."

Sarah gave a heavy sigh. "So you think I was an idiot to leave?"

"Put yourself in her place. Suppose she loves you, but she's not sure how you feel. You said you bumped her against the wall with your body, and that's what stoked your fire. It must have stoked hers, too, so she couldn't control herself. She kissed you. And what did you do?"

Sarah's voice was defiant. "I kissed her back."

"And I'll bet that got her hopes up. She was probably even too excited to sleep. She could see a door opening, and it likely half scared her. She was anxious to talk to you about it. But you slammed the door and ran away. No wonder she's angry."

Sarah's hand moved to her knee and her fingers began drumming. "Slammed a door? Lindsay said that same thing. Are you sure you two aren't in cahoots?"

"Maybe we are." Leah shook her head when Sarah's amber glance slewed quickly sideways at her. "Though not on purpose. I've never met your sister-in-law, but she sure sounds like she loves you and wants you to be happy. We both do."

Sarah sighed again. "I know that, and I appreciate it. But I can't go back after Faith again, Leah. I just can't take another rejection. If you and Lindsay are right, Faith should be able to figure out why I came back for her, and she can make the next move."

"And what if she doesn't?"

"Then I guess," Sarah said as she blinked back annoying tears, "it's over before it even got started."

"And you're happy with that?"

"Of course not!" Sarah said fiercely. "What the hell do you expect me to do? Go back and kidnap her? Drag her off by her hair like a caveman?" Her fingers flexed in time with her words, and her heart leaped as she realized the idea held some atavistic appeal. But Faith wasn't the kind of woman to be dragged anywhere she didn't want to go.

"I'm sorry, Sarah. I didn't mean to come in here and upset you even more than you already were. But I'm worried about you. You're not eating right or sleeping right either. I thought the trip home would fix that, but it didn't." Her voice turned pleading. "I know you're feeling bad right now, but please try to take better care of yourself. For Amy's sake and mine, if not your own."

Sarah's eyes went round. "You believe I'm endangering my health?" Leah nodded. Sarah considered that a moment. "I don't feel sick or anything, but I know I'm too thin. I'll try to eat better, all right?"

"Wonderful! For starters, I'll go make you another sandwich." She got up and leaned down to kiss Sarah on the cheek. "At least you gave Faith a try, Sarah. Don't give up. You're a very lovable person. You'll find that special someone eventually."

Sarah forced a grin. "I can count on one hand the people who think I'm lovable."

"See there." Leah frowned, then said sternly, "Your biggest problem is you don't believe you're lovable. But you are."

Sarah rose and walked to her drawing board. She pointed to the Rebel soldiers in her latest scene. The battle showed the soldiers caught in a Union ambush. "I wonder how lovable they would think I am." She sat on the bench, and Leah put a hand on her shoulder and gave it a little shake.

"Think of all the Union lives you saved. Those Confederate deaths made that possible. You have to accept that."

"Ah, Leah, I can convince myself intellectually, but emotionally it's a different story. I certainly can't convince my nightmares."

"You're still having nightmares?"

"Sometimes." She glanced down at her hands and lifted her gaze. "I had hopes that a loving partner could help me with that." She looked off into the distance. "Maybe being alone is my punishment for all those deaths."

"Stop talking such nonsense. It's not like you to feel sorry for yourself." Leah sat down on the bench and wrapped her arms around Sarah. "Keep your hopes up, Sarah. Things will turn out. I have faith in you."

Sarah's arms went around Leah. "I'd rather have Faith *with* me," she said with a sad smile. Both women leaned into their embrace.

Sarah stood in the kitchen, looking out the window. She blew into her coffee cup and took a careful sip of the scalding brew. A heavy rain shrouded the afternoon into gloomy gray and draped tiny, rapid rivulets against the glass with a soft tinging sound. "This storm certainly came up in a hurry. I barely had time to get Drummer into the barn. Looks like someone tipped over a river out there." She turned and walked back to the table, where Leah sat with a newspaper, occasionally resting her finger under a word as she read it. Amy was at the table, too, putting together a wooden puzzle of a colorful parrot. A fire in the cooking fireplace kept the room warm and cozy.

As Sarah approached, Amy looked up and smiled. "Aunt Sarah, what kind of bird is this?" She held up the box cover with the puzzle picture displayed on it.

"That's a parrot. Those birds live in a country far, far away from here. Some of them can be taught to talk."

Amy giggled. "Birds can't talk."

"Ah, but these birds can. They don't talk back and forth like we do, but at least they can learn a few words. Maybe I can find one for you some day. Would you like that?"

"I surely would." Amy's head jerked up and down in enthusiastic nods.

Sarah touched the top of Amy's hair as she passed by her. "I'll keep an eye out for one."

"Hey, Sarah, how do you say this word?" Leah's finger had stopped, and she had her head resting on her other hand, propped up by an elbow on the table. She spelled the word aloud, "P-o-i-g-n-a-n-t."

Sarah stopped next to her. "That's a tricky one. The 'g-n' combination in this particular word tells us that the 'g' is silent, but it gives the 'n' an 'n-y' sound. Want to give it a try?"

Leah scratched her head. "Poy-nee-ant."

"Close," Sarah said. "But the 'y' doesn't sound like one at the end of a word. It sounds like one at the beginning of a word, like 'yellow.' She reached past Leah's shoulder and put her thumb over the last three letters of the word, hiding them. "Say this part with the silent 'g.'"

"Poyn," Leah said.

Sarah moved her thumb. "Now say this part as though the 'y' were at the beginning of it."

"Yant. Poyn-yant."

"Right! Good work."

231

"What's it mean?"

"Oh, no, you don't," Sarah said with a laugh. "You have to look it up yourself. Where's the dictionary?"

"Well, it was worth a try." Leah grinned. "Amy, will you run into the study and get the dictionary, please?" Her daughter jumped up and hurried to do her mother's bidding.

Amy returned with the book. "Don't forget, Mama, you have to use the word in a sentence before the sun goes down."

"I will, sweetie." Leah glanced up at Sarah. "That was a perfect idea, you know. Both Amy and I are learning a lot of new words. Not to mention the grammar you're teaching us."

Sarah grinned. "You're quick to learn. With all the reading you're doing, pretty soon you'll know more words than I do." She set her empty cup in the sink. "I've almost finished my latest story. I'll be working on it the rest of the afternoon. Send Amy after me for supper, will you?"

"Sure. We're having the leftover roast from last night. We'll see you at suppertime." Sarah left for her studio while Leah riffled through the dictionary and Amy continued to put together her parrot puzzle.

About fifteen minutes had passed when a loud banging on the door roused Leah from her reading. She and Amy glanced at each other, then Leah went to answer the knock. When she opened the door, the force of the wind blew it inward, and she tightened her grip on the brass knob to keep the door from clattering against the wall. The struggle held her attention for a moment before she was able to look out at the figure standing on the porch.

"May I help you?" she asked.

Soaking wet from the downpour, the woman had both hands against her chest, holding her coat closed. Her sagging bonnet was pulled tightly about her face, and her eyes squinted against the swirling raindrops that pelted her even though she stood under the porch roof. Although Leah could barely see the woman's face, the voice she heard sounded surprised. "I . . . no . . . I think I've come to the wrong place. I'm sorry to bother you." She turned and hurried away, and Leah saw a mass of wet curls hanging down her back—red curls.

"Wait!"

As the woman continued to splash toward a horse and wagon that sat in front of their barn, Leah shouted, "Amy, get Aunt Sarah.

Tell her it's an emergency!" Amy bolted from the room, already calling Sarah's name.

Seconds later, Sarah came running. "What's wrong?" She saw Leah at the door, making no attempt to close it against the wet wind blowing in.

Leah pointed outside. "A woman just stopped here. I think it's Faith."

Sarah stepped quickly to the door and peered out. She stood like a statue, her eyes glued to the figure bent against the wind and moving toward the wagon. Leah punched her arm, hard. "Go, Sarah. Bring her back. For God's sake, at least get her in out of the storm."

Sarah dashed outside, not even stopping for a coat or hat. Drenched within seconds by the torrent, she ran as fast as she could, heedless of her aching leg. With her feet sliding and splashing water from the muddy yard, she caught up to the woman, grabbed an arm, and turned her around. Sarah's heart thudded against her chest as she shouted against the noise of the wind. "Faith, oh God, Faith, come into the house!"

Faith put a hand up above her eyes, and Sarah stepped closer to shield her from the rain. "I can't do that." The sound of Faith's voice, even raised as it was, stirred Sarah, body and soul. Her fantasy was no longer an impossible dream. Her love was here, right here in front of her.

"Why can't you? Are you crazy? It's pouring rain, and you're soaked. Come in and get dry before you catch cold."

"Let go of me. Don't you even speak to me. Ever." Faith jerked her arm free, slammed Sarah in the chest with the palms of both hands, and turned away.

Sarah stumbled backward and skidded on a tuft of grass in the quagmire that the yard had become. When her weak leg twisted and buckled under her, she went down. She landed flat on her back, and water splattered into the air down the length of her body. With her teeth clamped together to keep from screaming, she rolled over and pushed up onto her hands and knees.

She tried to get up, but her good leg kept slipping. Still on her hands and knees, she blinked to clear her eyes of the muddy water dripping down her face. She looked over her shoulder in despair as Faith climbed onto the wagon seat and jiggled the reins. With creaking and splashing, the horse and wagon turned to leave.

The rain suddenly lessened, and as the wagon passed by, Sarah could make out movement under a tarpaulin thrown in the back of it.

A hand reached out and lifted the tarpaulin's edge, hiking it into a tent over a dark head.

"Benjamin!" she called out and raised a hand toward him. Benjamin waved. She saw his mouth move but couldn't hear him over the combined noise of the wind and rain and the slap of the horse's hooves in the muck. The wagon slowed and stopped. Sarah's heart leaped, but a moment later, the wagon resumed its exit.

"Sarah!" At the faint sound of her name, she looked toward the house. Leah, wearing a black slicker with a hood that shielded her head and eyes, trudged across the yard. She stopped next to Sarah, but her gaze followed the wagon that continued on its way. A moment later, she turned back to Sarah. "Are you all right?" She frowned. "You looked like you needed help."

"Yes, I twisted my damn leg, and it doesn't want to work yet." Sarah reached up for the hand Leah offered, and with help, she stood erect.

Leah ducked under Sarah's arm and pulled it across her shoulder. "Let's get you inside. We can talk there." She wrapped an arm around Sarah's waist, and together they hobbled to the warm, dry house. When she got Sarah safely onto the kitchen chair nearest the fire, she peeled off her slicker and hung it to dry on a peg near the door.

Amy sat at the table, breaking green beans into a ceramic bowl. "Are you all right, Aunt Sarah?"

Sarah bit her lip and nodded.

Leah stepped into the bathroom, reappeared with some towels, and bustled back to the table. "Amy, honey, go play for a little while. I need to help Aunt Sarah get cleaned up." She wiped the green bean ends from the table and tossed them into a waste can as Amy left.

"That was Faith, I take it? I couldn't see her face well enough to be certain." Leah barely waited for Sarah's nod. "I confess I peeked through the window. Just as I looked out, I saw you fall. You stayed down, and she left, so I figured you could use some help. When you lifted your hand to the boy and he waved, that sure was a poignant scene."

If Sarah hadn't felt so bad, she would have grinned at Leah's use of the new word. She knew Leah was trying to lift her spirits, but her heart was in pain.

Leah wiped at Sarah's face with one of the towels. "You need a bath. As soon as you ran out without your slicker, I stoked the fire under the water." She nodded her head toward a black kettle hanging from a crane in the kitchen fireplace. The fire had responded to her quick actions, and flames licked at the cast-iron vessel.

"Sarah, how can I dry your face if you keep crying on it?" She put her arms around the seated woman's neck and pulled her close until Sarah's head rested against her warm breast. With a sob, Sarah wound her arms around Leah's waist. Leah stroked her hair and held her until the crying ended.

With a final squeeze, Sarah sat back and dried her tears on the end of the towel Leah still held.

Leah's voice was tentative. "Did she hit you?"

"No. Not exactly." She took the towel from Leah, scrubbed it over her hair, and tossed it onto another chair. "I was trying to get her to come into the house, and she pushed me away." She moved her leg, which caused a pinch of pain. "Pushed rather forcefully, I might add. And I slipped on the wet grass and mud." She scratched at her thigh, then an arm. The heat from the fireplace coaxed a mist from her wet clothes, and she suddenly had an attack of itching. "That bath sounds pretty good right now."

"Right." Leah grabbed a piece of cloth from a bin on the hearth and used it to protect her palms as she swung the crane away from the flames and lifted the kettle from its hook.

Sarah shook her head in puzzlement. "I don't understand the woman at all. She comes clear out here—I'm assuming to see me—but she slams me in the chest and takes off."

"Sarah . . ." Leah's voice trailed off as she walked into the bathroom, and Sarah heard the water splashing into the tub.

Leah brought the empty kettle back to the hearth, and Sarah prompted her. "What were you saying?"

Leah didn't answer at once. She pulled off Sarah's sodden boots and socks and assisted her to the chair in the bathroom. Once there, both women worked to strip off the wet pants and drawers plastered to Sarah's skin. "Do you need help with the tunic?"

"I can get it, but I'll need a hand stepping into the tub." Sarah pulled off the tunic and flinched when Leah's fingers touched her chest. She looked down and saw two red marks just below her collarbones.

"Faith hit you pretty hard. You've got a couple of bruises started there already."

Sarah snorted. "She's a strong woman. Knocked me the hell off my feet." In more ways than one, Sarah thought with a silent groan.

Leah supported Sarah's weight as she stepped into the tub and settled into several inches of warm water. She looked at the water, then at the mud on Sarah. "How about just washing your body. I'll put the kettle back on, and you can wash your hair in clean water."

"That sounds good." Sarah accepted the soap and washrag that Leah handed her. She dipped the washrag in the water, soaped it up, and ran it over herself. Leah went back into the kitchen to refill the kettle and set it in the fireplace to heat.

When Leah returned, Sarah asked, "What did you say earlier when you brought the kettle in? I couldn't hear you."

"That's because I didn't finish. I started to say Faith knocked on the door looking for you, and I was the one who opened it. She looked at me kind of funny." Leah moved one shoulder. "Maybe she thinks you and I are a couple."

Sarah scoffed at the idea. "But she knew you when you both lived in Cranston."

"Exactly." Leah folded her arms, and her lips twitched. "Let's face it, she knew me as a whore."

Sarah rinsed the soap from her body as ferociously as she spoke. "But you're not a whore anymore." Finished with the rinse, she stood up.

"But Faith don't—uh, doesn't know that." Leah got a towel from the closet and wrapped it under Sarah's arms. She helped her step from the tub and sit once more on the chair. "Maybe she thinks I like women."

"Oh, God, Leah." Sarah ran a hand through her still muddy hair. "You're probably right." She pulled her hand away and looked at it in distaste.

Leah's gaze followed Sarah's movements. "We can take care of your hair after I get your clean clothes, and I'm pretty sure I'm right. You should have seen the nasty look she gave me." She went out of the room, then took a step back in. "Maybe you should go explain to her."

"Like hell I will. I'm not about to go running after her and get knocked on my ass again. As angry as she was, she wouldn't listen anyway."

"Sounds like she's not the only one who's angry. You two will never get together if you keep hurting each other. Someone needs to straighten out this misunderstanding."

Sarah glared at Leah, but as she calmed down, she realized the advice made sense. "You're right. We've been chasing each other

236

around like a couple of fools. First thing tomorrow, I'm going to find her and explain about you, even if I have to hit her over her hard head."

"That's a grand idea," Leah said as she left, smiling.

Sarah sat there imagining her words to Faith and Faith's answers. In her mind, they fell together into a heated embrace and kissed. She switched her position on the chair and groaned, partly from the pain as she jostled her sore leg and partly from a more exquisite sensation that quivered through her body. I can do this, she thought. I can explain everything. How hard can it be?

Faith sat in her new home and unfolded the much-creased note from Lindsay Coulter. For the hundredth time, she read the words that seemed carved into her soul. *I know Sarah cares very much for you.* Those words had led her to make inquiries and discover, as Fate would have it, that Bonneforte was advertising for a teacher. She had applied and been accepted. So here she was, after leaving everything she knew, ready to join the woman she loved. Only, to her dismay, she discovered Sarah had found someone else.

Or had she? Leah was one of the girls from the tavern in Cranston. Had Sarah's self-esteem diminished to the point she needed to pay someone to love her? Faith found that hard to believe. In their short meeting in the storm, Sarah had seemed surprised but not guilty. Maybe she had actually fallen for Leah.

Perhaps I should have given her a chance to explain, Faith thought, then derided herself. Like my temper would have listened to anything she had to say just then.

A sob tore through her as she folded the note and put it away. She had foolishly pinned her hopes on finding Sarah waiting for her with open arms. Her own feelings were so strong, she had assumed Sarah's were, too. But it hadn't happened. If Sarah had found love with Leah, Faith didn't plan on coming between them.

At least, she had been wise enough to secure a teaching position, so she wasn't stranded. On the contrary, she was committed to teaching school for the year, during which she was liable to see Sarah occasionally. She would just have to avoid her and make the best of a bad situation. And try to put her heart back together. If that was even possible.

"Aargh!" Sarah groaned from her perch on the couch.

The previous night, Leah had gathered some bedclothes and Sarah had slept in the studio, loath to attempt climbing the stairs with a sore leg. Her choice proved wise. When she awoke near dawn, threw off her covers, and attempted to sit up, the movement stirred intense pain in her leg, giving rise to the groan. Resting on her elbows, she looked down past the edge of her cotton nightshirt at the offending limb. Damn! It was clearly swollen.

She dropped back to her pillow and grabbed the sides of her head in frustration, her fingers splaying through her hair. Now what? Leah was an early riser, too, and she might be in the kitchen. But could she hear a yell? Only one way to find out. Sarah took a deep breath and turned her head toward the open door of the studio.

"Leah!" She waited a moment and inhaled even more deeply. "Leah!" She heard movement coming toward her and sighed with relief.

Leah came dashing into the studio, drying her hands on her apron. "What's wrong?"

"I can't move my damn leg. Do you remember where the crutches are?"

"Sure, they're in the bathroom closet." She hurried out and soon returned to hand over one of the crutches. "Let me help you up, and I'll give you this other one." She set the crutch against the couch, leaned down, and let Sarah put an arm around her shoulders. Using one crutch and a boost from Leah, Sarah got upright and Leah gave her the second crutch.

Sarah's expression darkened. "I'd hoped I was finished with these blasted things."

"I know." Leah gave a spurt of laughter. "I'm glad I kept them when you wanted to toss them in the fire." She stepped back and took a good look at the leg. "It's swollen a lot. Should I take you to the doctor?"

Sarah's look was scathing. "Right. Jostling this leg around in the back of a wagon sounds like something I'd love to do." After taking two hesitant steps, she was right back into the rhythm of walking with crutches. "This has happened a couple of times before. The leg will be fine in a few days."

"What about Faith? You can't go after her today."

"Maybe I can. Should I let a little pain stop me?" Sarah tried to wiggle her foot, but gasped. "Who am I trying to fool? This leg isn't going anywhere, by wagon or by horseback. Does it seem to you the Fates are trying to keep me and Faith from getting together?"

Leah stepped toward the doorway. "Come get something to eat. I just took fresh cornbread out of the oven. Things always look better on a full stomach."

"I think it's going to be a while before this situation looks better, full stomach or not." Sarah slowly made her way to the kitchen. "I hope she stays in town a couple of days until I can see her."

"Maybe you should write her a note."

"No." Sarah sighed. "I'm certain this will take a face-to-face explanation." Shivering, she welcomed the warmth of the kitchen and chose a chair near the fire. She sat at the table and propped the crutches beside her. When she raised a hand to her brow, she was surprised at the sweat oozing along her hairline. She wiped her hand on the nightshirt. "Damn it, Leah, this leg is painful. Looks like I'll be off my feet for a couple of days."

"Well, when I go to town tomorrow to do the marketing, I'll see what I can find out about Faith." Leah fixed a plate for Sarah and set it in front of her. "Until then, you just remember to stay off that leg and give it a chance to get better. Time is a great healer."

Sarah nodded acquiescence even as Leah's words took on another meaning. Time hasn't healed me yet, she thought. But the possibilities are looking better.

Leah returned from the marketing on Monday with welcome news. She set down the bags of groceries and hurried into the living room, where Sarah reclined on the couch. Settling into the chair opposite her, Leah brimmed with excitement.

"I asked around, and it seems like your Faith is the new schoolteacher."

"I'll be damned."

"Yep, and she has her own house, right on the school property."

Sarah pushed herself into a sitting position and closed her eyes while a smidgen of hope danced in her mind. "That means I'll have plenty of time to convince her that you and I aren't lovers."

"But that's not the only problem you have."

Sarah's eyes popped open. "I know. We seem to feel a connection, but I'm not even sure she'll love me once she gets to know me better. At least now we'll have a chance to find out."

"Or you might not love her." Sarah opened her mouth to protest, but Leah held up a hand. "Do you really think you can just forget that she turned you in to the Union troops? You've suffered a whole lot from that, and I know you, Sarah. Honor means a lot to you. What Faith did wasn't honorable. I'm not sure you can put that behind you."

Sarah smoothed her fingers against the quilt covering her legs. She had constantly wrestled with that very question, until she had devised an explanation for Faith's actions that she could accept. "She thought she was doing the best thing for me. If she would just admit that she did it and apologize, I could forgive her. But she insists she never said a word, though her expression told me differently. We need to work that out."

"Be careful with your heart, honey. I don't want you to be hurting."

"I'm already hurting. I need to shake some sense into that stubborn woman." She looked at Leah. "What's that sly little smile for?"

"So far, you haven't done too good with physical action."

Sarah grabbed the edge of a pillow and tossed it at Leah, who easily caught it and threw it back on the couch. "At any rate, I'm not going to be happy until this situation is settled."

"Well, you have a happier situation to deal with right now." Leah stood up in order to reclaim a telegram from her skirt pocket. "At least, I think it's happier." She handed the telegram to Sarah. "It's addressed to both of us. I hope you don't mind that I opened it. I thought it must be urgent." Leah drew a surprised glance from Sarah when she said, "I even answered it."

The telegram was from Phillip. *Stegner seen in Brighton. Lindsay, Jessica, and I arriving Wiley Creek Sunday noon by train.*

Brighton was about thirty miles away. Wiley Creek was only five. "Here? They're coming here?" Sarah's face lit up. "How wonderful! I wonder why Scott's not coming?" Almost at once, she looked a bit shocked. "Tuesday, that's tomorrow." Before Leah could react, Sarah threw back the quilt and swung her legs to the floor, wincing a little. Her leg was still tender, but no longer so swollen. "We need to get the house ready."

"Sarah, relax. The house is always 'ready.' I'll just have to freshen up the beds. Phillip can stay in one of the bedrooms in the main house, and Lindsay and Jessica can stay in your wing. How does that sound?"

"Oh, Leah, that's perfect." She thought a moment. "Phillip might go straight to Brighton, since it's on the railroad line. But at least he can stay here if he needs to. Thank you for taking care of it. And for answering the telegram." It was considerate of Phillip to address it to both of us, she thought. Leah's bursting with pride. "Now if you'll start filling my belly with some food, maybe I'll be strong enough to meet the train tomorrow."

"Food's no problem. I just baked a ham. We can have it today and still have some for tomorrow. Phillip must be happy to get some news about Stegner. I hope it works out this time."

"Me, too." Sarah's face turned somber. "Stegner better hope Phillip sees him before I do."

"You let Phillip worry about Stegner. Right now, you need to concentrate on getting your leg better so you can enjoy the company that's coming."

"Hey, you're getting downright bossy—a regular termagant." She swung a hand at Leah's rear, but the laughing woman jumped out of her reach.

"A termagant? You know I'll look that up, and if it means what I think it means, you're in trouble, woman."

Sarah tried to look ferocious. "Watch those threats. I won't be weak forever, you know."

"That's right. I guess I better take advantage of bossing you around while I can." She waggled a finger at Sarah. "So, stay here and I'll bring you a platter." She left, and Sarah grabbed a crutch and limped toward the bathroom.

I'm so happy they're coming, she thought. And wait until I tell Lindsay about Faith!

Lindsay clapped her hands. "Faith is here? No wonder I couldn't find out about Redfire for you. I was tardy in sending a message over to her, and it wasn't answered. She must have been on her way. How wonderful!" A light danced in Lindsay's blue eyes. "Are things all right between you?" The two women were sitting on the couch in Sarah's studio, and Jessica, not at all shy, was climbing over and around her Aunt Sarah, grabbing pieces of long hair.

"No, but at least we're within hailing distance of each other." Sarah ducked to let Jessica loop some hair around her aunt's neck. "We have a few issues to settle, if we can." She explained Faith's unexpected arrival at the house, her probable misconception about

241

Leah, and how she'd knocked Sarah down. "The misunderstanding about Leah is the first hurdle to get over."

"I can imagine. When you told us on your visit home how you and Leah came to share a home, any thought of a physical relationship between you didn't even enter my mind. But I can see how Faith might interpret it differently." Lindsay attempted to halt Jessie's shenanigans, with little success.

"And apparently, she has." Sarah rescued her hair from Jessica's hands, pulled the squirmy child onto her knee, and bounced her up and down. "Tell me how you happened to come here with Phillip." As she'd anticipated, Phillip had gone straight on to Brighton.

"You know how Phillip's always been half obsessed with capturing Stegner? He had copies of your sketch printed, and he's been mailing one to every post office and sheriff's office in existence, I think. Every month, he sends out a stack. Last week, he got a letter from someone who claims to have seen the man in Brighton. He came over to tell us about it, and Scott remarked that the area was close to your place."

Impatient with her daughter's continued squirming, Lindsay got up, grabbed Jessica from Sarah's knee, and tucked her under one arm, giving her a tickle to keep her from yelling. While she continued talking, she gathered some paper and crayon pencils from atop Sarah's desk and got the child busy on the floor with them. At last, Jessica settled down.

"As soon as I heard that, I said I'd like to come visit you. Provided, of course, that Phillip wouldn't mind the company. They both said it was all right, and here I am!" She stopped a second for a breath. "Scott and a babysitter can do a good job of taking care of Pres, but I wanted to bring Jessie to see you, Sarah. You should be around each other more."

Sarah frowned. "I'm not so sure about that. You're her mother now. I have no claim on her." And, she thought, the more I see her, the more attached I'm getting. Maybe partly because I'm learning to accept that her natural father wasn't such a terrible man, in spite of the sordid circumstances of her conception.

Both women gazed toward the youngster. "She even looks a little like you," Sarah remarked.

"Yes, the black hair and blue eyes are a close match," Lindsay said, "but once beyond her coloring, she's Sarah-Bren Coulter through and through. And I'm glad she is."

Sarah's eyes widened. "You're glad?"

"Yes, glad." Lindsay reached over and squeezed Sarah's forearm. "You're one of the boldest, bravest women I know, and if Jessie inherits only a snippet of your character, I'll be happy."

Sarah's lips took on an ironic tilt. "I don't feel very bold and brave."

"You've lost some belief in yourself. You need someone to help you regain it." Lindsay's tone was scolding, but when Sarah's eyebrows rose, a grin fluttered at Lindsay's mouth. "Who knows, maybe Faith is the one who can do that."

"Lindsay, if they gave out prizes for persistence, you'd be the perennial winner."

Lindsay squeezed Sarah's forearm once more and released it. "You are going to talk to her, aren't you?"

"She told me not to speak to her ever again. I know she said it in anger, but I don't know how long that anger might last. Anyway, I plan to watch for a likely opportunity." She rubbed the back of her neck. "I wanted to dash right after her and take my chances, but my leg prevented that. Now I need to build up my courage." She touched Lindsay's arm with a fist. "I'll try to remember how bold and brave I am."

Lindsay chuckled. "I think I might just have an idea about how to approach her."

Leah knocked lightly on the doorjamb and stuck her head into the studio. "Dinner's ready."

"We'll be right there." Sarah turned toward Lindsay. "I'm anxious to hear your idea, but we better wait until after dinner." She stood and walked toward Jessica, limping only slightly. "Come on, Jessie. Let's go eat." She reached down, and when Jessica raised her arms, Sarah's heart constricted. She picked her child up and held her close.

The picture of mother and daughter reminded Lindsay of when they were all at Red Oak Manor just after Jessie was born. "Sarah . . ." Lindsay handed her a crutch, but Sarah brushed the offer away. "You really should keep in touch with Mother and Father Coulter. They're always asking for news of you, and I haven't felt free to tell them much. I think that's up to you."

"Oh, God. Let's take care of one problem at a time, all right? The less Mother knows about me, the better I feel." Sarah snorted. "The better she feels, too, I'm sure."

"Maybe so, but she is your mother."

243

"And she came through for me when I needed her. But you and I both know she'd never accept that I love a woman. I'm just not going to tell her unless it becomes absolutely necessary. I'm sure she'll be happier that way. Unless you want to tell her."

"Oh, no! You won't get out of it that easily. But you do realize it's possible Scott might say something."

"I can't live my life to suit Mother and Scott." Sarah paced in careful steps toward the kitchen with Jessie, for a change, resting quietly in her arms. "They'll just have to get used to that." Her tone softened a little. "But I will write to them and fill them in on everything else." She looked back at Lindsay, who was following her. "After I settle things with Faith."

"I'm anxious to see if my idea works."

Sarah could see that Lindsay was enjoying keeping her in suspense. "And I'm anxious to hear it," Sarah said dryly. "I hope it's a good one."

Lindsay's grin was downright ornery. "We'll find out."

CHAPTER FIFTEEN

Phillip slapped the dust from his hat and put it back on. His gaze roved Brighton's main street, and when he spied the word "Sheriff" painted in gold on a window, he headed there. He pushed through the door and entered an office. The man behind the desk wore a star on his chest, and a gold plate on a wooden stand provided his name.

"Sheriff Staumon?" When the man nodded, Phillip reached in his jacket pocket and pulled out the poster with Stegner's picture on it. He laid it on the desk. "I heard this man has been seen around here. Do you know him?"

The sheriff studied the picture and handed it back to Phillip. "Can't say as I do. He blew up a munitions train?"

"Yes. Hundreds of soldiers were killed and maimed." Phillip twitched up his pant leg. "Including me. I've been searching for him for a couple of years."

"A lot of soldiers did terrible things in the war," the sheriff said in a reasonable tone. "We can't punish them all."

"This man wasn't a soldier. He was a civilian working for the company that was shipping the munitions. He was one of the people responsible for its safe arrival." Phillip hesitated before continuing. "I grew up with him. As did a lot of the men who were killed."

"Just what is it you want me to do?"

"I want to take him back to West Virginia for trial. I'm hoping you'll arrest him and let one of your men take him back there. I'll go along, too."

"West Virginia? That's the new state that broke off from Virginia, right?"

"Yes. It became a Union state in1863, during the war."

The sheriff stood and limped from behind the desk. He grinned and slapped his pant leg. "I lost a foot in the Union cause. Let's take a walk up to the tavern and have a drink together. We can talk there about finding this traitor."

The two men strolled up the board walkway to the Gateway Tavern. Staumon held the door for Phillip and followed him in. Having entered the darkened atmosphere from the sunny street, Phillip couldn't see very clearly. He heard a curse and some quick shuffling as dim bodies scattered. He tripped over someone's foot. With the sudden shift of weight to his false leg, he stumbled. A shot sounded above the hubbub. Something burned his face as he fell to the floor. His head struck the hardwood floor with a loud crack.

Through the haze that suddenly clouded his mind, he heard two more shots ring out, followed by a thud. All noise ceased for several moments, then voices again lifted. Rough hands turned him over. When his blinking cleared his eyesight, he recognized Staumon. "What happened?" Phillip muttered.

"Your traitor was here, at the bar," Staumon said with a touch of awe in his voice. "He saw you right away and took a shot at you." Phillip struggled to rise, and the sheriff helped him. "Looks like he only grazed your cheek."

Phillip felt a little woozy from the blow to his head. He touched his face and looked at the sticky blood on his fingers. Staumon caught his glance. "You were damn lucky. We'll get the doc to put a plaster on that." He took Phillip's arm to lead him away.

Phillip stood his ground. "What about Stegner?" He looked past the sheriff at several men bending over someone on the floor by the bar.

"You can stamp 'Paid' on that poster of yours. I put two bullets in his chest."

Phillip slipped between the men who parted to let him see the dead man. Stegner's face was slack, his eyes vacant and wide open. He looked almost surprised. A vision of a younger Stegner, a barefoot boy wearing suspenders to hold up pants a bit too big for his scrawny frame, came to Phillip's mind. The man on the floor was heavy, his hair unkempt and his clothes too tight for his flabby body. How could he change so dramatically from a childhood playmate to a mass murderer to someone who would attempt to kill me? Phillip shook his head in amazement.

This time when Staumon urged him toward the door, he complied. He could hardly believe that his years of searching had ended so abruptly with Stegner's death. Thank God, the sheriff had been with him, or the death could have been his own. As he had lain dazed on the floor, Stegner could have finished him off. Phillip shivered as he realized the close call that had resulted from his lack of preparedness, and he could only imagine what Sarah would say.

A day later, the sound of a wagon brought Leah and Lindsay to the porch. "Sarah!" Leah called into the house from the doorway, "Phillip's here." She turned to Lindsay and put her hand to her mouth. "I'm sorry. I forgot Jessie is napping."

Lindsay tilted her head into the entryway, listening. "I don't hear anything. But Amy's there with her, reading."

"I noticed." Leah flashed a smile. "I think Jessie has taken Ree-Ree's place. Amy's watching over her like a little mother."

A moment later, Sarah, without a trace of limp, joined them. As the wagon came to a stop, Phillip stepped down, and the driver steered the horses back the way they had come.

The women rushed to greet Phillip, unable to miss that he had an adhesive plaster on one side of his face. He kissed each of them on the cheek and laid his arm around Sarah's shoulders as they walked onto the porch.

She smiled and yanked his hand. "I'm surprised to see you so soon, but it's wonderful to have you here."

"I'm thrilled to be here, in more ways than one," he said. He gave her shoulders a squeeze and dropped back a step to let her precede him through the doorway into the house. While the others took seats in the living room, Leah went into the kitchen and returned with a glass of water for Phillip. He gave her a big smile. "Just what I needed, Leah. Thank you. Traveling always parches me." He took a long swallow and set the glass on the table next to his chair.

Sarah and Lindsay were sitting opposite him on the couch, so Leah settled in the other stuffed chair. Sarah got right to the point. "Come on, Phillip, you know we're curious as hell to hear what happened to you."

"Curious as hell?" Phillip's eyebrows lifted. "Does wearing pants make you talk like a man?"

Sarah's cheeks reddened. "I'll talk as I please in my own home. And I'll wear what I please." She would have said more, but Lindsay quieted her with a pat on the arm and took up the conversation. "Please, Phillip, do tell us what happened. Did you find Stegner?"

"Yes," he said, and touched the plaster. "That's how I got this. I stopped at the sheriff's office, and he invited me to the nearest tavern to get a drink. I was blinded coming in out of the sun and didn't even see Stegner, but he was at the bar. I never gave a thought to what he would do when I finally caught up to him. Of course, he recognized me. I'm hard to miss." His grin was rueful. "Hard to miss with a pistol, too. I wasn't even armed. The idiot pulled a gun and shot at me."

Sarah snorted. "You went after a killer without being armed and he shot at you? Tell us again who the idiot was."

Phillip frowned in her direction. "I knew you would have some cutting remark to make about it. You just can't resist."

"Now stop it, you two." Lindsay spoke quickly. "You haven't seen each other in months, and here you are throwing barbs at each other like a couple of cantankerous youngsters. You should be ashamed of yourselves."

Sarah laughed. "You're right, Lindsay, but you've been away from our banter too long. Anyway, I apologize, Phillip. What happened next?"

Phillip was chuckling, too. "And I apologize to all of you. Somehow, manners don't seem to be as much in demand these days. But that's no excuse, I know." He bowed toward Lindsay. "Sarah and I will count on you to keep us civil." This brought a lifted eyebrow from Sarah, but she remained silent as Phillip continued.

"I tripped over someone's boot and staggered sideways, and that saved my life." He tapped his face next to the plaster. "The bullet just grazed my jaw. Lucky for me, the sheriff was right behind me. He pulled his gun and shot Stegner dead. I say 'lucky,' because when I tripped, my head hit the floor and I was dazed for a couple of moments. Had I raised up, I know Stegner would have fired again."

"So the bas—" Sarah stopped as her gaze flicked to Lindsay and back to Phillip. "So Stegner's dead." Phillip nodded. Sarah's voice roughened. "I hope he lived every single moment in dread of being caught. I know I wanted to shoot him down. But dying so fast was too good for him."

"Maybe so, but that wasn't up to us." Phillip shook his head. "I didn't expect such a quick—and dangerous—resolution after finding him, but I'm glad it's finally over."

Leah cleared her throat to speak and looked embarrassed when everyone turned to her. "Do you think he blew up the train all by himself?"

"We'll never know that answer," Phillip said. "Even with so much ignitable gunpowder on the train, it did seem like a lot for one man to handle. But we've never had evidence that anyone else was involved. Stegner took that information to the grave. At least we got one traitor."

They sat quietly for a moment until Lindsay spoke. "I've been waiting for you to get here so you could tell Sarah and Leah about Theo." She turned to Leah. "That's Phillip's older brother."

A wide smile on Phillip's face lightened his demeanor. "He's getting married."

Sarah laughed and clapped her hands against her knees. "You're not serious? Old bachelor Theo getting married? To anyone I know?"

"You remember Marcus Baronski who was killed in the war? Theo's marrying his widow next April."

"Janet Baronski is a fine-looking woman," Sarah said with definite enthusiasm.

Phillip's tone was dry. "Trust you to notice that." Immediately, he waved a hand as if to brush the remark away.

"Phillip . . ." Sarah met his eyes straight on. "I am who I am."

Their gazes locked, and Phillip pushed his fingers through his hair. "I've accepted that, Sarah. I didn't mean anything malicious by it." He waved his hand again.

Lindsay broke the tension between them. "Phillip, I guess you should be told that Faith's here in town."

"Faith?" Phillip hesitated for a moment and looked from Lindsay to Sarah. "Are you seeing each other?"

Sarah shook her head. "There's a misunderstanding. She thinks Leah's my girlfriend, and she doesn't want to speak to me."

Phillip sat up straighter in the chair. "You're not going to settle for that, are you?"

Sarah frowned. "What's that supposed to mean?"

"Damn it, Sarah!" Phillip glanced toward Lindsay, but she didn't say a word. "I called off my plans to marry Faith because you two were in love, and now you're telling me that you aren't even speaking to each other? Sitting here with your tail between your legs doesn't sound like the Sarah-Bren Coulter I know. Go after the woman."

Lindsay had been nodding at practically every word that came out of Phillip's mouth. "That's exactly what I told her. The old Sarah would be chasing after Faith on a white charger until she swept her off her feet."

Sarah looked from one to the other. "We know Lindsay is a matchmaker by nature, but you, Phillip, used to mind your own business . . . after a fashion."

Phillip's laugh boomed. "Between you and Faith, I became convinced I was minding the wrong business, so I decided to change my ways. Now everyone is fair game for my scintillating advice." He quieted his laughter. "Seriously, Sarah, I think you should explain things to Faith. You've both been through a lot, and you deserve some happiness. Maybe you can find it together." He smiled. "Look at Theo. He's willing to take the chance. He'd want—no, he'd expect—you to do the same."

Phillip's generous heart touched Sarah. He was so forgiving. What a pity Scott wasn't more like him. She beamed at Phillip's last remark. "Theo always did believe in me."

"He isn't the only one." Phillip leaned forward. There was no mistaking the earnestness on his face. "We all believe in you, Sarah. You've always accomplished whatever you set out to do."

"That's true," Leah said.

"We all believe in you," Lindsay echoed.

Sarah looked at each of them, and as she did, her resolve changed from formless, molten liquid to hardened metal. They believed in her. She could do no less than believe in herself.

"All right," she said with a firm nod, even though her heart skipped a beat. "I can do this. Tomorrow I set Lindsay's plan into action."

"In for a penny, in for a pound," Sarah muttered. She dismounted behind the schoolhouse and hitched Drummer to the rail where four other horses were tethered. After dusting off her soft yellow doeskin shirt and brown trousers, she tightened her slouch hat with a yank on the brim. She pulled a sketchbook and charcoal pencil from a saddlebag.

The yard had been scraped clean of grass to save on mowing, and several picnic tables sat just beyond the bare ground. Sarah ambled in their direction and chose a table Faith would have to pass on her way home. She laid her drawing paraphernalia on the tabletop and pulled at her trouser legs to ease the leather over her knees as she sat down on the bench. One hand scratched at her chest. Too hot for this shirt, she thought. But Lindsay had insisted she wear the yellow doeskin, said it made her amber eyes glow. Remembering, Sarah gave a mental snort. Lindsay the matchmaker.

The afternoon was warm for September, and Sarah tipped the slouch hat back past the front of her hair to cool her forehead, unconsciously presenting an attractive picture. She opened her sketchbook and began blocking out a proposed drawing, prepared to keep busy until school let out.

At the appointed time, the schoolhouse doors opened and about fifteen children trooped out in an orderly row. As soon as their feet hit the dirt, they scattered, some running and some walking off by themselves. Others gathered in twos or threes and strolled along, talking. A few untied their horses from the hitching rail, climbed on bareback, and rode off, most with an extra passenger aboard. Amy shared a ride with Elmer Grosse, an eleven-year-old who picked her up each morning and brought her home after school. He was a friendly boy who even stopped by the post office once a week to get the mail for his family and for Sarah's, too. Both children called and waved to Sarah as they passed her.

About fifteen minutes later, Benjamin came out, followed by Faith. As they approached, Sarah stood up next to the bench and tipped her hat. She grinned as Benjamin hailed her.

"Miss Sarah! Hello!" His face beamed, warming Sarah from top to toe.

"Hello, Benjamin. I've come to walk your mother home." Faith had given a slight nod in response to Sarah's hat tipping. She slowed for a moment, but her face remained as still as a frozen pond.

"But, Miss Sarah . . ." Benjamin looked puzzled as he glanced from Sarah to his mother and back again. He raised an arm and pointed toward a log-hewn house with a short porch that squatted about a hundred yards away. Sarah could see it clearly in spite of the bunch of trees growing haphazardly around it. "We only live over there." His voice lifted at the end, making the statement into a question.

Sarah's expression sobered, and she stroked her chin, as though in deep thought, before she nodded. "Yes, but you can't be too sure of being safe in these parts. A crazy buffalo or a rambunctious buck could come crashing through this very spot and hurt someone."

Benjamin realized he was being teased. He raised his hands with fingers bent into claws. "Or maybe a snarly bear." His smile widened when Sarah growled and mimicked his actions.

Faith turned and walked toward the house. Sarah scooped up her sketchbook and pencil and joined Benjamin as they followed her. The boy looked up sideways.

"I can protect my mother, you know." Sarah heard traces of tentative pride in his words.

She cuffed Benjamin's shoulder. "I'm sure you can. You're the infantry, the first and most important defense. Just think of me as the artillery. I'm there if you need me."

"All right." He gave her what she could only interpret as a speculative look. "May I ask you something?"

May I? Sarah smiled inwardly. You can tell his mother's a schoolteacher. "Certainly. Ask away."

"Why are you wearing men's clothes?"

His mother missed a step and almost stopped walking. Benjamin glanced her way, but his eyes turned back to Sarah, awaiting her answer.

"That's a good question, Benjamin. Seeing a woman dress like a man is hard for a lot of people to understand." Sarah rubbed the back of her neck. "When I wasn't much older than you, I took to riding my horse all over the countryside near my home, sometimes staying away even overnight. For which I often got yelled at." She smiled at memories of those innocent times. "I found out in a hurry that riding in trousers beat the dickens out of riding in a dress. So I started wearing trousers. That got me some scolding, too." Her wry smile drew an answering one from the boy.

"When I moved out here, I decided I would dress the way that's most comfortable for me. And that way is to wear trousers. The rest of the world be . . . danged. Can you understand that?"

As Benjamin nodded, they reached the house. Faith opened the door and went inside.

"You and Mama never spoke to each other," he said, obviously surprised.

Sarah rubbed her neck again. "Well, your mama is a little upset with me right now. She told me not to speak to her, ever. But I think if she sees me every day, she might change her mind." She winked. "I'll be by tomorrow again, all right?"

"All right, Miss Sarah. Goodbye." He went into the house and looked out with a wave before he closed the door.

"Goodbye, Benjamin." Goodbye, Faith. But Sarah felt good. Faith hadn't spoken, but she hadn't sent her away, either. And Faith had listened to the conversation between her and Benjamin, as witnessed by her startlement at Benjamin's question. Yes, Sarah felt good. Lindsay's plan of having her appear silently but constantly each day was off to a promising start.

The next morning, Sarah accompanied Phillip, Lindsay, and Jessica to town. While in the Bonneforte General Store, Phillip struck up a conversation with a customer who turned out to be a fellow carpenter. Their animated discussion resulted in an invitation to lunch. "You go ahead, Phillip," Sarah said when he told her about it. "We'll let Leah know not to expect you."

When the two men left, Sarah remarked, "It sounded like Phillip's taking an interest in the carpentry business in this area."

"It did, didn't it?" Lindsay slipped her arm through Sarah's as they walked toward their buggy. "Maybe he thinks the Showell house will be too crowded now that Theo's planning to get married."

"Thank goodness my home has room enough for Faith and Benjamin." Sarah marveled at how easily that thought had entered her mind. She glanced down into impish eyes as Lindsay squeezed her arm.

"That's the spirit! What woman could resist you?" Sarah raised one eyebrow, and Lindsay giggled. "You know what I mean. I'm sure you can work things out."

"I believe you might be biased, but I thank you for the encouragement. I'll keep following your plan and see what happens."

"When Faith sees how persistent you're being, it has to make her wonder if she misjudged you. I wager her curiosity will be our best ally."

After returning home, Sarah spent most of the early afternoon working on the drawing she had started in the schoolyard. She was standing at the window, holding it up to the light, when Lindsay tapped on the doorjamb and came in. She brought a tray of oatmeal cookies with her.

"You have to try some of these. Leah made them, and they're delicious." She set the tray on the desktop.

"If I ate every delicious concoction that Leah baked, I'd be as big as a buffalo cow." Sarah laid the drawing tablet on the desk and sat down.

"I guess I better take them back." Lindsay took hold of the plate, and when Sarah's hand rushed toward it, she tried to move more quickly. But Sarah snagged a couple of cookies before she whisked the plate out of reach. "I thought you didn't want any," Lindsay said with a laugh.

"I didn't say that, now, did I? Some things I just can't keep from wanting." Sarah laid the cookies on the desk for later and swiveled the chair away from the desk to face her sister-in-law.

Lindsay tilted her head and her lips twitched. "Like Faith?" She set the plate of cookies on a credenza that stood against one wall.

Sarah groaned and scratched the side of her head above her ear. "Lindsay, I know Faith and I need to settle some things, but I so want to kiss that woman."

"Then why don't you?"

"You mean just grab her and kiss her?"

"Why not? If she feels as you do, she probably wants to kiss you, too."

"I'm not so sure." Sarah grimaced. "She's not even speaking to me. If I grab her, she'll probably knock me on my tail end again."

Lindsay laughed and clapped her hands. "Faith sounds feisty."

"She is that." A tiny smile curled one side of Sarah's lips. "That's one of the things I like about her. She doesn't let anyone push her around."

Lindsay strolled to the desk and tilted the drawing to look at it. "Oh, Sarah, this is really good. You can tell exactly who each one is. No wonder people are starting to pay good money for your drawings." She looked up. "So is our 'walking Faith home' part of the plan working?"

Sarah jumped up. "Thank you for reminding me! School will be out soon. I have to go." She grabbed the drawing tablet and the cookies and ran toward the door. "I'll answer your question later. It's too soon to tell yet." As she went out, she yelled, "Tell Leah I'm headed to school, please."

"I will," Lindsay answered and waved her hands to shoo Sarah on her way.

Sarah waited at the school, sitting at the same table, drawing on the tablet she had plucked from Drummer's saddlebags. The school day was over and most of the children had left. Sarah was intent on her work and didn't see or hear Faith and Benjamin come out of the building. Benjamin ran to the table, his wide smile shining. Sarah's head jerked up when he spoke.

"Hi, Miss Sarah."

"Hello, Benjamin." Sarah meant to close the tablet, but Benjamin had put his hand on it. Faith slowly approached but didn't look toward the two.

"What are you drawing?" He walked around to Sarah's side and peered at the tablet. "Mama, look at this." He glanced up, and Faith gave a faint shake of her head and went on by them. Sarah gathered her belongings together and got up to follow her, while Benjamin fell into step alongside. He was unusually quiet.

"Something wrong, Benjamin?" As Sarah looked down at him, he danced out in front of her and walked backward, studying her face.

"Your drawing looks like some others I have." Her insides quivered when he spoke, but he didn't say anything more. When they were almost to the house, he turned around and ran the last few yards. "Please stay here, Miss Sarah. I want to show you something," he called to her before following his mother into the house.

Sarah waited, knowing what was coming and considering her options for how to handle it.

A short time later, Benjamin came out of the house carrying a leather-bound journal. He sat down on the porch steps and motioned Sarah to sit next to him. The boy laid the book on his knees and handled it reverently, softly running his palm along the facing that bore the words, *Personal Journal of Bren Cordell.*

Sarah's heart swelled just moments before her eyes filled with tears. Who would have guessed I'd be so sentimental, she thought. She wiped at her tears surreptitiously, but Benjamin looked up as she was in the act.

His dark brown eyes were very grave, and his gaze moved to the book in his hands. "This is what I wanted to show you. Mama just told me it's yours. Is it?" He looked up for her answer.

With her throat too constricted to talk, Sarah nodded. He handed her the journal, and she took it. Unconsciously imitating Benjamin's movements, she ran her hand over the cover and traced a finger along the words burned there.

Benjamin watched. "I could tell your drawing looked the same as what's in there." His brows furrowed as he struggled to understand. "But Mr. Cordell was a soldier. A man." His eyes examined her face. "He had a beard. How could that be?"

Sarah's voice was barely above a whisper. "I wanted to fight for my country, but women weren't allowed to be in the army, so I had to disguise myself as a man. The beard was glued on. I can show it to you someday if you like."

"You don't talk the same. When we were at your house in Fairmont, your voice was higher. Now it sounds more like Mr. Cordell's, but it's still different."

Sarah's throat had loosened a bit, and she slipped into a drawl. "You mean Mr. Cordell spoke something like this?" When Benjamin's eyes widened and he slowly nodded, she knew he had just accepted that she was, indeed, Bren Cordell.

"Did Mama know you weren't a man?"

"Not at first, but she was my nurse, so she found out soon enough." She tapped Benjamin's knee. "I was in danger if anyone saw through my disguise. I begged your mother not to tell anyone. I'm sorry we couldn't let you know."

Benjamin paled. "I saw the soldiers drag you away." His hands balled into fists, and he rested them on his thighs. "I wanted to help you, but Mama said I couldn't. She said you would be all right." His gaze moved to the damaged side of Sarah's face. "Were they the ones who hurt you?"

Struggling against a sudden knot, Sarah cleared her throat. "If they had turned me in to their commanding officer, as they should have done, I would have been all right. That's what your mama thought they would do." She cleared her throat again and heard the screen door behind her creak open. A hand offered her a glass of water. She laid the journal on the porch, took the glass, and looked up into Faith's eyes. She nodded a thank-you and drank the water down in one long draught. Afterward, she held the empty glass in her hands, twisting it around and around. "But instead, they shot me and left me for dead. The flash from the muzzle of the gun burned my face and head."

Benjamin started to cry, and Sarah set the glass down beside her and put an arm around his shoulders. "Hey, it's all right. I'm here. I'm alive." She squeezed his shoulders and touched her head against his. "Please don't cry." His tears affected her profoundly. "I'll tell you what. You know something that would make me really, really happy?"

Benjamin sniffled and made a valiant effort to stem his tears, wiping his sleeve in turn across his cheeks and nose. "What?" he mumbled. Sarah couldn't hear his question, but she saw his lips move.

"Tell me where in tarnation Redfire got to."

The boy jumped as though prodded. In a second, sunlight spread across his face, banishing the gloom. "He's here! We brought him with us! He's here!" He jumped up. "Can I go get him, Mama?"

"Yes, you may."

This was the first Sarah knew that Faith had remained behind them after giving her the water. She stood, turned, and stepped up onto the porch. She was two feet away from Faith, face-to-face, and the woman's nearness spread heat through Sarah with the speed of a brushfire. She reached up and took off her hat, holding it against her chest like a shield. But she didn't say a word.

Faith stood her ground. Though Sarah saw a pink blush move from her chest and up over her face, her voice remained flat. "You were very kind to Benjamin. I appreciate that." She turned and went back into the house.

Sarah remained standing there, pulling herself together, until she heard a horse coming into the yard. She shoved her hat on and walked down the steps.

Benjamin brought Redfire to a halt directly in front of her. The horse whinnied and hit Sarah in the chest as Benjamin slid off his bare back. She grabbed Redfire's neck and buried her face against it, unmindful of who watched as tears flowed down her face. Finally, she lifted her head to take a good look at her beloved animal.

Benjamin put the reins in her hand. "Do you want to ride him?"

Sarah didn't even bother answering. She threw herself across the horse's shoulder, swung her hips to settle on his back, and moaned at the familiar feel of her calves clasping Redfire's flanks. The slight pain in her bad leg barely registered. At her clicking sound, Redfire bolted out of the yard and into the surrounding fields. She was ecstatic as she flew across open fields and ducked among trees. All of her troubles were forgotten. A missing piece of her soul had returned. I could take you home right now and keep you forever, she thought. But she knew she wouldn't do that. She couldn't take Redfire away from Benjamin. If she did, he would lose a piece of his soul, too. But Redfire was within reach, and she knew she could ride him whenever she wanted to. That would be enough . . . for now.

She took Redfire back to Benjamin, walking the horse partway to allow him to cool down. When she dismounted, she gave Redfire another mighty hug and handed the reins back to a worried-looking boy. "Would you keep Redfire for me, please? And exercise him when he needs it?"

"Yes, ma'am!" Benjamin's smile rivaled the rising sun for brilliance. "I surely will. You come and ride him, too, all right? Mr. Svenson lets us keep him in his corral, just across the way." He pointed in the direction from which he had come. "We have your saddle, too. And your saddlebags." He tied the reins to a porch post. "I'll get the bags for you."

Before Sarah could say anything, he bounded up the porch steps and into the house. Several minutes later, he came out empty-handed. "Mama just made some iced tea, and she said I should ask you to come in and have some. She has your saddlebags for you."

As he spoke, Benjamin hopped on Redfire and nudged the horse to a trot. Sarah stood dumbfounded for all of five seconds, before she stepped up to the screen door and knocked. She watched Faith approach, and the nearer the redhead came, the weaker Sarah's knees got. By the time Faith opened the door, Sarah had to hang on to the door frame to keep her balance. She removed her hat, and Faith took it and hung it on a rack standing in the near corner.

"Come this way," she said, and walked toward the kitchen.

Sarah literally stumbled after her, entranced by the movement of calico caused by Faith's brisk strides. Her good leg clunked against a chair and Faith glanced back.

"Are you all right?"

Sarah nodded.

In the kitchen, Faith pointed to a chair and Sarah sat and watched her pour two glasses of tea over pieces of ice already chipped from the block in the icebox. Faith sat down and looked at Sarah. She took a sip of tea before she spoke. Her voice was low but firm, and Sarah heard her plainly.

"Talk to me, Sarah. Where do we stand with each other?"

Sarah's sense of focus had deserted her. She was edgy, distracted. Her fingers drummed on the table. She blurted out, "Leah's my friend and my housekeeper. She isn't my lover. She never was. No one ever was." She sucked in a breath, annoyed she had admitted her inexperience.

Faith hesitated as her eyes searched Sarah's. At last, she nodded. "All right. I'll accept that."

"You should," Sarah said, chagrin making her a bit touchy. "I don't lie. Not like some people." Her whole body twitched when Faith jumped up and walked away from the table. But the redhead didn't leave the room. She turned back toward Sarah, with her face flushed. She crossed her arms across her chest and her eyes narrowed.

"Sarah—" Faith stopped abruptly and took two deep breaths. "You act as though you're the only one who has any issues. We need to get them out in the open. You *have* lied to me." Sarah frowned and Faith continued. "You deceived me, and you deceived Benjamin, too. We both thought you were a Confederate scout."

"That's different," Sarah protested. "I couldn't tell you I was working for the Union. You were Rebel sympathizers. I had to protect my masquerade." She raised one eyebrow, and her tone became challenging. "Would you have sheltered a Union soldier?"

"I wouldn't turn away anyone who was wounded."

"Even though your husband served the Confederacy?"

Faith stamped her foot. "I have a mind of my own!"

"Hell, you turned me in even though you thought I was a Rebel. Am I supposed to believe you would have treated a Union soldier any better?"

"Stop turning this around! You lied to us. Is that why you're so determined to believe that I lied to you?"

Sarah bolted up out of her chair, but she cracked her bad shin on the leg of the table. Her zeal to confront Faith face-to-face turned into a loud groan as she lunged for the edge of the table to keep from falling. Faith grabbed her arm and steadied her. By the time she got Sarah settled back in the chair, both women were somewhat calmer.

Faith straightened up and stepped back. "I'd like to give a well-placed kick to that soldier who hurt your leg."

"No need." Sarah looked up at Faith, and her jaw tightened. "He's been taken care of."

"But how?" Faith blinked. Her face grew pale until the freckles stood out on her cheeks like sprinkles of cinnamon. "You killed him?"

Sarah scrubbed her hand across her face before answering. She wondered why she hadn't kept her mouth shut. But why was she embarrassed to tell Faith she had killed Angston? "Yes, I killed him." When she saw Faith's chin sag, she added, "It was a fair fight, I swear." She looked off into space, and her expression hardened. "Once before, I let him live, but I should have killed him. He hurt a lot more than just my leg."

She stood up, slowly this time, and stepped toward Faith. Her voice dropped to almost a whisper. "I'm not what you would call a forgiving person."

The rise and fall of Faith's breasts quickened with her breathing. "Sarah, I think I liked you better when you weren't talk—" Sarah's mouth closed over hers as long arms encircled her, gently pulling her close.

Sarah pushed her tongue against Faith's lips, and her body flashed heat as Faith sagged against her. Faith's mouth opened, and Sarah's tongue slipped into moist warmth and connected with Faith's.

An arm went around Sarah's waist and pulled them tighter together. She thought she would die of yearning. A hand clasped her breast, and they both moaned. Suddenly, Faith pulled away and gave her a shove. Sarah's heart plummeted. Oh God, she's changed her mind. She doesn't want me. She stumbled backward until a chair hit the backs of her legs and she sat down. Flustered and still breathing heavily, she didn't hear what Faith whispered.

Sarah's hand shook as she ran it over her scars. How could anyone love this face? It was too much to expect. She grabbed the glass of tea and drank it down without pause. Her heart lifted back into her chest when she heard Faith's next words.

"Go do your schoolwork, Benjamin, before it gets dark."

"All right, Mama." His bedroom door made a scraping noise as it closed.

Sarah sighed. "I didn't hear him come in. I thought you changed your mind. I thought you didn't—" She stopped and blinked several times, trying to cope with the painful bubble of emptiness that had expanded inside her chest.

Faith sat down opposite her, grasped her clenched hand, and rubbed her thumb across Sarah's knuckles. She let go of Sarah's hand and sat back, wetting her lips with the tip of her tongue. Sarah couldn't take her eyes off her. "So where do we go from here, Sarah?" A wry grin pulled at her mouth. "Even with the problems we have, we're obviously drawn to one another."

"I don't know where we go." Sarah shook her head. She raised her hand and ran her fingers through the white hair above her ear. "I do know I want to be near you." She wasn't yet ready to say she loved Faith. "As soon as I get close to you . . ." Sarah hesitated. She was such a novice at this. She had some things that needed to be said, but she was worried she might drive Faith away. "I don't want what's between us to be just physical." She gazed into Faith's eyes. "I want to work toward having—making—a lifelong commitment."

"I want that, too. I didn't follow you across the country just to go to bed with you." Faith blushed. "I came because I couldn't get you out of my mind. No one ever affected me that way before. I want to know you. I need to know you. It's like half of me is always with you. I need you close so I can feel whole again."

Faith looked so beautiful Sarah's whole body ached. Her lips were pink and pouty, and passion made her eyes look . . . Sarah searched for a word and could only think "smudged," as when she made a charcoal drawing and softened an iris with the tip of her little finger. Even Faith's hair looked a brighter, richer red, and some ringlets hung loose around her face and forehead. Sarah wanted to touch the curls to her lips and taste them, feel them trail along her body.

"I'm in a quandary, Faith." She could have cried at what her next words would be, but she couldn't see a way around them. "As long as you keep insisting you didn't turn me in, I don't know how I can get past it. It comes down to trust."

Faith sat staring at her for a long moment. Then she stood up. "I have to fix supper. Would you care to stay and eat with us?"

Sarah stood, too. Apparently, Faith was just going to ignore what she had said about the betrayal, and she herself was reluctant to say anything more right now. What if Faith never apologized? Sarah had no idea how she would handle that. Maybe she, too, should ignore it for a while and see what happened. Could she do that?

"I thank you for the offer, but Leah's expecting me." Sarah sighed when she saw the look that flitted across Faith's face at mention of Leah. She stepped toward her and reached for one of the long curls hanging in front of Faith's shoulder. She brought it to her face and inhaled its fragrance, kissed it, and twirled it around her finger. "Here we are, full circle. I swear to you, Leah is not my lover. You can come over and ask Lindsay if you don't believe me."

"Lindsay's here?" Faith touched Sarah's fingers and squeezed them, and Sarah felt it all through her body. Faith turned toward the icebox and opened the door. "Maybe we could all do something together Saturday." She lifted a smoked ham from the icebox shelf, and Sarah took it from her and set it on the table. Faith smiled her thanks. "A picnic would be nice. Ask her about it when you get home, all right?"

"I'm sure she'll agree. When I told her you were here, she was delighted. She has Jessica with her." She hesitated. "And Phillip's here, too. But he's all right with us," she added quickly. "In fact, he encouraged me to get in touch with you."

"I'm happy to hear that. Phillip's a good man, and I feel guilty about having hurt him." With Sarah following, Faith walked through

261

the living room to the front door. She lifted Sarah's slouch hat from the rack and handed it to her. They stood for a moment, just looking at each other. Finally, Faith said, "You'd better leave. Will I see you tomorrow?" A smile twitched at her lips. "I might need protection from those snarly bears."

Sarah nodded. "I guess I have to give you time to change your mind about apologizing. I owe you that much."

Faith's smile disappeared, and she stung Sarah's shoulder with a slap. "Get out of here before we get into another argument."

"Yes, ma'am," Sarah drawled. She bowed and put on her hat as she stepped out the door. "Goodbye." Why couldn't she be kissing Faith goodbye instead of just saying it?

Would that time ever come?

Sarah arrived home just in time for dinner. When she took her seat at the table with the others, Leah greeted her with, "Elmer brought you a letter from the post office when he dropped Amy off after school. Do you want it now?"

"Where is it?" Sarah started to rise, but Leah was already up. She grabbed the letter from the counter and handed it to Sarah, who opened and read it.

Jessica paid no attention as she attacked the slice of beef roast Lindsay had cut into pieces for her. Amy followed suit, keeping one eye on Jessica. But Lindsay and Leah gave up any pretense of eating and waited for Sarah to tell them her news.

"It's from a publisher." Sarah looked up with a big smile. "My book has been accepted."

Both women clapped their hands in approval, and the children joined in, not knowing why, but laughing and clapping anyway. Sarah bowed her head in acknowledgment.

"All right, confess." Lindsay prodded her for an explanation. "What book?"

Sarah raised a hand and kept reading. When she finished, she laid the letter on the table and gazed toward Lindsay. "I wrote and illustrated a book about one soldier's experiences in the Civil War. It's called *My War Remembered*."

Leah interrupted, "I told you it was good."

Sarah winked at her and continued, "I submitted it to a publisher in Philadelphia, and he wants to print it. He sent a contract for me to sign in the presence of a notary and send back as soon as possible. I'll have to take it into Cape Girardeau tomorrow and get that done."

Which means I can't see Faith tomorrow, she thought. And that reminded her of the picnic.

"I almost forgot. Faith suggested we all have a picnic together Saturday. And that includes everyone—Phillip, too. Can you two make arrangements about the food? As for where and when, I think at Maier's Point around ten in the morning should be good."

"That sounds like a lovely idea!" Lindsay said.

Leah said, "Maier's Point is a beautiful spot for a picnic. We'll take care of everything. Don't you worry about it."

"Thank you both. I have to send Faith a note about being away, and I'll let her know the time and place for Saturday."

Early the next morning, Sarah sat at the breakfast table, penning her note.

Dear Faith,

Both Lindsay and Leah welcome the idea of a picnic and suggest meeting this Saturday at 10 a.m. at Maier's Point. Phillip is agreeable, too.

Please excuse my absence from walking you home today. I've received a contract from a publisher in Philadelphia who wants to print my book, and I have to be away tomorrow to have my signature on the contract notarized. I will see you at the picnic.

Please ask Benjamin to watch carefully for snarly bears. I don't want either one of you endangered.

Very truly yours,
Sarah

Sarah's heart leaped at such a simple thing as writing "Very truly yours." She signed her name, blotted the ink, and folded the paper in thirds. She handed the note to Leah, who tucked it behind the apple in Amy's lunch kettle.

For the tenth time, as usual on school mornings, Leah looked at the clock on the mantel above the kitchen fireplace. "Get your things together, sweetie. Elmer should be here soon. And remember to give Mrs. Pruitt the note from Aunt Sarah."

"I will, Mama."

As Amy passed, Sarah touched her shoulder. "Thank you, darlin'. I appreciate your help."

CHAPTER SIXTEEN

Sarah drove the buggy toward Maier's Point on Saturday morning, listening contentedly to the chatter of the women and children in the back. Her publishing contract was signed, sealed, and sent off, and now she would be spending the day with Faith. Her future looked brighter than it had in years.

Too many years, she thought. Maybe it was time to let go of the war and all the pain and guilt resulting from her part in it. She cocked an eye at Phillip sitting quietly beside her. He'd been damaged also, but he'd been able to forgive and forget. Maybe she could, too. Maybe she could even forgive Faith, whether or not she received an apology. Well, she admitted, that still needed some work.

She nudged Phillip and tilted a smile at him when he turned toward her. "Beautiful day for a picnic."

"That it is."

"Are you sure you're all right with Faith and me?" Better to get this out into the open than to hurt Phillip all over again.

He returned her smile. "I wouldn't be here if I weren't. In fact . . ." He hesitated, and Sarah's ears perked up. "This probably isn't the best time or place to say this, but I'm more concerned about you and Scott."

"You mean about his reaction to Faith and me?" Sarah sighed as Phillip nodded. "I can't control what he thinks, just as I can't change who I am. Do me a favor, Phillip. If you have occasion to speak of us to Scott, please just act as though it's the most natural situation in the world. Can you do that?"

"Of course I can."

"Part of Scott's distaste comes from worrying about what other people will think. If he sees that some people can accept that his sister loves a woman, he might eventually accept it, too."

"You may be right." Phillip gazed at the ripe wheat fields through which they were passing. To their left, glimpses of the river were visible through a stand of trees. "At least it's worth a try."

"All we can do is try. See, I'm not the only Coulter who is hardheaded."

Phillip's booming laugh pleased Sarah. It always reminded her of earlier, happier times.

"Sarah," he said as the laugh ended, "next to you, Scott is a mere amateur at being hardheaded."

She slapped his thigh, but she knew he was right. "I'm working on that, Phillip. I'm determined to be less obstinate."

"Of course you are. Hmph."

She slapped his thigh again. "Just you wait and see. I can change."

"Sarah." Phillip's voice had lapsed into a serious tone, and her head turned to meet his gaze. "Don't change too much. I love you just the way you are."

A lump formed in Sarah's throat. She reached over and patted the thigh she had been smacking. Phillip grabbed her hand, squeezed it, and let it go. His gaze shifted away as Sarah steered the buggy off the path, through the trees, and brought it to a halt. A wide, green, open area lay bordered by the trees. Slightly elevated, the ground sloped toward a strip of beach next to a gleaming blue river. Upstream, a railroad trestle crossed the breadth of the river. Birds flitted among the trees or chirped and sang, accompanied by a woodpecker's incessant drumming. Several hawks glided soundlessly across a cloudless sky.

Phillip said, "I would assume we've reached Maier's Point."

Without her hat, Sarah sat under one of the trees, out of the afternoon sun. Her head was bent over her drawing pad as she contemplated an addition to the portrait she had worked on intermittently throughout the day. She added several strokes and stopped for a moment to look around. Faith and Lindsay sat near her on the blanket that had served as a spread for their picnic food. The meal had been consumed and the residue cleared, and the women were now relaxing and chatting.

Sarah and Faith were still a little edgy with each other. Sarah knew that Lindsay enjoyed Faith's company, so she had stayed in the background to give them time to visit with each other. Her own concerns about her relationship with Faith could be addressed later. Today, she was content just to have Faith near and be able to admire her wholesome beauty.

The children played at the edge of the trees, and off in the distance, she saw Phillip and Leah strolling along the beach. The day was too cool for bathing, but on arrival, everyone had shed their shoes and stockings and stepped barefoot into the water. Even Phillip had rolled up his pant legs, doffed one shoe and stocking, and dipped one foot in. Now all the shoes and stockings rested in a pile next to the blanket.

Sarah's eyes crinkled as she thought about Phillip and Leah. Now wouldn't they make a sweet pair? They were loving, generous, and forgiving people. Leah would be so good for Phillip, and Amy practically adored him, as all the children did. Sarah's gaze switched to Lindsay, who happened to be watching her. Lindsay gave a knowing smile and a slight nod. Sarah grinned broadly. With Lindsay on the job, Phillip and Leah didn't stand a chance.

Her glance moved to Faith, who looked away when their eyes met. Sarah restlessly shifted her position on the blanket.

"Mama!" Benjamin raced toward Faith, yelling loud enough for even Sarah to hear. "We can't find Jessie!"

Everyone jumped up. "What happened?" Faith asked.

"She ran into the woods, and she never came back out. Amy and I ran after her and called, but she didn't answer."

They all started toward the trees with Benjamin leading them. Suddenly, he slowed and pointed. "There she is!" he yelled and took off again at full speed. Sarah followed the line of his pointing arm and charged after him.

"Oh, my God," Lindsay screamed. "She's on the trestle."

"I hear a train!" Faith called out.

Sarah couldn't hear the train, but she heard Faith. "Go to the river!" she yelled back to the women. "I'll get the children."

Even with her feet bare, Sarah could run faster in trousers than they could in dresses. She reckoned that when she reached Jessie and Benjamin—oh, God, *if* she reached them—they might have to jump from the trestle into the river. She didn't know whether the women understood her thinking, but when she glanced back, she saw Faith grab Lindsay's arm and pull her toward the river with Amy following.

267

She slipped twice in the damp undergrowth. Her bare feet crunched over pebbles and dead branches, but she hardly felt it. Her leg pained her as though she had been stabbed. No matter what, she had to keep running. A young child crossing those ties without slipping and getting stuck would be a miracle. And with a train coming, they'd need a second miracle.

After an agonizing pursuit, she finally saw the two figures. Jessica was close to the other end of the trestle, and Benjamin was just picking her up. But the train was coming around a bend, about to block their escape. Even if the engineer saw them, he couldn't stop the train in time. Benjamin turned and ran toward Sarah, his strides timed to hit the cross ties. He would never make it. And Sarah couldn't possibly get to him.

In a full-out run, she flung her hands to the right in a tossing motion. "Jump!" The train chuffed so noisily, Benjamin couldn't hear. She could smell the engine's steam. She kept running and swinging her hands to the side. Benjamin wasn't looking at her. He was watching his feet land on the cross ties. Tears streamed down her face. The train would reach the children before she could. "Oh God, Benjamin, jump!" she shrieked.

She faltered, crushed by the futility of trying to reach them. Benjamin looked up, defeat in his eyes mirroring hers. She jolted back to life. Once more, she ran and tossed her hands, pointing to the river.

With his arms wrapped tightly around a wailing Jessie, Benjamin didn't hesitate. He jumped.

Sarah leaped off at almost the same instant. She flailed her arms to keep straight. If she hit the water sideways, it could knock her out. A groan escaped her as she saw Benjamin hit on his back just before she plummeted into the water. She kicked and pulled against the strong current as soon as she could, hurrying herself to the surface. She broke the water and swept it with her gaze. There! Benjamin was about thirty feet from her. She swam hard to reach him. He lay facedown in the water, unmoving. Where was Jessie?

She saw movement about twenty feet past Benjamin. Fear and the pain of impending loss squeezed her heart. She couldn't get to them both. She had to choose the closer child. She reached Benjamin and lifted his face from the water, just as he gasped for air and started choking and coughing. Thank God, she thought. With the air knocked out of him, he hadn't breathed in much water. His arms flailed wildly, and it took all her strength to encircle him with her arms and stop him.

"It's all right, Benjamin, I have you, I have you," she kept repeating until he quieted into a limp rag.

Her heart hurt as though it were being battered. Benjamin was too weak for her to let go, but how could she save both of the children? "Benjamin," she said, "can you hold on to me? I need to go after Jessie."

He nodded, but when she tried to swim with his hands fastened to her clothing, he kept slipping off and slowing her down. She was frantic. The daughter she had hated and had given away with such foolish willfulness was drifting away to her death. Remorse shuddered through her as she realized, too late, that she loved Jessie. Even beyond the grief she knew would come to Lindsay and Scott, her own grief filled her.

She turned to haul Benjamin back to her. Suddenly, she heard a yell, but she couldn't understand the words. It came again, louder.

"I've got her!" a man's voice shouted.

Phillip? Sarah had been so focused on calming Benjamin and keeping him afloat, she hadn't seen Phillip swimming out to Jessie, who now was a good hundred feet downstream of her and Benjamin. She cried when she heard his words. She had doubted that the other three women could swim, and she hadn't even considered the possibility that Phillip could help. He must have removed his artificial leg. A sudden thought stunned her. Had she saved Phillip's life so he could save Jessie's?

She paused a moment, treading water, and lifted Benjamin with one arm so they both could see Phillip heading to shore with Jessica. Benjamin's smile was happy, but tired. He leaned his head against her. Sarah gave him a squeeze. "Let's get us back to shore, too."

Exhausted from the furious run even before she went into the water, Sarah found it slow going to swim the short distance to shore with only one arm. When Phillip showed up next to her, she almost cried again. "Jessie?" she asked.

"Lindsay has her. She's fine. You look like you could use some help." He took hold of Benjamin's collar and released Sarah's fingers from it. "Let's go, Benjamin." He swam away with the boy in tow.

Indeed, Sarah made better time now that she had two arms free, but Phillip easily outpaced her. For the first time, she realized that her sore leg and her heavy pants were slowing her down. But she was almost to shore. No need to shuck the pants now. She'd worry about the leg later.

She saw Benjamin run through the last bit of water and land in Faith's arms. Leah had tucked her skirt up, and she came into the water to help Phillip hop to the riverbank. She came back into the water just as Sarah's feet touched bottom. Sarah waded to her and when they met, Leah flung both arms around Sarah's waist and laid her head on Sarah's shoulder. Through her tears, she said, "Thank God, you made it."

They stood in the water, embracing, and Sarah patted Leah's back and kissed her hair. "I'm all right, just tired enough to melt. Will you help me to shore?"

She looked up and saw Faith and Benjamin standing near the wagon in which they had come to the picnic. Faith's arm encircled Benjamin's shoulders, and the blanket used for the picnic draped his body.

Thank goodness, he's all right, Sarah thought. She saw that Faith was watching her with an odd expression. As Sarah and Leah moved toward shore, Faith waved and shouted something, then turned and helped Benjamin into the back of the wagon. She untied the horse's reins from the tree, climbed onto the seat, and they left.

"What did Faith say?" Sarah asked Leah.

"She said, 'Thank you. I'll see you later.' I'm sure she wants to get Benjamin home and into dry clothes."

Sarah nodded. "He's probably just as tired as I am."

"Most likely," Leah said. "You're both heroes. And Phillip, too."

Phillip had been sitting on the bank clad only in his drawers and shirt, with his pants and artificial leg lying on the ground nearby. Lindsay and Amy stood next to him with Jessica wrapped in a sweater and struggling to be released from Lindsay's arms. "Here comes Aunt Sarah, another one of your saviors," Lindsay said. Jessie stopped struggling and looked.

When they reached dry ground, Sarah decided her bad leg would hold her, and she and Leah parted. Leah gave Amy a hug, and Sarah limped toward Lindsay. She stepped into Lindsay's embrace, folded her arms around both woman and child, and leaned to give Jessie a kiss on the cheek. She grinned and was too worn out to duck away when Jessie's hand batted her in the face in an enthusiastic welcome.

"Thank God, she's all right," Sarah said.

"Yes, and thank you, and Benjamin, and Phillip, too," Lindsay added. She released Sarah and stepped back. "But more of that later. Right now, we need to get you all back home and into dry clothes." Sarah and Lindsay turned their heads toward a voice they heard raised in exasperation.

"This is no time for false modesty. I helped you take the dang contraption off, now let me help you put it back on." Leah was balancing Phillip's artificial leg in her hands and fitting it onto the stump of his leg. Amy stood next to them, holding Phillip's pants.

"Don't fight her, Phillip," Sarah called out. "Even I don't win many battles with Leah."

"That's right," Leah said. "Now just quit being silly and let's get you dressed, and we can all skedaddle back home and get warm and dry." By the time she was finished talking, she had the leg strapped onto the stump and was reaching for Phillip's pants.

Sarah caught Lindsay's gaze and winked. A connection between Phillip and Leah seemed increasingly possible. Maybe some good would come of the ordeal after all.

Once Phillip was ready, they all got into the buggy for the trip home. Leah insisted on driving. She pointed out that she was in better shape than either Sarah or Phillip, and besides, they would be warmer in the back. Lindsay, still holding Jessie, sat with Leah to keep her company, and Phillip and Sarah sat opposite each other in the back, with Amy huddled up against Sarah.

When Sarah mentioned she would get wet, Amy answered, "I don't care. You almost died." Sarah put an arm around her and pulled her even closer.

"Quite a day," Phillip remarked.

Sarah gave him a tired smile. "This time it was Phillip to the rescue."

"Not so," he said. "I was the second tier. If it hadn't been for you, those children would be dead."

"You mean if it hadn't been for Benjamin, they would be dead."

Phillip threw his hands in the air and laughed. "All right, so I'm the third tier." He leaned in to reach for Sarah's shoulder and squeezed it. "I'm proud to know you, Sarah Coulter. I saw you had to make a quick choice out there. You never hesitate to do the right thing, even when it's difficult."

Sarah was irritated at the tears that spilled over onto her cheeks, and she slapped at them. "Let's just forget about that, shall we? I still can't believe Jessie is all right."

"I'm going to tell you something you'll find hard to believe."

"Well?" Sarah said, when he hesitated.

He sat back and his face creased into a smile. "That little girl is cut from the same cloth as her Aunt Sarah. She didn't give up for one second. When I got to her, she was swimming."

Tired as she was, laughter bubbled from Sarah, and Amy giggled. "She *is* just like you, Aunt Sarah. Mama says you never give up."

Phillip agreed. "And she never does, Amy. That's one of the best things about her." His grin turned wicked. "And sometimes, one of the worst."

The next morning, Sarah waited as long as she could before appearing on Faith's doorstep at what she hoped was an acceptably decent hour. She had refused to show up using crutches, even though the pain in her leg was excruciating. She stood on the porch, hesitant to knock. Just as she raised her fist to rap on the door, it opened to an unsmiling Faith.

"Come in, Sarah."

Sarah gritted her teeth against her pain and stepped in. Faith took Sarah's hat from her hands and hung it up. Then she stepped forward, embraced her, and laid her head on Sarah's shoulder. It didn't feel like a lover's embrace, but it loosened Sarah's fragile hold on her emotions. She held fiercely to Faith while struggling to recover.

"Oh, Sarah, no matter what doubts I have about your feelings for me, you saved my son, and I'll be forever grateful for that."

Doubts? The word pushed Sarah closer to the edge, and her words leaped out without thought. "Your son saved my daughter." As soon as she uttered the words, she realized her slip.

Faith stepped back, and her head snapped up to meet Sarah's distressed gaze. She whispered, "Jessie is your daughter?"

Sarah didn't answer. She didn't have to.

"Oh, my God." Faith gasped and lifted her fist to her mouth as her eyes widened. "Of course, she is. From the soldiers who attacked you."

"Please, forget I said that. Lindsay and Scott are Jessie's parents now. I have no claim on her." Saying those words hurt Sarah more than she expected. But she knew they were true, and she needed to accept that.

Faith moved her hand to cup the scarred side of Sarah's face, stepping forward as Sarah stepped back. "How awful for you. No wonder you hated me."

When they heard Benjamin's voice, Faith's hand dropped like a heavy stone. "Why do you hate Mama?"

"Benjamin," Sarah said, relieved that he had interrupted a distressing subject, "I'm so glad you're all right. You were so brave yesterday, just as brave as any soldier could be. You risked your life for Jessie." She reached out to him and shook his hand, then she pulled him to her and embraced him. "Thank you for saving her."

Benjamin's tanned cheeks glowed with his blush. "You're welcome," he said, always mannerly. But as soon as Sarah let go of him, he repeated the question. "Why do you hate Mama, Miss Sarah? She never does anything bad."

Oh, God, Sarah thought. How can I explain without lying to him? I can only try my best. Maybe Faith will admit her guilt and get it out into the open.

"Benjamin, remember you said you saw the Union soldiers take me away from your home?"

"Yes, ma'am."

Faith's face was as closed as a slammed door. She waved her hand toward the couch and chairs. "Perhaps we should sit down," she said, and the Pruitts waited until Sarah limped to one of the chairs. Faith took Benjamin's arm and led him to a seat next to her on the couch. She looked at Sarah. "Are you sure you want to pursue this?"

Sarah ignored her and addressed Benjamin. "No one saw me come to your house, and no one but the doctor knew I was there. But the soldiers said someone had told them about me." She stopped to let Benjamin absorb this information before she continued. "Was it the doctor—and I don't think it was—or was it someone else? I think your mother knows who it was, and she won't tell me. That's why I've been upset." She threw a glance at Faith. "But I don't hate her. I could never hate her."

Benjamin frowned and turned to Faith with a child's directness. "Do you know who it was, Mama?"

Sarah had to strain to hear the low answer.

"I'm not sure, Benjamin."

In contrast, Sarah spoke too loud, with an edge to her tone. "The soldiers said a woman with red hair told them."

Benjamin turned toward Sarah as she spoke, but his gaze swung back to his mother. He looked puzzled. "The only lady with red hair is Mrs. Spain, William's moth—"

He stopped and stared at Faith. Sarah watched, appalled, as his young face crumpled. He pushed his hands against the sides of his face as though trying to hold it together, and Faith put her arm around his shoulders. "It was my fault," he said. He turned to Sarah and repeated it, almost shouting. "It was my fault." Sobs made his chest heave as tears ran down his cheeks. "I told William when I ran to get the doctor. Then when Mama said not to tell, he promised me he wouldn't say anything." He closed his palms against his face and wiped his tears back toward his ears. "But he must have told his mama. He lied."

Heartsick, Sarah limped over to Benjamin and grimaced in pain as she knelt in front of him. Sobs continued to shake him while he tried to keep his flooded eyes on her. "Oh, Miss Sarah," he said, "it's my fault you got hurt so bad. You should hate me, not Mama."

Sarah took his hands into hers. "Benjamin, listen to me. Listen carefully. I know you never meant for me to get hurt. That was two years ago, and you were just a little boy. You couldn't know your friend would tell. I don't hate you for it. I don't even hate William. He was just a little boy, too. And I truly don't hate your mama."

But I did, she thought. I hated Faith because I cared about her and I thought she had betrayed me. I let my distrust of her nearly ruin our chance at a life together. Now, I've allowed it to tear Benjamin's heart apart.

"I'm sorry. I'm sorry I was bad." Benjamin was crying so hard, he got the hiccups.

Sarah wept, too. "No, please don't cry. You don't need to apologize. You didn't do anything bad, Benjamin, and you're not a bad person. I'm the one who's been wrong, not you." She dropped her hands, placing one on Benjamin's knee and one on Faith's. "I should have trusted your mother. I've been a fool." Her breath caught as Faith's fingers covered hers. But the fingers stayed there, and a thumb brushed the top of her hand. She could breathe again.

Now, how could she make Benjamin feel better? Sarah lifted her hand from Benjamin's knee, wiped at her cheeks, and gazed up at Faith. Her eyes were on her son, and her cheeks were wet, too. Sarah looked back to Benjamin and poked him gently in the side.

"Think, Benjamin. You're a hero. Yesterday, you saved Jessie's life. No one else could have done that. You know I got there too late.

No matter how much I wanted to save her, I couldn't. Who grabbed her, Benjamin?"

Benjamin sniffled and swallowed, and his tears slowed.

Sarah poked him again. "Who grabbed her, Benjamin?"

"I did." He wiped his cheeks on the gray cotton sleeves of his shirt.

"So, who saved her?" She poked her finger at him several times without touching him, and Benjamin gave a teary smile as he jiggled from side to side to avoid the threatening finger.

"I did."

"That's right." Sarah slipped into Bren Cordell's drawl. "And do you think I could ever hate the young man who dashed through the woods to get to that trestle? Who gave no thought to his own life when he went charging across that dangerous footing to get to Jessie? Who saved her with that enemy train breathing fire down their necks?"

Benjamin's eyes never left Sarah's. His tears stopped, and a smile played at the corners of his lips.

"And," she said, "let's not forget how you followed orders without question and jumped into the river when I said 'jump.'"

"Which was especially brave," Faith added, "because he doesn't know how to swim."

Sarah was thunderstruck. The last iron band that had imprisoned her heart shattered, freeing her emotions. There on her knees in front of the boy, she opened her arms wide. "Please give me a hug, Benjamin." He slipped off the couch and nearly choked Sarah with the strength of his arms around her neck. "I love you, Benjamin," she said, "like you're my own son."

Benjamin spoke against her neck. "I love you, too, Miss Sarah. And I never ever want to hurt you again."

"That score is settled. No need to worry about it anymore." Sarah's hands moved to his shoulders, and she leaned away from him. "I think we've both had enough of this sweet talk. Don't you have a horse to care for?" She looked toward Faith who was using her palms to dry her face. "Is it all right for Benjamin to see to Redfire?"

"I think that's a good idea." Faith stood up. "Wear your brown sweater, Benjamin. It's a little cool out this morning." Benjamin lifted his sweater from the coat rack and started toward the door.

Sarah made an effort to stand but was hampered by the pain in her leg. Without a word, as naturally as though she did it every day, Faith placed her hand below Sarah's elbow and gave her a boost.

Sarah nodded her thanks and called to the boy. "Benjamin, when you finish your ride on Redfire, ride him again for me, will you?"

"Yes, ma'am."

"And you can stay out until lunch time," Faith said.

"Thank you, Mama!" He sped out the door.

Sarah watched through the window as Benjamin hopped down the steps. "He's a wonderful boy."

"You won't get any argument from me on that." Faith's soft ripple of laughter lapped gently at Sarah's sensibilities.

Sarah turned toward her. "I'm astonished that he can't swim. He never hesitated when he saw me motioning him to jump. He just jumped."

"He trusts you," Faith said. "We both do."

"I'm not sure what I've done to deserve it, but thank you. And I hope you'll forgive me for not trusting you." Sarah raised a hand and let it drop.

"It's been hard for me to understand how you could believe I would betray you." Faith shrugged one shoulder. "And you kept insisting that I admit it."

"That was a very trying time for me, and I came to some wrong conclusions. I'm truly sorry."

When Faith stepped closer, Sarah suddenly felt edgy, and she took a step back. "Faith, I know it's easy to say now, but I had made up my mind to tell you I didn't care whether you admitted your betrayal or not, I would forgive you anything." She rubbed her neck. "That near tragedy yesterday woke me up. Life's too unpredictable to waste time holding a grudge. You mean more to me than my own hardheaded, misplaced sense of honor. Besides, you were right. I deceived you and Benjamin, too. And I ask your forgiveness for that also." She took a deep breath. That was the most she had said at one time in months.

"There's nothing to forgive, Sarah." The twinkle was back in Faith's eyes. "I tend to lose my temper pretty quickly, and when I do, my tongue sometimes says things it shouldn't. I understand that you couldn't tell us the truth. I was just being defensive."

Sarah's tension eased as another worry lifted from her. Something else occurred to her, and she raised one eyebrow. "You knew all along, didn't you?"

"Knew what?" Faith frowned.

"That Benjamin had told someone I was at your house."

"I suspected it, but I couldn't be sure. He was in too much distress to question him about it. You saw how he reacted. I was trying to spare him that. And if my suspicions were wrong, questioning him could have done worse damage."

Faith lifted her arm toward Sarah's face, and Sarah flinched. The hurt that flickered in Faith's expression brought Sarah back within reach. "I'm all right with you touching my face," she said. "Pulling away was just a reflex."

Faith put her palm against Sarah's cheek and caressed the scars with her fingertips. "Benjamin does love you, you know. He grieved for months over your capture. He would open your journal and sit for hours trying to reproduce your drawings. Sometimes, he smoothed his fingers over the pages as though that could connect him with you."

Sarah put her hand over Faith's to hold it still, turned her head, and kissed the palm. "I love him, too." She dropped her arms to Faith's waist and pulled her close. Faith's arms twined around her neck. "And I love his mother."

Their lips met softly in a tender, searching kiss. Before it deepened, Faith leaned away. She grabbed the hair on both sides of Sarah's head and gave several short tugs. "There's one more thing to settle."

"Only one?" Sarah was undaunted. It felt wonderful to have Faith's hands entangled in her hair. "What is it?"

"Leah. Whether you admit it or not, there's something going on between you."

"Of course there is. Ouch!" Sarah laughed when Faith's hands yanked harder on her hair. "But not the way you think. Leah fusses over me like a mother hen, and I treat her like an ornery sister. I told you before. We love each other. We've been through some tough times together, and we've become very close, but we're not in love. She likes men. In fact, Lindsay and I are hoping Leah and Phillip might get together."

Faith's grip on Sarah's hair eased. "Now, that's an excellent idea."

"Leah and I are close, but we've never been this close." Sarah's arms tightened. She bent down and covered Faith's mouth with her own. Slowly, their tongues explored each other, fanning the passion that was on constant simmer. The kiss deepened and grew stronger. Their tongues touched and tasted and engaged in a mock battle that would end in mutual surrender.

Sarah's hands moved up to press her fingertips against the sides of soft breasts. Faith broke off the kiss and pushed her gently away. Stymied, Sarah opened her mouth to protest but clamped it shut when Faith took her hand.

"Come." She led Sarah to the bedroom. Once inside, she dropped her hand to work the bolt that locked the door.

Sarah cursed inwardly at the trembling she couldn't control. Faith's eyes were gentle. "Are you afraid?"

"No!" Sarah barked the word. "Yes." Her shoulders sagged. "I don't know what would please you. I've never made love to anyone else."

Faith's brows went up. "Anyone else?"

Sarah turned red. "I . . . uh . . . I asked Leah for advice." Faith's expression changed, and Sarah held up her hands to forestall Faith's remarks. "It's not what you think. You have to admit she knows a lot more about making love than I do."

"And just what did your mentor say?" Faith asked with a hint of sarcasm. "Or should I ask what she did?"

Sarah wondered how the hell she had got into this conversation. When she imagined making love to Faith, nothing like this had entered her fantasies.

"She laughed at me."

"That's it, she just laughed at you? That couldn't have been much help." Faith's expression was bland, but Sarah suspected she was being teased. As they talked, Faith steered Sarah to a chair and sat her down in it. She lifted Sarah's good leg and pulled off her boot and stocking. Sarah stopped talking and grit her teeth as she helped Faith remove the other boot and stocking. Well, she thought, at least we're making progress in the right direction.

Faith stood in front of Sarah and put her hands on her hips. "Did she say why she was laughing at you?"

"Yes, she did." Sarah was getting downright hot from blushing so hard. "I remember her exact words. She said, 'I'd bet my last dollar, darlin', that you've been making love to a woman for quite a few years now. You just never had anyone to share it with.'"

Sarah figured her humiliation was worth it when the room resounded with peals of laughter. Faith clapped her hands and nodded her head, shaking her curls loose around her face. She looked so beautiful that Sarah had to suck in some extra air to handle the pleasure that rippled through her.

"Oh, Sarah," Faith said when she caught her breath, "my whole attitude about Leah just changed. She's a treasure."

Sarah stood and pulled Faith to her. "You're the treasure," she whispered into a pink ear before kissing it. She nibbled the earlobe that she couldn't think about without imagining her lips on it. That brought images of other parts she wanted to kiss and nibble and suck on, and her fear disappeared. Her lips moved down Faith's neck, and the resulting quivers sent messages to her whole body. Her fingers moved lower, unbuttoning Faith's blouse, and her mouth followed and approached a rising curve. Faith's breast rose and fell against Sarah's chin while her lips moved farther along the soft rise that led to a rose-tinted nipple.

Suddenly, Sarah gasped as a hand slipped under her tunic and slid partway under her belt, flattening against her stomach. Oh, God. She had to stop her own journey and just bask in the unbelievable feeling. Moving a little away from Faith and leaning her forehead on Faith's shoulder, she offered freer access to the wandering hand. A thumb found her navel and played with it. In all of Sarah's dreams, she hadn't come close to imagining the excitement aroused by the touch of Faith's hand against her bare skin. And the hand was only on her stomach!

She concentrated on the absolute pleasure flowing through her, but a moment later, her belt was unbuckled and loosened. The questing hand flattened against her skin again and moved up between her breasts. There it stopped, and Sarah ached to be touched.

"Sarah," Faith said in a voice almost too quiet for Sarah to hear. She turned her good ear toward Faith, and the next words were still quiet but a bit firmer. "I want to take off your shirt."

She nodded dumbly, and as Faith's hands closed over the hem of her shirt, Sarah reached back and grabbed her collar and they removed the shirt together.

Faith gazed at Sarah's body, and the look of desire on her face increased Sarah's awareness of her disfigurement. She turned her head to put the undamaged side of her face toward Faith, but Faith put a hand on her chin, turned her head to the front, and looked into her eyes. Faith's voice was intense. "I don't want you ever to hide your face from me again." She rubbed her fingers over the scarred skin. "I love every bit of you. When I look at you, I don't even see these scars. I see the woman I love. And to me, you're beautiful."

"You are, too." Sarah reached for one of Faith's curls, brought it to her tongue and tasted it, then kissed it. Her voice thickened with emotion. "I love the way your curls spring loose around your face. Do you have any idea how many times I've imagined them tickling my skin as your mouth traveled down my body?" She tensed as Faith's hands moved, expecting them to touch her breasts. But instead, they dropped to her waistband and pushed down on her trousers. In a rush to help, Sarah hooked her thumbs in her drawers and removed them with the trousers.

While she was bent over from pushing off the trousers, she took hold of the hem of Faith's dress and kept lifting until it, too, was off. Faith removed her shoes and stockings and the camisole that she wore next to her skin. The women spent several moments just enjoying the sight of one another. When they stepped forward and entwined their bodies, Sarah thought her pounding heart would burst through her chest. Her hands moved over Faith's back to feel and smooth her skin.

"Wait, Sarah," Faith said in a voice that Sarah could feel vibrating through them both. "This is your first time, and I want it to be special. Let me show you how wonderful it can be." She loosened Sarah's grasp on her and stepped back, and Sarah had to fight the impulse to just shove her to the bed and fall upon her. Instead, Faith went to the bed and turned down the covers. She climbed in, turned on her side, and beckoned. "Come here. Let me make love to you," she said, her voice as passionate and inviting as her words.

Sarah lay down next to Faith and moved into her arms. The full length of Faith's body lay against her, and she trembled again. "I'm not afraid now. I just want you so much I can't stay still." She kissed Faith, and the trembling increased. Faith's tongue teased her and a hand rubbed across her breast. Faith fingered her nipple, rolling it and tugging against it. Sarah drew back, her breathing heavy and voice ragged. "I swear, if you touch me just once more, I'm going to come." Sarah's building passion simmered as Faith pushed her away.

"Not yet, not yet. I want to touch you in a way you've never been touched before." She slid halfway down the bed. As she lifted Sarah's upper leg and pushed it toward the side of the bed, she turned a still-trembling Sarah onto her back. She climbed between Sarah's legs, lay down, and lowered her head.

Sarah tried not to come right away, but as soon as Faith's mouth closed on her, she groaned and came in a rush of sensations. She grabbed fistfuls of red hair and bucked in a fury of motion while Faith accompanied her movements with her tongue and lips. Sarah nearly screamed aloud when fingers slid into her heat, filling her. Faith

280

plunged into the moist opening her tongue had already tasted, while she groped with her other hand to roll Sarah's taut nipples into submission. Desire and longing coalesced into a white-hot spot in Sarah's pelvis and exploded once more, sending sparks through her entire body.

Finally, her movements slowed, and Faith stopped. Sarah flung a hand over her eyes and sighed, but the sound of a voice made her move her arm. She looked down her body toward Faith and smiled at the picture she saw. Faith was resting her forearms near Sarah's knees while her red head rose into sight above Sarah's damp curls. With her hands splayed at the top of Sarah's thighs, she danced her fingertips against the soft skin at the junctures of thighs and belly, unfurling tiny ribbons of delight through the area.

"What did you say?" Sarah asked in a lazy voice as a satisfied smile spread slowly across her face.

"I wondered if you had your eyes closed the whole time." She smiled wickedly and dropped her head to offer one last touch of her tongue.

Sarah gasped as another jolt slammed through her. She ran her fingers into Faith's hair and hummed her satisfaction, tugging the hair for emphasis. "Mmm, I watched almost everything. I enjoyed every single movement I could see, and I took pleasure in every single touch. You are unbelievable." Sarah motioned with her arm. "Come here, woman. I want to reward you."

Faith laid her body against Sarah's as she slithered up to meet her. Sarah hadn't reckoned that tasting her own fluids on her lover's lips would be so erotic, but it was. "I want to make love to you now," she said, as soon as their kiss ended.

"Oh, God," Faith said in a voice suddenly hoarse with passion, "I want that, too."

Sarah rolled on top of her and began kissing her way down Faith's neck. This time, there was no cloth to impede her and she caressed Faith's breasts with her hands, then her mouth, then both. Faith moaned as Sarah kissed and sucked on her nipples, raising them into hard points, then flattening them again with her tongue. She lowered a hand to massage Faith's stomach, eliciting more moans. She touched damp hair with her fingertips, and Faith began to writhe.

"Sarah," she said with a quaver in her voice.

"What, my sweet?" Sarah whispered. Her whole being thrummed with the excitement of exploring Faith's body. Intent on pleasuring the woman she loved, she almost missed hearing her.

"My husband was a conservative lover."

Sarah vaguely wondered what that meant. Her attention was focused elsewhere.

Faith's next words rapidly refocused her attention. "No one's mouth ever touched me there, either."

Sarah smiled as Faith woke with a start. Her head lay between Sarah's breasts, with her arms twined around Sarah's body. Lifting her chin, she looked at Sarah, her eyes wide. "Oh, my God, it's not lunchtime yet, is it?"

"Not yet, darlin', but we better get moving." Sarah's smile widened.

Faith's gaze locked on hers, and she smiled back. "Do we have time for a kiss?" She moved up Sarah's chest, breast to breast.

"By damn, we'll make time. The bedroom door's locked. We can always tell Benjamin we were talking privately."

They kissed as though they would never get another chance. Sarah didn't want to ever let go of Faith, but common sense prevailed. They used the pitcher and basin on the bureau to wash up and got dressed.

"Seeing each other can be a problem," Faith said after they had helped each other with their clothes.

"We can work around it. We'll be discreet. Eventually, I hope you'll move into my house." Sarah pulled on a boot.

A puff of laughter came from Faith. "You call that being discreet?"

"We could pose as great friends. No one needs to know the truth. Besides, the town council would be so happy not to have to provide for you that they would overlook any gossip. As long as no one can point to anything specific, we should be all right." Sarah looked down at herself. "Of course, they might have their suspicions because of my clothing."

"We'll see. We can make those decisions later."

Sarah pulled on her second boot and winced as she stood up. "Funny. My leg didn't hurt at all for the last hour or so." She caught Faith's eye and they both grinned.

At the door, Sarah took Faith into her embrace. They kissed, and when they drew apart, both were breathing heavily. Sarah lowered her head for another kiss, but Faith pushed her away with a laugh. "Get out of here. If you had your way, you'd be kissing me when Benjamin walked through the door, and the devil be damned."

"Oh, really?" Sarah lifted one eyebrow. "You think you know me so well?"

Faith's expression sobered. "I don't know you well at all. In my more lucid moments, that scares me a little."

As Sarah lifted her hat from the rack, her expression turned serious. She twisted the hat in her hands and looked at the floor. "You have a right to be afraid. I have some dark places in my soul that affect my moods. Sometimes, I have pretty bad nightmares."

"Do they have anything to do with losing Jessie?"

"Some." Sarah rubbed the back of her neck and a look of anguish crossed her face. "I'm having a harder time adjusting to that situation than I ever thought I would." She inhaled deeply and let the breath whoosh out of her. "But what's done is done." With her head still bowed, she glanced up at Faith. "Most of my nightmares come from my guilt about the war. I tell myself I was only doing my duty, but the faces of men who died because of me still haunt me."

"Oh, Sarah, Benjamin and I will do our best to fill those dark places with light."

That answer fanned a flicker of joy that grew as Sarah raised her head to gaze intently at Faith. With the help of both Pruitts, how could she lose?

"Neither of us knows the other well," Sarah said. "But I hope we can spend the rest of our lives getting acquainted." A smile touched her lips. "You make me feel like I can do anything I set my mind to." She struggled down to one knee and held her hat over her heart. "I love you. I promise myself to you until death do us part. Will you promise yourself to me?"

"I will. I do," Faith said. "I think we just sealed that promise . . . for better or for worse." She put a hand on Sarah's shoulder and leaned close. They kissed one more time, and Faith helped Sarah stand. "Go now," she whispered. "Keep that love warm for me."

"You sure make it hard to leave." Sarah let her arms drop away from Faith. Opening the door, she looked out and could see Benjamin at a distance, coming home. She turned back to Faith. "That 'for better or for worse' part. We're both pretty strong-minded. Do you think we can live together without disagreeing very much?"

"I doubt it," Faith answered solemnly. Then laughter bubbled forth. "But I can think of a thousand wonderful ways to make up. So disagree with me whenever you dare."

"Dare, huh?" Sarah winked. "Somehow, I don't think I'll be the disagreeable one." Before Faith could form a rejoinder, Sarah hurried through the door and closed it, stuck her hat on her head, and stepped off the porch. She heard the door open as she limped toward Benjamin and saw his wide smile. She lifted a hand and waved, acknowledging the woman standing behind her and the boy running toward her.

Her heart soared. We can do this.

EPILOGUE

THREE MONTHS LATER—DECEMBER AT BONNEFORTE

I'm glad you and Benjamin came before the weather got so bad." Sarah pulled back the window curtain for a clearer view of the flakes coming down like bits of fluffy cotton.

Faith glanced up from washing their coffee cups at the sink. "Me, too. I guess we're in for a heavy snowfall." She pointed a wet finger. "Your woodpile is completely covered already. It looks like a hill."

"Luckily, we have plenty of dry wood in the side shed. You can barely see the footprints Scott and Phillip made going into the woods. Benjamin's have already disappeared. You might have to stay here for the weekend."

"Oh, what a hardship that would be." Faith's cheeks dimpled. "Two whole days with you." She dried the cups and hung them from hooks on an open shelf in the cupboard.

"Heh. Me and half a dozen other people." Finding time to spend with Faith over the past three months had been relatively easy. Finding time to make love to her had been a different story.

"You know you enjoy having your family here for the holidays, and I like it, too. Most of our Christmases were very solitary."

"Move in here with me and your Christmases will never be solitary again."

"I still haven't said anything to Benjamin."

"Obviously. Even if he doesn't know about us, he knows we're friends. You could still move in." This discussion seemed never-ending, but Sarah wouldn't quit asking. Maybe sheer persistence would win out.

"If we move in with you, Sarah, I want to feel free for you and me to put our arms around each other, and even kiss, without worrying that we might be found out."

"Ooh, you sound pretty bold, woman. I expect we'll still be discreet."

"Not bold enough to speak to Benjamin." Faith hesitated. "I just need to find the right moment." She nodded toward the window. "All that white makes everything look clean and pure. It's lovely."

Sarah recognized a change of subject when she heard one. She let go of the curtain, moved behind Faith, and slipped her arms around her. "You're lovely, too." She nuzzled Faith's hair aside and placed a kiss on her bare neck. Faith leaned into her and kept the contact as she turned around within the embrace.

"This *feels* lovely." Faith's arms lifted around Sarah's neck and they kissed. "Umm, and you taste lovely, too." She laid her head against a tan cheek, and Sarah kissed her hair.

"Let's go outside." Sarah thought that cold air sounded like a good idea at the moment.

"Outside?" Faith looked up, her expression a cross between a puzzled frown and a wry smile. "In this weather?"

"Yes!" Sarah's eyes gleamed as she pulled Faith toward the coat rack by the kitchen door. "Lindsay and Leah are upstairs with the children, and the boys are out hunting for the perfect Christmas tree. We can do our part by playing in this gift of snow." She helped Faith into her coat and donned hers as Faith pulled on galoshes. Sarah put a hand against the wall for balance, shucked her regular boots, and stomped into a heavier pair. "Let's get outside before we get too warm."

Sarah grabbed her hat, and they put on gloves as they went out. Faith blinked as some flakes stuck on her eyelashes. She spread her arms wide and inhaled deeply.

"Mmm. The air is invigorating."

"So is the snow." A handful of the chilly fluff caught Faith in the face.

Sarah laughed and jumped aside as Faith bent and swept a pile in her direction. After a few moments of wildly slinging snow at each other, they were both red cheeked and covered in white from the steady snowfall.

Sarah raised her hands. "I surrender." She removed her hat, stepped to Faith, and set the hat on top of snow-covered curls. "You're turning gray before your time," she teased.

Faith grabbed the brim with both hands and pulled the hat down until only the curls in front of her shoulders showed. "Well, Miss Sarah," she cackled, "even an old crone like me thinks you're an outstanding catch." Her eyes shone as her mouth turned down in a losing attempt to stop her smile.

"Your hair's too pretty to cover up." Sarah lifted the hat and put it back on her own head. She couldn't resist the picture Faith made with her curls all tousled, her freckled cheeks glowing, and her eyes sparkling with mischief. "And I'll still love you, even when you're an old crone." She pulled Faith to her and kissed her.

"Sarah—" Phillip's voice cleaved between them. The kiss halted abruptly, and the women whirled toward where Phillip stood at the edge of the woodpile. Sarah kept one arm around Faith's shoulders, and she squeezed her for courage as they saw Scott and Benjamin several yards away. The chosen tree lay abandoned on the ground.

Scott put a hand on Benjamin's shoulder, and a silence as heavy as the snowfall drifted upon them all.

Scott's icy tone shattered the quiet. "You ought to be ashamed of yourselves." In the corner of her vision, Sarah could see him scowling, but her gaze remained on Benjamin.

Faith opened her mouth as though to speak, but urgent fingers tightened on her arm, and Sarah spoke instead. "Benjamin, I'm sorry for not having told you this before, but I'm in love with your mama." Benjamin's face didn't change, and Sarah forged on. "And she's in love with me. I know that's different from the usual way of things— for a woman to fall in love with another woman. But it happens sometimes, and it happened with us. Being different is not something for us to be ashamed about." She glared at Scott and brought her gaze back to Benjamin. "What other people think about us being in love doesn't matter. But we do care what you think."

Faith spoke, then, in a sure and steady voice. "Miss Sarah and I are in love with each other, Benjamin, and she wants us to come live with her as her family." Sarah warmed at the pride that glowed from Faith's words, but chilled at her next sentence.

"But we won't do that if you don't want us to." Faith raised her arm toward her son, and he lifted his booted feet high to step quickly through the thickening snow. When he reached the two women, he

287

flung his arms around Faith as best he could. He leaned his head back and looked at her, his eyes squinting against the falling snow.

"Does Miss Sarah make you happy?"

"Yes. She makes me very, very happy."

"Then it's all right." He turned to Sarah. "You make Mama happy. You make me happy, too. I want to live here. I want to be your family." He spread his arms to try to embrace both women.

"Thank you, Benjamin." Sarah could hardly speak. Her hand trembled as she touched his head, her fingers tumbling snow from his knit cap. She glanced toward Scott, and to her satisfaction, he looked positively stupefied.

Just then a snowball hit Scott in the shoulder, spraying snow into his face. Almost immediately, one thumped Sarah in the back. "What the—" She turned her head and ducked as another ball just missed her. Benjamin laughed and grabbed at the snow.

Safely barricaded behind the woodpile, Phillip was pelting them with snow as fast as he could form it into balls. Sarah and Faith bent to the task of securing their own ammunition. When Sarah looked up, she saw Scott pointing.

"You and Faith get him from that side," he shouted. "Benjamin and I will flank him over here."

The four rushed behind the woodpile, showing Phillip no mercy. Within moments, Leah dashed out of the house to come to his rescue. The bombardment deteriorated into rubbing snow into faces and stuffing it down collars. At last, the skirmishers laughed themselves into exhaustion, calling a halt to the battle. They staggered inside and feasted on the sandwiches and cocoa that Lindsay had prepared and the younger children had already sampled.

For the moment, any unpleasantness remained under truce.

After lunch, Leah and Phillip volunteered to take the children outside for more play, but only after Phillip secured a promise that no one would try a sneak attack. He offered to put the tree in the shed— "If I can find it under all that snow." Sarah and Faith went to Sarah's study, leaving Lindsay and Scott to their own pursuits.

Sarah sat on her drawing bench, and Faith stood behind her, massaging her neck and shoulders. "That feels so good. Promise to do this every single day when you live here?" The hands moved to lift her hair, and she felt warm lips on the back of her neck. Delicious pleasure pulsed through her like a thousand inner caresses, and she shivered. "On second thought . . ." She reached back to tangle her fingers in Faith's hair and turned to almost meet her lips. "I might not get much work done." Faith's teasing smile made Sarah ache to touch her, but when Faith closed the distance between them, she settled for a kiss.

This feels so perfect, so right, Sarah thought. How could anyone, especially my own brother, believe it's wrong? She wanted to ignore Scott's disapproval, but it hurt. They had always been close.

A knock at the door separated the women, and Faith moved to sit in one of the chairs.

"Come in," Sarah called. Lindsay entered and closed the door behind her. Contrary to her usual manner, she appeared nervous.

"Sarah, Scott told me about the episode in the yard." Sarah waved her hand at a chair, but Lindsay shook her head no. "He's very upset about it."

"That's just too damn bad." Sarah spoke with such vehemence that Lindsay cringed. "I'm sorry, Lindsay, I know it's not your fault. I just don't understand who the hell he thinks he is to pass judgment on me. And especially when it's not his concern."

"You misunderstand," Lindsay hurried to say. "He's upset precisely because of his 'pigheaded ways,' to quote him. He muttered something about learning a lesson from a boy, and he asked me to come persuade you to talk to him. Or maybe 'listen' to him would be more precise." She tilted her head toward the door. "He's right outside."

Faith rose. "I'll come back later."

"Oh, no, please," Lindsay said. "He wants to talk to both of you."

Sarah beckoned Faith with her fingers. "Come, sit beside me, my sweet. We can do this together."

"That's the first you've called me 'my sweet,'" Faith said as she sat on the bench. "Except when—"

"That's enough." Sarah's cheeks colored and she swatted Faith's thigh. "That just shows how nervous I am," she admitted. She looked to Lindsay and nodded. "Go ahead. Send him in."

"Remember, Sarah, he's nervous, too. I don't want to hear any shouting match going on in here."

"I can't promise that, but I'll try." Sarah rubbed the back of her neck.

"There won't be any shouting," Faith said. She and Lindsay exchanged looks.

"Thank you. I'll send him in." Lindsay disappeared through the doorway, and a moment later, Scott entered.

"Have a seat," Sarah offered.

"If you don't mind, I'd rather stand. I can think a little better on my feet. Not a whole lot, but a little." His fingers twiddled with the edge of his jacket pocket. "I came to . . . to . . ." He stopped and cleared his throat.

Apologize? Sarah opened her mouth, but Faith squeezed her hand.

"Let him speak, Sarah."

Scott said, "Thank you. I wanted to speak to you both, because I'm finally beginning to understand how wrong I've been to meddle in your lives." His glance met Sarah's and flicked away. "Lindsay tried to tell me I should accept your decisions. Even Phillip tried." A grin quirked one side of Scott's lips. "He's talking about opening a carpentry business here, so I know your . . . situation . . . isn't bothering him."

"Leah might have influenced him a bit about coming here," Faith interjected.

"She has," Scott agreed, "but he warned me about meddling in your lives before he knew Leah very well. I didn't pay him any attention then or later."

Scott nodded to Faith. "It was Benjamin who opened my eyes." He paced a few steps and turned back. "You might find this hard to understand, Sarah. I'm not sure I understand it myself. But I feel responsible for you. Lord knows you've taken more care of me than I ever have of you, but the fact remains. I feel responsible for you and responsible for your happiness. I always have." He waved a hand. "Maybe it's because I'm a man." When Sarah remained silent, Scott cocked his head. "You aren't going to help me with this, are you?"

"Yes," Sarah answered slowly, "since you ask, I will. I feel responsible for you, too. And it has nothing to do with being a man. We're twins. We have a special connection. I've felt it all my life, and I know you have, too. That's why your disapproval has hurt me so much." Sarah's voice rose. She felt Faith's fingers entwine with hers and went on more calmly. "I guess I expected you, of all people, to accept me as I am. You know I've never pretended to be like other women."

"I do know that. You've always been honest and true to yourself. I'm the one who got on the wrong track, thinking I could tell you how to live. Society doesn't understand or accept women who love women and men who love men. Some call it an abomination, and I couldn't imagine you wanting to cope with that."

"It's not a case of 'wanting' to cope with it. I don't like the attitudes any more than you do. But I can't change my nature to satisfy society." Sarah's grin was wry. "I keep telling you, I am who I am. I'm in love with Faith, and we're going to make a life together. That's just the way it is."

"I know you don't need my blessing, Sarah, but you have it now. I saw your face when Benjamin said, 'You make Mama happy.'" Scott wiped at a tear trickling down his cheek. "That really says it all. I've been worried about you finding happiness, and you found it without me—even in spite of me." He walked to his sister, placed a hand on each side of her head, and kissed her cheek. "You've found it with Faith, and I'm happy for both of you."

He backed away as Sarah stood. She grabbed his shoulders, pulled him into an embrace, and returned his kiss. "You've just given me another measure of happiness."

They stood for a moment, hugging. Both fought to stop their tears, but neither succeeded.

They released each other, and Scott turned to embrace Faith. He whispered, "Take good care of my sister," and kissed her cheek.

"That's a solemn promise, Scott. You take good care of Jessica." Scott's head flew up, and when he met Faith's knowing look, he nodded.

"That's a solemn promise, too, Faith."

Sarah, intent on wiping her tears on her sleeves, didn't hear the exchange. She looked up as Scott stepped back, and a boyish smile widened his cheeks. "I better go show Lindsay I'm still alive." He pulled at his shirt to straighten it.

Sarah grabbed a handful of his shirt and yanked it awry again. "Don't let her think it was too easy," she said, her voice roughened by her tears. She kissed Scott's cheek again and gave him a quick hug. "Thank you, brother."

Scott didn't even try to speak. He tightened his lips, nodded his head several times, and left.

"Are you all right?" Faith moved to Sarah and embraced her.

"I am now." They kissed. As they held each other, Sarah could feel the tension draining from her. When she lifted her head, a smile of wonderment crept slowly across her face. "You and Benjamin are moving in, Scott's given us his blessing, and all my family is gathered under one roof. This will be the best Christmas I've ever had."

"Me, too," Faith whispered as their lips met again.

THE END

New Releases From
Intaglio Publications

Southern Hearts
By Katie Moore
ISBN: 1-933113-28-6

For the first time since her father's passing three years prior, Kari Bossier returns to the south, to her family's stately home on the emerald banks of the bayou Teche, and to a mother she yearns to understand.

At her mother's urging, Kari is begrudgingly forced to entertain Lani Trusdor, a sturdy woman with broad shoulders, solid thighs, and healthy birthing hips. At first they are an awkward pairing with little in common, though eventually they become friends, and as their friendship grows, Kari discovers a lot about herself and her family.

Will she give into her passion for Lani or will her seething lust towards another take hold and conquer her?

Misplaced People
By C G Devize
ISBN: 1-933113-30-8

On duty at a London hospital, American loner Striker West is drawn to an unknown woman, who, after being savagely attacked, is on the verge of death. Moved by a compassion she cannot explain, Striker spends her off time at the bedside of the comatose patient, reading and willing her to recover.

Still trying to conquer her own demons which have taken her so far from home, Striker is drawn deeper into the web of intrigue that surrounds this woman.

Together they are taken on a dark journey, on the run from London gangsters, leading them into a tidal wave of deception, mystery and ultimately murder, that will change their lives forever.

Counterfeit World
By Judith Parker
ISBN: 1-933113-32-4

Counterfeit World is a futuristic novel that mixes science fiction with elements of mystery and romance. The heroine is Shon Emerick, Lead Negotiator for Raimsee Enterprises, self-described as "a thirtyish professional, long body honed and spare, dark red hair tamed by a short bob, face disciplined to a pale mask, blue eyes as cold as my heart." The reality Shon inhabits is one where the U.S. government has been privatized, religion has only recently been decriminalized, the World Government keeps the peace on Earth—when it chooses—and multi-world corporations vie for control of planets, moons, asteroids, and orbits for their space stations.

Spring 2005 Releases From
Intaglio Publications

Murky Waters
By Robin Alexander
ISBN: 1-933113-33-2

The Illusionist
By Fran Heckrotte
ISBN: 1-933113-31-6